SWARM METAMORPHOSIS

Also by William Stubblefield

How Mother Rat Invented the World
(With illustrations by Merry Stubblefield)

SWARM METAMORPHOSIS

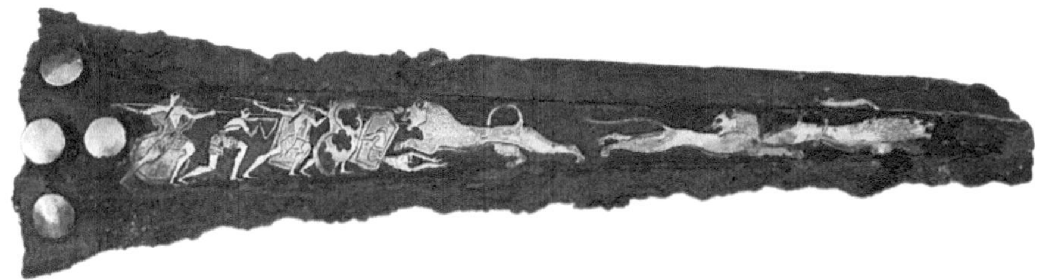

Circe and the Great Cat

William Stubblefield

Library of Congress Control Number: 2022910782

ISBN: 978-1-7375091-3-4 Hardcover
ISBN: 978-1-7375091-4-1 Paperback
ISBN: 978-1-7375091-5-8 Digital

Cover design by William and Merry Stubblefield.

The cover image is a late bronze age Mycenaean dagger,
bronze and inlaid with gold and silver, from the collection of the
National Archaeological Museum of Athens.
The image used on the cover is from Wikimedia Commons (File:Dagger_inlaid_Mycenaean_16_c_BC,_NAMA_394_1080834.jpg), and is
used under a Creative Commons Copyright.

Address all communications to
Practical Tales Publishing
PracticalTales@comcast.net
https://practicalTales.com

For Merry
And for all the wonderful animals
who have shared my life and inspired this book

I want to speak about bodies changed into new forms.

Ovid
Metamorphosis (Trans. A. S. Kline)

If a lion could talk, we could not understand him.

Ludwig Wittgenstein
Philosophical Investigations

Part I

Albuquerque and the East Mountains
Present Day

Chapter 1

It began with a tearing sound—narrow, sharply articulated, and quickly lost in a crescendo of shattered dishes and screaming animals.

"Fucking cats," Astrid Lund complained as she set her book on the side table and pushed herself up from the old blue recliner.

Since returning home to settle her mother's estate, Astrid had grown used to the occasional broken glass that attended Sigrid's five animals, but nothing had prepared her for the chaos she found in the kitchen. The counter had been swept clear, scattering pans, dishes, glasses, and the steel drying rack across the tile floor. As usual, the disaster's perpetrators had fled.

Swearing softly, Astrid began to pick up the surviving items. As she placed a handful of flatware in the sink, she noticed the source of the tearing sound: a triangle of torn plastic insect screen flapped in the open window. Astrid saw a smear of bright red on the white windowsill and, without thinking, touched it. She jerked her hand back, blood sticky on her fingers, and saw the translucent crescents of torn claws on the painted wood.

Squinting against the afternoon sunlight, Astrid searched the open space separating the house from the Cibola National Forest. As her eyes adjusted to the glare, she saw Audrey, a long-haired, tortoiseshell cat with the temperament of a bobcat, cross an opening in the scattered mesquite, her tail a dark flag over a barren frontier. In the seconds that followed, Astrid located each of Audrey's littermates. Greystoke, a tuxedo cat with fur the color of gunmetal and muscles like springs, sprinted across the field ahead of his sister. Chessie, the gray tabby who often seemed the wildest of the five, ran behind them. Spike followed, muscular and self-possessed, his dusty blond coat blending into the brown grass as Elizabeth, forever the chubby baby of the litter, ran to keep up with his elegant rolling trot, her long, ginger fur shining like polished copper. Astrid knew if they stayed outside after sunset, they risked becoming a meal for a coyote, bobcat, or one of the dogs that roamed the open space. With the chaos in the kitchen driven from her mind, she ran onto the porch as Elizabeth disappeared into the forest.

Astrid followed her, stopping a few yards into the trees to hold her breath and listen. She heard a feline cry and ran toward it. Entering a clearing, Astrid found the five cats gathered around a tall Ponderosa Pine. A blue jay taunted them from a low branch.

"A goddamned blue jay?" she muttered. "You tore through the window to chase a goddamned blue jay?"

Not wanting to frighten the jay and send the cats chasing it through the forest, Astrid paused to gather her thoughts and found herself transfixed by the contest playing out before her. Greystoke pulled himself up the tree's rough bark, with Chessie and Audrey close behind. He climbed onto the limb where the jay perched and lunged futilely at the bird. His sisters watched him fall to the ground as the jay flew to a higher branch, then continued their climb. Meanwhile, Spike and Elizabeth prowled the clearing below, eyes on the bird, ready to pounce should their siblings knock it from the tree. Above them, the jay danced at the fulcrum of chaos, jumping to safety as each cat drew near.

Unable to carry all five animals at once, Astrid decided to take two back to the house and return with cat carriers for the others. She knew Spike and Elizabeth would be the easiest to manage, and their littermates seemed preoccupied enough to stay near the tree—at least while the bird taunted them from its branches.

"It's okay, Spike," Astrid whispered as she crouched and stroked his back. She lifted him into the crook of her neck, forelegs draped over her shoulder, fur soft against her cheek. Astrid glanced up at the jay, who stared back with a seemingly analytic curiosity, then she kneeled beside Elizabeth, repeating the nickname she had given her when she was still a kitten. "Biffy. Come on, Biffy."

She did not notice the dog's approach until she felt Spike's muscles tense and his claws dig into her shoulder. Astrid heard a low growl and turned to see a black and tan gargoyle approach on a narrow path, muscles rolling beneath the fur raised along its spine. She recognized the corrupt Rottweiler-mix she had often seen prowling the open space, sometimes with a pack of other local toughs, but more often alone. She lowered Spike to the ground beside Elizabeth and stepped aggressively toward the dog.

"Go on," she shouted. "Git, you bastard."

The dog stopped and growled, measuring the threat posed by this lone woman, then it continued toward her, a single strand of saliva trailing from his mouth, a silver thread in the afternoon sun.

Astrid searched for a rock or fallen tree limb she could use as a weapon. She did not notice the blue light flashing through the clearing until an indeterminate wall of noise broke around her, and the ground fell from beneath her feet. She rolled as she struck the forest floor, pain radiating from her right hip. Astrid sat up and saw the dog stop and look past her, its lip curling into a snarl as a low growl behind her rose to a feral scream. The cry pulled her around like a string unwinding a top.

Astrid saw what appeared to be a mountain lion enter the clearing, head lowered, paws moving weightlessly across the dirt. It was at least eight feet long from its nose to the end of its tail—large even for the lions that still prowled the national forest. As the cat moved through the forest's patchwork of light and shadow, the colors of her mother's animals seemed to play across its fur. Shifting patches of gray parted tawny ripples, then gave way to flashes of orange and brindle before resolving into Spike's even buff. The dog froze, its eyes locked on the nightmare stalking toward it.

Astrid remained still—she knew running from a predator invited pursuit—and the great cat moved past her as gracefully as water flowing around a stone. It paused to study her through sage-green eyes—pitiless, penetrating, and coldly intelligent—then turned its attention back to the dog, a low rumble resonating in its chest. Astrid scanned the clearing but did not see her animals. Only the blue jay remained, watching from its perch with a bird's unbreakable focus.

As the cat continued up the path, the Rottweiler looked to each side, a bully gauging the consequences of his bravado. No reinforcements stood nearby, no pack to help or to judge. It bared its teeth and growled, holding its position on the narrow trail. The great cat stopped a few body lengths from the outmatched dog, muscles compressed, hindquarters rocking, palpating the ground beneath its paws. Astrid saw its jaw drop as if unhinged as the cat threw its head back and screamed. The scream seemed less a threat than a simple assertion of presence—a birth cry hurled against an indifferent world.

The dog backed away, cautiously at first, protecting its backside, then accelerating as it turned on the narrow path. It fell onto its haunch, hind legs skidding beneath it, scattering gravel across the grass before it recovered and fled back up the trail.

The cat turned toward Astrid after the dog crossed the top of the hill. It cocked its head as if in recognition, then padded toward her. Still sitting on the forest floor, Astrid crabbed back until a tree's rough bark pressed into her spine. She tried to rise, but her feet scraped ineffectually across the ground. The cat stopped less than a foot away from her and stared, more out of curiosity than menace, as Astrid sat frozen, unable to breathe, fingers digging into the dirt. The animal stretched its head toward her, and she smelled its breath, damp with the stench of digestion. She felt the wet sandpaper of its tongue against her cheek as her consciousness dissolved in a vortex of fear.

Astrid felt Greystoke's paws on her chest, his nose moist against hers. She gently pushed him aside and searched the clearing for the great cat, but she only found his littermates. Chessie rested beside her, and Elizabeth stood nearby, staring at her through half-closed copper eyes. Audrey looked up the path as if guarding against the dog's return, while Spike paced the clearing's perimeter. Astrid struggled to her feet, but her muscles remained unresponsive, detached from her will.

She shuffled forward as sensation returned to her limbs. "Come on," she said automatically, "we have to go."

She picked up Greystoke, tucked Elizabeth under her other arm, and called to their siblings. As she had hoped, the cats followed close behind. She led them across the open space, onto the porch, and through the house's still-open door.

Once inside, Astrid hurried through the house, closing windows to prevent a repeat of the cats' escape. She stopped at a wall of photographs she had framed for her mother in the months before her death—lovingly selected scenes of Sigrid Lund smiling with friends; climbing a ladder in her old straw hat and carpenter's belt to frame her house; lecturing at the university in a neat blouse and skirt; standing at the summit of Wheeler Peak, her blonde hair a tight braid against her red parka. Astrid's eyes rested on a picture of Sigrid in a T-shirt and jeans, sitting on the living room floor, back against the old recliner, legs stretched across the red Chinese rug. Five kittens swarmed over her as she laughed at the impossibility of keeping them in any kind of order.

"Ma," Astrid said softly, her fingers touching the glass as if feeling for a pulse, "what the hell just happened?"

Astrid sat on the edge of the recliner, elbows on her knees, watching the cats resume their habitual behaviors. Spike curled up on the warm surface of the ancient stereo that still played Sigrid's favorite classical music station. Elizabeth climbed onto the chair and wedged herself behind Astrid's buttocks. Audrey jumped onto the chair back in an arc so perfect she seemed to float into place and stretched across it. Greystoke pawed at Chessie until she hissed and ran up the stacks of books that buttressed the fireplace. She glared at him from the mantle.

Astrid watched them for a time, letting the currents of normalcy flow across her nerves. She lifted Elizabeth from behind her and leaned back in the chair, resting the cat on her lap. Astrid continued to seek reassurance in the room's familiar clutter, in the mismatched but lovingly selected chairs, end tables, lamps, artwork, and most of all, in the books overflowing the shelves, covering tables and unused corners of the room, leaning in stacks along the walls, their ivory pages and bright covers like strata of an imagined mountain escarpment.

When the afternoon light faded, Astrid walked into the kitchen, followed by five hungry animals. She watched their mealtime ritual of choosing a place among the mismatched bowls she put down on the white tile floor—smelling each other's food, hissing warnings, and finally, settling in to eat at their usual spots. They seemed unaffected by their experience in the forest. Astrid picked up Elizabeth and stroked her long, orange fur.

"What made you guys run off?"

Astrid touched her cheek where the mountain lion had licked her and stared at the five animals. After a time, she took her phone from her pocket and leaned against the counter, her fingers tracing a familiar pattern across the screen.

"It's me," she said as Claire Ortega answered. Claire was her oldest friend, and the only person Astrid could tell of her encounter in the forest—and trust not to question her sanity. "No, I'm okay . . . just a little cabin fever. Any chance of meeting for lunch or coffee? No, I just need to get out . . . Tomorrow would be perfect."

Claire's voice brought her deeper into life's comforting rhythms. They spoke for a few minutes, confirmed their meeting, and said goodbye.

Astrid walked down the hall to the bedroom. She removed her jeans—still dirty from the forest floor—and threw them into the laundry basket. She neatly folded her black sweater, placed it in the dresser drawer, and walked into the bathroom in her T-shirt and panties. Astrid studied her face in the mirror, searching for some slackness in its muscles, for some misalignment of her eyes, for an uneven dilation of the pupils—for anything that might suggest a neurological basis for what she had seen in the forest. She found nothing abnormal. *It must have been a stress-induced hallucination*, she told herself.

She took a deep breath and drew her hands slowly over cheekbones that reflected her father's indigenous heritage, past the small wrinkles at the corners of her eyes, and through her short, reddish-brown hair. She smiled at the contrast of her olive complexion with hazel eyes so much like her mother's. The smile gave way to a passing sadness as she recognized Sigrid's features in her straight nose and expressive mouth. Astrid stepped back from the mirror.

"Not the face of a hallucinating psychotic," she thought aloud. Astrid felt a pressure against her leg and looked down. Audrey stared up at her with demanding olive-green eyes.

"It isn't the face of a crazy cat lady, either," she said, picking up the small tortoiseshell cat and scratching her behind the ear. As was her habit, Audrey briefly enjoyed the attention, then squirmed away.

Astrid washed her face and arms, rubbed her skin briskly with a fresh towel, and took a last look in the mirror. The weeks she'd spent outside completing the large and small chores neglected during Sigrid's illness had tightened muscles grown slack from years spent in front of a computer. She flexed her bicep and pulled the sleeve of her T-shirt across her shoulder, taking pleasure in the curve of her muscles as they descended beneath the soft cotton.

Astrid changed into her red flannel nightgown, walked to the kitchen, and prepared a light dinner of bread, cheese, and a sliced pear. She washed it down with a surprisingly good Sangiovese she'd found in her mother's pantry. After cleaning up, she took the glass and bottle out onto the porch and sat in one of the old armchairs, the creaking of the wicker partitioning the silence as stars appeared over the mountains. When the air grew colder, she took a blanket from a nearby chair and spread it across her lap. Astrid pulled her knees against her chest and stared into the darkness, the cold air reassuring against her face. She imagined the great cat staring back, as patient as the mountains it inhabited.

Had she looked back when she'd returned home that afternoon, Astrid might have seen the blue jay fly to a high branch and watch her lead the cats across the open space. She would have seen it lift from the limb shortly after they'd gone inside the house and fly through the forest to land near the mouth of a small canyon.

Had she followed the jay, Astrid would have seen it walk forward with a bird's awkward gait, then rock back and forth as if preparing to fly. She would have seen a blue light surround it as the jay grew into the shape of a woman—slightly taller than she, with deep brown, almost black hair falling past her shoulders, brows tracking the curve of delicately slanted eyes, features reflecting no single human lineage but weaving countless threads into an elemental beauty.

If she had witnessed the transformation, Astrid would have seen the woman's lips part in release as she welcomed this accustomed form, pausing to straighten her navy-blue slacks and ivory silk blouse, brushing away a trace of dust that blemished the cloth. She would have seen her close her eyes and breathe deeply, raising her face to the sun with an unmistakably erotic expression of pleasure.

Had Astrid remained nearby, she would have seen the woman walk to the canyon wall and rest her hands on it, eyes closed, leaning forward until her cheek nearly touched the granite. She would have seen the woman remain motionless as if she were listening to the lichens growing into the stone—as if she were questioning the mountain itself. A few moments later, Astrid would have seen her walk along the cliff face, hands tracking its contours, searching for something both answer and question, both expected and anomalous, for something she would recognize as familiar, purposeful, but nevertheless, out of place.

Chapter 2

The wheels of Astrid's green Jeep Cherokee slipped as she accelerated from the gravel road onto Highway 14. It was a bright fall day, and she lowered the window to enjoy the brisk air and the scent of dying leaves. Astrid looked forward to seeing Claire, and to a few hours away from the solitude of Sigrid's house and the five acres of mesquite, scrub oak, and piñon that surrounded it. Most of all, she looked forward to moving past the incident in the forest—the urgency of the cats' escape, the Rottweiler's threat, the passing mountain lion, and the hallucinatory quality of the entire incident. She drove through Cedar Crest, a once small mountain town that had become a bedroom community for a growth-addicted city, took the ramp onto Interstate 40, and descended into Albuquerque's bland sprawl.

The late morning traffic moved quickly, and Astrid soon left the interstate, driving toward the coffeehouse Claire had suggested. Although it was part of a ubiquitous chain and located in a self-consciously upscale shopping development, it was clean and offered both decent espresso and a comfortable outside seating area.

Astrid found a table outside near a row of trees that almost hid the traffic on the nearby street. She sat in a sunny chair, enjoying the autumn air, and watching the people come and go from the coffeehouse—tired shoppers in groups or alone, couples enjoying a conversation, salesclerks grabbing a coffee on their break.

She saw Claire Ortega cross the parking lot, her stride as efficient and inevitable as a river in the spring. Claire wore one of the bright spring dresses she favored all year round, with life-sized orange tulips and yellow daffodils with green stems scattered across a white background—a striking contrast with her mahogany complexion. Her sole concession to the autumn air was the yellow cardigan she'd owned since college.

Astrid stood and embraced her. "It's good to see you."

Claire returned the hug, then held Astrid by the shoulders, examining her with concern. "How are you doing? You sounded stressed on the phone."

"I was just tired. How are Anthony and the kids?" Astrid asked, changing the subject.

Claire smiled ironically. "Anthony and Emily are in California visiting colleges, so Mark has to suffer the indignity of being alone with his mother."

"Is he still acting out?"

"Typical adolescent stuff. At least he spends most of his time in his room."

"How are his grades?"

"He barely tries, but he does fine. He seems to have inherited his mother's brains and his father's gift for bullshit."

Astrid smiled. She had long followed Mark and Emily's adolescence with a mixture of affection and bittersweet gratitude for the relative simplicity of her own life.

"How's work?"

"I'm enjoying the promotion. Raising two teenagers has prepared me for management," Claire said, laughing softly.

"I'm sorry to take you away on a workday."

"Don't be. It's not like I don't put in the overtime."

Claire draped her sweater over a chair to reserve their table. She ran her hands along the sides of her head, smoothing the black hair she wore in a simple ponytail and wiping away the stress of work and traffic. Claire stood in the sun for a moment, eyes closed, her features and bearing suggesting a woman in her twenties rather than a forty-year-old mother of two.

She took Astrid's arm and led her through the maze of outdoor tables, chairs, and patio umbrellas toward the coffeehouse.

"Come on. I'll buy."

Astrid and Claire had met when they were students in the Stanford Design Program. On the surface, they had little in common. Claire was finishing her master's in computer science and believed training in design could improve her software. Astrid had entered the program after the realities of an English literature degree left her wanting more realistic job prospects. Astrid had a comfortable, if mostly intuitive, proficiency with technology, while Claire struggled to move from the rigor of science to design's more subjective concerns. Claire and Anthony were raising two children in married student housing, while Astrid enjoyed all the temptations available to a pretty, single woman on a college campus.

Inevitably, they had built an enduring friendship.

When Astrid returned to Albuquerque to be near her mother, she persuaded an old boyfriend to help Claire and Anthony find jobs at Sandia National Laboratories. A few years later, Claire provided computer science advice when Astrid started her web design business—and emotional support when Astrid's divorce and Sigrid's illness forced her to sell it.

"How's life in the mountains?" Claire asked as she sat down.

"Quiet mostly, but I'm making headway on Mom's things." Astrid took a deep drink of her cappuccino and leaned back in the metal chair, enjoying the sunlight on her face.

"Is your father still in town?"

Astrid shook her head. "He went back to Taos after Mom's funeral."

Claire raised an eyebrow so slightly that only a close friend would notice.

"I enjoyed seeing him," Astrid reassured, "but we both knew it was time for him to go."

Claire took a long sip of coffee. "I always appreciate a man who knows when to leave. Speaking of which, have you heard from Alan? Has he gotten around to signing the papers?"

"Nice pivot," Astrid said, laughing. "No, but he's running out of excuses."

"Maybe what's-her-name is running out of patience."

Claire had long maintained that Alan was using his 'zombie marriage' as a firewall against a commitment-hungry girlfriend. "Any problems with the settlement?"

"He has conceded the business was mine, and he's agreed not to go after my mother's estate."

"So, he does have a decent streak . . . or maybe he's just afraid."

Astrid smiled ironically.

"You did put him in the hospital when you discovered his affair," Claire reminded.

"It was only the emergency room, and his nose was barely broken."

Claire sipped her coffee. "I saw on Facebook that you changed your name to 'Lund.'"

"I didn't want to keep Alan's name, and since I was changing it anyway—"

"You went full gonzo feminist?"

"No." Astrid laughed. "After Sigrid passed, it just seemed right to take her last name."

"What did your dad say?"

"He wasn't happy, but he tried to understand," Astrid said, tears pooling in her eyes. She dabbed them with a napkin from the rack on the table. "He has a son and a daughter up in Taos, but Sigrid only had me. Besides, it's not like I'd be passing the name along."

Claire reached across to take her hand. "Have you given any thought to coming back to town, Astrid Lund? Before you turn into some mad cat lady in the mountains?"

Astrid winced at the phrase 'mad cat lady.' It awakened memories of the cats' escape and her hallucinatory perceptions of the mountain lion.

"I think about it from time to time," she admitted, "but now I need to be there. Besides, five cats do not make you a mad cat lady . . . just a charming eccentric."

"My offer to help you get hired at the labs still stands. I need a good user interface designer. I could set up some interviews." Claire paused and smiled. "Maybe even clean you up a little."

Astrid looked down at her black sweater and worn jeans, then at Claire's bright ensemble. She took another sip of espresso. "I can afford to wait," she said as she leaned across the table and retrieved her shoulder bag from the empty chair. "There's something I want to show you."

Astrid took a flat cardboard mailer from the bag. It was the kind people used for mailing photographs in the days before digital cameras. She removed a photo and slid it across the table.

"I found this in one of Sigrid's drawers, between her recipe for vegan stroganoff and the manual for her table saw."

Claire looked at the picture wistfully. The black-and-white image showed Sigrid Lund at a party in her living room, wearing a long floral print dress and holding a glass of dark wine. She was smiling, relaxed, and was the only person in the crowd looking into the camera. The light caught her face in a way that left everyone else in shadows as if she and the photographer shared an impenetrable bond.

"I'd forgotten how beautiful your mother was," Claire murmured.

Astrid took a neatly folded note from the envelope. "This was with the picture."

Claire carefully unfolded the note. It was a high-quality paper, the kind sold in the few upscale stationery stores that survived in a digital world. The script was graceful and oddly formal, as if from a time when penmanship mattered.

> *This picture captures you perfectly—a bright spirit shining across time and worlds.*
> *I hope to return soon.*
> *Always*

"You don't hear that sort of thing these days," Claire said softly, not raising her eyes from the note. She turned it in her hand, looking at both sides of the paper. "It's not signed. Who was this from?"

"I don't know."

"She never told you?"

Astrid shook her head. "There's a date on the back of the photo from the development lab. It was a few months after I started grad school. Mom was teaching at the university, her class in Homer."

"I forgot she was an adjunct professor."

"A Harvard Ph.D. in classics, and she made more money as a carpenter."

"And she built your home."

"And someone loved her . . . and I never knew him."

"You can't be surprised," Claire said. "Sigrid was a beautiful woman."

"I just wish she'd told me. We never kept secrets from each other. Besides, there's something about this . . . It wasn't just a fling."

They sat for a long time, sipping coffee, watching strangers pass, and sharing the private space friendship creates. After a few minutes, conversation precipitated out of the silence.

"What are you going to do with the house?" Claire asked. "And the cats?"

"I'm thinking of keeping the house. It's paid for and in a beautiful place. I helped Mom build it, and I have good memories." Astrid spoke as if thinking aloud. "As far as the cats are concerned, they're the last thing I need right now, but it is their home, and they know me. When their mother disappeared—I think a coyote got her—they were just a week old and so small they'd fit in the palm of your hand. Mom and I had to bottle-feed them every three hours." Astrid paused. "I'll probably keep them."

"I suspect you will."

"It's weird, but Mom's death has affected them, too."

"Oh?"

"Yesterday, they clawed through a window screen and got out."

"All of them?"

Astrid nodded. "Mom called them 'the Swarm' because whenever one of them got into trouble, the rest seemed to appear from out of nowhere, like they shared a single mind."

"Swarm," Claire repeated, smiling.

"Claire," Astrid began, "something happened when they ran off. I need to talk about it, but I don't want you to think I'm crazy."

"I knew something was bothering you," Claire said, seriously at first, then laughing gently. "And don't worry, I've always known you were crazy."

"The problem is, this time, it may be true."

Helped by Claire's encouragement, Astrid described the events in the forest. She lowered her voice when she described the mountain lion's sudden appearance, its confrontation with the Rottweiler, and the hallucinatory intensity of its screams.

"Claire," Astrid whispered, "after the dog left, the lion walked up to me and licked my face."

Claire looked at her in shock, started to laugh, then recoiled in horror, her hand over her mouth. "My god, you must have been terrified."

"I passed out. The next thing I remembered was the cats being around me. There was no sign of the lion."

"Have you told anyone?"

"No one but you would believe me. I'm not sure I believe it myself."

"I believe you," Claire said gently, "but I also think you've been under a lot of stress . . . losing your mother, your divorce, your business. You need a break. How about we get out of here, hit the beach for a few days . . . just us girls, like old times. I've accumulated a ton of vacation time."

"Why the hell not?" Astrid said, taking her friend's hand. "Mexico? I'll line up a cat sitter."

"I'll talk to Anthony. We'll figure out a time."

Astrid tried her cup, but it was empty. She stood and stretched her neck and back. "You want another? I'll buy."

Claire reached across the table and grasped her forearm. "Don't get lost up there in the mountains. Okay?"

"Don't worry," Astrid smiled. "Besides, there's nothing wrong with getting lost from time to time."

Astrid worked her way through the maze of people, tables, and chairs. As she neared the coffeehouse, she saw a woman wearing navy-blue slacks, an ivory-colored silk blouse, and loaded down with shopping bags struggle with the coffeehouse door. Astrid moved Claire and her cups to one hand, her finger through the handles, and opened the door for her. The woman smiled and thanked her.

As Astrid followed her inside, the hot, moist air enfolded her. She gripped the door handle for support as her nerves caught fire and vertigo seized her. The jazz playing in the coffeehouse—every note, every drumbeat, the shimmer of cymbals, the clatter of valves on the saxophone, the squeak of the bass player's fingers on strings—flooded her awareness. Multiple conversations swarmed around her like hummingbirds around the feeder on her porch. A rush of scents joined the chaos—coffee, pastries, dishwasher soap, perfumes, and the commingled body odor of a dozen people in an overheated room. Astrid stepped back into the fresh air, still holding the door handle to steady herself. Her glance fell on a nearby tree, and it seemed as if she could see the sap running through its branches in rhythm with the slow respiration of its yellowing leaves. All these sensations came at once, wrapped in a soft, blue cloud. She leaned forward, her hand on her knee. The cups slipped from her grasp and shattered on the sidewalk. Claire rushed to her side.

"What happened?" she asked, taking Astrid's arm and helping her to a nearby chair.

Astrid described her vertigo, the heightened perceptions, and the strange blue color that covered everything like a watercolor wash.

"You mean like synesthesia?" Claire pressed.

"Isn't that when your senses mush together? You taste colors and stuff?"

"Yes. Has anything like this happened before?"

"Never."

Astrid heard the door open behind her. Her vertigo returned as fragmented images of the sky, trees, people, buildings and a dozen simultaneous conversations overwhelmed her. In the middle of it all, memories of the incident in the forest—of the cats and the jay, the Rottweiler, the mountain lion's sudden appearance—flooded her mind, as vivid as if she was experiencing them for the first time. Buried in the chaos, Astrid sensed an alien presence as if a stranger had invaded her mind and was rummaging through her memories, violently pulling them into her consciousness.

Astrid awoke to find herself lying on the concrete, Claire's yellow cardigan folded beneath her head. Claire kneeled beside her, holding her hand. A crowd formed around them as a man picked up Astrid's chair and set it on its feet. Claire spoke, but her words seemed distorted, indecipherable. Astrid could find no seams in the uninterrupted flow of sounds, no spaces to delineate words and meaning. A bolt of pain crashed through her left temple, and she cried out.

"My God, are you all right?" Claire asked in shock.

The words coalesced in Astrid's mind like a blurred image suddenly coming into focus. She tried to get up, only to fall back, her head spinning. "What happened?" she asked.

"You experienced an attack of vertigo. While you were telling me about it, you passed out." Claire paused as if to emphasize the seriousness of what had happened. "You need to go to the doctor," she pressed

"I'll be okay," Astrid said as she sat up.

Claire looked at her with the same 'don't give me that bullshit' look Astrid had seen her use on her children. The woman in the ivory blouse—the stranger Astrid had helped through the coffeehouse door—stepped out of the crowd. She set her bags on a nearby vacant table, kneeled, and put her hand on Astrid's forehead. Her touch was strangely soothing.

"She'll be all right," the woman said.

"Are you a doctor?" Claire confronted the stranger.

"No, but I've seen this before," she answered in an unidentifiable accent. "Family members." Her dark brown hair fell loosely around a face that combined Asian, European, and African features with echoes of cultures long forgotten. She turned to Claire. "Are you her friend?"

Claire stared mutely, annoyed by the woman's intrusion.

"It's good that you will be able to help her," the woman said, touching Claire's shoulder.

Claire looked down at the woman's hand, then glared back at her. The woman smiled back, gathered her packages, and left through the thinning crowd.

"I'm feeling better," Astrid said. She stood and stretched her neck and shoulders like a sprinter loosening up before a race. "I just need a little air."

"Sweetie," Claire insisted, "this is serious. You need to let me take you to the hospital."

"I don't think eight hours in a waiting room with a bunch of snot-nosed children will help. I'd rather go for a walk."

"You can't ignore this," Claire insisted.

"It's always worked before."

"Seriously?"

Astrid took her friend's hand. "I promise, if I have any more symptoms, you can take me to the emergency room."

Reluctantly, Claire accepted her terms. As they started to leave, Astrid saw the woman in the ivory blouse cross the street. A younger man in a perfectly fitted navy-blue blazer, an open-collared white shirt, and khaki slacks rushed to meet her. His light brown hair was carefully disheveled and only a little too long. He took her packages and escorted her to a silver BMW parked nearby. Astrid watched them drive away.

"Come on," she said, taking Claire by the hand. "Let's take a walk."

Chapter 3

Astrid turned onto the dirt road that led to her mother's house. Although the symptoms she had experienced at the coffeehouse had not returned, she was relieved to cross the drainage ditch that marked the edge of Sigrid's property. As she parked on the gravel next to the wooden porch and removed the key from the ignition, Astrid noticed the door to the house was ajar. The sense of relief left her immediately. Ignoring the knot in her stomach, she stepped to the ground and walked quickly, quietly, to the open door. She heard irregular footsteps and the cries of frightened cats coming from inside the house.

Astrid glanced through the narrow opening and saw no one in the entryway. Holding her breath, she slipped inside. Sigrid had kept a pistol, along with pepper spray, a Taser, and other home defense paraphernalia, in an oak sideboard near the door. Astrid opened the drawer quietly and found the .357 magnum revolver among the souvenirs of an old woman's fears. She checked that it was loaded and looked through the archway into the living room. A man dressed in work boots, jeans, and a red plaid flannel shirt stood with his back to her. He reached toward the bookshelf where Audrey crouched, hissing, fangs bared. Astrid cocked the pistol and stepped into the living room. "What are you doing here?" she shouted.

Astrid felt her breath catch as he turned to face her. He was shockingly handsome beneath his dark blond hair, and he moved with the effortless grace of a beloved adolescent. Only his eyes betrayed him—sharp and unsettling as if sequestered by pain and intensified by rage. He stared at her as if the revolver aimed at his chest was little more than a curiosity, then turned back to the bookshelves and dragged Audrey from her refuge. Howling in terror, the cat bit and clawed at his arms. The intruder did not react as he tightened his grip on the scruff of her neck, pulling the skin across her skull, drawing her eyes into slits, her lips into a grimace. Audrey stopped struggling but continued to growl.

Astrid steadied the revolver with both hands and aimed at the intruder. "Put her down," she demanded.

Ignoring the weapon, he walked toward the woman blocking his exit. Astrid lowered her aim away from Audrey, toward the stranger's right thigh, and squeezed the trigger. He cried out and stumbled as the bullet ripped through his leg. Breaking free, Audrey fell to the floor and ran toward the back of the house. The intruder looked down at the blood spreading across his leg and closed his eyes in concentration. The ragged wound closed, and the bloody jeans mended, leaving no trace of an injury that should have left him screaming on the floor. He glanced toward the hall where Audrey had fled, then walked quickly toward Astrid.

She cocked the pistol and fired again, aiming at the center of his chest. This time, the weapon had no effect. The shots did not drive him back, the cloth did not tear, and blood did not flow from a wound that would soon close. Each bullet left only a faint disturbance, spreading across his chest like ripples in a pond. Astrid fired until the hammer struck a spent round with an impotent click. The stranger closed the distance between them and knocked the pistol from her hands, sending it clattering across the room. Bringing his arm back around, he struck her hard on the cheek with the back of his hand, knocking her to the floor. Astrid fought to her feet as flashes of light danced in her eyes and her cheek started to burn. She saw the man walk toward the back of the house where the cats had fled.

Astrid ran to the entryway, hoping she could find some weapon in her mother's armory to use against this impossible threat. As she crossed the room, the floor seemed to move beneath her feet. She reached out to steady herself against the wall, turned, and saw a blue flash illuminate the hallway. The stranger backed into the living room as the great cat Astrid had seen in the forest stalked toward him.

The stranger showed no shock, no surprise as the cat approached in a predatory crouch, a low growl resonating in its chest. Instead, he stepped back and seemed to relax. Blue light swirled around him, and his body flowed like liquid into a form out of a nightmare. His limbs swelled with muscle and a thick tail extended from the base of his spine, curving across the floor. Skin, hair, flannel, and denim flowed together, hardening into bronze scales across his back, shoulders, arms, and legs. Black claws emerged from three stubby fingers on each hand, and his human features smoothed into a snake's elegant muzzle. He stood in a wrestler's stance, tail resting on the floor to brace against an attack or to thrust him forward at the great cat—the cat that now seemed small and vulnerable.

Astrid ran to the entryway and searched the sideboard, scattering pepper spray, keys, and tools across the floor. She found her mother's Taser—black with an ironic pink plastic trim that suggested a marketer's notions about women's self-defense. She slid back the arming switch, charging its capacitors, and ran into the room.

The cat's growl intensified, and Astrid realized she had to act quickly. Focusing the aiming laser on the intruder's back, she approached as near as she dared and pressed the firing button. The pop of compressed gas propelled two darts toward the creature, shining wires trailing behind. The darts struck its plated back and fell to the floor with no effect.

The lizard-thing turned and stared at her through yellow eyes. The cat leaped onto its back, claws digging into its shoulders, jaws clamped on the creature's neck. The intruder swung its snake's head from one side to the other, jaws snapping futilely. It reached for the cat, shoulders twisting, but could not grasp it. The monster screamed in rage and thrust itself back into the wall, crushing the cat against the adobe bricks, cracking the plaster from floor to ceiling. The cat's grip loosened for an instant; the intruder grabbed the skin at its shoulders and threw it across the room. The great cat struck the fireplace and collapsed to the floor, blood dripping from the side of its mouth as the reptilian nightmare moved toward it.

Astrid remembered she could use the Taser as a contact stun device. She charged the electrodes at the weapon's muzzle, ran forward, and pressed it hard against the intruder's back. It screamed and arched its spine in a violent spasm. Thrown back, Astrid somehow kept her footing. Holding the Taser with both hands, she pressed it once more against the bronze scales.

The monster shook violently. Astrid leaned into its convulsions, pressing forward with her arms, back, and shoulders, driving with her legs. Details of scales, limbs, and muscles flowed into one another as the nightmarish form seemed to melt. Suddenly, the creature collapsed upon itself, and Astrid fell forward, nearly landing on top of it. Throwing herself to the side, she rolled across the floor, stopping against the wall.

For an instant, Astrid saw a brutally injured man where the creature had fallen, a mound of burned flesh twisting in pain as he struggled to rise. Blackened scabs covered half of his body, and the bones of his shoulder and arm were held together by little more than charred cartilage. He raised himself on his uninjured arm and stared at her in rage. Half of his face was scarred past recognition, while the rest belonged to the beautiful youth she had confronted in her living room.

As quickly as the stranger had collapsed, a metallic bubble formed around him like a quivering ball of mercury. Astrid smelled a rancid chemical odor—a combination of burning hair, ammonia, and buried in it all, the musk and gardenia of cheap perfume. A rainbow of colors played across the surface of the bubble, like sunlight on an oil slick.

Still holding the Taser, Astrid rose to her feet. The great cat slapped the shining ball and growled at the ripples spreading across its surface. The ball increased in height and contracted in diameter as if struggling to regain its shape, then fell back on itself. After a few seconds, it extruded a tapered pseudopod and pulled itself like a giant amoeba across the floor.

As it crossed the room, a woman wearing an ivory silk blouse and navy-blue slacks appeared in the entryway. Astrid recognized the stranger from the coffeehouse. The woman jumped back, flattening herself against the wall as the quivering globule passed her and slid out the open door. It crossed the driveway as gravel, sticks, and other debris adhered to the rainbowed membrane. The woman watched it leave, then turned to enter the living room. Astrid saw a single tear cross her cheek.

Astrid's grip tightened on the Taser. "Who in the hell are you?" she challenged the stranger standing in the entryway.

The woman ignored her, surveying the chaos that had been Sigrid's living room. Chairs, end tables, and lamps rested like flotsam on the waves of the red Chinese rug bunched against the wall. Shards of flowerpots mingled with the soil and plants they had once enclosed. Books covered the floor like broken bodies. The woman saw the great cat, stepped toward it, and held out her hand, palm up and fingers relaxed.

"So, you're what has everyone so excited," she said as if speaking to an ordinary pet.

The cat padded toward her, then stopped just outside her reach and stretched forward to sniff her hand. To Astrid's astonishment, the animal walked to the stranger and rubbed against her leg like a housecat greeting a trusted visitor. The woman scratched behind its ear. Her hand seemed like a child's against its head. The cat leaned into her until she stumbled sideways.

"Who are you?" Astrid repeated.

The woman ignored her. "And who are you, little one?" she asked the animal.

The cat responded with the same combined meowing and purring sound Spike made when demanding attention.

"I think it's the Swarm," Astrid answered without thinking.

"Swarm," the woman repeated. Kneeling, she took the massive head in both hands and stared into the cat's eyes, her face inches from jaws that could bite through a two-by-four. "An odd name, but I think it suits you."

"No, Swarm is the five—" Astrid stopped in frustration and pointed at the great cat. "What the hell has happened to my animals?" Despite her efforts to suppress it, the name Swarm persisted in her mind.

"What was that thing that was in here?" Astrid demanded. "And who the hell are you?"

The woman kissed the cat on the bridge of its nose, then stood slowly, her hand on its massive head. Picking her way through the devastation—and with the great cat at her side—she walked across the room to the old blue recliner. She sat down, and the cat lay on the floor next to her, grooming itself contentedly. As it dragged its tongue across its paw with unbreakable feline concentration, Astrid saw the webbing between its toes—a feature it shared with Spike.

"I knew your mother," the stranger said.

Astrid noticed the woman's accent but could not identify it. It sounded vaguely like the Greek she had heard as a child when Sigrid read aloud from her beloved Homer but also suggested elements of Middle Eastern dialects, with nuances of the Baltic and the Orient, ultimately echoing the music of some long-forgotten people.

"My mother?" Astrid asked. "Then seeing you in town wasn't an accident."

"No."

"Did you have something to do with all this?"

"No."

"Then who was that man? And, what does he want with my cats?"

"Your cats are clearly of value to the man you fought," the woman said patiently, "but I do not know what he wants with them."

"He wasn't human."

"He's as human as you are . . . for the most part."

"But the way he changed shape . . . Bullets didn't harm him."

"Weapons may have some effect until he adapts to them. What you saw—the healing of the wounds, the reptilian form—were enchantments."

"What are you talking about?" Astrid asked, nearly shouting. She rubbed the side of her face, which was starting to throb where he'd struck her. "He didn't hit like an illusion."

"His enchantments are not simple illusions," the woman explained. "They can appear real in every way."

"Bullshit." Astrid pointed at the great cat. "What's happened to my animals? Is that an enchantment?"

"No, Swarm is real."

"Jesus, I must be losing my mind."

"You're not." The woman smiled ironically. "I would have noticed."

"'You would have noticed.' What the hell does that mean?" Astrid demanded. "Wait . . . At the coffeehouse . . . my vertigo, the syn—" Astrid stopped, trying to remember what Claire called her sensory chaos.

"Synesthesia?" the stranger offered. "It was necessary."

"Necessary?" Astrid glared at her. "You were fucking with my mind. What was it? Did you drug me somehow?"

"I did not drug you."

Astrid stared at her mutely, took her cell phone from the pocket of her jeans, and dialed 911. The phone did not respond.

"Is this your doing?" Astrid demanded, holding up the phone.

The woman said nothing. Astrid returned the phone to her pocket and inhaled deeply, her legs shaking from the adrenaline that saturated her system. The cat—Swarm, she found herself thinking reluctantly—lay next to the woman with its paws forward, its head resting on its forelegs, its eyes closed in contentment. The stranger continued to scratch behind its ear.

Astrid heard a sound behind her. The man who had met the woman at the coffeehouse stood in the entryway, nervously examining the room.

"What's going on?"

"Scott, darling," the woman said, "please wait in the car."

"I thought we were going to Santa Fe." He did not notice the great cat on the other side of the recliner.

"Please, Scott," the woman said in a voice not used to asking twice. "I have business here."

He stared at her as if trying to choose from a set of bad options. "I'll be in the car," he said finally, his voice thick with resentment.

Astrid watched him close the door carefully as he left, an absurdly ironic gesture amidst the house's devastation.

"Poor Scott isn't the brightest thing," the woman mused, "and, like most young men, he's terribly self-absorbed. Though, that does have advantages. He was probably checking his phone when your visitor crossed the driveway. Now that would have been hard to explain."

"But you're doing such a wonderful job explaining it to me," Astrid said sarcastically.

The woman ignored her and raised her finger to her lips. Astrid watched Swarm fall asleep, and she realized that the name had bound itself permanently to the great cat. She felt the room start to move as the woman reached into the shimmering blue distortions that surrounded the sleeping animal.

"I hate the noise that comes with these transformations," she said as the disturbance subsided. "It will lessen with time."

Astrid saw colors play across Swarm's fur. Audrey's tortoiseshell flowed like water through Spike's blonde coat, and Elizabeth's golden eyes orbited each other a foot apart in a swirl of orange. Eyes, ears, noses, mouths, and tails appeared as the distorted figures of Greystoke and Chessie joined their siblings in the kaleidoscopic transformation. It reminded Astrid of suddenly becoming aware of the details in an Escher painting of fractal animals—of birds composed of birds, of lizards composed of lizards—of Swarm composed of her five ordinary pets. The flowing colors solidified as spaces formed between them, and Sigrid's cats appeared on the floor.

Astrid stared, unable to move. Spike walked toward her and stared with sage-green eyes, asking for attention with his distinctive meowing and purring song. Astrid remembered the same sound coming from the great cat and realized she would never hear it the same way again. Chessie hissed at Greystoke as he pawed at her, then she ran to the bedroom, her brother chasing behind. Elizabeth began to groom herself compulsively as Audrey climbed to the top of a still intact bookshelf and surveyed the devastation around her.

"I know this is hard for you," the woman said, "but I will try to explain. Your animals belong to an age when the substance of life was less settled than it is now, as does the man you fought." She searched Astrid's face for some sign of comprehension but found none. "It is an age when physical form more closely reflected desire."

"What the fuck are you talking about? There was never a time when this could happen."

"Strictly speaking, this is not only about time."

"You said another age."

The woman shrugged. "That is a limitation of your language. Try to think beyond it."

"This is getting us nowhere," Astrid said, her frustration deepening.

"It's a start," the woman said patiently.

Astrid heard a noise from the entryway. Scott stepped into the living room, his hands on his hips.

"Something's happened here," he complained, gesturing angrily at the destruction around him. "I'll help if I can, but don't leave me outside like I'm your chauffeur."

"Scott," the woman said firmly, "go back to the car."

"Not without an explanation."

"Everyone wants explanations," the woman groaned. "I don't have time for this."

"Make time," Scott demanded.

The woman's dark eyes hardened—they seemed to take on the color and sheen of steel. Once again, Astrid felt a disturbance in the air. She saw Scott's face distort in pain. He lurched forward, his features contorted into a grimace, spasms bending his back into an impossible arch. He fell to his hands and knees as the convulsions intensified.

"My God!" he cried out.

Scott's legs shook inside the perfectly creased khaki pants, then drew up toward his buttocks, pant legs crumpling behind them. His polished loafers fell empty on the floor, and his arms shortened in the sleeves of his blazer, leaving it to cover his body like a blanket. Scott trembled beneath the cloth as if wracked by the chills of a terrible sickness. His voice turned to groans, then to something like an infant's cries, then to beastly squeals of terror. His soft eyes shrank and spread apart, his ears grew long, his nose swelled and flattened, nostrils pulsing.

Astrid saw a porcine head emerge from the carefully selected clothing, hairless except for a few scattered bristles, the shreds of Scott's white shirt hanging from its neck. The creature's squeals filled the room as it shook off the restraints of Scott's wardrobe and stood, panting amidst the room's devastation, a perfectly formed boar. It walked into the entryway on four short legs, snorting loudly, then turned and ran out the door. Hooved feet resonated on the wooden porch, then crunched across the gravel driveway.

Astrid found herself thrust from the chair, her movements as uncontrollable as the convulsions that had seized Scott. She thought she was being transformed into a beast herself until she realized rage was driving her at the woman, frustration hardening into violent purpose.

"God damn you," she shouted as she ran toward the seated stranger with her fists clenched. "God damn you to fucking hell."

The woman leaped to her feet and brought both hands up, knocking Astrid's arms apart. She slapped her hard across the face. Astrid landed painfully on her ass, legs spread in front of her like a child's, her face throbbing.

"Don't . . . Hit . . . Me," Astrid growled.

"You must be calm," the woman said, raising a hand and cocking her head as if listening for a distant sound.

"Calm? You want me to be calm?"

"Your visitor—the man you fought—is recovering faster than I thought."

Chapter 4

Astrid retrieved the Taser from the floor. "Are you telling me that thing is coming back?"

"That won't affect him again," the woman said.

"What the hell are you talking about?"

"He'll have learned."

"You can't learn to ignore an electric shock."

The woman snatched the Taser from Astrid's hand, pulled the neck of her blouse aside, and pressed the device against the skin below her throat. As the stun gun discharged, she took several short, fast breaths, then relaxed, inhaled sharply, and smiled. She handed Astrid the weapon.

"The man you fought has little experience holding a form here," the woman explained. "Your weapon distracted him, causing . . . well, you saw what happened. But he is highly intelligent, and it won't happen again."

"Holding a form here?" Astrid repeated as she disarmed the Taser and pushed the handle under her belt. "What the hell does that mean?"

"You wouldn't understand."

"Try me."

"Very well. The intruder and I are part of your reality, but a part you rarely allow yourselves to experience."

"You must be joking."

The woman looked at Astrid like a professor confronting a particularly dull student. "Our worlds are deeply interconnected."

"Interconnected?"

"Information flows between them."

"What information?"

"Everything."

"What do you mean, everything?"

"Everything from quantum states to stories."

"This is nonsense."

"You need to know where to look and how to listen."

Astrid gritted her teeth in frustration. "How did he get here? Can you send him back the same way?"

The woman held up a hand and cocked her head, listening intently. "You must leave," she said sharply. "Take the animals and go. Now."

"Is . . . is he coming?"

"Yes. You only have a few minutes."

"Won't he follow?"

"He'll follow until he gets what he wants."

"What the hell is going on? Can't you stop him?"

"It's not that simple."

Astrid stared in stunned comprehension. "You want to see what happens."

The woman said nothing.

"You're using me. You're using the cats," Astrid said in shock. "What are we? Fucking bait?"

"There are things you don't understand."

"Bullshit."

Astrid ran to the laundry room where Sigrid had stockpiled five cat carriers, ready for some sudden evacuation. She remembered the 12-gauge pump shotgun her mother had kept in a locked cabinet near the dryer.

"Not that simple my ass," she muttered as she dialed the combination to the locked door. She took the box of shells from the shelf, loaded the shotgun, and chambered a round. "Let's see how you adapt when you're scattered all over the wall, you son of a bitch."

She set the safety, leaned the weapon against the cabinet, and carried two cat carriers into the living room. She saw no trace of the animals. "Can you help me find the cats?"

"Of course," the woman said. She kneeled on the floor, and the five animals appeared from under the furniture, from the back of the house, and from the kitchen to gather around her.

"I could ask them to become Swarm," the woman offered as she stroked the cats. "She would follow you. It would simplify things."

Astrid laughed involuntarily. "This will do."

Making several trips between the laundry room and the car, Astrid put the cats in their carriers and loaded them into the back of the Jeep. When she returned to the house for the shotgun, the woman had vanished.

"Bitch," Astrid swore softly.

Astrid tried her phone once more, but it did not respond. She scanned the devastation of her living room, searching for anything she might be able to use. She looked for the pistol, but it was lost in the rubble. Astrid checked the Taser, then returned it to her belt. She picked up the shotgun, clamped the box of shells under her arm, and left the ruins of her home.

"Sorry, Scott," she said as she passed the boar who had overturned the trashcan and was enthusiastically devouring a fragment of take-out pizza.

Astrid placed the shotgun in the car, resting against the passenger-side door. She removed the Taser from her belt and lay it on the seat next to the box of shotgun shells. She glanced in the mirror to check the cat carriers in the back, then started the car and looked down the long driveway.

The man in the flannel shirt stood twenty yards in front of her. She pressed the gas pedal to the floor, gravel flying as she accelerated toward him. He made no effort to get out of the way. Astrid felt a thud as the car struck him, followed by jolts to the front and then rear wheels.

"Try ignoring that, asshole," she said as she slowed and looked in the rear-view mirror. She saw the stranger stand, his left leg hanging at an impossible angle. He reached down, pushed it back into place, and walked toward her.

Astrid downshifted and pressed the gas pedal to the floor. As she accelerated away, a large object filled the periphery of her vision. A tall Ponderosa pine fell across the road in front of her, its trunk bouncing as twigs and needles swirled in a cloud of dust. In reflex, she jerked the wheel to the right. The Jeep nosed into the drainage ditch at the front of the property, tilting violently to the left. Dirty water splashed across the windshield as the front bumper dug into the bottom of the ditch. The Jeep's rear end rose into the air, then fell back, landing on its left side as the airbag struck her face, sending a sharp pain through her neck. Astrid felt her left hand hit the dash as pain burned up her arm, through her shoulder, flooding her mind.

Astrid knew she had broken her wrist.

The car rested on its left side at the bottom of the drainage ditch. The shotgun had fallen against her, its barrel resting against her cheek. Astrid pushed the weapon away and released the seatbelt. She grabbed the passenger seat with her uninjured right arm and tried to pull herself free, only to fall back as pain overcame her. She heard a noise at the back of the car and looked in the rear-view mirror. The man in the plaid shirt had opened the rear hatch and was removing a single cat carrier. Astrid saw Spike's blonde fur through the steel grating of the carrier's door. She screamed in pain, in rage, in fear for her animal, but the stranger ignored her.

Astrid struggled to free herself from the wreckage as Spike's abductor climbed the ditch bank. She tried the switch to open the passenger-side window. Luckily, the mechanism still functioned, and the glass withdrew like a hatch over her head. She twisted in the seat, trying to get her feet under her. Each movement burned through her left arm, into her shoulder, consuming her awareness. Fighting through the pain, she climbed onto the hump that ran between the bucket seats, pushed the shotgun through the open window, and followed. She slid across the car door on her buttocks, pushing the shotgun beside her. Astrid tried to lower herself into the muddy ditch. She fell, desperately trying—and failing—to protect her broken wrist. For a moment, she feared she would pass out. Astrid closed her eyes, took a deep breath, and retrieved the shotgun from the top of the car. She fought through the mud and pain to the rear of the Jeep.

The rear hatch remained open, and the carriers lay in a jumble on their sides. Astrid heard small cries from inside them and looked through mesh doors at the cats. The four remaining animals were alive, conscious, and appeared uninjured. She straightened the cages but did not release the cats. Although they were frightened, she knew they would be safe while she went after Spike.

Astrid climbed the side of the drainage ditch, holding the shotgun across her chest with the stock clamped between her body and right arm, resting her broken left wrist along the top of the weapon, hoping to immobilize the injury even slightly, to reduce the pain that punctuated each step. As she climbed out of the ditch, she glanced back at the road where the Ponderosa had fallen. The tree still stood.

"Son of a bitch," Astrid swore. "It was an illusion."

She saw the stranger walk across the field toward the forest, Spike's pale blue carrier in his right hand. She forced herself to follow him, jolts of pain fueling the constant fire in her arm and shoulder.

Blinded by rage and injury, Astrid did not see the woman in the blue slacks and silk blouse walk to the back of the Jeep. The woman carried each cat to the top of the ditch bank, freed it from the carrier, and checked for injuries. Chessie raised her front leg and looked up at her. The woman took the cat's limb in her hand and closed her eyes in concentration. She released it, and Chessie stood normally. The woman took Elizabeth into her arms.

"Go, little ones, follow her," she said. She held Elizabeth close as she watched Greystoke, Audrey, and Chessie sprint across the field.

Astrid fought through pain and exhaustion to close the distance between herself and Spike's abductor.

"You son of a bitch," she screamed at him.

He turned to face her, holding the plastic carrier in his right hand, the muscles in his arm and shoulder alternately tensing and relaxing, his torso rocking as he compensated for Spike's struggles. He stood some five yards from where the national forest bordered the grass and mesquite of the open space and ten yards from Astrid. She released the safety on the shotgun, even though she could not fire it without endangering Spike. She made eye contact with the stranger.

"Why are you doing this?"

For a moment, Astrid saw a look of sadness shadow the youth's perfect features as tears dampened his cheek. He turned without speaking and walked away.

Astrid cursed and struggled after him, fighting through an aspic of pain. She heard a rustle in the dry grass and turned to see Chessie, Audrey, and Greystoke running toward her. The woman in the navy-blue pants and ivory blouse watched from the bank of the drainage ditch, holding Elizabeth in her arms, empty cat carriers scattered around her.

"Damn you," Astrid cursed.

As the cats encircled her, Chessie began to rub against her leg. She pushed the cat away gently with her foot. "Go back, Chessie," Astrid said sharply.

The gray tabby stared up at her. Astrid looked toward Spike's captor and saw him disappear into the forest. Although she knew Chessie and the others would follow, she continued forward, her only thought to recover Spike. Instinct drew her into the clearing where she had seen the five cats and the blue jay—the clearing where Swarm had first appeared.

"Spike," she called. "Spike, where are you?"

She heard a feline cry and hurried toward it, her throbbing left forearm resting on the shotgun for support. She longed to be still, to stop the pain, but she forced herself forward. She came to a clearing where the stranger stood near a canyon wall, Spike's carrier in his hand. He glanced at her briefly, then turned and walked toward the wall's granite face. Astrid saw the details of his form blur—flannel, denim, skin, and the blue plastic of the carrier stretched toward the cliff face as if pulled by some perversion of gravity. He froze for a moment, a surreal rendering of a man and his burden melting into stone, then snapped like a stretched rubber band, vanishing silently into the rock.

Screaming in anger and frustration, Astrid ran to where Spike and his abductor had disappeared. She leaned the shotgun against the cliff wall and frantically felt along the granite with her right hand, each movement sending a bolt of pain through broken bone and bruised flesh. She fell to her knees, trying to slow her breathing, to suppress the rage and confusion swirling in her mind. Chessie, Greystoke, and Audrey milled around her.

Astrid remembered that the woman in the ivory blouse still had Elizabeth. She struggled to her feet, retrieved the shotgun, and started back. After only a few steps, the pain engulfed her once more. Her legs collapsed, and she landed cross-legged in the dirt, the shotgun beside her. The cats gathered around her with Chessie meowing at her side, Audrey rubbing against her hip, and Greystoke reaching up to plant his paws on her shoulder.

Without thinking, Astrid pulled Chessie closer with her right arm. A tingling like a thousand pinpricks spread up her arm from where she touched the cat. She tried to pull her hand away, but her muscles did not respond. She felt the same tingling in her hip as Audrey leaned against it and again in her shoulder where Greystoke pressed his paws. A vortex of blue light surrounded her, so bright she could not see past it. The pinpricks spread through her body from each point of the animals' contact, electric pulses burning through nerves and throwing muscles into spasm. The spasms increased in frequency and intensity as if her flesh was melting. Astrid no longer felt the touch of the three cats against her skin, only their presence—intense, with neither boundary nor extent, unsettling in its intimacy.

Astrid felt the constant, implicit awareness of her limbs, her skin, and her viscera diffuse like mist, then collapse into a small knot in her brainstem, a vague pressure at the base of her skull. Only the pain of her wrist remained, orbiting the knot of sensation like a jagged moon. She fell backward, but instead of striking the ground, Astrid continued to fall into darkness, her vision collapsing into a diminishing circle of light.

Images from her past raced through Astrid's mind, each appearing briefly, vividly before receding into darkness. She relived the pain of learning her mother had died and longed to touch her one last time. For an instant, she saw her mother's reassuring smile and, just as quickly, saw it slip away. She fell through her past—through her divorce, through the years spent on her business, through graduate school—her fall accelerating with each memory.

She saw the face of her undergraduate literature professor, a brilliant woman who had taken the time to teach a confused freshman the magic of words. She saw men she had loved and felt each touch as if on a body not her own. She heard Claire's laughter and saw her smile, her dark skin shining with sweat as she held out a shot glass filled with amber liquid. Astrid felt the burn of tequila down her throat as Claire offered her a wedge of lime and then slipped away into the darkness. She felt Alan's hand on her skin and saw him as he once was, the fires of betrayal not yet ignited.

As the past unwound through the sharp pains of adolescence and the impressionistic recollections of childhood, memories not of her own making—wordless impressions, animal emotions, the joy of a developing body discovering itself—parted the cracks in her awareness. She found herself small, blind, and helpless, her face buried in fur as warm sweet milk flowed down her throat. She felt other bodies push against her and struggled to hold the nipple, her paws pushing rhythmically against the warm breast. She tried to crawl and fell onto her side, four legs paddling ineffectively in the air. She felt a familiar touch roll her onto her stomach as her mother's jaws closed around the scruff of her neck, carrying her back into the darkness.

She remembered growing stronger, her eyes opening as vision slowly joined smell, sound, and touch. Her legs carried her haltingly into the world, compelled by the intentions of a wordless mind. She hid in dark places, chasing small creatures across the ground. She felt a living form twist in her mouth and experienced an almost erotic thrill as it struggled, blood salty on her tongue.

The chaos of memories faded as vision, hearing, smell, and touch flowed into one another, coalescing into the pure presence of sun, wind, trees, and earth. She discovered a self without language or history, name or story, a mind indistinguishable from the movement of trees in the wind, the flicker of the sun through the leaves, the pressure of air and earth against her. Her vision became sharper, and she saw the world in shades of blue and green, in patterns of motion against an indistinct background.

Astrid looked down and saw fur covering her body, colors rippling through it—gray, brindle, black, and the reddish-brown of her own hair. She tried to find her center, but hers was only one of four minds swirling in shared currents of blood and breath. She clung to the knot at the base of her skull, the remnants of an almost forgotten physicality.

As the currents flowed together, Astrid felt stronger, her nerves more finely tuned, and a delicious mindfulness enfolded her, as intimate as a breath shared with a stranger. Three bright minds surrounded her in a dimensionless space. She became one of four facets in a polyhedral intelligence, four strings vibrating in an indecipherable chord, four currents flowing into a single stream of intention. The pain of her broken wrist faded to a distant ache as she joined Audrey, Chessie, and Greystoke in a shared body. The wills of the three animals carried her forward across the clearing.

As they neared the cliff face where Spike had vanished, Astrid felt the muscles of her legs tense as three feline minds enveloped her. She felt a surge of panic as the rock wall rushed toward her.

The disturbance passed from the cliff face, dispersing into the air and trees. The woman in the ivory blouse and navy-blue slacks entered the clearing, holding Elizabeth in her arms, idly scratching her behind the ears.

"See, it was just like I promised. Astrid has joined your littermates and gone to find your brother."

Elizabeth looked up at her through narrowed eyes.

"I know you miss them, little one, but everything will happen as the fates require."

She kissed the cat gently on the forehead. "I'm going to take you home with me. Would you like that? I know my ladies will love you. They'll give you treats." The woman smiled as she hefted the chubby body. "Fresh fish and saucers of warm goat's milk, followed by naps on soft cushions. Who knows, maybe we will learn how all this is meant to unfold." She looked into Elizabeth's copper eyes. "Don't be afraid, little sister. Creatures like us do not travel by smashing our faces through a cliff."

She gently set the cat on the ground, then turned and walked back into the forest, Elizabeth trotting beside her. For an instant, there was a disturbance in the air. The leaves fluttered as if touched by an inquisitive breeze, and the woods returned to silence.

Part II

Troy and the Aegean – Stranded Thirteenth Century B.C.E.

Chapter 5

Chessie sat beside Astrid's unconscious body, seeking comfort in the familiar rhythms of her breathing. A rustling of leaves and a motion at the edge of her vision pulled her head around, but it was only a low tree branch stirred by a random breeze. The perception resonated in her littermates' minds, carried by the persistent harmonics of sentience they had shared since before their birth. Just as Greystoke and Audrey felt Chessie's response to the wind in the trees, so did Chessie experience her sister sniffing the air near the cliff face and her brother searching the clearing's perimeter for Spike or Elizabeth's scent.

Spike and Elizabeth. For the first time in her life, Chessie could not fully engage the minds of her two littermates. The constant hum of their thoughts remained, though distant, attenuated, twin voids in her consciousness.

Turning into the breeze, Chessie opened her mouth and inhaled, channeling air over the scent receptors lining her palate. Mingled with the scent of dust and dying leaves, she detected an unusual salinity in the air, and her brother and sister shared the sensation. It joined other shared, anomalous perceptions—an increased humidity, a humic pungency in the soil, the absence of the constant hum of automobiles from the highway. A low growl resonated in her throat.

Chessie sensed a new presence at the edge of her awareness—complex, angular, and startling in its intensity, so unlike her liquid mind. It drew her attention to the woman lying beside her, and she saw her start to move. Chessie pressed against her, and Audrey and Greystoke returned to her side, drawn to the woman stirring on the forest floor.

Astrid awoke to the throbbing in her left wrist. It was the only fixed point in her awareness. Fragmented memories of the initial encounter with the blue jay, her struggles with Spike and Elizabeth's abductors, and most of all, the confusion of sharing Swarm's plural sentience whirled in her mind like trash in a tornado. Even language had abandoned her as she struggled to unearth words buried in the rubble of injury. She found her name in the chaos.

Astrid.

She tried to build on the familiar syllables, but words did not come.

"Fuck." She heard her voice like a curse from a stranger.

Astrid lifted her right hand from the ground and stared at the soil, rock, and plant residue clinging to her skin as if she could reconstruct her world from them. Gradually, the familiar structures of consciousness coalesced from the pain and confusion—the rhythms of her breath; the constant, implicit feedback of muscle, skin, and organs; the alignment of her senses with her surroundings; language's comforting doppelgänger. Audrey rubbed against her side, and Astrid remembered the spreading pinpricks and muscular spasms, the obliteration of her physicality, the experience of her memories being stripped away. She pushed the cat away.

No. That couldn't have happened, she thought. *They must have drugged me.* Audrey returned to brush against her again, but it was only the touch of a cat seeking affection. Astrid lifted the animal onto her lap with her right hand. "I'm sorry, honey. It's not your fault," she whispered,

She released Audrey and struggled to her feet. The clearing was as she remembered. Astrid's left wrist throbbed, grotesquely swollen, spreading pain through her arm and shoulder to consume her awareness. She pushed through the pain, forcing herself to think. She tried her cell phone. It showed no signal and did not connect when she dialed for help. Swearing, she returned it to her pocket. Astrid searched the clearing for the shotgun she had carried into the forest but could not find it. She wondered if the woman who had stolen Elizabeth had taken it as well. She started home, resting her broken wrist on her right forearm, pain harrowing her arm and shoulder with each step. To her relief, the cats remained close to her. When she emerged from the forest and saw her house, she took the phone from her pocket again, but it remained unresponsive.

As she started across the open space, Astrid heard the unmistakable sound of ocean waves. She turned toward it and stared in shock. Instead of her familiar foothills, she saw a grassy plain descend to a curved beach with a seemingly endless row of wooden ships drawn up onto the sand. Tents and makeshift huts sprawled along the shoreline as the smoke of campfires twisted into the sky. She smelled saltwater on the breeze that moved up the plain. Astrid closed her eyes in concentration. She found her center, the fixed hinge of her awareness, and held onto it by force of will. She held it in her mind, in the currents of her breath, in the tension that bound her joints. She opened her eyes slowly.

The shoreline had vanished, replaced by the familiar foothills of the Sandia Mountains, the open space with its native grasses, and mesquite separating the national forest from her home. Astrid continued toward her house with the cats following. She passed Scott's silver BMW, crossed the wooden porch into the house, and confronted her home's devastation.

She rushed to her mother's old phone with its reliable landline, but there was no dial tone. She flipped the light switch on the wall, but nothing happened. *Did he cut the power?*

Astrid walked to the kitchen sink and tried the tap, but nothing left the faucet. She found a bottle of spring water in the pantry and drank deeply. She remembered Scott's BMW and walked to the clothes he had worn, now a rumpled pile amidst the room's chaos. She shook the khaki pants with her uninjured hand, heard the jingle of metal, and removed his keys from the pocket. Astrid walked to the car and turned the key in the ignition. She fought back a rising panic as the engine failed to respond.

Okay, she told herself, *you're going to have to walk for help. But first, you need to stabilize your wrist.*

Astrid went back to the house and opened the bathroom cabinet. She found a bottle of Oxycodone left over from a surgery her mother had undergone a few months before her death. The brown plastic bottle contained several dozen pills, and she silently thanked Sigrid for her habit of keeping anything that might someday be of use. She tried to open the bottle with her right hand and swore at the child-proof cap. Frustrated, Astrid thought of smashing the plastic with her foot, but she stopped herself at the thought of pills scattering across the floor. With her left hand useless, she searched the bathroom for some way to secure the bottle while she removed the cap.

She thought of the vanity drawer and wondered if she could use it as a clamp. Astrid placed the bottle between the cabinet frame and the drawer front and held it closed with her hip. Working carefully, she managed to remove the cap with her right hand. The label said to take one pill every eight hours. She took two and left the open bottle on the sink.

With her nearest neighbor several hundred yards away, Astrid needed to immobilize the break before she went for help. She found an elastic bandage in the vanity drawer and remembered a length of quarter-inch plywood left from a minor cabinet repair. Taking the elastic bandage and a hand towel for padding, she crossed the driveway to Sigrid's workshop and found the plywood in a pile of scrap. It was as she had remembered: about fourteen inches long and three inches wide. Astrid folded the towel into a pad, placed it between her wrist and the plywood, and secured the makeshift splint with the elastic bandage.

Returning to the house, she cut a triangle from the bedsheet using scissors from her mother's sewing drawer and tied it into a sling. The combination of drugs and immobilization reduced the pain to an almost tolerable level. Astrid took a last look around the house and remembered the Oxycodone. She transferred the pills to a plastic bag and put it in the pocket of her jeans. Audrey, Greystoke, and Chessie followed as she went into the kitchen and filled their bowls from another bottle of water.

Astrid kneeled on the floor and reassured each animal in turn. "I need to go for help. I will be back. I promise."

She felt a strange connection with the animals, as if they understood not her words but her intention. She stroked each of them a final time, then left the house, closing the door behind her.

As she walked onto the porch, Astrid stopped in shock. Instead of the familiar path that wound through the piñon, mesquite, and dry grass to the neighbor's house, she found herself once more looking down a long, grassy slope. Two rivers crossed the plain, flowing to a beach where an impossibly blue ocean sparkled with refracted sunlight, polyhedral flashes dancing on the dark waves. Hundreds of wooden ships lined the beach, black with brightly painted decorations—the eyes, jaws, fangs, claws and wings of fantastic beasts. Tents and makeshift huts sprawled chaotically across the shore as if dropped by a storm's violent landfall. To her right—where the foothills of the Sandia Mountains should have been—the plain rose to a fortified city, its stone walls catching the sunlight like dull bronze.

She closed her eyes and breathed deeply, then looked again. The ocean, the ships, and the camp remained. It was a scene she remembered from her mother's many translations of *The Iliad*; an image she had first constructed in her mind as a child, her imagination ignited by Homer's terrifying song of honor and brutality, the ancient masterpiece that shaped the human soul like blood, nerve, muscle, and bone.

"No," she repeated the words like an incantation against madness. "No. No. No."

Astrid stared across the plains of Troy, descending from King Priam's tragic city to the camp of the invading Greeks—Homer's fearsome Achaeans. Transfixed, she forgot the pain in her wrist and the nightmare that had brought her here.

Her trance ended when she saw a half dozen men approaching from less than a hundred yards away.

Chapter 6

As the six men drew closer, the details of their appearance came into focus—including their weapons.

Swords and spears? Astrid thought, fear overcome by disbelief.

An older man walked at the head of the group, wearing a plain linen tunic and a purple cloak secured by a gold brooch. Gray hair fell loosely around his bearded face. Soft leather boots, like moccasins, covered his feet above the ankle. He wore a dagger tucked into his belt, its handle made of what looked like ivory, and carried a wooden spear with a polished bronze tip. He walked with a vigor that forced his younger companions to hurry after him.

A man in his early twenties walked confidently at his side. He wore a red linen tunic and a sheathed sword hung from a leather baldric. His long black hair fell to his shoulders, accented by thin braids decorated with golden beads. He carried a bronze shield with an embossed design but was too far away for Astrid to see the details. From time to time, he looked back over his shoulder to speak to the two men who followed behind him.

The taller of the two warriors wore a tunic dyed the color of wine. He carried a large shield slung over his back. It was made of white and black cowhide stretched over a wooden frame in the shape of a figure-eight—a design that protected him from his chin to his knees while allowing him to thrust freely with the spear he carried in his right hand. Bronze greaves covered his shins, and a leather helmet reinforced with curved white plates framed a bearded face. Astrid recognized it as a boar's tusk helmet, mentioned in *The Iliad* and sometimes found in the graves of Bronze Age warriors. It was a prize only the most deserving wore into battle.

He walked beside a shorter man whose beard framed an open face and full mouth. Long black hair fell from beneath his own boar's tusk helmet. He carried a spear, and a smaller figure-eight shield, which was covered in leather and reinforced with bronze plates. A boy of about thirteen followed the two warriors, carrying a short sword. He wore only sandals and a linen kilt wrapped around his waist.

A man Astrid took to be in his mid-twenties walked to the left of the others, close enough to belong to the group while remaining subtly apart. He was dressed in a short tunic and wore a leather helmet reinforced with bronze plates. A long plume of what looked like horsehair dyed red streamed from the helmet's peak. A short bronze sword dangled from a ring on his leather baldric, and he carried a circular, wooden shield covered with leather.

Astrid stepped to the edge of the porch. "Stop. Who are you?"

Staring nervously, they stopped ten yards away. The man in the purple cloak stepped forward, holding his spear in his right hand, and spoke in a language she did not recognize. The others spread out to stand on either side of him and remained silent, except for the man in the plumed helmet who gestured toward Astrid while talking excitedly to the warrior with the large shield. The tall warrior waved his hand, palm forward, silencing him. Plumed-helmet continued to glare at her.

"Who are you?" Astrid repeated. Although her wrist still throbbed, she sensed she should not show weakness and forced herself to stand straight.

The man in the purple cloak spoke in his strange language. His manner and tone of voice indicated he was the group's leader. He spoke to her once more, then turned back to his men. They gathered in a ragged circle, talking among themselves while occasionally looking back at her or gesturing toward the porch where she stood. Suddenly, the warrior in the plumed helmet broke from the group and started aggressively toward her. The older man called after him, but he continued forward. As he neared the porch stairs, Astrid ran back inside the house and locked the door behind her. She ran past the three frightened cats, into the kitchen and found Sigrid's chef's knife in the drawer. Astrid heard a crash and a splintering of wood. Carrying the knife, she ran into the living room as Audrey, Chessie, and Greystoke fled down the hall.

Plumed-helmet stood in the entryway, his right hand resting on the hilt of his sword as he stared uncomfortably at his strange surroundings. Taking a deep breath, Astrid confronted him with as much confidence as her pain-wracked body would permit. Holding the knife in her right hand, she shouted at him to leave. He lunged toward her. Astrid stepped back in reflex but failed to avoid his attack. He struck her right forearm with the edge of his shield, knocking the knife from her grasp and sending a sharp pain up her arm. He grabbed the front of her sweater, dragged her through the entryway, and violently threw her onto the porch. Pain exploded from

Astrid's broken wrist, and flashes of light pocked her vision. When her eyesight cleared, she saw Plumed-helmet standing over her, his sword raised, and his face contorted with menace.

The young warrior with the bronze shield ran onto the porch and pulled him away. Plumed-helmet shouted angrily at the man who faced him silently, eyes narrowed, sword still in its sheath. Even though their confrontation could determine if she lived more than a few more moments, Astrid found her eyes drawn to the scene embossed on the young warrior's bronze shield. A chariot and two horses filled its center. The rider of the chariot drove a spear into a fallen enemy as the horses reared above another warrior who faced them with a raised sword.

The older man in the purple cloak walked onto the porch and spoke in a voice accustomed to obedience. Plumed-helmet turned to him and continued to argue, his angry staccato landing like rocks against an ancient wall. After a time, the older man raised his voice in a short phrase, his muscles tightening with purpose, his chest and shoulders rising and falling with each breath to dominate the space around him. He tilted his bronze-tipped spear imperceptibly toward Plumed-helmet, who stepped back in silence, anger locked in his face. The other warriors watched from the foot of the steps, talking among themselves.

Trying to ignore the pain in her wrist, Astrid struggled to her feet and faced the group's leader. He was above average height and well-conditioned, although his muscles showed the lean quality often seen in older athletes. Astrid guessed he was in his late fifties or early sixties, and she noted the scars on his arms and legs—signs of a life spent in hard conflict. His gray hair and neatly trimmed beard framed a weathered face, still handsome, with prominent cheekbones and a straight nose marred by the angle of a poorly mended break. His dark eyes suggested a disciplined intellect. He stepped toward her, examining her face, her clothes, and her injured arm. He moved the spear to his left hand and reached toward the sleeve of Astrid's black sweater as if curious about the strange garment.

"What are you doing?" she demanded as she pulled back. "Who are you?"

As she spoke, the young warrior with the bronze shield began to laugh, and the laughter spread to the others. She heard a small cry behind her, turned, and saw Audrey step through the broken door onto the porch, with Greystoke and Chessie close behind. The man in the purple cloak looked at the cats, then back at Astrid as his face relaxed into a smile. He turned to his men and raised his hand. They lowered their voices but continued to laugh among themselves—all but Plumed-helmet, who aggressively stepped toward the animals.

Astrid moved in front of him, blocking his way. She realized the others were watching, judging her actions. Plumed-helmet glared at her, and she stared back coldly. He tried to step around her, but she stepped sideways, staying between him and the cats.

"Leave them alone," she demanded.

He reached out and grasped her left bicep to throw her aside. Ignoring the pain burning from her broken wrist, Astrid pushed against his chest with her right hand. She caught him off balance. Rage filled his eyes as he stumbled back. He started toward her angrily, then froze, his face slack with disbelief. He turned and ran from the porch. Audrey, Chessie, and Greystoke followed and ran through the grass to stop a safe distance from both the house and the Achaeans. Astrid remained on the porch, staring at her house in shock.

The house shimmered in front of her like crystal. Astrid saw through its walls into the ruins of her living room, into the kitchen, the bedrooms, the wires and pipes passing like shadows through walls of glass. The furniture, books, and possessions that had formed the physical armature of her life caught the sunlight like prisms, bathing the chaos of her living room, the cluttered kitchen, and the sanctuary of her bedroom and bath in a thousand rainbows. Astrid stood paralyzed as the house began to shimmer and dissolve into mist.

She felt a hand grasp her right arm and drag her across the porch. It was the young warrior with the bronze shield, shouting in his strange language and pulling her down the wooden steps. The older warrior left the porch beside them. Astrid and the young warrior fell to the ground as the last step dissolved beneath their feet. She watched her home vanish like fog in the heat of the day.

Astrid heard a rumble of voices and a clatter of bronze as the warriors reacted to the house's disappearance. Pain burned from her left wrist through her arm and shoulder as she tried to stand but fell back on the dirt. The warriors stood around her, their hands tightening on their weapons. The group's leader spoke sharply to them. They stepped back a few yards and continued to argue among themselves, gesturing toward Astrid and the empty ground where her house once stood. Their leader frowned and waved them away. They withdrew some thirty feet, watching her apprehensively.

The group's leader turned back to Astrid and laid his spear on the ground. Gathering his purple cloak around him, he sat across from her. He removed a worn leather bag from his beneath his cloak and handed it to her without speaking. Astrid felt it yield in her hand with the unmistakable weight of water. She drank deeply, despite its brackish taste.

"Thank you," she rasped as she returned the water skin.

He raised his hand in a reassuring gesture. Astrid allowed him to take the sleeve of her black sweater between his thumb and fingers. Surprise crossed his features as he felt the unfamiliar knit. He touched her injured left arm, fingers resting on the makeshift sling with surprising gentleness. Not taking his eyes off her, the man in the purple cloak placed his hand on his chest and spoke a short phrase while looking at her expectantly.

"I'm sorry," Astrid said, shaking her head. "I can't understand you."

He repeated the phrase slowly. This time, the syllables formed in Astrid's mind with stunning clarity. *Nestor.*

Astrid's breath caught in her chest. It was a name she had first heard as a child in the stories her mother had read to her. It was the name of Homer's great horseman, Nestor of Pylos, the warrior king who had led three generations of men into battle, earning respect for his mastery of strategy and his wisdom in council. Astrid wondered if he could possibly be the Nestor of legend and if the men with him could indeed be Achaean warriors.

"Nestor," she said to him.

Nestor smiled broadly, revealing even, white teeth, and the wrinkles at the edge of his eyes deepened. He gestured toward her with an open hand, palm up. She placed her hand on her chest.

"Astrid."

He looked at her inquisitively, and she repeated her name.

"Astrid," he said, struggling with the unfamiliar syllables.

"Yes," she said. "Astrid."

Nestor stood to his feet and held out his hand. Astrid let him help her up. He gestured to his warriors. They returned to his side but remained wary of this woman who had appeared from nowhere like a god or sorceress, and whose house had vanished like an exhausted enchantment. The cats remained nearby. For reasons she did not understand, Astrid knew they would remain close to her.

"Astrid," he said as he pointed toward the beach with one hand and motioned for her to follow him with the other. She looked down at the row of dark ships on the beach, the encampment sprawling from them, and the plain rising to the fortress-city. She turned and stared at the grass where her home had stood.

That's it, then, she told herself. She felt a gentle pressure on her right arm and turned to face Nestor. He gestured toward the beach and repeated her name. Astrid nodded and walked with him and his warriors down the sloping plain crossed by two rivers, descending to the long white beach and dark ocean.

Chapter 7

As Astrid followed Nestor down the slope, she heard him speak to the young boy who had accompanied him to her house. For an instant, she recognized the words "go" and "quickly" within the stream of unfamiliar sounds. A sharp pain pierced the left side of her head, colliding with the throbbing of her wrist. She stumbled and fell to one knee. Astrid composed herself as quickly as she could and returned to her feet. She took the plastic bag of painkillers from her pocket, removed another pill, and gestured toward the water skin Nestor carried. He handed it to her and watched, puzzled, as she swallowed the painkiller.

"Thank you," she said as she returned the waterskin.

Nestor spoke to the boy again, but this time, Astrid recognized nothing in his words. The boy ran down the hill toward the encampment.

As they continued across the plain, they passed the residue of war—fragments of shattered shields and splintered spear shafts, spent arrows, broken bows, and abandoned bronze swords littered the ground. Astrid noticed a piece of leather with boar tusks sewed to it and watched Plumed-helmet rush to pick it up. He tucked it behind his shield—a trophy for some boastful story, or perhaps, material for a boar's tusk helmet of his own?

Astrid saw a dog of no discernible breed pull on a long object like a puppy tugging on a towel, sinking to its haunches, shaking its head, and growling. The rest of the pack barked encouragement. She realized the dog was pulling on a human arm, the body buried in the sand, and she suppressed a wave of nausea. Astrid checked on Chessie, Audrey, and Greystoke, who had moved to keep her and the Achaeans between them and the dogs.

They reached one of the rivers crossing the field and waded through the shallow water. Astrid carried Chessie across, then returned for Greystoke. The young warrior with the bronze shield lifted Audrey across the stream and smiled when Astrid thanked him. She saw a chariot resting on its side in the water downstream, its wheel and axle in pieces. The bloated corpse of a horse lay halfway up the bank, still bound to its yoke, flies swarming around it. Nestor stared at the dead horse, his eyes growing moist.

He spoke to her in his strange language, and Astrid felt a sharp pain shoot through the left side of her head with brutal force. The blue haze and vertigo engulfed her, followed by the same sensations she had felt at the coffeehouse—the heightened perceptions, the dissolution of boundaries between her senses, the chaotic flood of memories. The flat light on the grassy slope, the scent of ocean and dust, and the voices of Nestor's men flowed together with painful intensity. She placed her right hand on her knee to steady herself as consciousness slipped away. Lurching to her right to protect her broken wrist, she fell into the grass.

Astrid awoke to find Nestor kneeling beside her. "Are you all right?"

"Yes," she said automatically. "Wait—you can understand me?"

"Yes, you are speaking my language," he answered with confusion in his voice. He turned to his men. "This is the work of a god."

Plumed-helmet scowled. "Or a sorceress."

"We must not act hastily," Nestor acknowledged, "but we must show her hospitality until we know the gods' will."

"And her animals?" Plumed-helmet pressed, spitting the word 'animals' out with contempt.

"And her animals," Nestor said firmly. "Immortals can appear in any form—human, beast, or even stones and water. Tonight, we will make offerings to the gods and ask for guidance."

Although Astrid understood their words, she somehow realized they were not speaking English.

Nestor turned to her and held out his hand. "Come. Do not be afraid."

"Where am I?" She took his hand and struggled to her feet.

"Troy," he said. "We are nearing my camp."

"Are you King Nestor of Pylos?"

He smiled and nodded.

"Then, this is the Trojan war?"

"Yes. We must return to my camp. It's not safe here."

Astrid looked toward the camp. She saw goats and cattle grazing near the sprawl of tents and a crowd of people gathering to stare at them. The cats had stopped some distance behind her, and Astrid sensed their unease. She walked back to them. Chessie and Audrey circled at her feet, and Greystoke looked up, crying softly.

She kneeled, stroking each cat. "What is it?" she asked softly.

Nestor approached her. "What's wrong?"

"My cats—they're afraid. I think it's all the people."

"Come," he pressed. "We must care for your injuries."

Astrid stood and walked with him a few yards, then stopped and called to the cats. They did not come but circled restlessly, answering her with frightened meows. Astrid seemed to feel their minds hovering at the edge of her awareness—their fear, confusion, and loneliness as immediate as her own.

"Don't be afraid," she said softly, kneeling in the sandy soil and holding out a hand. "Come to me."

The cats stared at her briefly, then ran to a wooden structure at the edge of the encampment. The structure stood above the ground on stilts, and a half-dozen cats prowled around it.

"It's our granary," Nestor explained. "The cats keep the vermin away. Your animals can wait there. No one will harm them."

Astrid watched her cats stop near the granary as a spotted tomcat stepped out and challenged them with an angry hiss. They stood unmoving as the tom approached, his nose raised, sniffing the air. He examined Astrid's animals one by one, accepting Chessie and Audrey as he confirmed their gender—despite their warning hisses. He growled a challenge at Greystoke, who neither responded nor backed away, but kept his face to the tomcat, protecting his back and flanks from attack. The spotted tom hissed again and withdrew. Astrid did not know if it sensed the risks of challenging her three cats—and Swarm—or was simply too lazy to start a fight in the heat of the day. She watched her cats retreat to crouch under a bush a cautious distance from the tomcat and his colony.

"They'll be safe," Nestor reassured her. He placed his hand on the small of her back and guided her toward the camp. Reluctantly, Astrid walked beside him, comforted by the strange connection she felt with her animals, the bond she hoped would bring them back to her.

As they entered the camp, the crowd parted, forming an entrance into a labyrinth of crude structures. Most were tents of varying sizes—a few were almost as large as Sigrid's house. Astrid also saw more permanent buildings, mostly rough wooden huts, some little more than lean-tos, while others were large enough to hold several rooms. A few were made of mud-brick or stone she assumed had been salvaged from the ruins of other buildings. The disorder suggested an improvised settlement, a presence that had lingered longer than planned. She looked inside several shelters as she passed, and was surprised at the comforts she saw, including tables, oil lamps, brightly colored rugs, and raised beds piled with fleeces, blankets, and animal skins.

A narrow stretch of sand separated the encampment from the endless row of ships beached along the water. The ships varied from under ten yards to more than thirty yards in length. The hulls were black from the bitumen used to seal them, and the smell of asphalt mingled with the ocean breeze. The ship's gunwales gracefully curved upward to elaborately carved bows and stern posts that confronted the plain with the painted eyes, teeth, and claws of predatory beasts—both real and imaginary.

As they made their way through the camp, men came out of the tents and huts to watch them pass. Women left their looms or cooking fires, talking excitedly. Astrid was surprised at the colors that brightened the clothes of men and women alike—reds, blues, purples, saffron, and other dyes lost to the archaeologists of her day. The women wore their hair up or in neat braids, accented with cloth headbands or bronze combs. Many wore flounced dresses that reached their ankles, with each layer a different color, while others were accented with fringed kilts tied around their waist, their blouses edged with strips of bright cloth. Astrid was startled to see several women with open bodices walking bare-breasted through the crowd while receiving no more notice than the others. She remembered seeing images of women dressed in this manner on pottery and frescoes from the Aegean Bronze Age.

The farther Astrid walked into the camp, the more the crowd grew, talking excitedly about her appearance, her clothes, and the strange circumstances of her arrival. The question of whether she was a goddess, a sorceress, or an escaped slave was already being debated throughout the camp. Trying to ignore the throbbing in her wrist, she walked silently, holding her head up and keeping her eyes forward.

Nestor led her into an open area surrounded by tents and huts. Rough wooden benches formed a rectangle around a large firepit. He gestured to a seat, and Astrid sat down. He sat beside her. Men began to fill the benches while the women remained behind them. Astrid watched silently, trying to understand the situation in which she found herself—and the impossible events that had brought her to it.

Nestor called to a tall woman in her twenties. She wore a white linen blouse and a long, flounced skirt with alternating layers of turquoise and dark red. A saffron headband held her hair up. Stray curls and the sheen of perspiration on her brow suggested she had been working. Her elegant carriage, black hair, and dark skin reminded Astrid of Claire, and she felt a sudden longing for her friend.

"What have you found, my king?" the young woman asked as she approached, the grace of her carriage mirrored in her lovely features. Her tone and manner were warm, relaxed, and self-possessed.

"That seems to be everyone's question," Nestor responded.

"What do you think?" she pressed gently, emphasizing the word 'you.'

"I think we must treat her with hospitality, Hecamede," he said. "Would you bring her food and something to drink, please?"

Hecamede. The name filled Astrid with a sense of excitement. Hecamede was Nestor's servant in *The Iliad.* She had been given to him as a prize—as a slave, Astrid reminded herself—after the Achaeans had destroyed her home. According to Homer, Nestor treated her with great respect and affection. As Hecamede disappeared into a large tent nearby, a muscular man in his late twenties stepped through the crowd and walked toward them.

"What have you brought us, little brother?" he asked the warrior with the embossed shield. Astrid noticed the family resemblance between them.

"Thrasymedes," the young warrior returned the greeting. "She was in the building that appeared on the hillside."

Thrasymedes, Astrid repeated silently, remembering Nestor's son who had accompanied him to Troy. She guessed he was talking to Antilochus, his younger brother, who was destined to die in the war. Astrid almost forgot the pain in her wrist as she stared in at these people out of legend.

Hecamede returned with a plate of food and a clay cup. Smiling, she placed them on the bench near Astrid, who thanked her self-consciously. She took a portion of cold meat from the strips resting on a mound of boiled barley. It was well-cooked and charred around the edges. Astrid washed it down with a sip from the cup—a sweet wine marked by the taste of wood resin and diluted with water. It reminded her of the Retsina she had tasted in Greek cafés.

The crowd parted as a man in his thirties made his way into the open space. He was dressed in a simple tunic, dyed the color of red wine, with a white border. He wore sandals on his feet, and was unarmed. Although shorter than most of the Achaeans, he was well-muscled, with a presence that dominated his surroundings. As he saw Nestor, a smile spread across his handsome face, teeth bright against a neatly trimmed beard. Black hair fell to his shoulders in thin braids decorated with gold, lapis, and amber beads. He greeted Nestor, and the men embraced.

"So, my friend, what have you found?" the newcomer asked, turning toward Astrid and staring at her thoughtfully. She saw no cruelty behind his dark eyes but no more than a little mercy. "The boy you sent to fetch me said she is a goddess. Perhaps she is only a woman, a refugee come in the hope of hospitality?"

"That, Odysseus, is what we must determine."

Chapter 8

Spike watched the two men argue across the rough wooden table—the man who had taken him from his littermates and a short, older man who smelled of wine and sweat. He leaned into the side of the basket, reeds creaking against leather straps. It was so unlike the blue plastic carrier with its smooth surfaces. His muscles tensed as he remembered how his captor had forced him into this rough prison.

Spike reached out with his senses into the small room, composing a world from the scent of dirt, fire, burned meat, and human body odors; from the glare of sunlight entering through the open door; from the voices of the men and the soft sounds of mice moving in the ceiling. A breeze flowed between the door of the hut and a small opening in the opposite wall. It passed through the reeds of the basket, and Spike turned into it, letting the fresh air from the outside wash over him.

Although his littermates were far away, their minds burned in his awareness. He sensed fear from Chessie, Audrey, and Greystoke, and the fur at the back of his neck rose in response. Although Elizabeth seemed safe, he sensed a loneliness in her that mirrored his own. He longed to be free, at their sides. He also found a new presence within the dimensionless space his mind shared with those of his siblings. He recognized the woman who had cared for him before his abduction, but he did not understand how she had come to join her consciousness with the minds of his littermates.

The short man kneeled on the floor in front of him and smiled with yellow teeth, his breath carrying the smell of wine, onion, and burned meat through his black beard. He touched the side of the basket with dirty hands, pulling the reeds apart to stare inside. Spike growled and retreated until the back of the cage pressed into his buttocks. His muscles grew tense, and his claws extended as his attention narrowed to the fingers pulling at the reeds of his confinement.

"Why do you bring me a cat?" Strachys stared into the basket, his fingers resting in the gap between the reeds. He jerked them back as Spike struck and frowned at the red beads forming a line across his dirty knuckle.

"Nasty beasts," he cursed, wiping the blood on his stained tunic.

"This one may prove valuable to both of us," Spike's captor said calmly. He reached across the wooden table and tore a piece of meat from the skeleton of a broiled rabbit, pushed it through the reeds, and watched it fall at Spike's feet. The cat hissed, ignoring the greasy offering.

"They're remarkable hunters," he continued. "Their senses, their unbreakable focus and persistence . . . all perfectly suited to their purpose."

"Then take its purpose and perfection to the village. It can hunt rats around the garbage with the others," Strachys growled, still rubbing his hand where Spike had clawed him.

"I want to show you something that may change your mind," Spike's captor said, pushing the pitcher of wine and the half-eaten rabbit aside. He poured a pool of oil from the unlit clay lamp onto the tabletop and held his hands over the spreading stain. It burst into flame. Strachys rushed toward it but stopped as it resolved into a three-dimensional scene, sculpted in a cold fire that left the wood unconsumed.

"What kind of sorcery is this?"

Spike's captor silenced him with a raised hand. "It's only a simple image, projected from my memory."

Strachys leaned toward the tabletop and saw five cats gathered around a tall pine, harassing a blue jay. A woman entered the clearing, followed by a black dog that threatened her and the cats. He saw the five small animals merge their bodies to become a great cat and drive the dog away. He watched the woman faint as the cat approached her. He saw the great cat become five small animals once more as the image faded, leaving one more stain on the dirty table.

"I wanted you to see what these animals can do," Spike's captor said.

"You were there? You saw this with your own eyes?"

"I was concealed nearby when it happened."

Strachys gestured toward Spike. "Is this one of the animals?"

"He is. I hope you appreciate my interest in him . . . and in you, Strachys."

"How do you know my name? What brought you here?"

"Your fame is not inconsiderable. Indeed, a certain minor king has offered a reward for the return of his former seer."

Strachys' eyes darted toward a neglected-looking bronze sword hanging on the wall. Spike's captor smiled.

"Don't worry, Akiala's reward does not interest me," he said, filling a cup with wine, "but you do. Akiala told me how his men caught you leaving his palace with a wagon load of valuables and an unfortunate serving girl—if you could call that pile of mud bricks and pig shit a palace. Had it been properly built, I doubt you would have burrowed your way to freedom."

"Who are you?"

The stranger looked at him in silence as if answering this ordinary question carried an extraordinary risk. "You may call me Phaethon."

"So, the bastard son of Helios, the sun god, has come to honor my palace." Strachys laughed with bitter irony. "What do you want, Phaethon, son of Helios? If that truly is your name."

"It's an old story and the name my mother gave me," the stranger said, taking a swallow of wine. "You may believe anything else you wish."

"How did you find me?"

"Akiala gave me some clues to your background and habits. After that, it was simply a matter of asking the right people the right questions," Phaethon explained. "What do you call this island?"

"Kyros."

"A few hundred people, goats, olive trees . . ." Phaethon glanced at the pitcher on the table, "a winemaker, and little else. Don't you tire of it?"

Strachys ignored him. "How did you come here? No ships have landed for weeks. A stranger passing through would have raised gossip, yet I've heard nothing."

"My modest skills include the ability to move quickly and unseen for great distances."

"What did Akiala tell you?"

"He showed me the 'treasures' you tried to steal—a few bronze cooking tripods, jars of olive oil, cracked clay lamps, dull swords, tarnished armor . . . a pathetic pile of junk. He introduced me to your serving girl, or what remained of her after her punishment."

"Claea? She's alive?"

Phaethon nodded. "She told me about your past."

"What did she say?"

"That you came from Crete, where you served as a scribe and left under circumstances much like your recent adventure. She said you were a learned man and were fluent in many languages. She also told me you were a seer, experienced with signs and enchantments."

Strachys shrugged.

"I need a man like you to help me understand how this animal and his siblings can become the great cat you saw," Phaethon explained.

"Tricks of the eye." Strachys scowled. "I learned them when I was a child; illusions to part a fool from his valuables, nothing more."

"I assure you, this was no illusion."

Strachys took a sip of wine from his cup and threw the dregs at Spike. The cat hissed and pulled back, rocking the basket. "Why do you care?"

"I was injured some time ago and have not returned to health," Phaethon said slowly, carefully. "I want to know how these animals can join their bodies and minds so completely. I believe it may help me heal my injuries."

"You have gifts; why do you need me?"

"My abilities are limited, and my injuries are severe. Even if I had the skills, it is unlikely I could work them on myself. I would be like a surgeon trying to cauterize his own wounds." He smiled. "I need you to be my surgeon."

"I'm not a healer."

"No, you are a thief and a fraud," Phaethon explained as Strachys scowled, "but you have skills I require, you need employment, and you are unburdened by scruples as to its nature."

He reached into his leather bag and removed a cylindrical object wrapped in fine linen. He unwrapped it carefully, revealing a scroll of extraordinary workmanship. Its olive wood spindle seemed not so much ancient as timeless, the wood darkened with great age. Carvings covered the knobs on each end—the right-hand knob showed people fighting, building monuments, and burying their dead, while the left showed them making love, farming the land, and raising children. It seemed as if a craftsman with skills surpassing mortal abilities had endeavored to represent all that is human in the burnished wood. Phaethon spread the linen on the dirty table, set the scroll at its center, and unrolled it to reveal a parchment of extraordinary quality. It had aged to the color of clay but showed no wear, no cracking, no fraying at the edges. The writing on it shined with gold's unmistakable luster.

"What is this?" Strachys asked.

"A book," Phaethon said reverently.

Strachys stared at the golden symbols. "This is the work of a god."

"Can you read it?"

The seer scratched under his beard thoughtfully—an affectation he had adopted long ago to build an image of wisdom. Over time, it had grown into a habit. "This matches no language I have seen."

Phaethon unrolled the scroll further to reveal a sequence of hieroglyphics written in the margin. "What about this?"

"I recognize the symbols. They're Egyptian," Strachys said, leaning closer. "They look like they were added later. They're written in ink, not gold, and are of a different hand, not as fine as the other."

"Can you read them?" Phaethon pressed, excitement rising in his voice.

Strachys continued to scratch beneath his beard. "Not easily, but I could find their meaning in time."

"I believe this book will show us how to unlock the animal's abilities."

Phaethon reached once again into his leather satchel, removed a smaller canvas bag, and emptied it onto the table. Rings, earrings, necklaces with gold, lapis, and amber beads, a brooch in the form of an owl, and a gold lamp of extraordinary workmanship fell across the rough wood.

"Help me, and there will be more," he said.

Strachys turned the lamp in his hand. The warriors and palace women engraved on its surface seemed as if they might step from the metal and continue their flirtations across the table. "This is of Egyptian origin. How did you come by all this?"

Phaethon did not answer. Strachys set the lamp down and ran his hands over the treasures, stopping to pick up a gold and lapis necklace. He thumbed the beads as his gaze moved back to the scroll. He reached toward it and paused, his hand above the parchment, his eyes lingering on it as if on a woman whose beauty he dared not approach. Finally, he gently touched the edge of the sheet, his reticence overcome by slight courage and overwhelming desire.

Phaethon smiled knowingly. "Will you help me?"

"It will be difficult," Strachys confessed, watching Phaethon's response like a merchant evaluating a customer.

"Let the book be your teacher and let the animal be your example," Phaethon assured him. "That should be enough."

Strachys stared at him. "I see no wounds. You walk well enough."

A shadow crossed Phaethon's face. "I feel my injuries constantly."

"Show me."

"No."

"If I am to heal you, I must know your afflictions," Strachys argued.

"Then you agree to help me?"

"Perhaps, but first, I must see your injuries."

Phaethon glared at the dirty seer. "As you wish," he said reluctantly.

He stepped away from the table and closed his eyes. His body relaxed, and a light seemed to emerge from his pores, flaring in a blue corona and vanishing instantly. Phaethon collapsed to the floor like a discarded carcass at a drunken feast. His entire left side seemed to have been consumed by fire. Bone and scab marked the blackened flesh like fragments of ivory and garnet scattered across a mound of ash, leaving the side of his face unrecognizable but for the eye staring through the scars. His left leg rested uselessly on the floor while his charred left arm hung at his side. He supported himself on his unburned right arm, staring up in pain. Only the right half of the face was untouched, remaining as handsome as the youth who had entered Strachys' hovel.

The blue light engulfed the broken body again, and Phaethon appeared as before. He grabbed the terrified seer by his filthy tunic. "Now, you know. Heal me, and I will give you more wealth than you can imagine. Fail me, and I swear, I will make you envy the pathetic creature you just saw."

"But you can already change your form," Strachys stammered.

Phaethon released him. "It is an enchantment, not a cure. The man you see is as I once was. I can walk, I can eat, I can lie with a woman, but I cannot hold it long. When I tire, the agony returns. It denies me any rest but drunken, pain-wracked exhaustion."

"Even if I learn the secret of these animals, I don't see how it could heal your injuries."

"My injuries cannot be healed," Phaethon said sharply. "One with powers far greater than yours has tried."

Strachys stared, his face slack with incomprehension. Suddenly, his lips tightened, and his eyes narrowed. "You want to join your body with another's . . . like the animals you showed me."

Phaethon nodded.

"But your injuries? How—"

"How would I heal them? When these animals merge, I believe a new body forms from their essences, not their appearance."

"But that's not possible," Strachys protested. "Enchantments cannot change a being's essence; they can only alter its manifestation."

"You talk like a philosopher, but I have studied these animals. The change you saw is not an enchantment. When they become the great cat, their essences change, as they do when they return to their original form. It is as if they are of a dual nature—the great cat and the individuals are equally real."

Strachys stared in disbelief.

"These injuries are not my essence," Phaethon continued. "They were inflicted on me by circumstance. They'll be left behind when I join with another."

"This is dark magic," Strachys warned.

"Are you going to talk about souls, eternal essences, the will of Zeus, and other nonsense? This is an animal," Phaethon shouted, angrily pointing at Spike. "Do you think the gods would deny us a power they have given him? Should I suffer while a mere animal holds the key to my healing?"

"I don't care about the animal," Strachys protested.

"Perhaps you worry about the person I will choose as my . . . what shall we call him? My healer? My host? I may simply consume him, or he may consume me. Who knows, we may both die, or we may become something greater than either of us."

"Some things are not meant for mortals."

"So," Phaethon laughed, "you do have scruples."

"You talk like you're a god. This will not bring anything good."

"Very well, my frightened little man. Enjoy your life with the other insects crawling in the dirt. I'll find another."

Phaeton stepped to the table and swept the golden lamp and other treasures into the leather satchel. He reached for the scroll, but Strachys grabbed his forearm. "Let me study the animal," he said, "and the book. I may find another way."

"So, you prefer to embrace your corruption by degrees," Phaethon laughed. He returned the valuables to the table. "Very well. I'll be back in a few days. I hope you resolve your metaphysical concerns and give me good news."

Phaethon stared at the seer as if he could see into his soul, his ambitions, his demons. "But I must warn you . . . the enchantments that hide my injuries have given me other abilities."

The blue vortex surrounded him once more, but Phaethon did not collapse in pain. Instead, he grew into a reptilian parody of a man, his features smoothing into the head of a snake, bronze scales covering an impossibly muscled body. He grabbed the seer by the tunic with three stubby fingers and pulled him close, claws leaving bloody tracks across his chest.

"Old man," the monster hissed, "if you hold anything back from me because of some fantasy of pleasing the gods, or if you try to cheat me, or steal the scroll, or tell anyone what you have seen here . . . know that I will find you. Do you understand?"

Strachys turned his face away in terror and nodded.

"Shall we seal our bargain with a kiss?" The lizard-thing drew a forked tongue across the seer's grimy cheek, then released him. Strachys stumbled backward to strike the mud wall. His hand covered the tongue's shining trail as if it were a wound.

Spike stared through the gaps in his cage at the monster walking into the daylight. The bronze scales on its back reflected the sun like fire into Strachys' hovel.

Chapter 9

Audrey, Chessie, and Greystoke remained near the granary in an uneasy truce with the spotted tomcat as Astrid's sentience resonated at the edge of their awareness. They sensed the direction they must travel to reach her and grew increasingly restless. After the sun disappeared behind the ocean, after the sounds of people preparing meals and conversing subsided, when all but a few had returned to their tents, the three cats left the colony. The spotted tomcat followed them for a dozen yards, then stood on a dune, ensuring they had left his domain.

The three cats crossed the salt meadow bordering the beach, following an arc around the encampment to avoid people. Confused by the strange place, by the chaos of smells coming from the cookfires, and by the salt air passing over the Aegean, they did not notice the dogs until they faced the pack they had seen on the battlefield. The dogs approached, growling menacingly, heads lowered, lips curled back, teeth catching the thin light.

Greystoke felt fear grow in his mind and the minds of his sisters. Chessie leaned into him, muscles tingling as their bodies flowed together, and Audrey quickly joined them. In Spike and Elizabeth's absence, Swarm displayed the slender physique shared by the smaller, faster siblings. Her fur took on the darkness of Chessie's black and pewter stripes, of Audrey's dark tortoiseshell, of Greystoke's gunmetal. Startled by the flash of blue light that preceded Swarm's appearance, the dogs froze. The great cat approached them in a predatory crouch, a low growl rumbling in her chest. The dogs growled and backed away, moving slowly at first, then scattering into the darkness.

Astrid's distant presence sang in Swarm's faceted mind, leading the cat toward the ships that lined the sand like stranded leviathans. Hiding in the shadow of the vessel farthest from the encampment, Swarm watched as the night deepened and people left the beach. Her mind settled into the liquid stillness of a cat at rest—eyes closed, body relaxed, senses attentive. Gradually, the facets of Swarm's mind separated, followed by the geometry of her flesh as Chessie, Audrey, and Greystoke returned to their individual forms.

A man stumbling drunkenly along the beach saw them by the ship. He found a rock and threw it in their direction. It bounced off the wooden hull as the cats ran to the next ship. The man did not follow. As time went on, fewer people passed by, and the night grew quiet. Illuminated by starlight reflected on seafoam, the cats moved from ship to ship, from one patch of shadowed sand to another, drawn to the beacon of Astrid's sentience.

Astrid groaned as pain pierced her left arm. She sat up and checked the splint, tightening the elastic bandage that held it in place. She heard a rustle of bedding and saw several of the women who shared the tent staring at her in the flicker of the oil lamp.

"My wrist hurts," she explained.

Astrid took the Oxycodone from her pocket, weighing her pain against her fear of running out of painkillers. Hecamede had explained how the Achaeans would pray to the gods that night for guidance in determining her fate, and Astrid decided not to spend what might be her final hours in pain. She took a pill from the plastic bag and washed it down with wine from a clay cup. She adjusted the bedding around her, elevating her broken wrist, and waited for the painkiller to take effect.

She remembered the women's reticence when she'd first come to the tent and how, under Hecamede's gentle persuasion, their fear of a stranger had given way to the guarded fellowship refugees share. They had welcomed her into their sanctuary and given her woven blankets and fleeces from their own rough bedding. Uneasy in her strange surroundings, Astrid had declined their offer of a linen bedgown and still wore her jeans and sweater.

Hecamede had told her how the women—all of them slaves, spoils of war—had taken possession of the tent after the warrior who owned it was killed. At first, they had gathered there informally when the men were raiding or feasting in honor of the gods. Eventually, they claimed it as a home for any woman who did not share a man's bed, whether because of age, injury, or a brief respite between the death of the warrior she served and the emergence of another to claim her. Currently, seven women lived there.

The tent enclosed some two hundred square feet, with two attached buildings providing additional space. The original occupant had constructed one of the buildings from stone and mud-brick taken in raids on nearby villages. The women had built the other themselves, using scavenged boards, tree branches, and driftwood. The dirt floor was smooth, hard, and reflected the lamplight. Astrid recalled reading how pioneer homes in New Mexico often used animal blood to bind their dirt floors, and she wondered if these women had done the same.

The beds consisted of rope nets supported by wooden frames, covered with animal skins and other bedding. Clay cups, pitchers, and other domestic comforts rested on wooden tables. Brightly colored rugs softened the spaces between the beds, and oil lamps provided light. Hecamede had proudly described the women's cunning in acquiring these small luxuries from returning raiders or the tents of dead warriors. Sweet smells filled the room—a combination of fragrant oils, cooking spices, and the constant presence of wood smoke and saltwater.

Astrid heard the rustle of canvas as Hecamede pushed the tent flap aside and entered, wearing a loose bedgown, her feet bare.

"How are you feeling?" she asked, sitting on the edge of Astrid's bed.

"I'm managing. Thank you for all you've done."

"Zeus is the protector of travelers," Hecamede explained modestly. "Hospitality to strangers honors all the gods."

"You've shown me more than hospitality."

Hecamede gestured toward Astrid's broken wrist. "Let me summon a healer. He will set the bone, apply poultices, say prayers—"

"Perhaps later." Astrid was not eager to experience Bronze Age medicine.

"It does not become easier with time," Hecamede warned.

Astrid nodded. "What's going to happen tonight?"

"The men have gathered, and the fires are nearly ready. Soon, they will bring a bull into the camp and sacrifice it to the gods."

Hecamede saw Astrid frown and seemed puzzled. "A bull will surely gain the attention of the immortals," she reassured. "Nestor and Odysseus will cut the finest parts from the animal, wrap them in fat, and burn them as offerings. They'll pour libations of wine and pray for a sign."

"They'll be asking what to do with me," Astrid pressed.

"Don't worry." Hecamede smiled ironically. "Nestor and Odysseus believe you are under the gods' protection, and I have never known the gods to contradict them."

Astrid squeezed her hand. "Thank you."

"Try to sleep. The men will eat, drink, and share stories through the night. Perhaps we'll get some rest." Hecamede smiled and pointed to an empty bed. "I'll sleep there tonight. Nestor wants me to stay near you."

All at once, the women in the tent began to talk loudly and gesture toward the entrance. Astrid saw Greystoke, Audrey, and Chessie standing just inside the tent, anxiously scanning their surroundings. Her heart rose as the cats ran to her bed, and she took them in her arms. Whispers and soft laughter spread through the shelter. A girl with a scar on her cheek, no more than eleven years old, approached her, walking with a limp.

"We do not let animals in here," she said shyly.

"I understand," Astrid said, "but these are my friends."

The women gathered around them.

"I have come from far away, and these animals have come with me," Astrid explained.

"Why?" an older woman asked.

"They watch over me, and I watch over them."

"Their bodies and markings are strange . . . different from the cats at the granary," Hecamede observed.

"Are they enchanted?" another girl of around twelve asked.

"Gods can take the form of animals," a frail, nervous woman added.

Astrid intuitively understood the risks of being mistaken for a goddess. "They're not ordinary animals," she said ambiguously, stroking Audrey's long fur. "They must remain with me."

As she spoke, the women began to laugh. Greystoke had stolen a piece of meat from Astrid's unfinished dinner and carried it to the end of the bed, away from his sisters. He growled as he tore hungrily into his prize.

The girl with the limp held her hand out toward Chessie, but the cat pulled back warily. "When I was little, I had a cat," she said.

Astrid offered her plate to her. The girl took a piece of meat, placed it on her open palm, and offered it to the cat. The child smiled as Chessie took the food and retreated to eat in safety.

"What's your name?" Astrid asked.

"Gilia."

"I'm Astrid." She set the plate on the bed near Audrey, who ate delicately.

Astrid sensed the women were starting to accept the cats' presence—at least until the men came back with the gods' judgment. Gradually, they returned to their beds, and Astrid rested back among the blankets and fleeces. Chessie reclined at her side, where Astrid could stroke her short fur, and Greystoke curled up next to her hip, away from his sister's sharp claws and quick temper. Audrey took her place near Astrid's shoulder.

Hecamede stepped toward the lamp that hung from one of the supporting beams and stretched upward to blow out the flame.

"Could you leave it?" Astrid asked.

"Of course," Hecamede said softly.

Astrid settled into the rough bedding, exhaustion and the effects of the painkiller covering her in a ragged insensibility.

Astrid sat up suddenly, startled by the screams of the sacrificial bull. As the animal's cries faded, drowned in a froth of blood, she heard male voices in the call and response of ritual prayer. Soon, the formal structure gave way to mingled currents of conversation, punctuated by shouts, laughter, and the occasional shattered cup or dish. Boasts and challenges rose from the noise, followed by the bluster of drunken contests. In time, the commotion faded to the low voices of young men sharing stories of conquests in battle and in women's beds. She saw a warrior stick his head through the tent flap and gesture toward a woman who rose quietly from her bed and left with him. Astrid checked the cats sleeping beside her, then returned to her rest, kept at the edge of sleep by pain, by worry for her animals and herself, and by memories of the dying bull's pitiful cries.

Chapter 10

Astrid awoke to a throbbing in her wrist and the sound of someone pushing the tent flap aside. She checked Chessie, Greystoke, and Audrey, who were staring in the direction of the noise, eyes wide and bodies tensed. Feigning sleep, she squinted toward the sound. The lamp burned fitfully, consuming the last of its oil, but Astrid recognized the man standing drunkenly in the entrance, holding the tent flap for balance. It was the man who had threatened her that afternoon—the warrior who had worn the red-plumed helmet.

Releasing the canvas flap, he staggered inside, dressed only in a short tunic, and lurched from bed to bed as women watched silently, frozen with fear. He stopped at a woman's bed, lifted a fleece to stare at her, then let it drop before he moved on. Plumed-helmet saw Gilia, the girl with the limp, staring wide-eyed. He grabbed her by the jaw and pulled her toward him, terror contorting her face as he examined her in the dim light.

"What are you looking at, you ugly cripple?" He cursed and threw her violently aside.

Hecamede rose from her bed, and Plumed-helmet staggered toward her.

"You don't belong here. Go back to your drinking," she challenged.

He glared back as if he would strike her, but Hecamede silently held her ground. "Be quiet, woman," he sneered. "Nestor isn't here to protect you."

He pushed her aside and scanned the tent. He saw Astrid and lurched toward her with a smile glazed in venom. "Bitch," he swore.

Astrid threw her bedding aside and started to run. He grabbed the hair at the back of her head—her scalp burned as he pulled her back and turned her face to his. Plumed-helmet tilted her head back and leaned forward clumsily, as if to force a kiss on her, then bit her cheek. He laughed as she pulled away, a streak of saliva crossing her face. He threw her onto the bed, grunting as he straddled her thighs, his weight pinning her in place. He grabbed her by the chin and forced her to look into his eyes, rage burning through the puffy flesh surrounding them.

"You made me look like a fool today," he growled. He held her chin like a vise as Astrid struggled. "Do you think the gods—or that old man—will protect you now?"

Still straddling her, Plumed-helmet pulled his tunic over his head, throwing it aside. Astrid saw his erection in the lamplight and felt her stomach churn with disgust. She groped on the floor beside the bed with her right hand, found her clay wine cup, and smashed it against the side of his face. He cursed and pulled back in reflex. Astrid pushed him aside, rolled from beneath his leg, and ran from the bed.

As she started to lift the tent flap, Astrid felt his fingers dig into her left bicep. The pain of her broken wrist exploded through her arm and shoulder as he pulled her back. She fought to hold onto consciousness, desperately clinging to the canvas with her right hand, her fingers scraping across the rough cloth as Plumed-helmet threw her back into the tent. Astrid landed on the dirt floor, pain radiating from her tailbone, from her cheek where he had bitten her, from her broken wrist.

As Plumed-helmet staggered toward her, Hecamede ran behind him and shattered a clay pitcher over his head. He fell to his knees, and for a moment, Astrid thought he would pass out. Instead, he recovered his footing and hit Hecamede in the face with his fist, knocking her to the ground. He stood unsteadily above her, his fists clenched, cursing.

Ignoring the pain in her wrist, in her face, in her back and chest, Astrid ran at him and struck him with her right shoulder, driving him into a nearby bed as its occupant fled. She helped Hecamede to her feet, and they started toward the tent's opening. Despite his drunken state, Plumed-helmet recovered quickly, grabbed Astrid by the arm, and threw her back into the tent. He hit Hecamede hard across her face until she fell. He kicked her in the stomach, and she doubled up in pain.

Plumed-helmet stalked Astrid like she was a cornered animal, staying between her and the tent's opening, the venomous smile returning to his face. She backed away, searching for some weapon she could use, for some way to escape. Plumed-helmet ran at her with surprising speed and threw her to the floor. He fell drunkenly on top of her and forced his knee between her legs as his right hand closed around her throat. Astrid's screams became a desperate rasp as his fingers tightened around her trachea. He squeezed her breast painfully with his left hand. She clawed at him with her uninjured hand and felt skin collect under her nails as she raked his cheek. He released her throat and hit her in the face. Astrid fought back from oblivion and saw him rub his hand across his cheek, stare at the blood on his palm, then hit her again. He grabbed her right forearm and pinned it against her chest as he drunkenly groped at her crotch. Frustrated by her belt and denim jeans, he released her arm and tore at Astrid's pants with both hands, cursing as she hit him repeatedly with her right hand.

Plumed-helmet stopped and looked up as a blue light flashed through the tent. The dirt floor quaked beneath him, and a feral scream filled the air, turning his rage into terror. A dark form swept across Astrid's vision, eclipsing the lamp's dying flame and closing like night around her attacker. Plumed-helmet struggled ineffectually as Swarm pushed him across the floor, a cat toying with its helpless prey. Somehow, he found his feet and stood naked, bleeding from the wounds crossing his chest, back, and upper arm. He stared in shock at the horror growling before him, tail twitching, white fangs and green eyes bright against dark fur. He turned to run toward the tent's opening.

Before his foot left the ground, the cat leaped on his back, knocking him onto the dirt. Plumed-helmet screamed as Swarm clamped her jaws around his neck and shook violently. Astrid heard a muffled snap and saw his body convulse. Swarm continued to shake him as the spasms faded, her jaws locked around his neck. Finally, the cat released him, and he fell to the floor, his cheek resting motionless on the dirt, eyes wide, frozen in surprise.

The tent flap parted, and Nestor entered with Odysseus at his side. A crowd of warriors and a few women jostled behind them. Swarm stood over the dead warrior, growling in warning, her tail twitching, a predator guarding her prize. Astrid saw Odysseus reach for his bronze sword and rushed forward, fighting through her injuries to reach Swarm's side. She grabbed the loose skin on the cat's shoulders with her right hand and forced herself to stand as straight as her broken wrist and bruised flesh would allow.

"Do not harm her," she commanded.

Odysseus stopped and stared at her in astonishment, his hand on the hilt of his sword. Astrid felt Swarm's tripartite mind burn at the edge of her awareness. Instead of the vague, constant sense of the cats' presence she had experienced since coming to Troy, the panic of a cornered predator surged through her mind in a torrent. Astrid's breath caught in her chest as Swarm's emotions filled her awareness, nearly overpowering her. She held the scruff of Swarm's neck tightly as the cat growled another warning and repeated in her mind the soft reassurances she had used to calm her five animals in the past.

Astrid realized she had been holding her breath. She inhaled suddenly, involuntarily. As her lips parted, blood from the wounds on her face flowed into her mouth, and Swarm's emotions surged once more at the sweet, saline taste. She felt an urge to surrender to the purity of the cat's blood-lust, to strike out at the madness around her, to end her pain and confusion. Astrid resisted the impulse, closed her eyes, and forced herself to breathe steadily. Gradually, Swarm's emotions diffused through her consciousness like a rapidly flowing stream entering a wide shallow. Astrid opened her eyes and saw that Odysseus and the crowd had barely moved. Her struggle with Swarm felt like it had lasted several minutes, but she realized it had only taken seconds.

Odysseus looked into her eyes. Astrid knew the Achaeans would follow his lead, and she returned his gaze, even as she fought to control Swarm's panic and instinctive aggression. She sensed Odysseus working through alternatives, weighing Swarm's threat against his estimate of the woman who seemed to control the great cat.

"What happened here?" he demanded.

Hecamede stepped forward, careful to keep Astrid between her and Swarm. Blood ran down her cheek from a cut above her eye, falling in drops on her bedgown. Despite her injuries, she stood tall, defiant.

"He tried to rape her. The cat appeared out of nowhere and killed him." Hecamede pointed at Plumed-helmet's body. "You asked for a sign—here it is." She faced the crowd, head high, daring them to challenge her.

"What she says is true." Nestor's voice filled the tent. "Only the gods could have done this. Does anyone doubt that this woman and her animals are under their protection?"

The men talked among themselves, their voices filling the darkness. Most seemed to agree with Nestor, though a few demanded vengeance for their dead comrade.

"He was our friend," Odysseus declared, trying to calm the crowd, "but he acted foolishly and displeased the gods. Prepare his body for a warrior's funeral. We will offer libations to the gods in thanks for this sign and to honor his courage. We will cremate him with a warrior's honors and carry his ashes home in a bronze container I'll select from my own prizes."

"The great cat serves this woman," Nestor added. "She can turn its rage against the Trojans. Protecting her will bring us good fortune."

Astrid heard a rumble of assent from the gathered warriors. She stepped back, still holding the loose skin at Swarm's shoulders. To her relief, the cat followed, backing away from its kill. Two Achaeans approached cautiously, grabbed the body by the arms, and dragged it from the tent.

"Remember this and tell everyone," Astrid told the warriors. "No one may harm the animals that came here with me. This great cat protects them as it protects me—even when it cannot be seen. Now leave—all of you. No one may remain but this woman," she said, nodding toward Hecamede.

The warriors and the few women remaining in the tent left quickly. Only Nestor and Odysseus remained, staring in disbelief at the strange woman and the great cat standing beside her.

"I'll be all right," Astrid told them. "Please go."

Nestor placed his hand on Odysseus' shoulder. "Come," he said. Reluctantly, Odysseus left at his side.

As the tent flap closed behind them, Astrid limped to the nearest bed and sat painfully on the edge of the wooden frame. Swarm climbed up beside her, circled twice to create a depression in the bedding, and lay down. Astrid began to sob convulsively and vomited, spraying partly digested meat, barley, and wine like a fan across the floor. She sat, doubled forward, her right hand across her stomach, breathing heavily. The pain of her broken wrist, forgotten in her struggle with Plumed-helmet, rushed through her. Hecamede sat beside her on the bed, keeping Astrid between herself and Swarm.

"Are you all right?" She placed her hand on Astrid's shoulder.

Astrid nodded, still shaking from the spasms that wracked her body. Gradually, her breathing came under her control. She touched Hecamede's face gently where Plumed-helmet had struck her.

"Did he hurt you?" Astrid asked, her face damp with tears.

Hecamede shook her head. "No. The wine had weakened him."

Astrid began to smile, then winced at the pain. She touched her cheek where he had bitten her and was relieved to find no blood on her fingers. Hecamede looked nervously at the great cat lying calmly on the bed.

"It's true . . ." she said. "You are a goddess."

For a moment, Astrid found herself unable to respond, but then she began to laugh. She laughed as uncontrollably as she had wept. She laughed through the pain of her broken wrist, through her injuries from the attack, through the terror, grief, and rage she had suppressed since coming to Troy.

"I don't think a goddess would have puked all over your floor," she said.

"If she had taken a human form, she might," Hecamede explained, at first earnestly, then struggling to finish as she, too, began to laugh.

She put her arms around Astrid. They held each other as the laughter faded, and they cried in each other's arms like lost children. Astrid felt a pressure against her hip. Swarm pushed against her, purring loudly.

"Are you Artemis?" Hecamede asked.

"Artemis?"

"Animals obey her."

"I thought she preferred hounds." Astrid smiled through her pain.

Hecamede stared at Swarm. "This is the work of the gods."

"Perhaps it is, but I am only a woman like you, and I don't know what is happening."

Hecamede weighed Astrid's words, then nodded. "I'll bring water and towels to wash the blood away," she said as she rose from the bed.

"Could you bring something I can use to clean this up?" Astrid asked, gesturing at the barley and fragments of meat scattered across the floor. "And, please, more wine."

Hecamede smiled and started to leave the tent.

Astrid felt a tremor in the bedding. "Wait," she said.

Hecamede turned back, her eyes growing wide as she saw a vortex of blue light engulf the great cat.

Astrid walked to Hecamede's side and took her hand, leaving Swarm alone in the swirling light. "I cannot explain what is happening, but I think you should see it."

The two women stood together, watching three small cats take form in the shimmering gyre.

"Do not be afraid," Astrid reassured her.

Chapter II

Annape floated alone in the clear water, staring into the moonless sky. A freshwater Naiad, born at the spring's subterranean source, her eyes were well suited to the starlight. She preferred it to the full moon that draws her sister nymphs to lie in the soft grass and gossip endlessly of their dreams and intrigues, that raises the blood of the wolves who share Aeaea with the bears, great cats, deer, swine, and other animals in Circe's menagerie, calling them to howl through the night.

The starlight illuminated the spring in silver hues—the moss that lined the pool, the trout and tadpoles that swam around Annape's pale limbs, the dragonfly nymphs, crayfish, worms, and all the blind, beloved creatures who shared her waters. She watched a small trout swim between her fingers and remembered how she had once flowed softly across fertile mud, springwater herself. The thought returned Annape to her original liquid state, and the trout swam through the bottom of her foot. Ticklish since birth, she laughed and felt her leg twitch in reflex, returning her body to solidity. She raised her hand from the water and watched a silver rivulet—a reminder of her elemental past—flow down the curve of her forearm.

Annape heard a twig snap and saw one of the lions who roamed Aeaea pad across the moss toward her, his dark mane framing his face. She offered him water in her cupped palms and felt his rough tongue and the hard ivory of his teeth against her skin. He emptied her small offering and pushed his muzzle past her hands to drink deeply from the spring. When the lion returned to the meadow, Annape walked beside him, naked in the starlight, water shining on her skin. Deer, owls, swine, wolves, and other beasts came from the forest to surround them, all hoping for one of the delicacies she sometimes stole from Circe's kitchen to share with them.

"I'm sorry, little ones. I don't have anything tonight," she said as she caressed a black bear's rough fur. The animal nudged her insistently, sending her stumbling across the damp grass. Annape remembered the bear had given birth recently and was nursing two rambunctious cubs. She took her great head in both hands and stared into her dark eyes. "I'm sorry, little mother. I know you need extra food. I promise, tomorrow night."

In no hurry to return to her bed, Annape walked the long arc of the meadow's perimeter. She listened to the large and small creatures moving in the forest and inhaled the fragrances lifted from the grass by Aeaea's warm breezes. Her retinue thinned as the animals learned she carried no treats and wandered off to test the forest's promise. Annape climbed a small rise, accompanied only by the ever-hungry mother bear, and looked down on the palace spreading low across the meadow. It was the home of her mistress—Circe, the enchantress; Circe, the trickster; Circe, the author of endless schemes and wonders.

Annape saw a light shine suddenly from the palace, spraying green pigment across the silver grass. It came from the chamber where the small orange cat slept—the cat Circe had brought from the distant age.

"It's past midnight," Annape said to the bear. "Something's wrong."

She ran through the soft grass toward this latest of Circe's enigmas. As she approached the palace, Annape heard a cry, the thin howling of an animal in distress. She ran down the marble colonnade with its walls open to Circe's gardens, through the atrium, to the chamber where Lara, her sister Naiad, sat among the fleeces and brightly colored cushions. The cat sat wide-eyed beside her.

Lara looked up, concern shadowing her face. "I was sleeping with the cat as our mistress asked when she began to cry for no reason."

Annape sat beside them and gently stroked the cat. She remembered her strange name and spoke it in reassuring tones. "Do not be afraid, Elizabeth."

She heard footsteps and turned to see Circe enter the chamber, wearing a long dressing gown. The enchantress adjusted the fabric around her as she kneeled beside them. Elizabeth cried out again, and the goddess took the cat into her arms. "What's happening?"

"I don't know," Lara said. "I was sleeping, and she began to cry."

"What is it, little one?" Circe asked as she ran her fingers through Elizabeth's fur, first in long, comforting strokes, then probing with a physician's touch into her muscles, joints, and abdomen. The enchantress' examination ended with her hands resting at the base and sides of Elizabeth's head.

"The animal is frightened. Did you hear or see anything?" Circe asked Lara. "Anything that could have disturbed her?"

"No. I fed the cat as you asked and watched her go to sleep. I would have noticed anything unusual."

Circe nodded thoughtfully.

"What do you think happened?" Annape asked.

"Nothing within these walls. It comes from her mind."

"A nightmare?"

"Perhaps . . . perhaps something more. Annape, bring my extracts."

"What could it be?" Annape asked as she started from the chamber.

"Let us hope it's a message," the goddess said softly. "Now hurry, and Annape . . ."

"Yes?"

"Put some clothes on."

Annape blushed and hurried down the hall, first to her bedchamber with her small wardrobe, then to the vault where Circe kept her herbs and extracts, her scrolls and totems, her medicines and poisons.

Elizabeth rested on the cushions beside the enchantress, calmed by Circe's touch. "What is it, little one? Have your brothers and sisters reached out to you? Are they safe?"

Elizabeth began to purr. The sound reflected neither rest nor contentment, only a frightened animal's efforts to comfort herself.

"No matter," Circe reassured her, "we'll know soon."

Annape returned to the chamber, carrying a wooden box, a tangle of vines carved into its lid. She wore a linen shift, free of the bright dyes her sister nymphs favored, its weave as thin as a sheen of water on her skin. She set the box on the marble floor near the enchantress' feet. Circe raised the lid, revealing neat rows of clay jars.

"Her mind is joined to the minds of her littermates," Circe said as she ran her fingers over the box's contents. "That is where her distress originates."

She lifted a jar, removed its carved wooden stopper, and poured a drop of oil into her hand. It shone like peridot in the lamplight. She returned the jar to the box and rubbed her hands together, spreading the oil across her palms. Circe cupped her hands over her mouth and nose and breathed deeply, her immortal breath commingling with the carefully prepared extract.

She lifted Elizabeth onto her lap and stroked her gently. The cat's eyes closed in sleep, Circe's in meditation. The enchantress sat as still as stone with Elizabeth's head in her palm. Two Nereids, awakened by the commotion, approached the chamber and watched sleepily from the entrance. One yawned, and Annape raised a finger to her lips. After several minutes, Circe opened her eyes and moved Elizabeth to the soft bedding. The cat remained asleep.

"What is it?" Lara asked.

"Her littermates have come to our world," Circe explained. "Her connection to them is strong."

"What frightened her?"

"A man attacked the woman who followed them here."

Annape looked at her in concern.

"All is well," Circe reassured. "The attacker is dead."

The enchantress rose from the cushions and spoke to one of the young women in the doorway. "There is fish leftover from my supper. Bring it here. The cat will be hungry when she awakens." She then turned to the other. "Bring wine to my chamber. I have much to think about."

They hurried on their errands.

"Lara," Circe said, "stay close to the animal. Come for me if you see anything strange."

"Where are the woman and the other animals?" Annape asked.

Circe smiled at her. It was a smile that could shatter empires, a smile that could raise men's ambitions to the level of the gods or imprison them forever among the demons that inhabit their souls.

"They are at Troy," the enchantress whispered.

Chapter 12

Crouched in the shadows of the single oil lamp, Spike gnawed patiently, silently on the straps that bound his prison. He heard his captor move and froze. Strachys shifted in his chair, stretching his back, then leaned forward into the circle of lamplight and the scroll that had held his attention through the night. Spike resumed gnawing on the leather band and felt a flush of pleasure as it parted in his mouth. He pressed against the side of the basket, and the reeds yielded, creaking in protest.

"What are you doing in there?" Strachys said, turning stiffly from the table and holding the lamp over Spike's cage. He did not notice the severed strap. "Our friend was right. You are persistent," he said wearily.

Strachys returned the lamp to the table, retrieved the clay cup, and took a long drink of wine. He stared at Spike as if he were a stranger in a tavern, and the cat stared back silently.

"This man who calls himself Phaethon—as if he were the bastard son of a god—is a strange one," Strachys said. He leaned toward Spike with drunken earnestness. "But he has brought me something interesting." He lifted the scroll from the table and held it in front of Spike's cage.

"This is a mystery," he said. "It is unlike any language I've seen. As to the symbols in the margin, they are Egyptian. I can read them easily, but I didn't tell our employer. You see, I long ago learned two things that have served me well . . ."

He lowered his voice conspiratorially and glanced around the empty hut, a practiced gesture to accompany an often-told story. He held up a dirty finger. "One, never let others know what you are thinking, and two," he said, raising another, "when others are in a hurry, your best tactic is always to delay. Their urgency will cause them to make mistakes."

He unrolled the scroll, exposing the hieroglyphics left in the margin by an unknown hand. "These are nothing more than names," he explained to the indifferent cat. "Some are the names of Egyptian gods, while others I do not recognize. What do you think, my friend?"

Strachys read the symbols in a loud voice. "Just as I expected. Nothing."

The seer returned the scroll to the table, took a deep drink of wine, and stared drowsily into the darkness. He did not notice the vague motions on the scroll's surface, the symbols that moved on the parchment like insects waking from a long sleep, nor did he comprehend Spike's uneasy growl.

"Don't worry," Strachys said, leaning toward the cat, "I'll think of something to tell our employer."

With his back to the table, Strachys did not see the golden symbols move across the parchment, at first slowly, as if exercising long-neglected joints, then with increasing speed. He did not see them leave the scroll and cross the table like ants swarming over a carcass, nor did he see them shine in the lamplight as they moved down the table leg to the floor, flowing over each other in golden waves—thousands of individuals governed by a single purpose. He noticed nothing until they swarmed over his sandaled feet.

"Gods!" Strachys screamed as he frantically brushed at the golden writing covering his legs. His hands had no more effect on them than they would have had on shadows as the inhuman writing moved up his legs to his torso. The symbols grew as if nourished by contact with his skin, then split in two and split again, continuing to multiply, spreading across his shoulders, his arms, and his neck. An indecipherable golden scripture covered Strachys' dirty face, blinding his eyes and sealing his ears and nostrils. Words that had gone unspoken for millennia filled his mouth. He shook as if seized by the chills of a horrible illness, then bent forward in spasm as if his body would turn in on itself. Strachys fell unconscious to the floor as the characters arranged themselves in a seamless mosaic across his skin, covering him in a golden sheath.

Frantically, Spike threw himself at the sides of his cage. It gave way where he had chewed through the leather strap, and he forced his face through the broken reeds. Their jagged ends dug painfully into his skin, pulling it tight across his skull, drawing his eyes into slits, his face into a grimace. His right shoulder and foreleg followed his head through the opening, reeds snapping under his efforts. All at once, his body slipped through, and exhausted, he fell to the floor.

Spike stood panting, staring at the gilded sarcophagus lying motionless beside him. Suddenly, the golden sheath vanished into Strachys' flesh like water sinking into dry sand. Spike hissed and withdrew to a dark corner. The seer remained motionless. Spike heard no breathing and saw no trace of life. He carefully walked around the seer's body, then ran from the hut into the safety of the night and the surrounding trees.

The sunlight entered through the small window, shining mercilessly on Strachys' face. He held his forearm over eyes sensitized by drink, then he groaned and rolled over, raising himself stiffly from the dirt floor. He stumbled to the clay water jar he kept just inside the doorway and lifted the ladle to drink. He poured another portion over his head and stepped into the sunlight. Strachys felt strangely displaced from his body and blamed it on his hangover. He remembered the nightmare of golden insects crawling over him and once again swore to stop drinking.

Strachys looked down at his hands, expecting to see the tremors that possessed them on such mornings. To his surprise, they remained steady. He frowned at the network of wrinkles, dirt, and broken veins that covered the back of his hands and his forearms. The sense of physical displacement intensified as he watched his skin grow taut over newly curved muscle, free of dirt, wrinkles, and dark spots. Thinking it was only an alcohol-induced hallucination, Strachys closed his eyes, squeezing his eyelids desperately together. He opened them, and the delusion remained. He felt a strange presence within himself. It was not one of the familiar demons that drink summoned from the darkness of his soul. This was something new, sharing his body, filling his joints with power. He moved his limbs slowly, testing each joint, exploring each sensation, muscle pulling against muscle, strength against strength.

Strachys stared down at his dirty clothes with revulsion and tugged at them with unblemished hands, tearing them away to stand naked in the morning sun. He turned in the warm breeze, stretching his arms toward the sky, moving his back and limbs into positions that only yesterday were blocked by age and affliction. He moved like an athlete before a competition, merely to enjoy the erotic sensation of life flowing through his body.

He walked back into the hut to the table with the scroll spread across it. It was blank, except for the hand-written symbols that remained in the margin. Strachys smiled in understanding. He walked to Spike's empty cage and examined the broken reeds protruding from its side like shattered ribs.

"Clever beast."

He saw blond fur caught in the sharp ends of the broken reeds and felt a compulsion to touch it. The urge came from the strange presence that shared his mind and body. Strachys reached out, felt a tug at his fingertips, and turned his palm upward. Gold filaments, thinner than a spider's strands and more plentiful than the grass in the fields, extended from his hands to penetrate the fur and skin left by the escaped cat. He gasped as the golden threads reached through the tissue left on the reeds to enter the mind of the animal who had left it there, binding it to Strachys' consciousness with a terrifying intimacy. The seer seemed to lose possession of his limbs, the sense of his body, the constant, unconscious awareness of his extent and position in space. He found himself inhabiting a wild, instantly responsive body, a mind unencumbered by the buzz of human pretense. He walked on four legs beside the stream that flowed nearby, even as his own body remained in the dimly lit hut, motionless as if in a trance. He leaned down to drink and saw the cat's broad head reflected on the water's surface. He lapped up the water with a rough tongue and felt it cold in his mouth.

Strachys pulled his hand away from the cage. The golden threads withdrew, and his body's constant affirmations of nerve and muscle returned to a human geometry. Still, the echo of the embodiment he had shared with the cat remained. He felt a rumble in his belly as he reached for a portion of cooked rabbit left from his dinner, stared at it, and realized the hunger was not his own. He returned it to the platter and smiled. He knew he would be able to locate the animal wherever it went on the island.

"Enjoy your freedom, my little friend," he said softly. "There are subtler forms of confinement."

Spike landed on the soft loam of the stream bank and watched the bird fly away. He retreated under a nearby bush and waited for some new prey to come to drink or eat the berries that grew by the water. Spike felt a strange movement beneath his consciousness and reached out to his littermates with his thoughts. Although distant, they remained in his mind as always, familiar tributaries of his sentience. He sensed the woman who had followed them to this place. She seemed restless, pained by injury. He also felt something new, unwelcome, sharing his consciousness.

Spike struggled to push the intrusion from his mind. He spread his attention across the trees, grass, and sky, across the sound of flowing water, the distant calling of birds, animals, and insects, and the smells penetrating his nostrils. He pushed his senses down through the pads of his paws into the soft, mossy earth of the stream bank and outward into the breeze passing through his whiskers. As Spike reconstructed his world from these realities, the alien presence seemed to vanish.

He did not notice the traces it left behind, as subtle as the scent that remains when smoke vanishes into the air or the conversations that linger in the walls of an abandoned house.

Chapter 13

Akiala's kingdom occupied a narrow valley some four days march inland from Troy. It was a backwater of interest only to traders stopping over on their way between the empires to the east and the wealthy cities lining the coast from Mycenae to Troy to Egypt. Akiala's subjects lived clustered along the river—little more than a stream—that fed the struggling groves of olives and figs, the sparse pastures, and the fields of barley.

Phaethon paced the anteroom of Akiala's megaron—the great hall of his palace—while the two warriors who guarded the king's inner chamber watched him indifferently. The great hall and throne room, the stone floors, and the barrel roof followed the pattern of the megarons found at the heart of all Mycenaean palaces—even in backwaters like Akiala's kingdom. The frescoes that covered the walls expressed the same themes—men and women eating and drinking in the company of their king, heroic battles on imagined fields, stories of the gods—all the tales mothers told their children to teach them their place in a world of gods, kings, warriors, and slaves.

He paused near a fresco of young acrobats, male and female alike, vaulting naked over charging bulls, their hands upon the beasts' horns or shoulders, their backs and legs arched in effortless grace. It was a traditional entertainment of Minoan royalty. Phaethon noted that these were only mediocre copies of the grand Minoan frescoes, not even of a quality achieved by the itinerant artists who wandered the Aegean seeking commissions. They were probably the work of some inexpensive local—garish copies drawn from the memory of other garish copies, painted by an artless hack to impress the rustic subjects of a provincial king. The leapers lacked grace, and the bulls seemed more like fat cows than the sinewy beasts that raged across the walls of Crete's grand palaces.

Phaethon turned as the captain of Akiala's guards entered the anteroom with four men following in a ragged formation. He noted that the guards' tunics needed mending and their armor was haphazardly polished. Only their captain showed the discipline in dress and carriage—the union of man and weapon that marked a warrior. For a moment, contempt dimmed Phaethon's anticipation of the coming contest.

The captain of the guard motioned for him to remove his sword. Phaethon placed it carefully on the stone bench near the entrance to the great hall, precisely at the center of the marble top. The captain took the leather bag from Phaethon's hand and examined its contents—gold lamps, cups and bowls, ivory carvings, and jewelry of gold set with lapis, amber, and other gemstones. He removed a polished bronze dagger with gold and lapis inlaid in its ivory handle.

"You cannot take this into the hall," the guard captain said as he placed the knife under his cloak and returned the bag with its remaining treasures. Phaethon knew Akiala would never see the decorated blade—a minor but potentially useful insight into the guard captain's character. Phaethon followed him and his four warriors into the throne room and the waiting king.

"So," Akiala said eagerly, leaning forward on his throne, his paunch resting between spread legs, "have you found my former seer?"

The guards watched, hands on the hilts of their swords, as Phaethon stepped toward the throne and nodded.

"Where is he?" Akiala demanded.

"In his home. Where I left him."

Akiala leaned forward, his eyes narrowed beneath shaggy brows.

"I have come to offer this ransom for his safety," Phaethon said as he placed the bag on the dais near the king's feet.

"Is this some kind of joke?" Akiala laughed uneasily. "Will I find his head in that bag?"

"No. Strachys is in my employ. I ask you to withdraw the reward you have offered for his capture and accept this ransom in its place. I think you will find it more than generous."

Akiala rose to his feet, his face red with anger. "Suppose I take your ransom . . . and your head?"

Phaethon heard the rattling of swords and armor as the guards moved into position behind him. Without turning, he adjusted the map of the hall and its occupants he held in his mind.

"I had hoped you would be reasonable," he said. "The seer has skills I require, and I want him to work without the distraction of a price on his head. Not only is this ransom generous, but you will also have my gratitude."

A smile crossed Akiala's face before melting into a sneer. "Kill him," he told the guards as he slumped on the throne, a petty tyrant anticipating an afternoon's entertainment.

Phaethon heard two soldiers draw their short swords and move toward him. Gauging their locations by the sound of their footsteps, he pivoted toward the nearest of the two, moving inside the radius of his strike. Phaethon grasped the guard's arm as it passed and, using his opponent's momentum, threw him over his hip. He stripped the sword from the guard's hand as the man fell. Phaethon ducked under the second guard's attack, the sword passing harmlessly over his head. Still kneeling, he struck into the man's belly with his borrowed weapon. Phaethon felt a thrill of release as it cut through muscle into unresisting viscera.

As the man fell, Phaethon glanced at the captain of the guards, who held back, assessing his opponent. He motioned the two remaining guards forward. They approached slowly, with an excess of caution, and Phaeton sliced through their hesitation. He brought his sword across the neck of the closest guard, blood spreading over the man's tunic as he fell. The other guard struck at him clumsily, like a shepherd hitting a sheep with a stick. Phaethon grabbed his wrist and pushed it aside as he brought his sword down across the guard's shoulder, shattering his collarbone and continuing into his ribs.

The guard Phaethon had first disarmed rose to his feet and retrieved a fallen comrade's sword. He looked to the captain of the guards who directed him to fall back. The two guards who had flanked the entrance to the great hall rushed in, staring wide-eyed at the three bodies lying on the floor.

Phaethon backed toward the throne, his eyes on the four remaining warriors. As he heard the king rise behind him, Phaethon turned in a blur, slicing his bronze sword through Akiala's neck. His momentum carried him around to face the guards before they could move—before the king's porcine head hit the floor. Stunned, Akiala's men watched their king's head roll off the dais as his body collapsed at the foot of his throne, blood spreading across the white stone.

"I have no quarrel with you," Phaethon told the guard captain. He gestured toward the king's head with his sword. "And, we no longer have cause to fight."

"I will avenge my king," the guard captain said sharply.

"If we must fight, will you tell me your name?"

"Etagama."

"Why avenge him, Etagama, when you can replace him?"

Etagama smiled broadly. "Why not do both?"

Phaethon spoke to the guard he had first disarmed. "You came for me bravely while the others held back. Why waste your life fighting for no purpose but revenge?" He saw doubt cross the guard's face and turned to Etagama. "We can continue this and see what happens, or you can hear my proposition."

Etagama dipped his sword almost imperceptibly, signaling a willingness to bargain while keeping his weapon in play. Phaethon backed toward the throne, picked up the leather bag, and slid it across the floor toward him.

"You might kill me," Phaethon said calmly. "I'm willing to discover if you can . . . or we can help each other."

"You knew Akiala would refuse the ransom," Etagama observed.

"Yes," Phaeton acknowledged, "just as I hope you will accept it."

"All this for that fraud of a seer?"

"My business with Strachys is mine alone," Phaethon said, "but it is important to me, and I require he not be disturbed."

Etagama laughed. "If that was all you wanted, why did you bother to come here? No one has taken the king's reward seriously."

"I also need a place where I can reside safely as my plans unfold," Phaethon admitted.

"Why should I trust you?" Etagama asked.

"You've seen my abilities. Had I wanted to take this palace, I could have come with spear and sword and soaked the floor in blood. I only want a place where I can rest undetected from time to time. My real interest lies elsewhere."

"Continue," Etagama said.

"I need a host who will protect . . ." Phaethon paused and searched for the right word, "my sanctuary as I come and go, as well as my privacy when I am here."

"For how long do you need this . . . sanctuary?"

"A few weeks, perhaps more. I will not be a permanent guest," he said, smiling.

"What else do you want?"

"Are we coming to an understanding?"

"Perhaps."

"The woman who helped Strachys try to escape, the one your king punished. I believe her name is Claea?"

Etagama nodded.

"Give me a room, the woman to attend me, and freedom to come and go as I please. All the rest is yours—the ransom, the kingdom, and should you need it, my sword in your defense."

"Why do you want that one? She's not desirable—she has not even recovered from her injuries."

"I have my reasons," Phaethon said as he lowered his sword.

"As you wish." Etagama gestured toward a doorway near the king's dais. "That is where the king entertained his women," he said contemptuously. "You may have it."

Keeping his face to the guards, Phaethon sidestepped to the rough wooden door, the sword still in his hand. He opened the door cautiously and glanced inside. "This will do," he said. "My final request is that when I am here, I must not be disturbed."

Etagama nodded. "What is your name?"

"My name is not important, but my privacy is."

"As you wish," Etagama said reluctantly.

"Now, please send the woman to me and leave us."

The newly made king nodded toward one of the guards, who scuttled off to fetch Claea. He gestured at the bodies on the palace floor. "Remove them," he told the remaining guards. "Bury them with warriors' honors and prepare a royal funeral for the king."

"Leave Akiala with me," Phaethon interrupted.

Etagama looked puzzled.

"I wish to speak with him," Phaethon said, smiling ironically.

Etagama stared at him. After a time, he nodded. He watched his guards remove their comrades' bodies, then followed them from the throne room.

Phaethon watched them depart, then walked to where Akiala's head rested on the floor. He lifted it by the hair, raised it to eye level, and contemplated the fat, ashen face, dull eyes, and shocked expression.

"Killing you was . . ." Phaethon paused like a poet struggling to express a subtle emotion, "disappointing. I would have thought a king's death might carry some sense of importance, perhaps signify something?"

His voice hardened. "Instead, you died like a pig in a slaughterhouse, and another took your place immediately."

Phaethon walked to the throne and took the king's seat. He placed Akiala's head on the floor between his feet, facing up, and leaned forward with his elbows on his knees.

"Is that all the death of a king means? Another takes his place, and things go on as before. Etagama saw himself on your throne before your head hit the floor."

He nudged the head with his foot as if considering it from another angle might produce some additional insight.

"I have no illusions about Etagama," Phaethon mused. "He'll be as cruel and as stupid as you were. He will grow fat from food and wine, softened by women, as did you. Will he then fall to someone younger, more ambitious?"

Phaethon stared at Akiala's face as if contemplating a theorem from some nascent geometry.

"I wonder . . . how do you think a god would die? They are said to be immortal, but that means nothing. Anyone can be killed—if a king, why not a god? Or does mere belief in their immortality change things?"

Phaethon stepped over the king's corpse to pace near the throne. "Would a god's death bring some sense of finality? Something worthy of ceremony? Would birds sing out in sorrow, or clouds form over the ocean and sweep across the land, dropping tears from the heavens?" He stared at the king's head lying beside the dais as if awaiting a response.

"Would a god die prettily, like a hero in a play, with no blood or excrement staining his immortal robes, just an immaculate catharsis spoken in perfect meter? Would we exit the theater with moistened eyes, stumbling into a world without gods? Or would the fools simply create a replacement, perhaps choose one of their own, some Etagama to become their new god?"

He heard a sound at the entrance to the throne room, looked up, and saw Claea, the woman Akiala had beaten for her role in Strachys' attempted theft. He gestured for her to approach. "Come in, Claea."

She stopped before him, staring with a slave's emotionless gaze. A filthy tunic hung from her shoulders, hiding the contours of the young woman's body. Her dull brown hair fell in greasy strands around the slackened muscles and grayish skin of what should have been a youthful face. A brutal swelling below her left eye pushed her nose to one side. She stared at Akiala's head resting on the floor.

"I will not harm you," Phaethon said.

She neither responded nor took her eyes off Akiala's face.

"That is the man who hurt you," he said. "I have killed him."

Claea looked at Phaethon, then turned and spit on the face framed in Akiala's dark curls. She kicked it and watched the king's head roll like a child's ball as a scream of rage split her slender form. She ran after it and fell to her knees, tearing at the king's unmoving face. She beat it with her small fists, sobbing like a wounded animal, her body convulsing as if it would crack.

Phaethon watched as exhaustion overtook her rage. "Stand."

Claea took her feet without questioning—a slave's reflex. She faced him, tears streaking her dirty cheeks. Phaethon took her by the arm and turned her toward Akiala's battered face. "Look at it. You must never forget."

"Who are you to tell me to remember?" she screamed, jerking her arm from his grasp. "Do you think I will ever forget what he did to me?"

"I understand more than you realize."

"You understand nothing."

"My scars are not visible; that only means they cannot heal."

"What do you want of me?" Resignation and defiance mingled in her voice.

"I will be coming here from time to time to rest. I want you to attend me."

"Why me?"

"Perhaps a whim, perhaps something more . . .." He paused for a moment. "Perhaps no reason at all."

Claea nodded without emotion and wiped her bloody hands on her tunic. She reached down and gathered the dirty cloth, then pulled it over her head and dropped it to the floor. She stood naked, offering him a body marked by Akiala's brutality. Phaethon surveyed her bruises and noted that some were new—swollen and only starting to discolor—while others were older, already faded to a dull yellow. A bend in her forearm told of a poorly treated break. She stared at him knowingly.

"No," he said, retrieving the tunic and placing it in her hands. "That is no longer your life."

She held the cloth bunched in front of her breasts.

"I have learned healing arts beyond the abilities of your physicians," he said. "I will treat your injuries, and I will teach you how to be beautiful."

She stared at him, puzzled.

"You see, Claea, beauty is only a kind of enchantment . . . or should I call it art? It can be learned. In return, you will serve me."

He climbed the king's dais and sat on the throne. "I will tell Etagama that no one may harm you, and only you may enter my room," he explained, gesturing toward the door of his sanctuary. "You will maintain it and serve me when I am here. I may come at any time, without warning, so you must keep it ready always. When I am here, you will bring my food and care for my belongings. I will ask for nothing more. I will not use you in any cruel or dishonorable fashion. Do you understand?"

Claea nodded, her confusion masked by a servant's indifferent obedience.

"My only requirement is that when I am here, you will not enter this room without first receiving my permission." He waited until she confirmed with a nod. "Now go. I would like to be alone."

She put on the dirty tunic, bowed slightly, and turned to leave.

"And Claea," Phaethon called behind her, "tell Etagama I would be grateful if he gave you clothes that suit your status as my attendant."

She looked back at him. Phaethon thought he saw a smile cross her lips, but the mask quickly returned, and she walked from the throne room. As he watched her leave, Phaethon leaned back to rest, drained by his confrontation with the guards. As he closed his eyes, he felt a sharp displacement, like the moment immediately after slipping on the wet rocks of a streambed before gravity's acceleration overwhelms the senses. He grasped his left bicep and saw his forearm dissolve into a blackened stump.

"No," he groaned, "it's too soon."

He shook as the concealing enchantments continued to fail. Through an act of will more than of magic, Phaethon stumbled into the sanctuary Etagama had given him. He locked the door with a final, painful effort before he fell onto the bed, his broken body trembling among the blankets and fleeces that stank from the desperate physicality of Akiala's affairs.

Chapter 14

Unable to sleep because of the pain in her wrist and the trauma of the attempted rape, Astrid left the women's tent before dawn while Hecamede and the others slept. She walked to the shore and watched twilight reveal the details of the camp, the ships, the ocean, and the hillside rising to Troy's impenetrable walls. She removed the improvised splint to examine her injury and soaked her wrist in the ocean's cool water. The swelling and discoloration had worsened, and her arm bent sharply above the wrist joint, an egg-sized lump marking the site of the break. Worried about the consequences of delaying medical treatment but unwilling to trust Bronze Age medicine, Astrid replaced the splint, tightened the elastic bandage, and took another Oxycodone. She returned to the common area at the center of Nestor's camp and sat on the rough bench, waiting for the painkiller to take effect.

She felt a pressure on her hip as Chessie rubbed insistently against her. Astrid lifted the cat onto her lap with her right hand.

"So, little one, we've had our house torn apart by a monster from a bad horror movie, I have a broken wrist, and Spike and Elizabeth are missing. We're stuck three thousand years in the past, and I have no idea how to get us home. Our one stroke of luck is that I was only *almost* raped to death. Without you and your friends—without Swarm—I would have been."

Swarm. Astrid thought about the great cat and looked down at Chessie, purring softly on her lap. "For all I know, I'm laying drugged in some psych ward, and this is all a nightmare," she said to the sleeping animal.

She ran her fingertips over the bruises on her face. *No,* she thought. *This is real.*

Astrid held Chessie close, rubbing her fur in long, calming strokes, and watched Audrey and Greystoke explore the common area, scrounging for food among the feast's leftovers.

"You're at the center of all this, aren't you? You and your brothers and sisters?" she mused as Chessie purred softly. "And you don't understand it any more than I do."

As the sun warmed the camp and the medication masked the pain in her wrist, Astrid watched people step from their tents into the remains of the feast—the cups and plates littering the ground, the scattered bones with cooked meat still clinging to them, the cloaks and other possessions left behind by drunken young men. She saw the blood-stained ground at the head of the commons and remembered the dying bull's pitiful screams.

Chessie began to squirm in Astrid's lap. She set the cat on the ground and watched her walk behind one of the tents to perform her morning toilet. Astrid hoped she would cover it well. She saw a woman, barely in her teens, stumble out of a tent, her hair and clothes in disarray, squinting in the sunlight. The women who followed seemed to have taken more time to prepare themselves. Some wore simple tunics of plain or brightly dyed linen—wine red, blue, saffron, turquoise—while others wore bright dresses with flounced skirts, the layers of color swirling around them as they walked. A few left their breasts exposed as they walked into the morning air.

"It is the Minoan style."

Astrid turned toward the voice. Hecamede stood near, her dark hair gathered under a turquoise-colored headband.

"I saw you were staring." Hecamede smiled as she sat beside Astrid.

Astrid saw the bruise on her cheek. "Are you all right?"

"Sore." Hecamede rubbed her side where the attacker had kicked her. "But no broken ribs."

"How can I ever thank you?"

"It was nothing," Hecamede shrugged. "I saw you were staring," she repeated, changing the subject.

Astrid understood Hecamede's need not to linger on the attack. "What did you mean, 'Minoan style?'"

"The open bodice has long been the fashion among Minoan women," Hecamede explained. "It has spread to other places, particularly among women of wealth or position—or those who claim to be. I do not care for it." She began to laugh. "I find they get in the way when I work."

"You say 'women of wealth or position,'" Astrid said, watching a young woman dressed 'in the Minoan style' bring water to a man stumbling into the sunlight. "Does that include her or other women in the camp?"

"She claims high birth," Hecamede whispered, "but she's only trying to impress the man she serves. She hopes he'll take her to his home and give her a position of importance, perhaps as a wife."

"Tell me about her," Astrid said, gesturing toward another woman, similarly dressed, sitting alone at the far end of the common area. Her clothing was torn and stained, and her hair fell randomly from a clumsy effort to put it up in a red band. She stared vacantly across the ocean.

"She was a woman of some importance, the wife of an advisor to a king," Hecamede whispered. "That's what she was wearing when the Achaeans sacked her city."

"They killed her husband?"

"And her children—she saw it happen. Her mind has gone to the underworld with them. Sometimes she talks to them, though mostly she sits and cries. She tries to command us as if she were still the lady of a house. Some of the younger women laugh, but most of us do as she says out of kindness."

"And the men?"

"They leave her alone. They fear that harming her would anger the gods."

"What about you, Hecamede? How did you come here?"

"The Achaeans raided my home at Tenedos. Achilles took me in the raid and gave me to Nestor." Sadness shadowed Hecamede's elegant features.

"Did you have a husband? Children?"

Hecamede shook her head, a tear moistening her cheek. "Just my father, Arsinous. He died defending our home."

Astrid squeezed her hand.

"It is the way of things." Hecamede shrugged. "I was fortunate to be given to Nestor. He is kind and does not force me to share his bed. I serve him and prepare his food. The others don't know it, but sometimes he seeks my counsel."

"He is wise to do so," Astrid said. "Hecamede, how long has this war been going on?"

"Almost nine years. It seems like forever."

Astrid remembered that *The Iliad* had taken place in the tenth year of the siege. The pivotal incident of Homer's story—the disastrous feud between Achilles, the Achaean's greatest warrior, and Agamemnon, their vain, self-serving supreme commander—had yet to occur.

"How are things in the camp?" she asked.

"The men are growing impatient while Agamemnon does nothing," Hecamede said in a low voice. "They cannot breach Troy's walls, so they spend their time raiding nearby cities or shouting insults at the Trojans, daring them to come out and fight. Sometimes, the Trojans join forces with their allies—the Achaeans have made many enemies—and try to drive them away. Those days are the worst."

"Are many killed?"

"The lucky ones," Hecamede said. "Others die from their injuries, the stench of death spreading from their wounds. Mostly, the men wait, feast, and pray to the gods . . . and argue among themselves. Nestor tells me that more of them are challenging Agamemnon in council."

"What does Nestor say about it? Odysseus?" Astrid asked.

"They try to keep order. The alliance would fall apart without Agamemnon, and they fear the consequences."

Astrid reminded herself that although the theft of Helen, the wife of Agamemnon's brother Menelaus, by the Trojan Paris was the rationale for the Achaean alliance, Agamemnon's military power was its foundation.

"What about Achilles? Does he oppose Agamemnon?" Astrid asked.

"Achilles, most of all."

Astrid felt a familiar pain and looked down. Greystoke was biting her ankle gently, his way of demanding attention. She lifted him onto her lap.

"King Nestor," Hecamede said suddenly, rising from the bench as Nestor approached, dressed in a simple tunic, unarmed, his feet bare. His sons, Thrasymedes and Antilochus, walked with him.

"Could you bring us a pitcher of water, please?" Nestor asked Hecamede. "Perhaps some food?"

Hecamede nodded and walked across the commons to Nestor's tent. Astrid saw her limp slightly, a consequence of the attack.

Nestor introduced his sons, not realizing that Astrid had already recognized them from her readings of *The Iliad*. He sat on the bench beside her; Thrasymedes and Antilochus found wooden stools nearby and sat facing them. Hecamede returned with a bronze tray carrying a clay pitcher of water, cups, and a bronze bowl of figs. Nestor offered the figs to Astrid, who ate one and found it delicious—smaller and sweeter than those she had tasted in her own time. She took a handful and returned the bowl to Nestor. He did the same and passed it to his sons, who ate enthusiastically.

"Can I bring you anything more?" Hecamede asked.

Nestor shook his head. "Could you leave us? I would like to talk with our guest."

Hecamede smiled reassuringly at Astrid, then returned to the tent. Nestor chewed a fig thoughtfully and watched Audrey, Chessie, and Greystoke circle Astrid's feet.

"Hecamede has told me about your animals," Nestor said after a time, "how they transformed into the great cat that killed Dymenos."

"That was his name? Dymenos?" Astrid had never thought of her attacker as having a name. The syllables ignited memories of the attempted rape like a final violation.

"He was a cruel, undisciplined fool," Nestor swore. "Always rushing in, driven by anger or lust or the vanity I see in too many young men. I knew he would not return home when he came to Troy. Few of them will." He put his hand on hers. "I am sorry for what he did to you."

"And to Hecamede," Astrid reminded him.

"Yes, and Hecamede." Nestor frowned and stared at the sandy ground. "Astrid." He spoke her name slowly. "It is a strange name. How did you come here? And what is the nature of these animals? How is it they have such abilities?"

"King Nestor—"

"Just Nestor," he interrupted, smiling.

"Nestor, Hecamede told you the truth about my cats, but I don't understand it myself. The animals belonged to my mother."

"Your mother?"

"She died, and they came to me. I did not learn of their abilities until recently—they had always seemed like ordinary cats. The three who are with me belong to a litter of five."

Astrid told him of her coming to Troy, omitting any details that might raise questions about her origins in the future. She told of the cats' escape into the forest, their encounter with the dog, and their initial transformation into Swarm. She described Spike's abductor, his metamorphosis into the lizard-thing, and how he had nearly killed Swarm and her. She told of the strange woman who had appeared at her home, and how she had transformed the unfortunate Scott into a boar. She described how the intruder had taken Spike and broken her wrist.

"He changed his shape?" Antilochus asked in astonishment.

"Yes. When Swarm fought him—"

"Swarm?" Nestor interrupted.

"I'm sorry," Astrid said, "that's the name I gave the great cat you saw in the women's tent."

"Swarm," Nestor repeated. He looked down at the three cats and smiled.

"The man took one of my cats and vanished. The woman took another. They were not together . . . they seemed to be rivals."

"How did you come here?" Nestor asked.

"When I tried to follow them, something happened—I assume it was another enchantment. I lost consciousness and awoke beside these three cats. At first, I thought I was in my home, then you found me and . . ." Astrid struggled to calm her emotions. "Well, you know the rest." She did not tell him of her merging with Swarm.

"These are dark enchantments," Thrasymedes said.

"Did you know this man and woman?" Nestor asked.

"No, I'd never seen them before. I don't even know their names."

"Do you know where they could have taken your animals? Or why they wanted them?"

"The woman told me that the cats' abilities made them valuable to the man, but she did not know why," Astrid explained. "I don't know why she took Elizabeth."

"Elizabeth?" Thrasymedes asked.

"That's my other cat. I must find them."

Nestor looked at her with concern. "You have no idea where your animals are, or even if they still live."

"I know they live," Astrid insisted.

"Our desires often deceive us," he cautioned.

Astrid thought of the strange connection she had come to feel with the cats. "I can't explain how, but I know my animals live, and I must find them."

"Is it worth risking your life?"

"They're my friends," Astrid said.

He looked at her for a time, then nodded. "Astrid, there is little we can do without knowing more. But I do know you are in grave danger here—from the war, from these dark enchantments," his eyes lingered on the bruises on her face, "even from the men in this camp. Let us take you home to your family. Perhaps they can help you. My sons can accompany you in one of my ships."

"Nestor, I have no family."

He looked at her in disbelief. "No husband? No father or mother, brothers or sisters? Where is your home?"

"An enchantment brought me here. I don't even know what direction we would take."

He stared at her in frustration.

"There must be a reason I was brought to Troy, some purpose I do not understand," Astrid argued. "I must not leave here until I learn how to find my animals—or at least, why I was brought here."

"There might not be a reason. Gods and sorcerers often behave out of whim. Or, you could have been sent here by those wishing to harm you, believing that you would be killed or enslaved . . . and you almost were. Do you understand how dangerous this place is?"

"I know the danger." Astrid held up her broken wrist. "I did not let this stop me. I did not let Dymenos stop me. I won't stop now."

Nestor sat upright on the bench and stared out across the Aegean. "Talking to you is like arguing with Achilles," he said in exasperation.

Astrid saw Thrasymedes and Antilochus glance at each other and smile.

"I know it seems hopeless," she said, "but there must be something we can do."

Nestor took a fig from the bowl and turned it thoughtfully between his fingers. "You say this woman and the man were rivals, and she seemed friendly to you?"

Astrid nodded. "She's my best hope."

"Very well," Nestor said in surrender, "you may stay here for now, and we will wait for some sign. In the meantime, we may be able to learn more about these people through their enchantments. Such things leave traces that cannot easily be seen, but there are traces, nonetheless. I will consult our seers."

"Thank you," Astrid said.

"But I will not wait indefinitely," he warned. "If we cannot locate your animals, or if no sign appears, or if I decide it has become too dangerous for you to stay—you will have to leave. If you cannot tell us how to find your home, I will send you to my home in Pylos, where my wife can care for you."

Astrid forced herself to remain silent.

Nestor pointed to her left arm as he rose from the bench. It was still in its makeshift splint and sling. "Hecamede tells me you're reluctant to let our healer treat your injury."

"I'd hoped to have it treated when I returned home," she evaded.

"Don't wait too long." Nestor smiled knowingly. "In my experience, our healer can sometimes help—if only by accident."

Chapter 15

Astrid watched Nestor and his sons leave the common area. She took an Oxycodone from the bag she carried in her pocket and washed it down with a cup of water Hecamede had left on the bench. She had no idea how to find Spike or Elizabeth. Frustrated, she nibbled on the last of the figs and watched the camp continue its slow awakening.

A young warrior dressed in a linen kilt walked barefooted from a tent, carrying a leather bag. He sat on a bench nearby and arranged the bag's contents neatly beside him. Astrid recognized them to be grooming tools. He raised a polished bronze mirror to his face and began to scrape his teeth with the flattened end of a stick, occasionally picking between them to remove some remnant of the night's feast. He smiled broadly into the mirror, then took a clay jar and poured what looked like olive oil into his hand. He rubbed it on his body, then scraped away the excess oil and dirt with an elaborately carved tool that appeared to be made of ivory. He finished by vigorously wiping his skin with a cloth, occasionally smiling in Astrid's direction. Astrid felt relieved when a young woman approached him, took an ivory comb from the bench, and began to groom and braid his hair. He turned his face, eyes closed, toward the morning sun.

While she waited for the painkiller to take effect, Astrid watched people fill the commons, some doing morning chores while others came into the center of the camp for breakfast and gossip. Many stole guarded glances in her direction, turning away when their eyes met hers. In Nestor and Hecamede's absence, she felt self-conscious, her feelings of vulnerability intensified by the crowd.

"Let's take a walk," she said to the cats.

Moving slowly and hoping not to draw attention to herself, she left the common area and walked past the long row of ships down the beach. The cats followed, bound to her by the psychic connection that lingered from her merging with Swarm as much as by their fear of this strange place. The crowds thinned as she reached the edge of the camp. Astrid waited until no one was watching and ducked behind the last of the ships that lined the beach.

Grateful to be alone, she sat with the cats in the shade of the ship, her back resting against the black hull, digging her feet into the moist sand, staring out across the water, and listening to the surf. Even as she began to relax, Astrid sensed that the cats remained anxious. She tried to reassure them, petting each animal in turn. Her connection to them seemed to strengthen with touch.

"What is it, little ones? Should we go back? Or should we stay away for a while? Clear our minds; maybe try to sort things out?"

Another encampment stood about a hundred yards away. A river flowed between the camps, down through the salt meadow, widening as it crossed the beach and entered the ocean. Astrid guessed it was the Scamander, generally assumed to be the site of the Achaean encampment. A band of green lined the river, at first no more than a thickening of the salt meadow's coarse grasses but growing denser upstream as tenacious coastal shrubs and grasses took hold. Further inland, where the river had washed away the salt of the ocean and the humus of decaying plants and animals had nourished the soil, a forest spread into the hills.

Astrid waited until she could see no one on the beach and hurried to the river's edge, Chessie, Audrey, and Greystoke staying close beside her. She looked back from the cover of the low shrubs to make sure she had not been seen, then led the cats along the river into the thickening foliage. She came to a small stream that fed the river and, lured by the sound of cold water flowing over stones, followed it into the hills that looked down on the chaos of Agamemnon's war.

Elizabeth rested on the brightly colored cushion, a partly eaten bowl of fish nearby. She watched Circe stare into the hemisphere of light that swirled on the marble tabletop. The cat did not see the figures moving within it—the images of Astrid, Greystoke, Chessie, and Audrey walking into the trees— to her, it was merely a swirl of light. Instead, she drifted into sleep, and her attention settled over the familiar contours of her littermates' minds. She smelled the salt air and felt the sand under her siblings' paws as they ran across the beach. She sensed Astrid's presence, the pain in her wrist, and her connection to the minds of her littermates. She also knew Spike had escaped his imprisonment, and she shared both the joy of his freedom and the aching loneliness of his separation from her and his littermates.

Circe lifted the cat into her lap. "Tell me, little one," she mused, "can you see your friends in the light? Or are your eyes immune to Circe's enchantments?"

Elizabeth purred.

"I suspect they are," she said. "You lack the webs of self-deception that make humans so easily enchanted."

She lifted a piece of fish from the nearby bowl and held it as the cat ate. "I think you are more closely tied to your littermates than even I can understand."

Circe ran her hand meditatively across Elizabeth's long fur. "What am I to make of you? Animals who can join to form a new creature and then return to what they were. Even the gods who change their shape at will cannot join their minds and bodies with each other. Are you freaks? Formed out of my indiscretions to shine briefly, then vanish into forgetfulness? Or are you fated to bring about some great change in the world, some new thread in the tapestry of creation?"

She lifted Elizabeth's chubby body and kissed her on the head. "And what of this woman? She joined with your bodies when she traveled here and remains bound to you. What is her role in your fate . . . or your role in hers?"

She eased the cat onto the soft bedding. "Such questions do not trouble you, do they, little one?" Circe said as she rose from the cushions. "But they are of great importance to a goddess, and we are not going to answer them here on Aeaea."

A young woman approached as if she anticipated her mistress' call.

"Annape, I must go and ask a favor of my uncle."

"Proteus?"

"Dear Annape, how is it you always know my mind?" Circe mused. "Will I ever fully understand your gifts?"

Annape blushed, her pale skin revealing her embarrassment instantly.

"Take care of the cat while I'm gone," Circe instructed.

"Proteus can be difficult," Annape observed as she took Elizabeth into her arms.

"Yes, but he can see farther into people's fates than I, and he may help me to unravel this mystery. I do not think he will refuse me. Despite his rough temper, he finds my little adventures . . ." she paused, searching for the right word, "shall we say 'interesting?'"

Part III
Troy and the Aegean – Circe Intervenes
Thirteenth Century B.C.E.

Chapter 16

strid continued to follow the stream into the hills above Nestor's camp, following the narrow, worn trail that passed through the trees. From time to time, the path departed from the water's efficient line of descent to pass around rock formations and patches of dense brush, always returning to the stream's seductive murmur.

Astrid felt a pain in the palm of her right hand. When she stopped to examine it, Audrey limped toward her with her right foreleg raised. Astrid kneeled and felt the pad of her paw. She found a thorn and removed it—as she did, the pain in her palm vanished. Since arriving at Troy, Astrid had felt strangely attuned to the cats, sensing their proximity, their moods, their drives. She watched Audrey lick her paw and remembered her struggles to control Swarm's rage after the great cat had killed Dymenos. She felt the cat's minds intersecting her own, faint voices at the edge of her consciousness, waiting to flood her mind with tempests of animal emotion.

A throbbing from her broken wrist interrupted Astrid's thoughts; she had delayed her next painkiller for too long. She followed the trail to rejoin the stream where it accelerated through a narrow channel and took a pill from the eight remaining. She knew they wouldn't last more than two days, possibly three if she rationed carefully.

"Hurt now or hurt later," she muttered as she placed the pill on her tongue and washed it down with water from her cupped hand. She found a mossy spot nearby and sat in the shade with her back to a tree, adjusting the sling and makeshift splint that immobilized her wrist. She released her thoughts into the stream's calming music, waiting for the painkiller to take effect.

Audrey, Chessie, and Greystoke felt the sharp complexities of Astrid's mind soften as the drug flowed across her nerves, carrying her into a restless sleep.

Audrey remained at Astrid's side, her liquid mind touching Astrid's thoughts. Greystoke explored the shaded area around the stream, while Chessie found a deep pool a few yards downstream to the side of the central currents, where the quickly flowing water slowed into a lazy spiral. She leaned forward on the moss, careful not to fall into the dark pool, and drank, her rough tongue lifting the cold water into her mouth. She saw a school of small silver trout approach the surface and batted at them with her paw. Water splashed on her face, and the trout vanished into the pool's depths.

Chessie crouched near the edge of the stream, waiting motionlessly. The fish returned, a silver flash followed by more silver flashes. She felt her heart quicken and her muscles tense as fish filled the pool. She sensed a presence among them—steady, calm, curious. Chessie slapped at the fish with her claws extended. The trout scattered as water splashed across her fur.

Astrid opened her eyes, awakened by the splash. She saw the gray tabby backing away from the stream, droplets on her fur catching the sunlight.

"What happened, honey?" she asked, still drowsy. "Did you get too close to the water?"

She looked up through the trees. The sun was high, and she wondered how long she had slept.

"We should get back. Hecamede must be worried."

As Astrid stood to leave, she noticed a strange rock formation on the other side of the water. Its symmetries suggested a human origin. Curious, she jumped a narrow stretch of the stream and waited for the cats to follow, but they remained on the bank, staring uncomfortably at the running water. Astrid sensed their anxiety and lifted them across, one by one. They followed her to stand in front of a crudely constructed shrine.

Two rough but carefully stacked stone pyramids flanked a large, flat rock to form a simple altar. A tangle of brush formed a wall behind it. A variety of objects lay like offerings on the flat rock—a clay cup of water, wildflowers from nearby meadows left to dry on the stone, a rough clay figurine, and a piece of pink quartz that probably came from the stream bed. Astrid picked up the statuette and examined it. It was a rough terracotta, with ashes still embedded in its surface. The body's contours were female, its face framed by what looked like long hair or a shawl.

"It is a shrine to Artemis."

Startled, Astrid turned toward the voice. An old man stood a few yards away, leaning on a gnarled walking stick, wearing sandals and a simple tunic. He was bald, with an unkempt white beard. His legs were thin and bowed, but his knotted calf muscles suggested he was not weak.

"Who are you?" Astrid challenged.

He walked toward the shrine while Astrid backed away, the statuette still in her hand.

"I'm a friend of Nestor's. He told me about you," he explained. He stopped in front of the shrine. "There's a girl who lives in these hills. She fancies herself to be a disciple of Artemis. I've seen this before—girls wishing to escape the world of men often hide here, surviving on small game, wild berries, and anything they can steal. They build these shrines to Artemis. Artemis the huntress, Artemis the virgin—Artemis the protector of foolish young women. Few of them survive long, but this one seems to be tougher and more resourceful than most."

"Did you follow me here?"

"No, but it seems I've found you," he cackled. He walked to a fallen tree and sat wearily, then removed a sandal and began to massage his foot.

"Don't be afraid," he said, his smile revealing as many gaps as teeth. "I still like pretty young women, but I no longer think they're worth the trouble. I come here every day to rest and soak my feet in the cold water."

Astrid walked to the shrine and returned the figurine to its place. "How do you know Nestor?"

"When the Achaeans first came, I visited their camp. Some of the men tried to drive me off, while others called me an old fool and laughed. Nestor gave me hospitality and respect . . . and wine."

"That sounds like him," Astrid said. "What did he tell you about me?"

"That you were a mystery, possibly under the protection of a god." He nodded toward the shrine. "Artemis, perhaps?"

"I don't think so," Astrid said uneasily. "I should get back. It's getting late."

"I'll walk with you. These hills can be dangerous." He replaced his sandal and laughed. "You can protect me."

They followed the stream through the forest. Astrid accompanied him, first at a cautious distance but drawing closer as the old man showed no threat. They followed the trail to where the stream joined the river.

"We should cross here," he said.

He picked up Audrey, carrying her across the water. Astrid was surprised that the high-strung cat allowed him to handle her.

"She's a beautiful animal," he said, petting her long fur as he lowered her to the bank.

Astrid carried Chessie across with her right hand, jumping the widening stream, and then she returned for Greystoke. As she brought him across, she slipped on the wet moss of the bank. Greystoke jumped to safety as the old man grabbed her right hand. She thanked him and released her grip. He did not let go, and Astrid pulled sharply.

"Let me go," she demanded.

"Do not be afraid," the old man reassured her without releasing her hand.

He stepped into the stream, the water flowing around his knees. Astrid cursed as he pulled her toward him—and into the deep water at the center of the stream. He seemed to grow stronger as she resisted. She fell into the water, fighting to keep her head above the surface as the current and the old man pulled her downstream toward the river. She saw the cats run along the bank beside her. Astrid found her footing on the rocky stream bed, the water swirling around her waist.

"I mean you no harm," the old man repeated.

Astrid saw a blue light on the bank as Swarm took shape, and she tried to pull the old man toward the cat. Swarm approached the stream, teeth bared, then drew back and growled as water splashed across her face.

"Shit," Astrid swore.

The stream joined with the river, and the old man pulled her into the strong currents at the river's center. The water deepened and lifted her from her feet. Swarm followed along the bank, growling restlessly, occasionally approaching the river's edge, only to pull back from the cold depths. Astrid felt the old man pull her underwater, and she fought against his grip. For a moment, he seemed to loosen his hold, but his bony fingers only gave way to something thicker, stronger, wrapping coldly around her arm. Astrid's feet touched a shallow place in the riverbed, and she stood, the water now up to her chest.

Instead of the frail old man, Astrid found herself face to face with a man in the late prime of life, graced by age but untouched by its frailties—and covered with silvery scales that shone in the sun. Tentacles branched from his shoulders—only the man's face and muscular torso remained human. A silver tentacle encircled her arm, and Astrid felt a serpentine grasp enfold her hips. He pulled her under the water, ignoring her struggles.

Astrid held her breath and fought against his grip. She felt a tentacle cover her face like a band of hard rubber, and a blue haze filled her mind. It was the same haze she remembered from the coffeehouse when she had encountered the strange woman, but this penetrated her consciousness with a harder intention. Astrid panicked as she exhausted the air in her lungs and tasted salt in the water. He had carried her to where the river flowed into the Aegean. She struggled desperately to the surface and filled her lungs with the damp air.

The creature pulled her back under the water as a flood of memories filled her mind, memories reaching past her arrival at Troy, back through her struggle with the stranger at Sigrid's home to her first encounter with

Swarm. She felt a cold presence reach into her earliest recollections, chambers of memory she rarely entered. Astrid lost the will to fight, her panic giving way to a strange calm. She felt no anxiety, only sadness as a deep peace enfolded her, calling her to rest, to release the pain, to end her struggles. She felt detached from her body, unconcerned with the water overcoming her—until an intense pain in her left wrist pulled her back from the soft indifference.

Astrid clawed with her right hand at the tentacle tightening around her broken limb, but she failed to loosen its icy grip. Somehow, he had torn the splint and sling from her arm, and she felt the tentacle tighten around the swollen flesh like a steel cable. Astrid felt bone fragments move, tearing through the scar tissue and edema that surrounded them. She screamed in pain, only to be silenced as water filled her mouth.

Suddenly, the pain stopped, and the sea creature pushed her through the water. She felt herself accelerating as her head broke the surface. Astrid gasped for air, saltwater following it into her lungs as he ejected her from the ocean to land on the beach with a bone-jarring thud. She gasped for air through aching lungs, shaking uncontrollably, leaning on all fours, vomiting seawater onto the sand.

On all fours?

The realization overwhelmed her as she raised her left hand before her eyes. The splint and the bandage, the swelling and bruises, the pain and deformity had vanished. She made a fist and then opened her fingers without pain. She sat in the sand, opening and closing her fist, laughing as saltwater ran from her hair, across her face, trickling into her mouth.

Astrid saw Swarm run across the beach toward her and started to her feet. The great cat barely slowed as it jumped to greet her, front paws on her chest, knocking her onto her back. Swarm pinned her against the sand, licking her face with her rough tongue. Laughing, Astrid turned her face to the side and held Swarm's great head with two perfect arms. She rolled over and crawled from under the cat. Astrid took her feet, and Swarm rubbed against her, knocking her sideways. The cat crouched, shoulders lowered, hindquarters subtly rocking, tail twitching. It was the same posture her cats had assumed in a thousand games they had played since birth. Astrid ran in circles on the beach as Swarm playfully chased her, scattering the sand with her great paws.

Spike crouched among the branches of a low bush. He had prowled the shoreline for days, searching for a way to reach Astrid and his siblings, but the dark ocean always blocked his way. Spike closed his eyes, and his attention dispersed through his resting mind, his consciousness touching the minds of his littermates.

Spike awoke suddenly. He felt Chessie, Audrey, and Greystoke join their bodies together, and their combined strength surged through him. He sensed Astrid's struggles with a strange, powerful creature, and he shared her panic, helplessness, and pain as the river's currents carried her beyond Swarm's reach. He cried out as she disappeared into the ocean, then he sensed her relief as she suddenly returned to land.

As Swarm ran toward her, Spike experienced the salt air as if through his own lungs. The soft sand pulled at his feet, and he felt Astrid's emotions as Swarm knocked her to the ground. He felt her embrace the great cat and an almost forgotten emotion filled the faceted consciousness he shared with his littermates—the consciousness he shared with Astrid.

Joy.

Chapter 17

Circe sat on the bank near the improvised shrine to Artemis, her arms around her knees, feet bare, toes curling into the soft moss, her face raised to the sunlight that danced through the leaves overhead. She saw a silver flash under the water, and a small trout breached the surface to land on the bank. It struggled, its tail arching toward its head, then snapping back to propel itself randomly, futilely toward the stream. A dozen more followed, then a hundred, until a thousand small fish breached the water like a geyser—a silver arc that ended in the shape of a man.

"Well done, uncle." Circe smiled. "I wondered how you would manage such a narrow channel."

She leaned back, arms straight behind her, legs stretched across the moss as Proteus, The Old Man of the Sea stood before her. Seaweed entangled a beard and flowing hair the color of seafoam. His silver flesh shone, scales damp from the stream. Proteus shook his head, scattering water across the bank. Circe closed her eyes and turned away, laughing as the spray dampened her linen tunic. Proteus walked naked across the moss to sit cross-legged near her.

Circe nodded toward the rough shrine. "Tell me, uncle, why do I see so many shrines to Artemis in woods like this? Why do these girls never build monuments to me?"

"Perhaps because Artemis defends the virtue of young women," he scowled. "I have never known you to defend even your own."

The enchantress laughed softly. "I find that too much concern for virtue can blind one to the larger picture. What have you learned about the woman and her animals?"

Proteus stared impassively through the trees toward the ocean.

"Uncle, your silence suits the company of fish," Circe said after a time. "I am asking for your counsel."

"Their future is unclear," he said reluctantly. "I see patterns form briefly, then dissolve in shifting possibilities."

"Is this just your legendary reluctance to share your visions? Do you really see nothing?"

"I see nothing you don't already know."

Circe frowned. "I had hoped for more."

Proteus shook his head. "This woman is not of our world."

"No, but she is in it. What about the animals?"

"Their minds lack a human's layers of pretense. They are simple to read but too fluid to reveal details. " He frowned at the enchantress. "I know of their abilities and their origins. Their fate is tied to the woman's . . . and to yours. I see nothing more."

Circe leaned forward, pulled her knees into her arms, and rocked thoughtfully on the moss.

"What is your game?" Proteus demanded.

"My game, uncle?"

A wave of darkness crossed his skin, silver scales turning the color of lapis. "You ask me to read this woman and her animals, but you do not say why. When I say I cannot read them, you show no surprise. You ask for my help to understand why they came here, but I sense you already know. I even sense you are behind it."

"Have you seen nothing that can help me?"

"You traveled beyond our world," he accused, ignoring her question.

"It was necessary."

"You create your own necessities."

"And those necessities require that I ask for your help."

"You have enchantments enough to see the Fates' tapestry."

"You see beyond what's written," Circe argued. "Your visions come from the living soul of an immortal, not from extracts and incantations. I had hoped you might see more."

He shook his head. "Child, I can see the contours of time, the obstacles and openings that will shape a life. What I cannot see are what one will choose to love and choose to scorn."

"It was love that brought this about," she confessed.

"It usually is. I assume you have not told Zeus."

Circe shrugged. "Zeus knows more than we think—certainly, more than he admits. Over the ages, he has learned to give me a certain latitude. He understands that surprise and invention—even disobedience—are as important to the unfolding of the universe as his designs."

"Do not play games with me, child," Proteus cautioned.

"Uncle, these games are all that make life matter. This woman and her animals are unique. You walked this ground as an aged human, then became something part man and part sea beast. You appeared to me as a school of fish and now you assume a human shape—soon, you will return to the Aegean as water yourself. You exceed all the gods in your ability to change form. Can you achieve what these animals do effortlessly?"

"You know I cannot." He scowled and pointed to the ocean. "The ocean is my single, essential being. All the rest, even this," he said, passing his hands over his body, "are only enchantments. But both forms these animals take— as individuals and as the great cat—are essential, genuine."

Circe smiled. "That is what I have seen. How can you know that they are new to all of creation and deny that they are as important as the men camped on this beach and their tiresome war? Can you tell me anything that may help me?"

"I have told you . . . their future remains unclear."

Circe stared across the Aegean, rocking on the soft moss. "Astrid and the animals are weaving their own threads into the fabric of reality," she said softly, thoughtfully.

Proteus rose and started toward the stream. "I've done what you asked."

Circe ran behind him and grabbed his elbow.

"What are you not telling me?" She spoke over his shoulder, her breath warm against his ear.

"What do you mean?"

"I did not ask you to heal her injury."

Proteus turned sharply to face her. "What of it?"

"I've never known you to care for mortals. I've seen you let sailors drown when you could have easily saved them. You won't even share your visions with a mortal unless he captures you and demands it as a ransom for your release. What is your game, uncle? Why did you help this woman?"

"She would not have survived with a broken arm," he said, looking toward the Achaean beachhead. "Not on this wasteland."

"Why do you care?"

"Perhaps I'm curious to see what will happen," he said dismissively.

"Why?" she pressed, holding the shape-shifter by his arm. "Why does she matter to you?"

Once more, Proteus' skin turned a deep blue. "Can't you see? For all their abilities, these animals are incomplete—as is the woman."

"As I have thought," Circe said, smiling.

"I do not know their fates, but they are intertwined. They must be allowed to realize their future—both the woman and the animals."

He touched Circe's cheek with an icy hand, his brow furrowed with concern. "Be careful, child," he cautioned. "You're playing with forces that could destroy even you."

Proteus turned and dived into the narrow creek, breaking into a thousand small fish. Circe watched the Old Man of the Sea return to his home, a band of silver moving through the narrow creek, through the Scamander River to spread upon the Aegean surf.

She sat on the soft loam by the stream, deep in thought, watching Astrid play on the beach with the great cat. She watched them tire of their game, then rest beside each other on the beach, staring across the Aegean. She watched Astrid stand, brushing the sand from her damp clothing, and saw Swarm separate to become three bright creatures who followed her back to Nestor's camp.

Chapter 18

Phaethon stood in the doorway of Strachys' hut. "What do you have for me?"

"Come inside," Strachys greeted him.

Phaethon stepped into the single room where the seer ate, worked, and slept. He examined the tapestry hanging on the wall, the freshly swept clay floor, the new fleeces on the bed, and the bowls and cups neatly arranged on the shelves. He walked to the wooden table where he had first shown Strachys the five cats joining to become Swarm, and he ran his fingers across its surface. The stain where he had poured lamp oil to ignite the vision of Swarm's first appearance had been scrubbed clean.

"You look well. I see you have new clothes." Phaethon looked out the doorway at the woman working at a loom under a shady tree. "And a new companion."

"I have been reborn," Strachys said with an ironic smile. "Come, let me share my good fortune and my gratitude."

He took a second chair from its place near the hearth and set it at the table as Phaethon watched impatiently. Strachys brought two cups and a clay pitcher from the shelf. He poured wine for himself and his guest, diluting it with water from a similar pitcher on the table.

Phaethon remained standing. "What have you learned?"

Strachys frowned, a host facing a graceless guest. "The cat is bound to his littermates by invisible threads. Their minds are both independent and always joined, sharing impressions and emotions."

"Yes, yes. Have you learned how the animals join their bodies together?"

"There is work to be done."

"Work to be done," Phaethon repeated menacingly. He looked around the hut, and his eyes rested on the scroll stored on the highest of Strachys' new shelves, still in its cloth covering. "I bring you the wisdom of the gods.

I bring you an ignorant animal, pay you well, and ask you to duplicate its abilities. Now, you say there is work to be done?"

"These are not ordinary cats—" Strachys began.

Phaethon grabbed him by the folds of his tunic and pulled him so close their faces nearly touched. "Where is the animal?"

"He is nearby."

"Nearby? What do you mean, nearby?" He threw the seer into his chair and grasped the hilt of his sword. "Where is the animal?"

"He is near the village," Strachys said, clearing an area on the table. "I watch him constantly. Let me show you."

"You let him escape!" Phaethon pulled Strachys from the chair and threw him to the floor. He drew his sword, drove his knee into the seer's abdomen, and pressed the edge of his blade against his throat. "By the gods, I will end you," Phaethon raged.

Strachys stared impassively as Phaethon felt the sword's grip writhe in his hand. The blade raised from the seer's throat, curving upward in the form of a serpent, hissing angrily. Phaethon recoiled as the snake struck, missing his face by the thickness of the blade he'd recently held. He threw the snake aside in horror, only to see his sword clatter across the floor, coming to rest near the mud-brick wall.

Strachys pushed his stunned attacker aside and rose to his feet. "Much has changed since your last visit," he said, wiping the blood from his face.

Furious, Phaethon ran at him, only to fall as if a spear thrown from an onrushing chariot had struck him in the belly. A blue corona surrounded him and his flesh seemed to melt. Strachys stepped back as the charred, twisted body collapsed at his feet.

Phaethon awoke to the touch of water on his lips. He sat up quickly, knocking the cup from Strachys' hand. "What did you do to me?"

"Nothing. I changed the appearance of your sword to protect myself, but the rest was not my work."

Phaethon sat on the floor, breathing heavily.

"I restored your enchantments," Strachys explained. "When I did, I learned that you . . ." He paused. "Well, you already know."

Phaethon nodded. "It's grown difficult for me to sustain my appearance. I must rest frequently."

"Your anger at learning I did not have your cure drained your enchantments. When I restored your appearance, I also strengthened the forces that enable you to hold it. You will find it easier for a while."

"For a while?"

"I can only help a little. Your underlying injuries are growing worse. If we do not find a cure—"

"I will die," Phaethon interrupted bitterly.

"Yes."

"Why didn't you kill me?"

"I'm not a murderer."

Phaethon laughed sarcastically. "That's not your only reason."

"The scroll has given me great powers, but I have much to learn. I, too, want to understand these animals' abilities. We can help each other."

The seer helped Phaethon to his feet and gestured toward the table. Phaeton collapsed into a chair, and Strachys sat across from him. He slid a cup of wine across the wooden surface, and Phaethon drank deeply.

"I've penetrated the mind of the animal you left here," Strachys said. "I always know where he is. He cannot leave this island, and I can capture him at any time."

"Why did you release him?" Phaethon demanded.

"I didn't. The cat escaped." Strachys smiled. "As you said, they are remarkable animals . . . but I've learned more."

"Continue."

"The minds of these animals are joined, even when their bodies remain separate. I sensed the others after I first engaged with the cat's awareness. Each animal has its own will, its own perceptions, its own desires . . . but they share a single sentience."

"They cannot share a single mind; it would mean chaos."

"Not at all," Strachys said. "We experience our minds as a single awareness, but they consist of many different thoughts, emotions, and perceptions, all existing simultaneously—usually beneath our consciousness and often competing for our attention. Our minds combine the many threads into a single sense of the world. Even when we focus on certain perceptions or ideas, others continue to work beneath our awareness. We can speak, listen, walk, watch our surroundings, feel hot and cold, experience emotions . . . and even draw a sword," he smiled at Phaethon, "all without confusion. The animals are no different. Each animal shares the minds of its siblings effortlessly, ignoring them when it acts as an individual or combining them into a larger picture of reality as it suits them."

"This is all very entertaining," Phaethon said impatiently, "but what does it mean?"

"Just as we are unaware of how our minds make sense of the chaos inside us, the cats are not conscious of how they join their bodies. When they are apart, they are just ordinary animals, except for a vague sense of their siblings' presence. Their abilities sleep until something—fear or anger, I assume—awakens the great cat. I must have another cat so I can place them together and observe what happens."

"I'll bring them all," Phaethon said, draining his cup.

"No," Strachys laughed, "one is enough. I do not wish to face the monster they can become."

"Do you know where they are?"

"I've been able to trace the others through the animal you brought me. They are at Troy with their mistress, in the camp of Nestor of Pylos."

"Their mistress?"

"Yes, a woman is with them. Her presence is strong in their minds."

"Could it be the woman from the other age?" he mused. "Could she have followed them here?" He looked up at the seer. "You say they are at Troy?"

Strachys nodded.

"There is a war there," Phaethon thought aloud. "It's chaos—that will be useful. Can you tell me more?"

Strachys shook his head. "I cannot sense details."

Phaethon stood from the table. "Very well," he said, "I will return with the animal you require."

"There is something else you may want to know."

Phaethon returned to his seat.

"Every object carries traces of its history and of the people who have handled it," Strachys explained. "I've learned to read those histories. Do you remember the gold lamp you gave me when we first met? It still carries impressions of its former owner, a young Hittite woman of some nobility. It was her prized possession. I experienced her panic when soldiers raided her home. I remember how she hid in her room, clutching the lamp, listening in terror as her captors approached. I remember her grief when they tore it from her hands." He paused, tears shining in his eyes.

"So?" Phaethon pressed.

Strachys wiped his eyes with his sleeve. "In the same way, I have learned that the scroll you brought me belonged to Circe, the enchantress. I know you stole it from her. I also learned of your relationship . . . and your hatred for her."

Phaethon's features hardened. "Circe caused this misery."

"I know she once loved you."

"She should have let me die."

"Perhaps, but I have learned something else that may interest you. Circe is destined to love Odysseus."

"The Ithacan king?"

"Odysseus is at Troy. When the war ends, he will visit her island."

"And he will be the bitch's lover?"

"Yes."

"Does Circe know this?"

Strachys nodded. "She has foreseen it. She already loves him deeply."

Phaethon walked across the room and retrieved his sword.

"What are you going to do?" the seer asked.

"Go to Troy. Steal a cat. Kill a king." Phaethon walked to the shelf where Circe's scroll rested. "Perhaps I will hold this until you need it again," he said, placing the scroll inside his leather bag.

"No," Strachys cried out, rushing from his chair.

Phaethon raised his sword, holding its point against the seer's chest. "Don't try me, old man. I won't fall for your tricks a second time."

Strachys stared in horror as Phaethon turned and walked from the hut. He ran after him in panic, tripping on a chair leg in his haste. As Phaethon crossed the clearing outside, he heard a scream from the woman sitting under the tree. He turned and saw the seer lying on the ground, his body wracked with convulsions, digging at the dirt with hands like claws, gasping silently, screams dying in his throat, his skin turning the color of dried meat and falling away in pieces.

Phaethon ran to his side. The convulsions slowed as he drew near, and the brown flakes stopped falling from Strachys' flesh. Those that had fallen to the ground turned from brown to the color of dull bronze. When Phaethon reached Strachys' side, the flakes began to shine in the sunlight like scales shed by a golden snake. They returned to Strachys' body one by one, disappearing into his skin.

The seer rolled onto his side, reaching toward Phaethon. "Please, do not take it. I will die."

Phaethon reached into his bag and removed the scroll. He unrolled it and stared in shock at the blank parchment.

"What have you done?" he shouted, his face red with rage. "Where is the writing? Have you destroyed it to keep the knowledge for yourself?"

He dropped the scroll and grasped his sword.

"No. The writing is in me," Strachys croaked, clutching the blank scroll to his chest. "The writing did not tell of the power . . . it is the power."

"No more tricks, seer," Phaethon growled.

"The writing is alive," Strachys pleaded. "It's inside me. I tried to interpret the scroll. I did everything I could to understand it but failed. Then one day, the characters left the parchment and swarmed over my body. They penetrated my flesh, becoming part of me . . . with their knowledge."

He did not mention how speaking the Egyptian characters awakened the golden text, nor did he tell of the strange presence that shared his mind and body.

"They give me much power," Strachys continued, his words coming in short bursts as he continued to gasp for breath, "but I am still learning how to use it. I can create illusions, read the history of objects—I can even penetrate the cat's mind. I was able to restore your strength, but only temporarily. There is so much more. I must continue to learn."

Phaethon stared at the seer in disgust and took his hand from the hilt of his sword. "It seems our partnership has found a life of its own," he said bitterly. He gestured toward the scroll Strachys held. "Very well, keep it." Phaethon kneeled on one knee and stared into the seer's eyes. "It's of no value to me as it is, but never presume to deceive me again."

He stood and glanced at the woman who stood beside the loom, still trembling in fear, then he started down the mountain. Strachys held the scroll to his chest and felt the ancient presence stir once more within him. He watched Phaethon disappear below the ridge.

Since escaping his confinement, Spike had followed the bond that would lead him to his siblings and the woman who had come to share their minds. He prowled Kyros' shoreline in a widening arc, living on whatever he could find in the dry hills—mostly insects and the occasional bird, lizard, or mouse. He'd found his way always blocked by the dark ocean.

Now, he crouched, hidden in a patch of scrub oak, watching the stream that flowed past Strachys' hovel, down the mountainside, and into the Aegean. A village sat just inland from the beach, where the stream bed widened, and the water slowed to deposit its alluvium over the earth. Days ago, Spike had discovered the village—a cluster of mud-brick homes, struggling olive groves and vineyards, animals grazing the sparse grasses, and with it, the promise of food found in human places. He'd also found a colony of cats that did not welcome strangers. Spike remembered the large striped male who guarded his territory and the shoulder wound he had received in their first encounter. The memory faded as his empty belly drove him forward.

Spike saw the striped tomcat step into his path and hiss. His muscles tightened, and the fur on his shoulders, back, and tail raised in defense. The constant presence of his littermates receded in his consciousness as a predator's focus seized his attention. Spike knew instinctively that a careless move could end things disastrously. He also knew that a stalemate would deprive him of the food he desperately needed. Spike inched forward, keeping his head and shoulders low, his hindquarters compressed for a strike.

As he approached, the big tomcat growled. Spike sensed the coming attack but held back, waiting. The tom's warning growl rose into a scream as he pounced.

Spike saw that the tom had leaped too soon and leaned back as the attack fell short. His opponent struck at him in desperation, claws parting the fur of Spike's face but not breaking his skin. As the momentum of the tomcat's strike carried him around, Spike lunged forward and drove his canines into the soft skin where the tomcat's cheek met his throat.

Chapter 19

Astrid sat alone on the beach near Nestor's ships, her toes digging into the warm sand as Audrey, Greystoke, and Chessie explored nearby. She watched them drive a mouse from beneath a bush and chase it into a hole under a clump of dry grass. They gathered around the burrow, pawing at the sandy ground.

She ran her thumb and fingers over her left wrist, pressing into the tissues, searching for some evidence—a roughness of the bone, a tenderness in her muscles, a trigger point that would send a twinge up her now perfect limb—anything that might explain the healing of the break. She felt only the familiar contours of her forearm. Had the broken wrist been an illusion, like the falling pine that had sent her car into the ditch? Or was its healing a trick of the mind that could vanish at any time, leaving her in agony? She took a handful of warm sand and rubbed it over her wrist and forearm. The small points of pain affirmed the unmistakable character of reality.

Astrid's encounter with Proteus had taken a toll on her clothes. Although her jeans would return to normal after being rinsed in fresh water, the sweater was irrecoverable. She brushed sand from the linen shift Hecamede had given her and felt the cloth between her thumb and fingers. It was unlike the clothing to which she was accustomed—the imperfections of the hand-woven fabric seemed strangely luxurious, almost intimate.

She thought of how Hecamede had offered to share her small wardrobe. At her insistence, Astrid had tried on a layered, Mycenaean dress like many of the women in the camp wore. The artistry and colors—mostly blue, with red and white accents—bore the touch of patient female hands, and Astrid had drawn her fingers lovingly along the seams. Hecamede's offer had moved her deeply, but she found the layers of cloth too confining. Not wanting to hurt Hecamede's feelings, Astrid had praised the dress lavishly before choosing the simple, unrestrictive shift. Once her jeans dried, it would serve as a blouse, but now, she enjoyed the warm breeze passing through the loosely woven linen to touch her skin.

Astrid heard a noise and turned to see Nestor approach, barefooted, his bronze dagger scabbarded on his belt. He sat cross-legged beside her as Audrey, Greystoke, and Chessie returned from their explorations to greet the man they had come to trust.

"I'm not used to such friendly cats," he said, stroking Audrey's long fur. "They're not like the cats at the granary."

"She's usually more aloof. She seems to like you," Astrid said, smiling.

"I forget these are not ordinary animals."

"Right now, she's just a cat."

"Hecamede told me your wrist has healed," he said, holding out his hand.

Astrid let him take her arm. He probed it like a physician, thumbs pressing through muscles to follow bone and tendon.

"How did this happen?" he asked.

Astrid told him about the old man she had met in the hills above the beach, how he'd changed shape into something part human, part sea beast, and carried her down into the ocean. She described her pain when his tentacles had constricted around her wrist, as if repairing the break by force alone, and the ferocity with which he had thrown her onto the sand.

"Could it have been Proteus?" Nestor mused.

"You mean the Old Man of the Sea? I've heard stories but did not believe he was real."

"I have seen many childhood stories reveal themselves on this plain. They say he can foretell your future."

"But only if you capture him and force him to talk."

"You know the old tales," he said, smiling.

"My mother taught me when I was little. But, Nestor, there's something else. When he grabbed me, I could sense a presence in my mind, like he was reaching into my thoughts . . . No, it was more like he was searching through my memories."

Nestor frowned. He picked up a handful of sand and rubbed his thumb across it thoughtfully. "The gods have an interest in you. Do you have any idea why?"

"Only that it involves my cats."

"Did he tell you anything that may help us find them?"

Astrid shook her head.

"It's not always good for the gods to take such an interest in a mortal," Nestor said, staring out to sea. "They have their own plans and desires, and our needs are of little concern to them."

"What do people in the camp think?"

"Word has spread," he said, holding a hand toward Chessie, who sniffed his fingers cautiously, "especially after the great cat killed Dymenos. Now, the news of your arm has left little doubt that you are special to the gods—if not an immortal yourself."

Astrid exhaled heavily.

"It does make people think before harming you," he said. "On the other hand, it draws their attention, which is not always a good thing."

"I had hoped I would find a way to locate my animals and leave before too many people noticed."

"I've asked my seers. They offered nothing but their usual riddles."

"You don't trust them?"

"I find their pronouncements are either things that anyone who thinks carefully would discover or are so vague as to be useless."

"That's been my experience with such men in my homeland."

The horseman took her hand and sat quietly, looking out across the water.

"Nestor," Astrid asked after a time, "why do I feel there's something you want to tell me?"

He frowned and nodded. "Agamemnon has taken an interest in you."

Astrid felt a knot in her chest as she remembered Homer's account of the Achaeans' supreme commander. How his greed, arrogance, and misjudgments had brought them to the edge of disaster.

"Odysseus and I are trying to convince Agamemnon that it's best to leave you alone, that giving you hospitality and protection, but otherwise letting you follow the gods' intentions, is our safest course. We argued that any interference might bring their wrath upon us. For now, he seems content to let you remain with me. Agamemnon does not like to take risks, especially when he sees no advantage to himself—but that could change."

"What should we do?"

"Keep quiet and continue trying to locate your animals."

"Nestor . . ." she began.

"Try not to worry," he said, squeezing her hand, then releasing it slowly, "but you must stay close to the camp."

"But I encountered Proteus in the hills. I may learn more there, something that could help us."

"It's too dangerous."

"Trojans?"

"I'm more worried about bandits. This war has taken everything that makes them men; now, they live like animals."

"What about the Trojans?" Astrid asked.

"What do you mean?"

"I've seen no fighting."

"You've never been in one of Agamemnon's councils," he said, smiling.

"Do you fight often?"

"It's been a long siege—nine years so far—and we wait. Sometimes small bands of Trojans venture out, looking to prove themselves. Sometimes we do the same, driving chariots around the city, shooting arrows and insults over the walls, challenging Hector and his warriors. Occasionally, we meet them on the field, but mostly, we wait. Still, you should stay in the camp."

"I must find my animals."

"If you must leave," he grumbled in surrender, "ask one of my sons to go with you."

"I understand."

He looked at her skeptically.

"Nestor," Astrid said, changing the subject, "when I was walking in the hills—before I encountered Proteus—I found a makeshift shrine. I asked Hecamede about it, and she thought it might belong to a girl named Myia, who lives in the woods and claims to follow Artemis. What do you know about her?"

"I remember her from several years ago. She was taken in a raid on a nearby village and given to one of the warriors. The next day, he was found dead near his tent, his throat cut. The girl said a band of Trojans had attacked in the night and killed him. She said they had taken his weapons and other possessions. Shortly thereafter, she disappeared. The rest is gossip."

"What sort of gossip?"

"Some believe her story while others think she killed her master and took his belongings."

"What do you think?"

Nestor stared thoughtfully across the Aegean. "I think this war has left many people lost."

He stood and held out his hand. Astrid let him help her to her feet, and she walked beside him back to the camp.

Chapter 20

Astrid and Nestor parted as they returned to the camp. She walked to the women's tent, took a clay jar of water from the row of vessels lined up in the shade outside, and entered the shelter. It was late-morning. Soon, the heat of the day would drive people into the tent, but now she was grateful to find herself alone. The chaos the three animals brought with them—the stolen food, the hairballs coughed up in people's bedding, the late-night hissing and fights, the excrement that escaped Astrid's efforts to keep the sand around the tent clean—all had strained her relationships with the other women. Agamemnon's interest in her only increased her desire to find Spike and Elizabeth and return home. She filled the clay bowl she used for the cats' water, poured herself a cupful, and sat on the edge of the bed, watching the animals drink.

"What do we do now, little sister?" She reached down to stroke Chessie's black and pewter stripes.

Draining the cup, Astrid lay back among the fleeces and blankets, hoping to clear her mind. She felt something hard under her shoulder and reached into the bedding. She found the clay figurine from the shrine in the forest.

"What the . . .?" she mumbled as she turned the statuette in her hand. She looked around the tent but saw no one.

Astrid lay back in the bed, rubbing her fingers across the crudely fired clay, remembering Nestor and Hecamede's accounts of Myia, the girl who lived in the hills. Greystoke crawled onto her stomach and relaxed into the contours of her body, purring loudly.

"It seems we've been invited out," she whispered as she stroked his fur.

Astrid rested in the bedding, thinking about the mysterious young woman—the rumors she might have heard and the possibility she might know something about Spike or Elizabeth.

She also remembered Nestor's warnings.

"I see no reason why Myia—or whoever made this statue—would want to hurt us," she told Greystoke as she scratched behind his ear. "We have to talk to her, and I don't think she'd be happy to see an Achaean bodyguard."

Astrid placed Greystoke on the bedding beside her and found her jeans, still damp but wearable. "Besides," she said to him, "if anything happened, you could always become Swarm."

She pulled her jeans on under the linen shift. The denim felt cool against her skin, and she remembered Swarm's refusal to follow her into the river with Proteus.

"Unless it happened in the water," she added as she laced her shoes.

Although Astrid thought it unlikely bandits would prowl the forest in the heat of the day, she did her best to remain hidden in the trees and shrubbery by the river. She also paid close attention to her psychic connection with the cats, in case they sensed danger. After a short climb, she reached the shrine by the stream.

Whoever put the figurine in my bed expects us, so she's probably watching, Astrid reasoned. She returned the statuette to the flat stone, found a tree near the stream, and sat down with her back against the trunk.

She did not wait long. A young woman—a girl, perhaps fifteen years old—stepped from a rock formation near the shrine and walked warily into the clearing. She wore sandals and a linen shift, much like Astrid's, but of a rougher cloth. A short sword hung through a ring attached to a leather baldric, and she held a bow in her hand. The feathered ends of more than a dozen arrows protruded from a quiver at her back. Her black hair was cut short, and her body was slender and athletic, accented by the soft contours of female adolescence.

"Who are you?" the girl asked cautiously.

"My name is Astrid."

"The people in the camp say you're an immortal."

"I'm as mortal as you are."

The young woman looked at her nervously.

"What's your name?" Astrid asked.

"Myia."

"I've heard of you."

"What have they said?"

"They told me you escaped the camp, that you live in the hills, and you follow Artemis. Why did you leave the figurine in my bed?"

"To bring you here."

"Is it a statue of Artemis?"

"Yes." Myia shifted her weight from one leg to the other. "I thought you might be her."

"Artemis? I'm sorry, I'm just a woman, like you. Come and sit with me."

Myia looked at her, hesitating.

"Please, I won't hurt you."

Myia sat on a boulder about five yards away, keeping her weight forward over the balls of her feet, ready to run.

"How long have you lived in these hills?" Astrid asked.

The girl looked at the ground as if trying to recall some distant memory.

"I heard it was a long time," Astrid prompted.

Myia nodded.

"How do you live?"

"I hunt and fish. Some of the women in the camp give me food and other things. Sometimes," Myia added cautiously, "I steal things."

"Tell me how you left the camp."

"Trojans killed the man who had taken me in a raid," she said flatly. "I ran away."

"Some people say you killed him."

Myia stared silently.

"It's all right," Astrid said. "I know what it must have been like."

"I am still pure," the girl said.

Astrid remembered Dymenos' attack and felt a knot in her stomach.

"Are your cats enchanted?" Myia asked. She seemed to relax a little.

"I don't know. Perhaps."

"How is it they can join together to become a lion?"

"You know about that?"

"Some of the women in the camp talk to me. One of them told me how your animals became a great cat and killed the man who tried to rape you. I didn't believe her, but then I saw them do it myself."

"When Proteus took me into the water?"

"That was Proteus?"

"I think so."

"He is powerful. Are you certain you're not a goddess?"

"Yes," Astrid smiled, "I'm certain. The cats are special, but I'm as human as you. They protect me, and I protect them. Would you like to pet them?"

Myia hesitated, then walked toward Astrid and the cats. She kneeled a few yards away and held her hand out, palm up. Greystoke came forward and sniffed at her fingers while Audrey and Chessie remained behind. Myia sat motionless as Greystoke meowed and looked up at her; she scratched him below his ear, at the hinge of his jaw.

"You understand cats," Astrid observed.

"I had one when I was little . . ." Myia said, not taking her eyes off the cat, "before the Achaeans came."

Astrid closed her eyes in sadness at the implications of Myia's words. She watched as Audrey approached the girl. Soon, Chessie joined them, and Myia smiled at the game of trying to satisfy the three animals with only two hands. She looked like any teenage girl from Astrid's own time.

"Why are you here?" Myia asked, not taking her eyes from the cats.

"Because you invited me."

"No, I mean, why did you come to Troy?"

"A man and a woman came to my house and took the cats' brother and sister. I came here to find them."

"They may be dead," Myia said matter-of-factly.

"I don't think so. The man and woman did not want to harm them."

"Do you know who they were? Where they took your cats?"

"No. Have you heard anything that could help me?"

The girl shook her head.

"Any rumors? Or something you might have seen, something out of the ordinary?" Astrid pressed.

"Perhaps Artemis or another immortal could help."

"They haven't been in touch," Astrid said ironically.

"Proteus helped you," Myia said. "It means the gods are interested. You must be patient; they will show you the way."

Astrid remembered how the woman who had taken Elizabeth had turned Scott into a pig. She thought of Homer's account of Circe doing the same thing to Odysseus' sailors in *The Odyssey*.

"Myia," she said, "have you heard of a goddess named Circe?"

Myia looked at her with concern. "She is an enchantress. Her magic is very dark."

"What do you know about her? Could she have taken them?"

"They say she lives on an island called Aeaea, surrounded by animals—some of them were once men . . . Why do you ask?"

"Just a feeling." Astrid shrugged. "It probably means nothing."

Myia went back to stroking Greystoke's soft fur.

Astrid watched her for a time. "You could help me" she said.

Myia looked up at her warily.

Astrid gestured at the cats circling the girl. "They like you. You could help me care for them. Why don't you come back to camp with us?"

Myia took her feet quickly. "No. I won't go back there. They'll make me a slave . . . or kill me."

"I can protect you," Astrid pressed. "You can't live alone in the woods forever."

"I must go." Myia ran past the shrine into the trees and brush.

"Wait. Please. Don't be afraid."

Astrid ran after her but could not match her speed. She stopped, out of breath, and stared into the forest where the girl had vanished.

Circe sat back from the ball of light swirling on her marble table as Astrid walked down the hill to Nestor's camp, the cats close behind. The ball collapsed back into nothingness as she drank deeply from a golden goblet. Elizabeth purred on the cushion beside her.

"Astrid is getting restless," Circe mused, stroking Elizabeth's soft fur, soothed by the rise and fall of the her purrs. "She's starting to put things together. She even suspects I am part of this . . . She has promise, Sigrid's daughter, more than I'd imagined," the enchantress said thoughtfully. "She's intelligent, persistent, and not afraid to act."

She looked down at Elizabeth with a conspiratorial smile. "Perhaps it's time to help her along."

Chapter 21

Phaethon stood on the narrow path, staring up the hill at the small cabin. He could see the location had been chosen to protect its occupant's privacy and security. The nearby village was neither wealthy nor close to trade routes, larger cities, or anything else that might draw large numbers of people. The house was far from the town and the roads that served it. The one-room dwelling was made of stone rather than mud brick and rested against the mountain, with its cliffs and rocky talus discouraging an attack from the rear. Anyone approaching from the front would have to climb the open hillside, making them visible to the occupant. The slope was steep and rocky enough to be impassible for chariots—even challenging for men on foot. The stream passing near the house guaranteed a reliable supply of fresh water.

Phaethon followed the directions the village winemaker had given him—directions wrapped in a warning. He climbed the trail that wound up the rocky slope, not attempting to conceal his approach. He stopped fifteen yards from the house with its narrow windows and held his hands open, visible at his side.

"I'm looking for Proxonos," he shouted.

He heard a stirring inside the house, followed by a woman's voice, sharp with concern, and a man's short syllables. A man appeared in the doorway, well-muscled and naked, except for the sword in his hand. Although shorter than Phaethon, he was tall enough to stand above most men. He wore his hair cut close, free of the braids and beads favored by young warriors, and his dark beard was neatly trimmed. His face was well proportioned, even handsome, except for the scar that crossed his cheek and the cruel metal in his gaze.

"Who wants him?" the man in the doorway challenged.

"I have work that might interest him. I can pay well."

Phaethon noticed a movement in the house behind the man and saw a woman, also naked, retrieve a garment from the floor and hastily pull it over her shoulders. The man in the doorway looked back into the house.

"Wait there," he told Phaethon.

He followed the woman into the shadows, and Phaethon heard a hasty exchange before the man returned, wearing a simple kilt, still carrying the sword. "What brought you here?"

"Are you Proxonos?" Phaethon squinted up at the sun when the man did not answer. "It's hot, and I'm thirsty. I would think a man they call 'the ambassador' would invite me to refresh myself before we discuss business."

Proxonos hefted the sword, his grip alternately relaxing and tightening, his eyes narrowing as he evaluated his visitor. "Or I could kill you and take that bag you carry over your shoulder."

Phaethon threw the bag onto the ground near Proxonos' feet. A gold bowl rolled out, trailing jewelry of gold set with lapis, turquoise, and other stones.

"Trinkets," he said. "Take them if you're easily satisfied, and I'll be on my way. Or you can hear my offer."

Proxonos glanced at the bag, then at the man standing opposite him, judging his bearing, his weapons, and his intent. He scanned the field descending from his house, looking for warriors hidden in the trees. Satisfied that the stranger had come alone and was neither a fool nor an immediate threat, Proxonos gestured toward a table and benches in the shade of a nearby tree. He walked back into the house and returned with two pitchers—one of wine, one of water—and two bronze cups. His sword hung at his side. He straddled a bench and poured the wine.

Phaethon sat across from him and drank deeply.

"What's your name?" Proxonos asked.

Phaethon told him. The mercenary did not react to the name out of legend. Phaethon wondered if it was out of ignorance of the old stories, a warrior's self-control, or the habit of a man accustomed to dealing in aliases.

"What brought you to me?" Proxonos asked.

"Your reputation is well known, and I need a man with your abilities. I asked in the village, and the winemaker sent me here."

Proxonos smiled broadly.

"Did I say something funny?" Phaethon asked.

"No." Proxonos lifted his cup and drank.

Phaethon heard a noise from the house and saw the woman rush out, holding an empty basket to obscure her face. She ran past them, down the narrow trail that crossed the hillside.

"She wouldn't be related to the winemaker by any chance?"

Proxonos shrugged. "Why do you ask?"

Phaethon took a sip from the cup and placed it on the table. "She became upset when I called out to you but seemed more interested in hiding her identity than in covering her nakedness. You brought the wine out yourself rather than ask her to serve us; therefore, she is not a wife or a slave. As soon as you sat down, she grabbed her things and ran off, hiding her face behind an empty basket. This confirmed that she did not want to be recognized, and the empty basket suggested she had brought something to your home. When I asked if she was related to the winemaker, you challenged me with a question, but not a denial."

Phaethon poured more wine into his cup, and took a drink. "I would guess the empty basket had held several jars of wine, and the fat winemaker does not enjoy the long hike to your home, so he sends his wife to make deliveries. She seemed too young to be satisfied with her old husband. Perhaps you added a few items to the payment in exchange for additional services? Also, the winemaker seemed agitated when I mentioned your name."

Proxonos' smile broadened. "What else do you know about me?"

"That you are the equal of any warrior on the plains of Troy but choose not to take a side, even though you have received offers."

"I have no interest in serving any king," Proxonos sneered.

"You did once."

Proxonos' eyes narrowed.

"They tell me you earned the nickname 'Ambassador' when you served a king to the south," Phaethon said. "As the story goes, he sent you to collect taxes that a subject village had withheld. Instead of simply extracting payment, you killed everyone in the village, bringing their valuables—and their heads—to your employer in a wagon. He did not approve."

"He was a fool. They would have deceived him again. I gave them what they deserved and made an example for the other villages."

"And he gave you that scar."

"And I killed him."

"But you did not take his throne," Phaethon observed. "I need a man who has no interest in serving kings or in being a king but who will not hesitate to kill a king."

Proxonos stared across the table silently.

"There is an Achaean named Odysseus. Do you know of him?" Phaethon asked.

"The Ithacan king. He is at Troy with the Achaean invasion. He is a formidable warrior. You want him dead?"

"If I simply wanted him dead, I would have done so myself."

Proxonos looked him over, gauging whether his visitor could fulfill his boast. He did not reveal his assessment.

"I have business in the camp of Nestor of Pylos," Phaethon continued, "and I would like you to draw attention away from it."

"What is this business?" Proxonos demanded.

"Does it matter?"

Proxonos drained his cup, stood, and started back to his cabin.

"Very well," Phaethon said. "There is a woman in Nestor's camp who has an animal I must acquire."

Proxonos returned to his seat, his curiosity aroused. "An animal?"

"A cat."

"A cat?" Proxonos laughed, barely holding his balance on the rough bench.

"It is not an ordinary cat. It is enchanted and of great value," Phaethon explained.

"Enchanted?" Proxonos spoke the word like a curse as his laughter died. "I do not involve myself with enchantments."

"You will not have to," Phaethon insisted. "We'll approach at night. I will go to Nestor's camp to carry out my business, and you will go up the beach to attack Odysseus. You will face no enchantments; you will only fight men like yourself."

Proxonos frowned and stared at Phaethon. "You will have to pay more if enchantments are involved," he said, "even indirectly."

"The price doesn't matter."

"If all you want is a diversion, why go to the trouble of killing Odysseus?"

"Let me say I want to rid myself of two problems at once," Phaethon explained. "Can you make it look like a Trojan raid?"

Proxonos ran his finger around the rim of his cup thoughtfully. "I'll need men. I know some who will come if you pay well."

"Local men?"

Proxonos laughed. "I thought you wanted this done properly. My men come from the north. They serve no one, but they will do as I ask—for the right payment."

"Sea people?"

Proxonos nodded.

Phaethon took a deep breath. The sea people had come from the plains to the north. Fearsome horsemen who had dominated their native grasslands, they had learned the ways of the sea and raided cities and villages through-out the Aegean. They showed mercy to no one.

"How many can you get?" Phaethon asked.

"There are about fifty nearby. I could find more."

"Fifty will do. Do they have a ship?"

"They call them sea people for a reason."

"Name your price. I need this done quickly."

Proxonos retrieved the bag Phaethon had thrown to the ground. He spread its contents on the table.

"These are trinkets—to trade for wine or a woman. For each man, a bag like this, but add something worthy of a warrior—a fine sword, a bronze cooking tripod, or a gold goblet. Five times that for me." Proxonos looked across the table at Phaethon and saw no hesitation at his demands. "Make it ten times for me . . . because enchantments are involved."

Phaethon raised his cup. "I'll return in two days with your payment," he said, draining the wine and rising from the bench. "Gather your men and have them ready to sail for Troy."

Proxonos watched his visitor walk the rough path that descended from his cabin and turn onto the trail that led to the village. He gathered the pitchers, cups, and Phaethon's initial payment from the table and returned to the cool darkness of his home.

He did not see his visitor turn from the trail into the seclusion of a grove of fir and cedar trees. The mercenary who hated enchantments did not hear the words that came from Phaethon's mouth, nor did he see Phaethon collapse into a ball of light no larger than a small bird and fly away over the village and across the surrounding plains.

Phaethon entered the great hall of Etagama's palace. Two guards challenged him; he smiled approvingly at their polished weapons and crisp demeanor.

"Let him pass." Etagama's voice came from the inner chamber. Phaethon walked past the guards and approached the new king.

"King Etagama," Phaethon said, smiling as he crossed the throne room and approached the white stone dais.

"My mysterious friend, I am happy you have returned to us. Was your journey difficult?"

"No, but it was long, and I need rest. Is Claea here?"

"When she learned of your arrival, she hastened to your quarters and has prepared it for your comfort."

Phaethon nodded.

"You must join us tonight," Etagama said proudly. "We will sacrifice an ox to the gods in thanks for your safe return."

"You honor me, but I am weary and must rest."

"Tomorrow night, then," Etagama said, a gracious affect concealing his resentment.

"Tomorrow night," Phaethon agreed. He dipped his head in a gesture of respect and then walked to his sanctuary.

Phaethon paused as he entered the windowless room and his eyes adjusted to the candlelight. It was cool and smelled of flowers. A young woman knocked and entered at his invitation, her hair held up by a plain gold band, her skin clean. She wore a skirt layered in blue and saffron, with a plain white blouse and a white fringed kilt around her waist. She moved gracefully—unlike the frightened, dirty slave he had left in the palace.

"My Lord," she said, smiling shyly.

"Claea, you look well." He settled into a cushioned chair. "Have the salves and extracts I gave you helped your injuries?"

"They are almost a thing of memory," she said as her hand unconsciously moved to the side of her face, touching a faint scar.

Phaethon looked around the small room. Fresh candles lit a space decorated with brightly dyed tapestries and carefully arranged bedding. He saw the flowers she had placed on the table near the bed, the golden cup filled with wine, and the plate of cooked meat and bread.

"You have done well, Claea," he said. "Does Etagama treat you well? Has he been unkind or harmed you in any way?"

"He has been very kind. He has given me the freedom of the palace."

"That is good."

"Have I pleased you?" she asked softly.

"Yes, you've pleased me greatly, but now I must rest. Tell the guards I am not to be disturbed."

Phaethon watched her close the door as she left. He rose wearily from the chair, secured the bolt, and sat on the edge of the bed. He stared at the plate she had left for him, less like a hungry traveler returning home than a man contemplating a prize he could not possess. His body flickered in the dim light of fading enchantments as he lay back on the clean bedding and blew out the candle Claea had lit. He pulled a single fleece across his charred body, the warrior who had won his sanctuary replaced by the broken demigod who ruled it.

Chapter 22

Astrid heard a woman's frustrated cry, turned toward it, and saw Hecamede lying on the ground in front of the women's tent. Her red headband had fallen over her eyes, and dark curls escaped to cover her face. The clay jug she had carried from the stream lay on its side, water seeping into the sand as Audrey, Chessie, and Greystoke disappeared into the camp's maze of tents, firepits, and workspaces.

"I'm so sorry," she said, helping Hecamede to her feet.

"It's not your fault." Hecamede straightened her headband and arranged her hair beneath it. "The cats came running around the tent and startled me. I lost my balance."

Astrid saw the sweat on her face. The stream was not close, and the late-morning heat was rising. She lifted the nearly empty jug from the damp sand. "Let me refill it."

Hecamede took the jug from her. "It's nothing. Go find your animals."

Astrid scanned the area near the women's tent, but did not see the cats.

"Go," Hecamede insisted.

Embarrassed but worried for the cats' safety, Astrid thanked Hecamede and began searching for the perpetrators of this latest disturbance. In the days since she had spoken with Myia, Astrid had made no progress toward finding Spike or Elizabeth. She'd spent her time helping Hecamede with chores, sharing meals with Nestor and his sons, walking alone on the beach, and cleaning up after the three impulsive animals. She remembered their previous misadventures—they had always hidden nearby while Astrid made her apologies and cleaned up the mess. Now, she exhausted their usual hiding places and continued through the camp, looking among the beached ships, inside each tent, and behind each basket or amphora, her anxiety increasing.

"They went up there."

Astrid turned and saw Gilia—the child who had befriended the cats—limp toward her, pointing to the grove of trees above the camp.

"Are you sure?" Astrid asked. "They wouldn't go that far without me."

"I saw them," Gilia said. "Can I help?"

"No, honey, I can get them. But it would help me if you told Hecamede where I've gone."

Astrid watched Gilia start back to camp, then hurried toward the trees, anxiety for the cats driving caution from her mind. Sweating in the rising heat, she struggled uphill through the sand to reach the riverbank with its firmer ground. She looked back to make sure she had not been followed, then walked quickly beside the water, stopping where the stream joined the river. Astrid opened her mind to the connection she'd come to share with the cats and felt a pull on her consciousness—an instinct to take the trail that followed the stream. She followed it past Myia's shrine, going deeper into the forest than before.

Astrid heard a voice ahead and froze. She left the trail to make her way through the cover of the brush. Approaching quietly, she came to a small clearing and looked across it in disbelief. A cluster of metal tables and chairs rested in the shade of a tall cypress. They were identical to those at the café where she had seen Claire Ortega on a morning that now seemed like a dream. Claire sat at the nearest table, laughing as she leaned down to pet the three cats who brushed eagerly against her legs.

Astrid rushed into the clearing. "Claire? No. No, it can't be . . ."

Claire looked up nonchalantly. She wore the same bright dress Astrid remembered from the last time they'd met. Claire gestured toward the opposite chair, where a second cup waited. "I thought you'd never show up," she said casually. "I went ahead and ordered for you."

"This isn't happening . . ." Astrid said. "I thought you were home, safe."

"What the hell are you talking about?" Claire laughed.

Astrid struggled to speak through her shock and worry. "Claire, is it really you? Do you know where you are?"

Claire began to speak, then stopped as she noticed the trees and sandy soil, the empty tables, the blue expanse of the Aegean, and the rows of beached ships showing through gaps in the foliage.

"That's strange," Claire muttered, although she seemed unconcerned.

Astrid pulled her from her seat and threw her arms around her. "I'm so sorry. I never wanted you to be part of this."

Claire held her close for a moment, then stepped back and looked at her with concern. "It's okay, honey. I'm fine."

"It's not fine. How did you get here?"

"I'm meeting you for coffee."

"No," Astrid insisted. She felt her knees tremble as a terrifying possibility struck her. "My god, this is in my head. I've lost my mind."

"Sweetie, it's okay," Claire reassured, taking her hand. "You're as sane as the day I met you—for whatever that's worth." She laughed as she guided Astrid toward the empty chair.

"Look around," Astrid pressed. "We're at an outdoor café, but there's no café. Look at the forest, the ground—it's not concrete, it's dirt. There aren't any cars. Look at the ocean. We're not at home."

"No, we're not . . ." Claire's voice trailed off as she looked down and to her left in thought. Astrid had seen Claire withdraw like this when she was analyzing some hard technical problem. She waited silently.

Claire looked up. "I'm not here."

"What do you mean?"

"I'm home, in bed. I'm dreaming."

"Claire, I know it feels like a dream—sometimes I feel the same way—but you are here."

Claire seemed simultaneously calm and attentive, as if she was listening to a distant voice. "I'm here and I'm not. It's hard to explain."

"Take your time," Astrid probed gently, as if dealing with a sleepwalker she dare not awaken. "Am I dreaming, too?"

"No, you're really here."

"I don't understand. How can your dream put you in my reality?"

"You're overthinking it. Drink this." Claire pushed the second coffee cup across the table toward her friend. "Tell me what's going on."

The white ceramic cup came from Astrid's time and held a hot, perfectly prepared cappuccino. She took a sip. "God, I've missed that," Astrid said. She drank deeply and tried to compose her thoughts.

She reached across the table and took Claire's hand. "Do you know where we are?"

"Troy." Once more, Claire seemed to repeat words from a distant source.

Astrid remembered her own confusion on coming to Troy. "Claire, how do you know that?"

"I think I understand what's going on," Claire said thoughtfully. "It feels like someone is speaking through me. I hear my voice, but the words aren't mine. I don't know where they came from or even what they mean."

"Like some sort of suggestion?"

"Yes, but the voice goes away when I talk to you . . . Let's try something. I'm going to clear my mind and relax. I want you to ask your questions, and I'm going to say the first thing that comes to mind."

Claire closed her eyes and adjusted her posture as if in meditation.

"You said someone was speaking through you," Astrid asked. "Who is it?"

"Circe."

"The enchantress," Astrid said thoughtfully, as if adding a new piece to a puzzle. "I'd wondered if it was her . . . Claire, you said you weren't really here, that you were dreaming. Could you explain it to me."

"Circe brought me here in a dream so I could speak to you. My real body is at home."

"Thank god you're safe. Do you know how I came here?"

"Yes. You merged with Swarm and followed Phaethon."

"Phaethon?" Astrid leaned back in her chair in surprise.

"Should I know who that is?" Claire asked. She opened her eyes and seemed to return to normal.

"Only if you'd stayed awake in lit class."

"No offense taken. Who's Phaethon?"

"Phaethon was the bastard son of Helios, the sun god in Greek myth. He tricked his father into letting him drive the chariot of the sun—"

"Chariot of the sun?"

"It's a long story, but he was the son of Helios, who drove the sun across the sky in a chariot pulled by flaming horses. Phaethon wanted to show his friends that he was truly the son of a god. He tried to drive the chariot against his father's wishes and died when Zeus struck him with a thunderbolt . . . But this makes no sense."

"Why not?"

"Phaethon isn't real. Even these people think of it as a myth. Besides, if he was real, he'd have died long ago. He wouldn't be here."

"But he is real, and he is here," Claire explained. "That's the problem."

"What do you mean?"

"It's hard to explain. You'll understand in time."

"OK," Astrid said. "Did Circe bring me here—to Troy?"

"No," Claire said, returning to the dream-like state.

"I saw her with Elizabeth before I came here. Is she all right?"

Claire nodded. "She says the cat is well and will return to you soon."

"Did she send Phaethon to my home?"

"No. Phaethon came to steal one of your animals, and she followed him."

"Why did he take Spike?"

"She says she isn't sure, but it has to with your animals' abilities."

"You mean joining their bodies to become Swarm? But they were just ordinary cats until she and Phaethon showed up."

"Your cats were never ordinary," Claire said.

"What are you—what is she talking about? They were born in Sigrid's barn," Astrid insisted. "Their mother was just a cat . . . Never mind. What do they have to do with Circe, Phaethon . . . with the Trojan war?"

"This is where their story begins," Claire said. "That is why you're here."

"Why I'm here? What can I do? I'm barely staying alive."

Claire returned to her normal waking state. "It's all right, honey. I don't understand this myself. I can't be sure, but get the feeling she means you no harm—she means the cats no harm."

"Why can't she just send us home?"

"First, you must reunite your animals," Claire said.

"I must reunite them? Why can't she? I have no idea where to look. Nestor keeps threatening to send me to live with his wife—"

"That's why she brought me here—to help you," Claire interrupted. "You need to listen, we don't have much time."

"Why? What's happening?"

"Anthony's waking up. He'll go out and make coffee, then he'll bring me a cup, and I'll have to leave you."

"He brings you coffee in bed?" Astrid said, astonished. "You never told me about that."

Claire shrugged guiltily. "You need to find Spike and Elizabeth."

"Can you tell me where they are?"

"No, but they can," Claire said. She gestured at Chessie, Audrey, and Greystoke resting quietly at her feet.

"What?"

"They can lead you to the others."

"How?" Astrid asked.

Claire kneeled and gathered the cats together. "Give me your hand."

Astrid leaned forward in the chair and held out her right hand. Claire placed it on Audrey's back. The other cats came to stand beside their sister.

"Clear your head," Claire instructed. "If a thought comes to mind, let it pass. Focus only on the animals, on their presence."

Astrid felt a tingling across her skin, the pinpricks that had preceded her merging with Swarm. She pulled her hand back in reflex.

"What happened?" Claire asked.

"They were starting to pull me in, to join with me like before."

"I know it's scary, but you can control it. There's a still point in your mind. Go there. Stay calm."

"Is this you speaking? Or Circe?"

"It's me, it's Circe—I don't know, maybe both of us," Claire said, laughing. "Trust me."

Astrid left the chair to sit on the ground among the cats. She took a deep breath and exhaled slowly, closing her eyes and focusing her attention on her solar plexus. Claire placed her hand on Chessie's shoulders. Astrid began to feel the tingle once again, the spreading pinpricks, the three animal minds—pure, focused, insistent.

"It's okay," she heard Claire say, "I'm here."

Astrid steadied her breathing, envisioning the air filling her lungs, well-being spreading through her body. The pinpricks faded, but the three presences remained in her awareness, three voices singing wordlessly in an otherworldly harmony.

"What are you experiencing?" Claire asked softly.

"I hear voices," Astrid said, "like they're singing."

"Good. Can you distinguish them?"

"Yes. They're like the different voices in a fugue."

"Those are the minds of these cats," Claire explained.

Astrid opened her eyes. Audrey, Chessie, and Greystoke rested in front of her, huddled together, sleeping like when they were kittens. A shimmering blue light surrounded them. Astrid felt a growing excitement, and the glow intensified. She felt the pinpricks start up her arm and took another deep breath. The tingling faded.

"Can you still hear the three voices?" Claire asked.

"Yes."

"Go deeper. Listen carefully."

Astrid closed her eyes. "There is a lower tone, steady like a drone."

"Yes, that's Swarm."

"Is it always there?"

"Yes, but now she's sleeping. Listen for two more voices."

"I can't hear anything. Wait . . . they're faint . . . I can barely hear them. Are they Spike and Elizabeth?"

"Yes."

Astrid held her breath and tried to listen past Audrey, Chessie, and Greystoke, past the drone of Swarm's sleeping presence, as if searching for a single voice in a choir. She heard a distant song and sensed it was Elizabeth. Astrid discerned another, weaker voice, coming in and out of perception. She guessed it was Spike. She also sensed a direction. Astrid withdrew her hand as the blue glow faded and the cats began to move.

"There," she told Claire as she pointed across the Aegean. "That way."

Claire smiled. "That's the direction you must follow."

"But it was so faint, I'm not sure if it was Spike or Elizabeth. I don't know how far away they are. I—"

"It will get easier over time,' Claire interrupted, "but the connection is there. As you move closer, it will strengthen, and you can adjust your course."

"Claire, why am I the only one who can sense their location?" Astrid said. "Why can't Circe? She has Elizabeth. I would guess she used her to find me. She probably used her to send you here."

Claire nodded. "Circe's ability to read the cats is limited. She can touch their minds, but it cannot compare to your abilities."

"But why? What makes me so special."

"The cats decide who can share their thoughts. They chose you."

"Chose me? I don't understand."

Claire picked up the cappuccino and handed it to Astrid. "Drink this. I think you need it."

Spike stepped from his hiding place near the granary and turned into the breeze, mouth open, pulling the air across the scent receptors lining his palate as well as through his nostrils. He smelled the cats in the colony, the sweet smell of drying grain, the stench of humans in the village, all carried on the moist, salt air.

Since his last encounter with the striped tomcat, the two animals had formed a barely stable truce. If Spike avoided the main body of the colony—particularly the females—the tom left him alone to hunt rodents and scavenge among the scraps of food the villagers discarded. The two cats exchanged glances as Spike walked toward the ocean.

He looked out across the water and felt the minds of his siblings resonate with his own. He once again sensed the woman who had lived with them before his abduction. Her mind seemed more closely joined to theirs than before, resonating like a newly added harmonic. Their combined presence filled him with rising joy and deep longing.

Chapter 23

Astrid took a long drink of the cappuccino. The coffee was as hot as when she'd first found Claire in the clearing, and she noticed that the cup remained full. She smiled and took another swallow.

"Here, this is for you."

Astrid opened her eyes and saw Claire holding out her old rucksack—the pack that had taken her across Europe when she'd finished undergraduate school and into the Rocky Mountains whenever she could find the time.

"What? How did you . . ."

"How did I bring this with me? Damned if I know." Claire seemed to have grown comfortable with her role as the enchantress's voice.

Astrid lifted the pack into her lap—it was stretched tight and sat heavily on her thighs. Inside, she found clothes from home: clean socks, underwear, two T-shirts, a blue cotton work shirt, two sweaters—one red and one black to replace the sweater that had been ruined in the salt water—a pair of jeans, and her hiking boots.

"My god," she said. "Thank you."

"Don't thank me." Claire laughed. "I'm just a meat puppet."

Astrid looked in the pack's side pocket. She found her toothbrush, a tube of toothpaste, and several bars of soap.

"Claire, this is heaven." Astrid rubbed her hands thoughtfully over the pack. "Any chance of getting a gun? Or if not, at least a proper knife?"

"No technology. It doesn't belong here, and the consequences could be grave. Your clothes don't belong here either, but you're already wearing them, and the universe seems to be surviving." Claire rose from her chair. "There is something else. Wait here," she said as she walked behind a nearby cluster of boulders.

Claire returned, leading two perfectly matched horses—a stallion and a mare. Astrid felt her breath catch as she saw them, powerful, elegant, their muscles gliding beneath coats that shined like polished copper. Their eyes revealed an intelligence both deeply grounded and always on the edge of exploding in a blur of acceleration. They danced at the end of their rope leads as if constant motion was their resting state.

"Take these to Nestor," Claire said. "Tell him they're a gift. Tell him you know how to find your animals. He'll understand and will help you."

"Circe, if it is you—why do all this? Why can't you simply come with me yourself?"

Claire started to answer, then stopped as if a thought had faded before she could speak.

"I'm sorry, honey," she said. "I think she hung up on us."

Astrid felt a push on her shoulder, almost knocking her off her feet. The stallion nudged her again. She grabbed the rope where it joined the leather halter and rubbed his cheek, making rhythmic shushing sounds.

"Thank you," Astrid said as she turned back to Claire. She was gone. Tears filled her eyes. "Thank you," she whispered.

Astrid stroked each horse's head, her hand following the lay of the fur down the long, hard bone to the nostrils' improbably soft velvet. She looked into their eyes—dark, with an expansive intelligence—so unlike the cats' narrow, predatory focus.

"Come," she said softly, taking the rope leads and starting down the hill. The horses followed as if they had walked with her a thousand times, while the cats remained a discrete distance to the side. As she neared the edge of the clearing, Astrid looked back. The tables and chairs had vanished.

Astrid led the horses past Myia's shrine to Artemis. She continued along the stream to where the water widened before joining the river. The horses jumped the stream effortlessly, and she lifted the cats across. As she led the animals from the bank, Astrid stopped suddenly.

Two men stood on the path, swords in their hands. One wore a leather helmet, a filthy tunic, tattered moccasins, and carried a small round shield slung over his back. The other was similarly dressed but carried no shield and wore no helmet. The tangles of his black hair surrounded a dirty face. Astrid noticed that he was missing an eye. She knew instinctively that they were neither Trojans nor Achaeans.

"What have we here?" the man with the helmet asked menacingly, a yellow smile crossing his dirty face.

"What are you doing up here . . . all by yourself?" One-eye asked, leering.

"Let me pass." Astrid felt the horses pull against their leads.

The men stepped forward. "Not so fast," the man with the helmet warned.

"Let me pass," she repeated.

One-eye laughed and turned to his companion. "What do you think?"

"I think she does not deserve these horses. They should belong to warriors," the man with the helmet said, "like us."

Astrid felt the cats' presences intensify in her mind, and she saw them circle each other.

"These horses belong to Nestor," she asserted, stalling until Swarm could take form.

"'These horses belong to Nestor,'" the man in the leather helmet mocked. "The old man means nothing." His tone shifted to a snarl. "Besides, he isn't here, is he?"

Astrid glanced at the cats. Chessie stared up at her as Greystoke and Audrey moved closer.

"Why don't you leave us alone?" she asked, hoping Swarm would take shape quickly.

"Why don't you give us the horses, and maybe we'll let you live?" the bandit with the missing eye said.

The helmeted bandit started toward her, raising his sword menacingly. As he took his first step, he cried out in shock and lurched back, dropping his sword to grasp at the shaft of an arrow that protruded from his throat. Astrid heard a gurgling cry as blood gushed from his mouth and flowed across his tunic. He fell at her feet, his body convulsing violently.

Before Astrid could find the source of the arrow, One-eye ran forward and struck at her with his sword. She ducked instinctively, and her backpack took the brunt of his blow, its force knocking her to the ground. One-eye grabbed the mare's lead rope as the stallion leaped over the stream and ran back along the path.

Astrid saw the helmeted soldier's bronze sword on the ground near his body and rolled toward it. She picked up the weapon as the frightened mare reared again. One-eye held the mare's rope lead, and it raised his arm above his shoulder. Astrid stepped toward him and swung the sword with both hands, driving the blade against his exposed side. She felt it strike bone and slide across his ribs. One-eye screamed in pain as blood oozed from a gash on his side.

Furious, he dropped the horse's lead and turned toward Astrid, sword raised. As she stepped back, holding her sword in both hands, an arrow pierced his chest, just below his right collarbone. He dropped the horse's lead rope and staggered away, cursing, clawing at the shaft, blood spreading across his filthy tunic. He disappeared into the trees.

Astrid saw Myia standing near a large pine about ten yards to the side of the path, her bow in her hand.

Astrid grabbed the mare's dangling lead. The horse reared, tearing the rope from her hand, then leaped the stream and ran after the stallion. She heard a low rumble and saw what had caused the mare to panic. Swarm stood nearby, growling, her fur a dark mixture of Audrey's, Chessie's, and Greystoke's coats, her green eyes staring up at her.

"A little late, aren't you?" Astrid told the cat.

She heard the growl resonate in Swarm's chest and sensed her unease. Astrid took Swarm's head in her hands and scratched behind the cat's ears in a soothing rhythm. Myia stood frozen, unable to take her eyes off them.

"It's all right. She won't hurt you."

Myia took a step back as if she was about to turn and run.

"Please wait," Astrid shouted. "Don't go. Don't be afraid."

Astrid sensed Swarm's tripartite mind at the edge of her awareness, three distinct but connected intentions, with the constant drone of Swarm's presence sounding beneath them. She focused her thoughts on calming the great cat. Gradually, Swarm relaxed, and the three minds grew apart. Astrid raised a hand to reassure Myia as a swirling ball of blue light enveloped Swarm, then faded. Myia stared in disbelief as Chessie, Audrey, and Greystoke appeared where the great cat had stood.

The helmeted bandit began to stir, rocking groggily in the sand despite the arrow protruding from his throat. Myia ran and kicked him in the face, knocking him back, blood bubbling from his wound as he struggled to breathe. She kneeled on his chest, pinning him down as she took the knife from her belt and cut his throat in a single stroke. She stepped away as blood sprayed across his chest.

"The cats obey you," Myia said incredulously.

Astrid turned toward her, still shocked at the violence of the attack.

"Do they obey you?" Myia repeated, gesturing at the three cats milling around Astrid's feet.

"No . . . yes . . ." Astrid stammered as her mind cleared. "I mean, I have a little control."

"Then you are a goddess," the girl declared.

Astrid shook her head. "No."

"Then the woman you spoke to—"

"You saw her? The tables and chairs?"

"Yes. She was a goddess."

"No, but I think one sent her."

The girl seemed confused.

"I promise I will explain everything, but first, I need to find those horses," Astrid said. "Will you help me?"

Myia pointed to the other side of the stream. Astrid turned and saw the animals standing side by side. The stallion pawed the ground nervously as the mare stared at her intently.

"Please don't leave," Astrid said as she approached the horses.

The animals let her take the lead ropes and followed her back over the water. Astrid found Myia standing over the dead outlaw, pulling his belt from his body. The girl turned him over, removed the shield he wore across his back, then lifted the helmet from his head. She added them to a pile of his possessions and continued searching the corpse.

"What are you doing?" Astrid demanded.

Myia looked at her in surprise, then gestured toward the dead man's weapons, neatly stacked beside her. "These are useful. He won't need them." She pointed to the sword Astrid had used against one-eye, lying on the ground where she had dropped it. "You should take it."

"I'm not sure that's a good idea. I'd probably hurt myself."

"You fought well," Myia said. "I doubt he'll survive his wounds." She took the dead man's dagger and gave it to Astrid. "Take this—as a prize from your victory."

Astrid took the knife. She picked up her backpack and frowned at the gash in its side where the bandit had struck. It was only a few inches long, and the clothing beneath seemed undamaged.

"It could have been worse," Myia said. "The sword was dull. These pigs take no pride in their weapons."

Astrid put the dagger in the pack's side pocket. She felt her knees tremble from the adrenaline still in her veins and took several deep breaths, trying to calm herself.

"Myia, do you remember when we first met? How I told you that a man and woman had stolen the cats' brother and sister?"

Myia nodded.

"The woman you saw in the clearing showed me how to find them."

"How?"

Astrid gestured toward the three cats milling nervously around her. "They can sense where their brother and sister are. She showed me how to use that to find them."

Myia looked at the cats, then back at Astrid.

"I know it sounds incredible, but you have to trust me," Astrid said. "She also gave me these horses as a gift for Nestor. He'll take it as a sign to help me find my animals."

"Then, you'll be leaving."

"Come with me. You're strong, you're, smart and you understand animals."

"No," the girl said warily.

"Please. What do you have here? You live alone, barely sheltered from the weather. These woods are full of bandits, Trojans, Achaeans, and god knows what else. It is only a matter of time until something happens to you. Come with me."

"I can't. The men in the camp will remember me. They'll . . ."

"I won't let them," Astrid insisted.

"Then, you are a goddess."

"I'm not, but the people in the camp fear me. I can protect you."

Myia stared silently.

"I promise, I won't let them hurt you. Please, I need your help."

Signs of struggle played out in Myia's face.

"Can't you see how everything that has happened here," Astrid pressed, "the woman in the clearing, the horses, your help in driving the bandits away . . . these are all signs."

Astrid felt a tinge of guilt at using superstition to influence the girl. Almost immediately, she wondered if her words might not be true. She stared at Myia in silence until the girl finally nodded.

"You must leave your weapons," Astrid said.

"I will not."

"Myia, I can't protect you if you walk into the camp armed. The men will see you as a threat, and I won't be able to stop them."

Myia stared at her, conflict on her face, then she gathered up the outlaw's weapons and walked to a thick patch of scrub growing in a nearby pile of rocks. She cleared a space and used the outlaw's sword to dig a shallow trench. She arranged the arms in it carefully—first the outlaw's weapons, then her bronze sword, bow, and quiver, with the shield on top to protect them. She covered them with dirt, returned the rocks to their place, and scattered leaves and twigs over all traces of her work. When she was satisfied, Myia walked back to Astrid and the horses. Astrid saw the dagger still in Myia's belt—the expression on the girl's face indicated that it was not open for discussion. She handed Myia the mare's lead rope.

Circe lay back on the cushions and stared thoughtfully at Elizabeth resting next to her. The enchantress strained as she lifted the cat into her lap. "No more treats for you," she said, smiling.

She stared into the ball of light that shimmered on the table and watched Astrid and Myia lead the horses down the hillside. "It won't be long now. She has a few more tasks to perform, then will leave Troy in Nestor's ship."

Circe took a long drink of wine from a golden cup.

"I never thought the girl would help her," she said as if Elizabeth understood. "I should have expected this. Astrid is Sigrid's daughter, and she can be as persuasive as her mother. She is right in thinking the girl can help—she is strong and courageous—but she is wrong when she says she can protect her. The men in the camp will recognize her, and many believe she killed their comrade."

Circe moved Elizabeth gently back onto the cushion and leaned into the ball of light.

"It seems we have another enchantment to perform," she said as she reached into the shimmering light and cupped her hands around Myia's figure. Circe closed her eyes, her features settling into something like sleep. A faint aura surrounded Myia's image as the enchantress opened her eyes and withdrew her hands.

"The nimbus that surrounds her will not change her appearance," Circe said as Elizabeth purred loudly. "Neither she nor anyone else will notice it, but it will alter the perceptions of those who look on her. They will see her, hear her, and accept her without question, but they will not recognize her from the past."

Circe leaned back into the cushions and closed her eyes. She stroked Elizabeth's soft fur, letting the calming vibrations of the cat's purrs and the rolling changes in its volume flow across her nerves as the ball of light collapsed.

"It won't be long now . . ." she whispered.

Chapter 24

Astrid led the horses through Nestor's camp, Myia and the cats walking warily at her side. A crowd soon gathered around them, drawn by the seemingly magical beasts, and grew as they made their way to the weathered tent Nestor and his warriors had pitched on the beach nine years ago. A building of mud bricks and stone adjoined it, like an anchor holding a sail against the wind.

Before Astrid could call out to Nestor, Antilochus left the tent.

"Antilochus . . ." Astrid began, Her words faded as he walked past her and Myia, barely acknowledging their presence.

"Where did you find these?" he asked incredulously.

He did not wait for an answer, his attention completely absorbed by the almost luminous animals. Antilochus stroked the stallion's chest, his hand carefully working down its foreleg past the knee. He lifted the hoof from the ground for inspection, released it gently, then stood and stroked the animal's shoulder. He moved on to the other foreleg, continuing until he had examined each animal, running his hands over their back and legs, their head and neck. The horses stood patiently, honoring the touch of an experienced horseman. Antilochus took the rope leads from Astrid, one in each hand, and spoke softly to each animal in turn. The mare tossed her head, copper mane flowing. He kissed her on the nose.

"They're wonderful," he said to Astrid, sounding more like a man speaking of his beloved than a hardened soldier evaluating a beast of war. "Where did you find them?"

Astrid surveyed the crowd and glanced reassuringly at Myia. "Is your father here?" she asked Antilochus.

Antilochus called to his father, and Nestor walked into the sunlight with Thrasymedes at his side. As their eyes adjusted to the glare, they stopped, mouths open.

"They're perfect," Antilochus called to them. "A stallion and a mare. I don't know if they're trained for the chariot, but they let me handle them."

Nestor approached the animals slowly, ignoring Astrid, Myia, and the crowd that surrounded them. He circled the horses—neither touching them nor speaking—examining them with experienced eyes. Nestor seemed oblivious to his surroundings as he studied every aspect of the animals. He looked at Astrid inquisitively but said nothing. To her surprise, he did not seem to regard Myia's presence as unusual. He barely noticed her at all as he turned his attention back to the horses.

"Move away," he commanded the crowd.

The crowd moved back, leaving Nestor and the horses inside a human fence. He nodded toward Antilochus, who dropped the rope leads and stepped away. Nestor stood in front of the animals, motionless as Astrid stood with Myia, Antilochus, and Thrasymedes.

"What is he doing?" she whispered.

"Watch," Thrasymedes said softly.

Nestor stood about three yards in front of the horses. Astrid heard the hum of the crowd drop to inaudibility and felt a pressure against her arm as Myia moved close to her. She checked the cats and saw Audrey, Greystoke, and Chessie resting at her feet. Nestor stood motionless as minutes passed. The stallion and mare watched him restlessly, shifting their weight from side to side, alternately raising their heads to smell the air, then lowering them to the ground as if searching for some trace of vegetation, their exhalations raising twin vortices of dust beneath their nostrils. Nestor remained as silent as the darkness between dreams.

Astrid felt a twinge in her back and shifted her weight quietly. After what felt like at least twenty minutes, the stallion took a step forward, stopped, and stared at Nestor through liquid brown eyes. He tossed his head and snorted, then stepped back. Nestor did not move, and the stallion once again approached with the mare at his side. He stretched his head toward the horseman and began to paw the ground with his hoof.

Nestor held out his right hand, and the stallion sniffed his open palm as the mare drew beside him. He gently stroked each animal in turn, running his hands along their cheeks and noses, whispering the sweet nonsense humans speak to cherished animals. After a few minutes, he took hold of their lead ropes.

Nestor did not take his eyes off the horses when he asked, "Where did you find these animals?"

"Nestor, they are a gift for you," Astrid said softly. A rumble of voices passed through the crowd.

He smiled. "You did not answer my question."

Astrid moved close to him and whispered, "Could we talk alone?"

Nestor turned to the crowd. "Haven't you seen a horse before?" he challenged. "Or are you so eager to avoid work that you poke your faces into other people's affairs?"

The crowd shifted, but only a few departed.

"Thrasymedes, Antilochus, see to it these horses are cared for but keep them apart from our animals. Feed and water them, check them for injuries," he scanned the crowd, "and post guards around the corral."

His sons took the lead ropes and led the horses away. The crowd parted to let them pass, still talking in hushed tones. Eventually, people began to leave, some singly, most of them talking animatedly in twos or threes, spreading out to be absorbed into the sprawling camp. Astrid was once again surprised that no one seemed to notice Myia.

Nestor took Astrid by the hand—gently, as if she retained some lingering connection to the shining horses—and led her toward his tent. Myia walked unnoticed at her side. Hecamede held the tent flap open as they entered. Astrid sat on one of the benches, placing her backpack on the ground nearby. Myia sat beside her, and the three cats milled at their feet.

"Nestor," Astrid said, "this is Myia. She is going to help me with the cats." She watched for Nestor's reaction. He smiled at the girl, unconcerned with her sudden appearance.

Hecamede offered her water. Myia thanked her and drank deeply.

"Where did you find these horses?" Nestor asked.

"My cats ran from the camp this morning." Astrid glanced at Hecamede, who smiled, not revealing the chaos the animals had created. Astrid told them how she had followed the cats into the forest and described meeting Claire in the clearing, including the gift of the stallion and mare. She did not mention the metal tables or her encounter with the bandits.

"You knew this woman?"

"She's a friend from home . . . but she wasn't really there."

"What do you mean?" Nestor asked, puzzled.

"My friend told me that she was at home, asleep. She said she was dreaming and that someone else was speaking through her. When I asked who it was, she said 'Circe.'"

"Circe," Nestor said, his expression darkening, "the Enchantress?"

Astrid nodded.

"Where is your friend now?"

"She said she was only here in a dream, and after she gave me the horses, she vanished."

Nestor frowned. "This enchantress . . . she is known for dark magic."

"My friend—or Circe speaking through her—said that the man who took my animals was named Phaethon."

Nestor crossed his arms thoughtfully. "Are you saying he could actually be the son of Helios?"

"I don't know."

"Do you know the story?"

Astrid nodded.

"Even if the stories are true," Nestor said, "Phaethon lived long before the world was as we know it existed. And the legend tells how Zeus killed him with a thunderbolt."

"I know. I can't explain it."

Nestor led Astrid through her story once more, stopping her at each step and questioning her with surgical precision. She answered carefully, walking a line between the trust she had come to feel for him and the need to avoid details specific to her origins in the distant future. Occasionally, Nestor glanced at Myia, who said little, mostly nodding and confirming Astrid's account of meeting Claire in the forest. Nestor and Hecamede continued to treat her as if she had always been at Astrid's side.

"There is something else," Astrid said. "My friend told me that these cats can sense where their brother and sister are. She showed me how to draw that knowledge from them."

Nestor sat upright, his eyes alert. "How?"

"It's hard to explain, but the abilities that let them become Swarm bind them when they're apart. She showed me how to sense that bond."

"Then, you can track them?"

Astrid nodded. "It gives me a direction, but not a distance."

Nestor took a deep breath and exhaled slowly. "That is enough. As usual, my seers have given me nothing but riddles."

Astrid smiled.

"The gift of these horses," he said, "the strange appearance of your friend in the woods . . . They can only be signs from the gods telling us how to find your animals. Hecamede, Antilochus is at the stables with his brother. Tell him to come to me when he has finished."

Hecamede pulled aside the cloth that covered the tent opening and left.

"Astrid," Nestor said, "you must tell no one this story. You must avoid talking about the origin of the horses or your encounter with the woman in the forest. If anyone asks, tell them that you found the animals wandering on the beach."

"Has something happened?"

"Agamemnon has called a council tonight to decide what to do with you and your animals."

A look of concern crossed Astrid's face.

"Try not to worry," he reassured. "This may help us."

"How?"

"People in the camp have grown restless. Rumors have spread about you—not all of them are good."

"Am I in danger?"

"No one will act before Agamemnon's council."

"And after?"

"The council will run late, and we can leave a day or so after. Agamemnon believes you are under the protection of the gods. I think we can convince him to let us help you on your way."

"What if he tries to stop us?"

"Don't worry. Odysseus and I can deal with him," Nestor reassured.

Astrid heard the tent flap rustle and saw Antilochus enter.

"Well, my son," Nestor smiled at him, "it seems it is time for us to help our friend find her lost animals . . . and perhaps her way home."

Antilochus smiled broadly. "I thought it might be so."

"How long would it take for you to gather a crew and prepare a ship?"

"I've already spoken to a few of your warriors, and they are eager to join us. I've asked some of them to prepare one of the ships for sea. They're checking the sails and the caulking on the hull."

Nestor smiled. "Select twenty-five men—not just our finest warriors, but also some younger men who will learn from the voyage. When can you be ready to leave?"

"It will take a day to finish preparations and to load and organize our supplies. We could leave on the tide the day after tomorrow."

Nestor stood with his arms open. Antilochus rose from the bench, and they embraced before he left through the canvas flap.

"He seems to know what I want before I do," Nestor said, moisture filling his eyes. "He will be a fine leader someday."

Astrid felt a knot in her chest, once again stricken by Homer's account of Antilochus' death at Troy.

She turned to Myia. "Could you wait outside?"

The girl paused nervously.

"I'll be here," Astrid reassured her. "If you need me, call out."

Nestor walked to the tent flap and held it open as Myia reluctantly left. He returned to sit beside Astrid.

"Nestor," she said, "why are you doing this?"

"I told you. The horses are a sign."

"It isn't just the horses."

Nestor looked into her eyes for a time. "Why are you risking your life to recover your lost animals?"

"They saved my life when . . ."

"When Dymenos attacked you?"

"Yes."

"But that isn't the only reason."

"I can't leave them," she said.

"I am helping you for the same reason. We cannot do otherwise." Nestor paused in thought. "Over the years, I have come to know men, and I have come to know horses. I prefer the latter."

Astrid smiled.

"I came here at the call of a brother king to recover a faithless wife," Nestor said thoughtfully. "Now, I find myself in the ninth year of a war that will not end, where that purpose is all but forgotten. When men speak of it, they do so without conviction, as if their true reasons for fighting lie elsewhere, with plunder and adventure . . . I've grown tired of waiting in plain sight of the city that has frustrated us for so long . . . I'm sick of doing nothing but fighting the occasional band of Trojans. I'm sick of the excesses and cruelty of ignorant young men, of watching them sail off to raid some helpless village." He paused, sadness shadowing his face. "I'm tired of watching them die. I'm tired of prayers and ritual sacrifices that become nothing but drunken feasts. Most of all, I've grown tired of our supreme commander, of his greed and shortsightedness."

"But this must seem insane to you," Astrid argued. "I come here from nowhere. I bring cats that have impossible abilities. I tell you incredible stories of monsters and enchantments, of gods healing my injuries—"

He laughed. "The things you say must be true. No one would tell such unbelievable lies."

"I've faced these people already," she said. "Phaethon, Circe . . . they are dangerous."

"I've faced death all my life," Nestor said, taking her hand. "It no longer frightens me. I've lived almost sixty years and have led three generations of men, some to victory and honor, others down to death. I long to spend the time that remains to me in some noble work, not this charade of a war. You have brought me a gift."

Nestor sat quietly, staring at the tent flap as if contemplating what lay beyond it. "Now, I must go and explain these horses and my departure to my people," he said, rising wearily from the bench.

Astrid stood, placed her hand on his shoulder, and kissed him on the cheek. Nestor looked into her eyes for a time, then touched the side of her face gently. He turned and left the tent; the heavy cloth fell between them, leaving Astrid alone in the dim light. After a few moments, she walked out into the sunlight.

Myia hurried to her. "Is everything all right?"

"Yes." Astrid took her hand. "Myia, when you were out here by yourself, did anyone approach you?"

"No."

"When we walked through the camp with the horses, did anyone look at you with recognition? Or surprise?"

"A few glanced at me, but I didn't sense anything unusual."

"Doesn't that strike you as odd? Even if no one remembered you, the sight of a stranger should have drawn their interest."

"There was nothing," Myia confirmed. "What does it mean?"

"I feel like someone—probably Circe—has a hand in this, but I don't know how," Astrid said slowly, "or why."

Chapter 25

Strachys' calloused feet scraped the clay floor as he struggled from his bed and stumbled across his one-room cabin. Once more, he had slept into the afternoon. He reached for the pitcher on the table and poured the last swallows of wine, his hand trembling. He drank deeply, then walked stiffly through the doorway and found a fresh jug of water just outside—the woman had come to the cabin while he slept. He looked for her at the loom under the tree but she had left. Although she still attended him, she had grown distant as the power of Circe's scroll consumed his thoughts and actions—and his moods.

He took a ladle of water and poured it over his head, then drank deeply from another. He hurried back into the house like a man reaching the shelter of a cave after hours in the desert heat. Strachys found a partly eaten loaf of bread on the wooden table and sat down. As he ate, he stared at the scroll resting before him.

"Is it time to resume our work, my friend? Or . . . are you more than a friend? Perhaps even more than a lover?"

Strachys touched the scroll's wooden spindles. He sensed Circe's lingering presence and realized she had never spoken the words that would free the golden writing from the parchment. He understood the conflict between her desire for the scroll's power and her fear of the price that power would demand—he remembered his agony when Phaethon had removed the scroll from his possession.

"If we are separated when your words are within me, I will die," he said softly. "That has never been true of a lover. They leave all too easily, and I seem to recover soon enough."

He unrolled the scroll and ran his fingers over the parchment.

"You consume the spirit within me when we are joined for too long. That is very much like a lover," he said ironically. "Then, when I grow weary, the same words that brought us together return you to the parchment, and I become as I was before." Strachys looked down at the dirty nightshirt and wrinkled flesh on his arms and legs.

"Lovers do not come and go so willingly when commanded," he exhaled wearily, "but like them, you leave me with a void only you can fill. It increases each time we part."

He stared through the narrow doorway at the sunlight baking the ground outside, at the unattended loom, at the path where the woman would descend to the village when his enslavement to the golden writing became too hard for her to bear.

"I think that soon, I will lose myself completely in your embrace."

He did not rise from his chair but recited from memory the syllables a stranger had written long ago in the scroll's margin. He watched the golden writing crawl from the parchment like a phalanx of insects, bleached to a metallic sheen by the sun. He did not move his hand as they crawled up his arm and swarmed down the table legs toward his feet. His muscles twitched involuntarily, and he closed his eyes as the characters covered his ankles, then his calves, and disappeared under the nightshirt. He trembled as the writing emerged at the fabric's opening to cover his neck, and finally, his head in a golden mask.

Strachys awoke, still seated at the table. He looked down at the muscles of his hands and forearms, firm and curved like the arms of youth.

"So, my friend, we start our little dance once more."

Strachys removed the dirty nightshirt and threw it onto the bed. He walked to the shelves and found a neatly folded tunic the woman had left for him. Dressed in the soft linen, he returned to the table and reached forward as if to grasp some invisible ball. A swirl of light formed beneath his hands, and he stared through the cold fire at the blond cat prowling through the grass near the granary and the feral colony that guarded it.

"What is this?" He closed his eyes as if listening for some faint sound in the image shimmering before him.

"So, the woman who followed you here has discovered the thread that binds you to your siblings. She is coming for you." Strachys relaxed as the ball of light faded, then walked out into the sunlight.

"Fate is moving things along," he murmured. He stretched his limbs like an athlete approaching a race, finding delight in the pure physicality of movement, in the interplay of nerve and muscle, of sunlight and air.

"Our employer will bring one of your siblings to us, or they will come on their own. Either way, we will have what we need."

Chapter 26

Astrid followed Nestor and Odysseus past the endless row of ships that lined the Trojan beach, making their way through the night toward Agamemnon's council. Telemachus and Antilochus walked protectively at her side. Myia had remained with Hecamede at Nestor's camp—women, except those suspected of being a goddess, were not welcome at the council. At Agamemnon's insistence, Astrid had brought Audrey, Greystoke, and Chessie. She engaged the minds of the three frightened animals and felt their weariness from the long walk. She also felt their unease at the crowds surrounding them and their instinct to merge their bodies and find safety as Swarm. Astrid lifted Chessie into her arms to let her rest from the walk. She also hoped to strengthen her bond with the littermates through touch—and prevent Swarm's unwanted appearance.

"Don't worry," she told Greystoke and Audrey, "you'll get your turns."

She had seen the Achaean beachhead from the hillside when she first came to Troy, the long curve of the Trojan Bay all but obscured by the dark ships and the corruption of human activity spreading from them. It was not until she walked through camp after camp that she fully understood the scale of the Achaean invasion.

As they passed each encampment, Nestor told Astrid of the men who had come to Troy, of their lives and their homelands. His words awakened her memory of *The Iliad* and Homer's catalog of the ships in the Achaean force. She passed through the camp of the Athenians who, long before their city had entered its golden age, sent fifty ships to Troy—one of the smaller forces in the great army. Astrid followed a winding path among the tents of the Cretans, whose leader, Idomeneus, fought at the front of the Achaean ranks and served as one of Agamemnon's closest advisors. She saw the encampment of Ajax, son of Telemon, known for his size, strength, and ferocity in battle. She walked the sand where Diomedes' ships rested.

Diomedes was second only to Achilles in his prowess as a warrior, and his aristeia—his deadly rampage through the Trojan ranks—still lives in Homer's tactile poetry.

Astrid followed Nestor through the sprawling camp of Menelaus, Agamemnon's brother, whose betrayal by his wife, Helen, and the Trojan Paris had provided the rationale for this war of greed and brutality. She remembered from *The Iliad* how Menelaus would almost kill Paris in single combat, until Aphrodite's intervention saved the Trojan prince and prolonged the war.

The list continued, almost without end, but nothing thrilled Astrid like seeing the camp of Achilles, the greatest of the Achaean warriors. His feud with Agamemnon and angry departure from the field of battle almost cost the Achaeans everything—just as his eventual return shifted the war back in the Achaean's favor and ended his own tragic life.

Astrid also saw the heartbreaking realities of the war. Stolen treasures shined inside tents—pottery, fine cloth, gold, and skillfully wrought bronze picked off the bones of broken homes and cities, giving the lie to the war's justification of restoring Menelaus' honor. She saw women who'd been taken from their families and enslaved look up from their labors and watch her pass, a free woman in the company of kings. She saw wounded warriors dying in their beds, numbed by drink, their dirty bandages covering the infections that would end their lives in the stench of rotting flesh.

Passing among the flickering circles of light engraved in the darkness by torches, braziers, and lamps, Astrid also discovered the extent of her own fame. Men and women, warriors and slaves, all stopped what they were doing to see this woman said to be an immortal.

As they neared a large complex of tents and stone buildings, Astrid and her friends slowed their pace as if restrained by a single will. Countless fires illuminated the brightly dyed tents, their canvas rippling in the ocean breeze. The stone and workmanship of the buildings exceeded any she had seen on the Trojan beach, and Astrid realized it was the camp of Agamemnon, king of Mycenae, supreme commander of the Achaean forces, whose greed and hubris brought tragedy to those who followed him. She felt the tension rising among the cats and wondered if it was a response to her own anxiety. She nuzzled Greystoke—the cat she now carried—and called the three animal minds into the shelter of her own self-control.

At Nestor and Hecamede's insistence, Astrid had worn one of Hecamede's flounced dresses—layers of red and saffron, with a fringed kilt of fine, white linen wrapped around her waist. She wore her hair up in a jeweled headdress, and a gold necklace shined against a white blouse closed with golden pins. Her feet were bare, covered with sand from their long walk, and she wore a gold anklet above her right foot. Astrid lowered Greystoke to the ground with his littermates and checked the unfamiliar garment, straightening the seams and brushing away the sand. She felt Odysseus' hand on her shoulder.

"How do you feel?" he asked her.

"Like a Mycenaean princess," she said ironically.

"Goddess would be helpful."

"I'll try," she said, smiling. "What's our plan?"

"Astrid," Nestor said, "you must let Odysseus and me do the talking. We've dealt with Agamemnon in council many times. He may seem impulsive, but he always has some goal in mind. He will avoid risks to himself and challenge others, setting warrior against warrior, creating conflict, and dividing men until he sees a path to his advantage."

"I've seen leaders behave like this in my homeland," Astrid observed. "It usually ends badly."

Nestor took her hands in his and looked into her eyes. "You must remember who you are at all times. Do not show fear or anger—behave like a woman chosen by the gods. Agamemnon is boastful, but inside, he fears for his hold on power. You must not bow to him, but be careful not to threaten him, or he will lash out."

"That's a hard needle to thread," Astrid worried.

"Goddesses are used to dealing in contradictions," Odysseus joked. Astrid glared at him mockingly.

"If he asks a question," Nestor continued, "answer with confidence. Do not be afraid to look him in the eye, but do not reveal your feelings when you do."

"So," she said, "we're improvising."

Odysseus smiled.

Astrid followed Nestor and Odysseus into Agamemnon's council. Telemachus and Antilochus walked at her side. They entered a large common area, circumscribed by stone benches and carefully positioned fires. The kings and warriors of the council took their places on the benches while a crowd gathered behind them. A man she assumed was Agamemnon sat at the head of the common area. The lines on his face suggested a man in his late forties, although the curve of his shoulder and arm muscles could have belonged to one much younger. His long hair and beard were streaked with gray, and Astrid recognized the shine of gold in his rings and bracelets, and in the ornaments braided into his hair. He held a bronze-clad spear in one hand—a symbol of authority—and golden pins held the wine-colored cloak around his shoulders.

She stepped closer to Antilochus and whispered. "The red-haired man beside Agamemnon . . . is that Menelaus?"

Antilochus nodded.

"What about the tall, muscular warrior near them? Is that Ajax?"

"How do you know him?"

"I recognize him from stories I've been told. Where is Diomedes?" she asked, remembering the man whose courage and skill in battle were second only to Achilles.

Antilochus nodded toward an imposing figure leaning forward on a bench, his elbows resting on his knees, staring at her with penetrating curiosity. Astrid returned his gaze and felt an ancient calling—the inter-woven feelings of deep familiarity and irreconcilable strangeness that bound her to Homer's twin masterpieces.

She continued to survey the warriors of Agamemnon's council. Her eyes stopped on a confident, athletic man in his twenties, with dark blonde hair falling to his shoulders. He sat across the open area from Agamemnon, thriving in his distance from the other man's power rather than seeking proximity to it like the other members of the council. His physical beauty drew Astrid's gaze, but what held her attention were his eyes. Unlike the curious, darting glances of the men in the crowd, he stared at her with deep understanding—and the sorrow such understanding brings.

"Is that Achilles?" she whispered.

Antilochus nodded. It was clear he felt it improper for them to talk in the council, but Astrid could not stop as a lifetime of imagining these warriors consumed her thoughts. Her reverie dissolved as Agamemnon stood and began to speak.

"Come, good Nestor, Odysseus. Do not stand in the shadows. Let me see this woman I've heard so much about."

Astrid walked between Nestor and Odysseus to an empty bench near Agamemnon, the cats close beside her. Nestor's sons took places behind them, just as the other lieutenants stood behind their kings. Agamemnon walked across the commons and motioned for her to come forward. Astrid stepped out to face him, returning his gaze. His small, darting eyes carried a sharp, feral intelligence but seemed devoid of empathy or depth of under-standing.

"What is your name?" he asked, smiling.

"Astrid."

He tilted his head. "It's a strange name."

She remained silent, not releasing her focus on him. Agamemnon looked down at the cats who stared up from around her feet.

"Are these the animals I've heard about?"

"Yes."

He reached down to touch Audrey, who hissed loudly. The supreme commander of the Achaeans pulled back quickly as she struck him, her claws extended. He rubbed blood from the back of his hand, then smiled and turned toward the council, laughing, as Astrid took Audrey into her arms. Most of the warriors joined his laughter, but a few looked at their comrades—and at Astrid—with concern.

"How did you come here?" Agamemnon asked.

Astrid paused, unsure of what she should reveal.

"She came to Nestor's camp with her animals, seeking shelter and assistance," Odysseus answered as he stepped forward to stand at her side. "She was injured, and we helped her. We have also sworn to protect her."

"At ease, brave Odysseus," Agamemnon said, still smiling. "She is in no danger here."

He returned to his place at the head of the council and took his seat. A young girl, little more than a child, brought him wine. "But, my clever friend, there is much you are not telling your commander."

"What do you mean?" Odysseus asked.

"I have learned that she summoned a great cat to kill Dymenos," Agamemnon said, and a low murmur spread through the council.

"Only when he attacked her."

"Some say the cat sprang from her small animals."

Odysseus held his response.

"I've also been told that Proteus healed her injuries," Agamemnon added, "and that she has spoken with Artemis . . . perhaps even Athena, Apollo, Hera, or Zeus himself."

"I agree she is favored of the gods," Odysseus acknowledged. "But do not believe everything you are told, or Olympus may be emptied entirely."

Laughter spread through the crowd as Agamemnon frowned. Odysseus walked into the center of the council, waiting for the voices to fade.

"You do yourself great credit," he said, addressing Agamemnon directly. "A leader should always know what is happening in his army, and we have kept nothing from you."

"Shouldn't you inform me if an immortal enters the camp? Or if lions spring from small cats to kill one of my warriors?" Agamemnon protested.

"We do not know her to be an immortal," Nestor said, stepping forward. "We found her lost, hungry, and injured . . . like a mortal woman."

"What of these horses she brought as gifts for you . . . horses that could only have come from the gods?"

"I have given her the protection due to one whom the gods favor," Nestor said, "and I have accepted their gratitude."

"Yet none of her favor, none of these honors have come to me," Agamemnon complained. He looked around the council as if for agreement. The men talked among themselves quietly, ambiguously.

Ajax stood, towering over those around him.

"Agamemnon," he began, "Nestor and Odysseus are right. If she truly is under the gods' protection, it is best we offer help and not interfere with her wishes. The ways of the gods are not ours to question. I do not know why she selected Nestor from all the kings and warriors gathered here, but I take no offense, nor should you."

Menelaus rose from his seat. "Perhaps the gods are testing us," he challenged Ajax, "to see if the Achaeans honor their supreme commander and would bring her before him."

"And so, we have," Odysseus reminded him.

"Only after your commander demanded it," Menelaus countered.

Achilles stepped into the sandy commons, smiling. "Perhaps she fears our leader's appetites and prefers to stay with gentle Nestor?"

Laughter rippled through the council, and Agamemnon glared at him. "Do not test me, Achilles."

Achilles gestured toward Astrid. "She is attractive and very different from the women we've taken in our raids. Perhaps a king might be tempted?"

"As Briseis tempted you?" Agamemnon scowled.

"Briseis is of noble birth, and I love her," Achilles said in a voice tempered with resistance.

"She was taken in a raid, and I gave her to you," Agamemnon warned. He stared at Achilles for a time, then spoke once more, his words an icy staccato. "Do not forget that I can withdraw my gifts."

Achilles started toward Agamemnon, rage clouding his face. Astrid remembered how, in *The Iliad*, Agamemnon ultimately took Briseis for himself—an offense that led to Achilles' refusal to fight and the story's great tragedy.

Odysseus stepped between them as the gathered warriors began to talk loudly. "My commander, brave Achilles, the gods are watching our treatment of this woman," he said. "This argument will not please them."

Agamemnon nodded toward Odysseus, then turned back to Achilles. "Do not let your love for Briseis interfere with your duty to me."

Quickly, before Achilles could answer, Agamemnon addressed Nestor. "I am surprised that you have said so little." He spoke like a man about to tell a joke. "Such brevity is not your habit."

A smattering of laughter passed through the crowd, and Agamemnon seemed pleased with himself. Astrid remembered Homer's portrayal of Nestor as loquacious, often tedious in counsel—qualities so unlike the man who now walked the perimeter of the assembly, silently commanding the attention of each man he passed. She leaned toward Antilochus. "Why does Agamemnon mock your father?"

"He knows the men respect Nestor," Antilochus whispered, "perhaps more than they respect him. He feels he must assert his superiority."

Nestor finished walking the perimeter of the common area and stepped into its center.

"Is this how we hold a council?" He spoke in a voice of earned authority. "Bickering like children over some imagined slight?"

He stood before Achilles as an equal. "Great Achilles," he said, "our leader forgets that once a jest escapes his lips, it flies on its own wings and can turn to a harder purpose. He means you no dishonor."

Achilles placed his hand on Nestor's shoulder and faced the great horseman. He nodded and, after a final, chilling glance at Agamemnon, returned to his place among his warriors.

"Is this your famous wisdom?" Agamemnon challenged Nestor. "An insult to your commander?"

Nestor crossed the commons to address Agamemnon directly. "No. It is a defense of my commander, for I know you would not risk bringing the gods' wrath down upon this army."

Nestor turned and stepped once more into the center of the commons. He looked across the gathered warriors as if he could make eye contact with each man in turn. "You are correct in stating that this woman is not an ordinary mortal. I have seen her small animals become a wild beast, capable of tearing the greatest of us apart, and I have seen her bring horses suitable for Apollo's own chariot from the forest above our camp."

A low rumble spread through the crowd.

"Although she has demonstrated great power, she has also shown herself to be as human as any of us. I have seen her suffer from her injuries and weep with longing for her home—like so many of us. But whether she is a goddess or a mortal lost in this war, the reasons she came to me would still belong to the immortals. They are not ours to question."

He paused as a murmur of assent passed through the assembly, then turned to face Agamemnon. "Do not risk the gods' wrath by interfering with this woman . . . or her animals," Nestor said, his voice taking on a tone of warning mixed with respect. "Let her rest in my camp and leave when she desires. In that way, you will earn the gratitude of the gods."

Agamemnon stared at him for a time from his seat at the head of the council, weighing Nestor's arguments against his own schemes and desires. Eventually, he stood, carefully arranged his cloak around himself and spoke in a loud voice. "I have listened to your counsel, and I thank you all—especially wise Nestor—but I have decided that the woman and her animals will remain with me. The immortals will rejoice at the honors I'll bestow upon her—the bulls I will sacrifice in her name and the gifts I will give her. They'll smile upon our war against the Trojans."

"My commander—" Nestor protested.

Agamemnon held up a hand to silence him, then turned to Astrid. "Do you not agree?"

Astrid struggled to contain the anger rising within her as she walked into the center of the commons. She did not answer Agamemnon but called silently to the three cats. Astrid sensed their anxiety as they ran to her side but did not try to calm them. Instead, she drew them close, kneeling and touching each animal in turn, welcoming the metamorphosis surging through them. She felt a tingle in her hands and quickly pulled away as a blue gyre engulfed the cats. A rumble passed through the crowd as Swarm took shape where the three small creatures had stood. The psychic connection she'd come to feel with them intensified.

Stay with me, little ones. Astrid repeated the words silently, hoping to calm the three animals who shared Swarm's—and her—mind and prevent the great cat from raging in panic among the armed warriors. She rested her hand on Swarm's muscled shoulders, fingers digging into her deep brown, almost black coat. Swarm's green eyes scanned the crowd like a cornered panther, and her teeth caught the fire light as she growled in warning.

Be calm. Stay by me, Astrid repeated in her thoughts, embracing the animal emotions surging at the edge of her awareness, attempting to absorb them into her own self-control. She walked the perimeter of the council with Swarm at her side. Most of the warriors she passed stepped back in fear while a few grasped their swords.

"Would you raise arms against me?" she challenged them as she endeavored to contain Swarm's emotions. "Do any of you dream you could prevail against this beast born of the gods' power?"

Do not be afraid. I am here with you. Astrid formed the words silently, a reassurance aimed at Swarm's anxiety. She stopped in front of great Ajax, who stood to face her, his presence dominating the warriors around him.

"I will not forget that you spoke on my behalf. I will always look upon you with gratitude and protection. Our strength—the cat's and mine—will flow through your arms and guide your spear."

Ajax nodded silently as Astrid continued along the line of kings and favored warriors. She approached Diomedes, whom Antilochus had pointed out when they had entered. Unlike the others, he had neither moved from his original position nor touched his weapon. As Astrid came near, he stood and faced her, his features revealing neither fear nor threat.

Do not fear, my loves. She repeated soothing Swarm's tripartite sentience.

"Diomedes," she said for all to hear, "do you wish my blessing and the power of this animal?"

"Yes," he said simply, a warrior accepting his due.

Astrid rested her open palm on his cheek and felt the tension in his jaw. "The cat and I will always be at your side in battle—unseen."

Be calm. Do not be afraid. She repeated the words silently as she walked from warrior to warrior, always careful to stay between Swarm and the crowd, drawing on her will to insulate the animal from the storm of human emotions. As she passed, she made eye contact with as many men as she could, stopping to bless those who mastered their fear and approached her.

When she came to Achilles, she pressed her fingers deep into Swarm's fur and looked at the great warrior with compassion.

"Achilles," she said. "Your greatness will not come easily, but I will always be at your side."

She motioned for him to approach, repeating silent reassurances to the great cat as he came near. Achilles showed no fear of the beast at her side but kneeled and extended his hand, palm up. To Astrid's surprise, Swarm sniffed his fingers, then leaned into his touch as the greatest of warriors ran his hand along the side of her head, caressing her as if she were a kitten. The steady hum of men's voices fell silent, and Agamemnon stared impassively, revealing nothing except for a quiver in the muscles of his jaw. Astrid heard the cat purr and felt Swarm's anxiety give way to trust.

After a time, Achilles turned his attention from the cat to Astrid. She searched his face, hoping to see what had calmed Swarm. She found the eyes of a man, but they were eyes from which she could not turn away. Astrid touched his cheek and kissed him softly on the lips.

"I will not forget that you have defended me," she whispered so only he could hear.

Astrid stepped back as the council's constant murmur swelled to shouts of approval. She watched Achilles, the tragic son of a Nereid and a mortal king, return to his seat. She felt Swarm's anxiety rise once more and knew it was time to leave the council of the Achaeans.

Be calm, my loves. Stay with me. Astrid repeated the silent reassurances as she crossed the open commons to stand squarely before Agamemnon. She pressed on Swarm's shoulders while envisioning a seated cat. To her relief, Swarm sat beside her. Astrid saw anger and fear contend across Agamemnon's cruel features, his eyes burning with resentment.

"The animals and I will stay with Nestor until my father calls us home," she declared.

The word 'father' raised the rumble of the crowd into a chorus of shouts. Agamemnon's eyes darted around the commons as if he was looking for an escape.

"You must let the great cat stay with us," he argued. "It will drive fear into the Trojans and their leader, Hector, who torments us in every battle."

"The great cat serves no one," Astrid declared. "It does not care whether it devours Hector's liver . . . or yours."

"It serves you," Agamemnon challenged.

"And it must remain with me," she said. "The cat and I are one."

Be calm, my loves. Stay with me, she repeated in her mind. "Great king," Astrid said, inserting a note of deference into her voice, "you have honored us by calling this council. Now, I ask you for one more gift. In a few days, the great cat and I will leave. King Nestor will take us to a place of our choosing, and from there, we will return home. The night after we leave this beach, I ask you to call your warriors together and pray for the gods to bless our journey. If you do as I ask, the cat and I will be with you in battle, unseen but always present."

I am here, my darlings. You are within me. Astrid repeated the words silently as the council members began to argue—first among themselves, then shouting at their commander, demanding that he grant her wish.

Do not be afraid. Astrid grasped the loose skin at the scruff of Swarm's neck, squeezing it gently. She repeated the reassurances as much to calm herself as the great cat.

"It shall be so," Agamemnon said as if the decision had been his from the beginning. "We will call a great assembly, sacrifice fat cattle—enough to feed everyone in our ranks—and we will pour libations to the gods. We will ask their blessings on this woman, on these animals, and on noble Nestor, who will carry her across the ocean. We will pray for her to favor our efforts against Troy."

Stay with me. It won't be long. Astrid repeated the calming words in her mind as she nodded to the commander of the Achaean forces. She turned back to Nestor.

"Now, good Nestor," she said, loud enough for all to hear, "I shall return to your camp." Astrid walked past him, Swarm at her side, as he and Odysseus stared, speechless, lips parted in astonishment.

Come, my children. You are safe. She repeated the words in her mind as she left the council ground, neither pausing nor looking back, exhausted by the effort of confronting the gathered warriors and controlling Swarm's violent instincts. She walked as if in a trance, not daring to release her psychic connection with the great cat. As she passed, the constant murmuring of voices grew silent, and the crowd parted. She walked until she found a space safely outside Agamemnon's camp, away from people, sheltered beneath the prow of a beached ship. She fell to her knees and threw her arms around Swarm's muscled neck.

Come to me, Audrey, Greystoke, Chessie. She called silently to the three littermates, her forehead resting against Swarm's shoulder as she felt the cat begin to relax. *Come, Chessie. Come, Greystoke. Come, Audrey.*

The beast shook in her arms as Swarm's faceted sentience began to separate. Astrid fell back onto the sand, grasping at the grains pressing into her palms, releasing the animal minds she had struggled to control. She felt them withdraw to the edge of her consciousness as her cats took shape, emerging from the beast that had confronted the Achaean council. Astrid heard footsteps and saw Odysseus, Nestor, Thrasymedes, and Antilochus approach.

"You took a great risk," Nestor said. He frowned as he held out his hand.

Astrid let him help her to her feet, her legs trembling.

"Agamemnon was furious," he continued. "We are lucky to be alive."

Odysseus looked down at the cats. "So is Agamemnon," he mused.

"I could not let him take me into his camp," Astrid said.

"What if he had ordered his men to attack?" Nestor challenged, his voice thick with worry. "What made you think you could get away with that?"

Astrid did not have an answer—she had acted impulsively, on instinct. The words left her mouth as if of their own will.

"You and Odysseus cannot read a roomful of men like I can."

The two warriors stared at her in shock. Odysseus began to laugh, and Nestor glanced at him as if asking for help. He turned back to Astrid, his voice and manner softening.

"I feared for your safety."

She touched the side of his face and looked into his eyes. "I know, but I saw no other way."

"We shouldn't linger," Odysseus interrupted, looking back at the light coming from Agamemnon's camp, the voices rising in the night as the council's deliberations gave way to the shouts of young men enjoying the wine now flowing freely among them. "Besides," he added with a smile, "I find myself with a growing thirst for several cups of Nestor's wine."

As they started back to the camp, Odysseus rested his hand on Nestor's arm, slowing his pace, letting Astrid, Nestor's sons, and the cats move ahead. "Tell me your thoughts," he whispered.

"We were fortunate tonight, but I'll feel better when we're at sea."

"No, about the woman."

Nestor stopped and turned to him. "She is under the protection of the gods—it is my role to protect her."

"I have eyes. I can see how she looks at you—and you at her."

"The gods chose me for a reason. They know I will not be . . ." He paused, measuring his words. "Distracted. I will honor my duty—above all else."

"I know you will, but I also know the gods reward those they love."

Nestor laughed and shook his head. "You always were the rash one, my old friend."

He placed his hand on Odysseus' shoulder. "Come, let's go back to my camp. I seem to remember you saying something about sharing a few cups of my wine."

Odysseus held back and watched Nestor go ahead to walk with Astrid and the others. He smiled as he followed them through the night, rejoining them as they reached the waiting fires of Nestor's camp.

Phaethon and Proxonos stood at the bow of their ship, listening to the shouts from the Achaean camp. They had lowered their sails and rowed in silence, oars straining against the leather straps that secured them. They followed the shoreline, unseen in the darkness.

"It is as I told you it would be," Phaethon whispered, gesturing at a collection of ships and dwellings. "That is Nestor's camp. I will leave you and wade ashore. Odysseus' camp is just ahead. Sail past it to the rock outcropping. You can land there and conceal your ship."

Proxonos nodded.

"There is a council at Agamemnon's camp. After it ends, the Achaeans will feast and return to their beds. Attack just before dawn when they are still asleep."

Proxonos scowled. "And sodden with food and drink."

"Will you recognize Odysseus?"

"Kings are easy to spot."

"Are your men ready?"

Proxonos looked back along the deck at the rows of mercenaries, bandits, and hired killers that filled the benches. "Many of their friends have died, skewered on Achaean spears. They are eager to avenge them. We'll give you your distraction," he said sarcastically, "while you go steal a cat from a girl."

Phaethon ignored him as he hung a leather satchel over his shoulder to carry his prize. He checked the sword hanging at his side, balanced the bronze-tipped spear in his hand, and swung his legs over the gunwale as the ship passed a tongue of sand.

"Start your raid at the first light of dawn," Phaethon said as he slipped into the water.

Chapter 27

Astrid awoke to the chaos of shouting men and clashing bronze. As her eyes adjusted to the flicker of the tent's lone clay lamp, she saw Myia sitting up nearby. The other women sat startled in their beds or were throwing their covers aside to rise; a few were dressing hastily. Astrid checked the cats: Audrey and Chessie remained near her, frightened and alert. Greystoke sat upright beside Myia, his eyes wide.

"Myia," she said as she pulled her jeans on under her loose linen nightdress, "are you all right?"

"Yes," the girl answered, stress hardening her voice.

Astrid saw Hecamede hurrying to leave the tent. She wore only sandals and a loose bedgown, her hair a dark tangle.

"What's happening?" Astrid called to her.

"I don't know. It could be a raid."

"What should I do?"

"Stay in the tent. The women will help you," Hecamede said as she lifted the tent flap. "I must go to Nestor."

Astrid nodded. After Hecamede left, she laced her shoes and placed Chessie and Audrey on Myia's bed next to Greystoke. She sensed the cats' unease.

"Stay with the cats," she told Myia.

Disregarding Hecamede's warnings, Astrid started toward the tent's opening. She saw Myia take a short bronze sword from her bedding.

"Where did you—" Astrid started to ask. "Never mind. Protect the cats—and yourself."

As she walked into the twilight, Astrid saw warriors running through the open area outside the women's tent, some adjusting their armor and weapons, others scanning the crowd as if they shared her confusion. A boy of about eleven ran barefoot through the camp, dressed only in a short kilt, carrying a torch and lighting the lamps and braziers scattered among the tents. Astrid ran to him as he added kindling to the coals that glowed in the pit outside the women's habitat and kneeled to blow the wood into flame.

"What's happening?" She took him by the arm as the kindling ignited.

"A raid," he said in a frightened voice. He pulled free from Astrid's grip and added logs to the fire.

"Where?"

The boy pointed up the beach, then ran, the light of his torch disappearing in the twilight. Astrid saw Antilochus step through the confusion, wearing a bronze cuirass, greaves, and a boar's tusk helmet. He carried a bronze-tipped spear and the embossed bronze shield she remembered from the day she'd arrived at Troy. A sword hung at his side.

"Are you all right?" he asked her.

"Yes. Myia and the cats are in the tent. What's happening?"

"There's a raid at Odysseus' camp," he shouted over the chaos. "Nestor's taken most of his warriors to help. I stayed behind with the rest to guard the camp."

A crowd of warriors gathered around him. Antilochus picked out three men and directed them to positions in front of the women's tent. He sent the rest to Nestor's tent to wait for him.

"These men will protect you," Antilochus said, gesturing toward the three warriors. "I must rejoin my men."

As he turned to leave, Astrid grabbed his arm. "Wait," she said, pointing at a figure approaching through the early half-light.

Phaethon stepped into the open space, fully armed with a shield and spear, a short sword at his side. He wore no helmet.

"It's the man who stole my animal," she told Antilochus.

Nestor's son gestured to the three warriors standing in front of the tent, and they came forward. One of them stood beside Antilochus on Astrid's left, and the other two took positions to her right.

Phaethon stood in the fire's light. "Why so unfriendly?" he shouted.

"Where's my cat?" Astrid demanded.

"Prowling a granary on a nearby island, growing fat off rats and scraps of fish. He's lonely. He wants a companion." Phaethon rested his hand on the leather bag hanging at his side.

"Bullshit," Astrid cursed. She felt Antilochus' hand on her arm, holding her back.

"Why must we do this? I mean you and your animals no harm," Phaethon said impatiently.

"Go to hell," she shouted.

Phaethon threw the leather bag on the sand in front of him.

"This is a terrible way to transport an animal. I have no desire to use it. Select one of your cats and come with me. I know enchantments that will let us fly like Hermes, and you can carry the animal in your arms. You will be my honored guests, and I swear by Zeus that I will return you and both animals in a few days—unharmed."

He gestured toward the Achaeans. "And these men do not need to die."

"Liar," Astrid shouted. "Your promises mean nothing."

Antilochus spoke a sharp command, and the two warriors at the ends of the line stepped forward, shields raised, spears projecting forward, bodies centered above their feet. Antilochus and the third Achaean remained protectively beside Astrid.

The warrior to Phaethon's left was the first to strike, lunging with his spear. Phaethon knocked it aside with his shield but did not counterstrike. He adjusted his position to remain equally distant from the warriors who bracketed him. The first Achaean attacked again; his companion struck simultaneously. Moving with inhuman speed, Phaethon ducked beneath one spear and turned the other aside with a wave of his shield.

It was not until the Achaean to Phaethon's left dropped his weapon and grasped the shaft protruding from his thigh that Astrid realized what had happened. Phaethon pulled on the spear, but the Achaean would not let go, screaming in pain as he endeavored to disarm his opponent. When the second warrior pressed his attack, Phaethon released the spear. The injured man fell back, still holding the spear, blood spreading from his thigh.

Phaethon caught the second warrior's spear thrust on his shield, deflecting it upward. As the spear's tip passed by, it cut Phaethon's neck, and blood gushed from the wound. The bleeding stopped quickly, and the wound closed. The Achaean stepped back in shock as Phaethon drew his sword.

Antilochus and the third Achaean hurried forward to join the fight, with Antilochus taking the center as his two warriors attacked Phaethon's flanks. Despite the ferocity of their attack, Phaethon remained untouched, pushing each strike aside with blurred motions of his shield and sword.

Astrid ran to the fallen warrior. He had pulled the spear from his thigh, and it lay on the ground beside him. She checked his wound and saw no venous or arterial bleeding, only the steady pooling of blood from torn flesh. She tore a strip from the hem of her nightdress to bandage the wound. He grabbed her hand and smiled grimly. "I will recover," he said. "Go."

Astrid grasped his spear's wooden shaft at its center; she felt the warrior's blood sticky on her palm. "Bind the wound to slow the bleeding," she said, handing him the strip of cloth.

"By the gods!"

Astrid heard the voice behind her and turned to see Myia standing in front of the tent, sword in hand. The three cats stood frozen a few feet in front of her, staring at Phaethon and the Achaeans.

"Myia, take the cats back into the tent," Astrid shouted.

"I tried . . . They ran to you."

Still holding the injured warrior's spear, Astrid saw the cats gather together as a blue light enfolded them and a tremor passed through the ground. She watched Swarm take shape a few yards in front of Myia, as black as if the rising dawn had forged night itself into the contours of predatory rage.

She turned back to the fight and saw Phaethon explode forward, his sword gashing one of the warriors on the shoulder just above the edge of his shield. The man fell back; his arm—still holding his shield—dangled uselessly at his side. He wavered on his feet, then lost consciousness and fell to the ground. Phaethon drove his shield into Antilochus, knocking him onto the sand, then attacked the third Achaean. The force of Phaethon's blow shattered his spear. The warrior retreated and drew his sword.

As Antilochus and his remaining warrior regrouped, Swarm moved between them, a low growl rumbling through her chest. Phaethon saw the cat and stepped back quickly. He lowered his hands to his sides as a vortex of blue light engulfed him.

"Stop him," Astrid screamed.

She grabbed a tree limb that protruded from the fire burning in front of the tent and thrust the burning end into the vortex. The flames exploded as if enveloped in pure oxygen, knocking her back. Astrid saw Phaethon's twisted form convulse within the blinding corona and heard him scream in pain. He recovered and threw the burning log aside. Astrid stared, frozen as the blue vortex returned, and his broken body grew into the reptilian nightmare she remembered from her home. A snake's smooth head stared at them impassively, and bronze scales covered the impossibly muscled body.

Astrid did not notice the monster's tail until its blow sent her skidding across the ground, the pain of broken ribs burning through her left side.

Swarm lunged at the Phaethon, moving low across the sand to strike with extended claws, then retreat before it could react. Her blows scraped across the scales without effect until she found the softer flesh of the monster's belly. Blood gushed from torn muscle as Swarm repeatedly struck at the vulnerable flesh. The monster fell back in shock, even though his wounds closed almost immediately.

Antilochus, Myia, and the uninjured Achaean joined Swarm in the attack. Instinctively, they circled Phaethon, each striking then retreating when he turned toward them, allowing another to attack his unguarded flank. Ignoring the pain in her left side, Astrid joined them. Holding the fallen warrior's spear in her right hand, she repeatedly struck at the vulnerability Swarm had discovered.

Initially, the tactic seemed to work as Phaethon lurched from one attacker to the next, steadily driven backward. Although his wounds quickly closed, the monster seemed to weaken, drained by the effort of healing its injuries. Suddenly, the lizard-thing feinted toward Antilochus, leaving his flank exposed. Myia ran forward, sword raised to strike.

"Myia, no," Antilochus shouted.

As Myia ran within the radius of the monster's deadly tail, it struck her hard on the side. She skidded across the ground to collide with a stone bench, her back bent at a terrifying angle.

Enraged, Astrid intensified her attack, thrusting with the spear until she felt her arm go numb, her vision a narrow circle through which she struck at the armored nightmare. She did not see Phaethon strike Swarm until the cat fell at her feet, blood spreading from her shoulder down her dark fur. Astrid reached instinctively to touch the wounded animal and felt the tingle of transformation run up her arm. She pulled back in reflex.

Astrid saw the last of Antilochus' warriors fall, his throat torn out by the monster's bronze claws, blood flowing across the sand. Antilochus pressed forward alone, the ferocity of his blows driving the reptilian monster back. She knew he could not sustain the effort—just as she realized she could do little by herself to help him.

Astrid placed her hands on the injured cat, embracing the transformation. Unlike her first merging with Swarm, this was urgent, convulsive. Astrid did not resist as her physicality collapsed into the knot at the base of her skull and her mind accelerated through layers of memories, through the metamorphosis of her body, falling blindly into the singularity of Swarm's undiluted fury. The cat's wound and her broken ribs faded to a distant ache.

Watching through the green and blue hues of Swarm's feline vision, Astrid saw Antilochus fall back, weakened by exhaustion and driven by the monster's inexhaustible strength. She felt the combined wills of Swarm's faceted mind carry her forward as the cat prepared to attack. Desperately clinging to her reason, hoping to guide Swarm's attack, Astrid searched for some weakness in the armored nightmare. A tremor under the soft skin of its belly caught her attention, and she concentrated on the spasm.

As she did so, the scaled body seemed to lose its solidity, appearing as a projection of light surrounding a shadowy, vaguely human form. The injured body convulsed in a clumsy parody of the monster's fluid movements, and

Astrid recognized the broken puppeteer who guided the monster's attacks. Somehow, she had penetrated Phaethon's enchantments. Suddenly, Astrid felt Swarm's rage fill the dimensionless space her consciousness shared with the three animal minds as the cat prepared to strike. Overwhelmed by the predator's instincts, her focus evaporated, and the scaled body returned to solidity, hiding the dark kernel of Phaethon's true form.

Astrid felt Swarm's legs uncoil with exhilarating power, driving her sharply forward, jaws seizing the vulnerable tissue where the monster's belly met its legs. She tasted the sweet saline of blood, a feral thrill overwhelming her human revulsion. Swarm's jaws held muscle and sinew tightly, staying inside the deadly radius of the thick tail, its bone-crushing blows thudding ineffectually on the ground behind her. Suddenly, the muscle itself tore from the reptilian body, and the cat fell back.

Astrid saw the monster strike Antilochus on the shield, throwing him across the sand. As it closed on Nestor's unconscious son, Astrid embraced Swarm's instincts and drove forward. She felt the cat's teeth—her teeth—penetrate the unprotected skin on the inside of the creature's thigh. Blood filled her mouth—as sweet as life, as salty as death. Astrid felt as if she would lose herself completely in Swarm's fury.

Phaethon screamed in pain, his goal of carrying a living cat to Strachys lost in his rage. "Separate, by the gods, separate or I will separate you."

Phaethon clawed at Swarm's back, ignoring the jaws clamped on his muscles, tearing at her as if he could expose the three littermates by force alone. Pain exploded through the body Astrid shared with the cat as the monster's repeated blows broke bones, as they separated her ribs from her spine. Her jaws released their hold as a final blow sent her rolling across the sand. Swarm tried to find her feet, but her torn muscles and broken bones failed to respond. Staring through the cat's eyes, Astrid saw the bronze claws shine in the low sunlight, accelerating toward her in a killing blow.

The blow did not come. The stubby hand with its three claws stopped above her as if the monster had turned to stone. Astrid joined her will with the cats and tried to roll away, but Swarm remained frozen in place. It seemed as if she had fallen into a merciful insensibility at the approach of death—almost as if time had stopped.

Astrid saw a woman enter her field of vision, crossing the frozen carnage with immeasurable grace.

Chapter 28

Immobile as a painted lion fallen beneath a painted hunter on a buried potsherd, Astrid—still sharing Swarm's body—could only watch as the woman passed before her. The woman wore a warrior's armor over a long tunic the color of the Aegean. Tight braids trailed from a gold helmet that reflected the light of dawn like burning magnesium across the camp. She carried a spear and shield, the muscles in her arms swelling with strength modulated by grace. A broad sash—little more than light and shadow—flowed across her gold cuirass. When Astrid saw it, the pain of her injuries faded, and she felt a bloodlust rise in her chest, a feral urge to strike at Phaethon's frozen form.

Astrid recognized the sash from Homer's description—it was the Aegis, worn into battle by Athena, the warrior goddess. The Aegis overcame reason to drive men into bloody slaughter, engulfing their bodies, minds, and souls in a lust for combat, filling their ears with the roars of a thousand beasts. An ancient horror seemed to float across the shimmering cloth—a woman's face twisted by torment and framed in a storm of venomous serpents, crying out in wrath against the world, against life itself. It was the face of Medusa.

Astrid watched Athena move with terrible beauty through the carnage surrounding her. A look of revulsion crossed the goddess' face, and her grip on the spear tightened in a spasm of rage as she walked past Phaethon's reptilian manifestation.

"Who brings this abomination to my battlefield?" The goddess glared at the nightmare standing frozen before her.

Turning from Phaethon's immobile form in disgust, Athena walked to the warrior whose shoulder he had slashed. She kneeled in the blood-soaked sand and touched the injury with a mother's caress. The wound closed, and the warrior struggled to rise, only to fall back in sleep as Athena placed her hand behind his head. She lowered him gently to the sand as if laying a child in its crib. She performed the same healing ritual on the warrior who had fallen with Phaethon's spear in his thigh.

The goddess walked to Antilochus, who still held his sword and shield. Seeing no external wound, she ran her hands over his unconscious body like a physician, pushing fingers deep into his unresponsive flesh. Suddenly, he gasped for breath, his back arching, limbs pressing against the dirt, only to fall back into sleep as the goddess placed her hand on his forehead. "Rest, brave Antilochus," she said. "It is not your time."

Athena walked to the warrior whose throat Phaethon had torn away. She kneeled at his side like a nurse soothing a dying patient and stroked the man's brow. "I cannot help you," she grieved, tears spreading across her cheek. "You have already gone to the underworld, murdered by this . . ." Athena glared at Phaethon's reptilian form, "this thing."

She saw Myia, laying broken beside the stone bench, looked down at the sword still in the young woman's grasp, and smiled. Athena touched her forehead, and Myia stirred fitfully, her back straightening as she rolled away from the stone and fell into a peaceful sleep. "You will awaken, healed and refreshed, my warrior princess."

The goddess walked past Phaethon to stand at Swarm's side. She kneeled beside the great cat, looked into her eyes, and ran her hands over her fur. Athena's touch resonated through the nerves Astrid shared with Chessie, Greystoke, and Audrey.

"Why do I sense you are more than the beast you appear to be?"

Still paralyzed but not numb to pain, Astrid felt Athena's fingers burn into Swarm's shoulders, welding torn flesh and bone in a divine fire, pressing separated ribs into their junctions with the great cat's spine. Screams of pain filled her chest, unable to escape the paralysis that held her. The pain subsided as the healing progressed, and well being surged through the body she shared with Swarm, followed by soft darkness as three feline minds drew apart and settled into sleep. Astrid felt her own physicality expand from the tangled nerves of her brain stem, and she returned to her human form. She found herself sitting in the dirt, her three cats sleeping beside her.

Athena stared in shock. "What enchantment is this?"

Astrid crawled from beneath Phaethon's frozen attack, leaving her animals to sleep. She took her feet and faced the goddess. "Are you Athena?"

Athena stepped back. "How can you see me when I have become invisible to human eyes? How can you speak when I've frozen time itself?"

"I don't know," Astrid said awkwardly.

"Who are you? How did you take the form of this great cat?"

"My name is Astrid," she said as the goddess looked down from more than a foot above her. "These animals are my companions. I do not know how, but they can join their bodies and minds to form the great cat you saw. Sometimes, they merge with me as well."

"Did you bring this abomination to my battlefield?" Athena demanded, gesturing at the monster with her spear. As the goddess raised her arm, Astrid's eyes fell once more on the Aegis. She fought to contain the blood-lust rising within her. Athena smiled, and the Aegis faded to a shadow.

"No," Astrid said, "he came to my home and stole one of my animals. I came here to recover it and was befriended by Nestor, Odysseus, and—"

"You know these men?"

"Yes. They're my friends."

"Your friends?" Athena laughed in surprise. "Like the great cat, you are more than you seem." She gestured toward Phaethon with her spear. "How did this monster come here?"

"He wanted to steal one of my animals. I don't know how he found me."

"And you fought him?" The goddess asked, like a teacher seeing a trace of promise in a dim student.

Astrid nodded.

"Then, what is this thing?" Athena mused as she touched the creature with the tip of her spear. Blue light spread from the golden blade to engulf the beast, and the reptilian head writhed like a snake caught in a trap, jaws snapping futilely in the air. The bronze scales dissolved, and the muscled limbs and tail withered, leaving a man's broken remains at Athena's feet. She stepped back in horror.

"Surprised to see me, auntie?" Phaethon challenged in a pitiful rasp.

"I do not know you."

"These family reunions can be awkward. We really should get together more often."

Athena's gray eyes narrowed. "Phaethon?"

"No welcoming embraces? No joyful tears and kisses?"

"How is it that you live? What enchantments brought you here?"

"I'm touched. You do care."

"Impertinent mongrel," she swore. "Have you learned no humility?"

"Oh, I have learned much, auntie. I've learned what happens when the gods amuse themselves with mortals. I've learned how they deny their own offspring—"

"Silence."

Phaethon stared up at her, a smile on his charred lips. "I've learned the worst Zeus can do. Why would I fear you?"

Athena pressed the point of her spear against his throat. Struggling against his injuries, Phaethon presented the unburned side of his neck to the blade. "Come, auntie, end me. Do you think I would count it as a loss?"

The goddess lowered her weapon. "You do not deserve my spear."

"Bitch," Phaethon cursed, the words turning into cries of rage against her, against the gods, against life itself. Athena raised her spear toward the sky, sunlight reflecting from its tip like nuclear fire across the ocean where a dark cloud gathered.

"I do not know what enchantments brought you here," Athena said, looking down at Phaethon's broken body, "but if you ever return to this field, I swear by Zeus, I will inflict such torments on you as to make what is coming feel like a lover's kiss."

The cloud approached like an incoming storm.

"A swarm of insects?" Phaethon smirked. "How trite."

Astrid sensed the fear beneath his boast.

"Can't you think of anything original?" Phaethon mocked. He raised the blue vortex of enchantments as Athena's curse engulfed him.

For a moment, the protective ball Astrid had seen at Sigrid's home formed around him, only to collapse as countless insects threw themselves against its surface. Some penetrated the oily rainbows that swirled across it, though many more fell broken to the sand. Their deaths did not diminish the cloud swarming around him. Screaming, Phaethon dragged himself to the ocean, the buzzing, swarming cloud following until the metallic ball disappeared into the surf. After the span of a held breath, a blue light boiled beneath the water, and the snake's head crested the surface, only to be driven back underwater. The scene repeated as the cloud followed him out to sea.

The goddess turned to Astrid. "How is it you can see me? Why haven't my enchantments left you sleeping like the others?"

"I swear, I don't know."

"I pray you're not lying." Athena placed her hand on Astrid's forehead, The pain of a dozen migraines crashed through her brain as Astrid felt an alien presence probe her awareness, her emotions, her memories. The goddess removed her hand as Astrid fought through the rubble of sense and memory swirling in her mind.

"Circe . . ." the goddess said the syllables slowly, weighing each sound. "I should have known."

Astrid trembled on all fours, fingers digging into the sand, holding onto the earth itself, waiting for the her mind to clear. She rolled onto her hip and looked up at the goddess. "I could have told you that," Astrid said as she caught her breath. "You didn't have to turn my mind inside out."

"Don't be impudent," Athena said crossly. "Remember who I am."

Astrid tried to take her feet. A synesthetic spiral engulfed her senses, and she fell back.

"I'm not sure my cousin fully understands the web she has spun," Athena said, frowning, "but it seems she has entangled us both."

Astrid tried to stand once more. She raised herself to a single knee and waited as the world and her senses realigned. She took her feet.

"Help me," Astrid pleaded to the goddess. "I just want to find my animals and go home."

"Tread lightly," Athena warned. "There is more at play here than you understand."

"What is it? Why won't you help me?"

Athena did not acknowledge Astrid's pleas but lifted from the sandy ground like a great sea bird. Her body grew as she rose into the sky, first casting a shadow across the women's tent, then blocking the sun from all of Nestor's camp. As the goddess continued to rise, she spread herself across the sky, becoming as thin as mist. Astrid's breath caught in her chest as the sun shined through, and Athena vanished.

Astrid saw the cats awaken and kneeled among them. She felt their bodies for injuries but found none. She closed her eyes and touched them as Claire had shown her, calling their minds to the foreground of her awareness, searching for some lingering trauma, but Athena's touch had erased it from their memories.

"Why have you forgotten what I remember?" she asked as she stroked the animals in turn. She recalled Phaethon's crushing blows and the pitiless fire of Athena's healing touch. "It's just as well."

She saw Antilochus, Myia, and the surviving warriors stir. Astrid rushed to Myia's side and kneeled beside her. "Are you all right?"

"I feel fine," Myia said as she sat up and tested her body for injury. "No, I feel better than that . . . strong, rested. What happened?"

"It's over. The monster is gone."

Myia looked at her with a puzzled expression. "Monster?"

Astrid heard voices cry out. She saw Antilochus kneel beside the dead warrior, his comrades joining him in a chorus of grief.

She turned back to Myia. "What do you remember?"

"There was an intruder. He fought well and killed one of the Achaeans. I joined the fight, and we pushed him back."

"Is that all?"

Myia paused. "I remember him striking me with his shield. I lost consciousness."

Antilochus approached the two women as the surviving Achaeans remained beside their fallen comrade.

"Are you hurt?" he asked.

"No, I'm well," Astrid said. "Did you see her?"

Antilochus seemed puzzled. "See who?"

"Didn't you see—" Astrid began, only to stop herself as she saw the confusion on his face. "Nothing, I'm just babbling. I must have been knocked unconscious. What happened?"

"We defeated the stranger," he said. "He ran through the ships into the water and escaped."

"There was nothing else? Nothing unusual?"

Antilochus turned the question over in his mind. It seemed as if he was struggling to articulate a thought that would not take form. "No," he said, "other than his speed. He fought like Achilles himself. Why do you ask?"

"It's not important," Astrid said as she noticed the crowd gathering around them. She saw Nestor and a party of warriors push through the crowd and ran to the horseman. She threw her arms around him as tears filled her eyes. "Thank god you're safe."

Nestor held her close, his cheek pressed against hers. "Raiders attacked Odysseus' camp," he said. "We drove them off." He grasped her shoulders and looked into her eyes. "Are you all right?"

Astrid nodded. "What about Odysseus? Your men?"

"Odysseus is well. We lost not a man but killed many of the raiders."

"Who were they? Trojans?" Antilochus asked.

"No," Nestor said. "I believe they came from the north."

"Sea people?" Antilochus asked in surprise.

"What do you mean, 'sea people?'" Astrid asked.

"Tribesmen from the plains to the north have moved into our lands—fierce, merciless people. They sail these seas, raiding as they please," Nestor explained. "They've been growing bolder, but such men would not attack an encampment like this. They prefer to prey on the defenseless."

"Nestor . . ." Astrid said, "I think this has something to do with me."

"With you?"

"The man who took my animal came here. He tried to take another."

Nestor stared at her with concern. "Tell me what happened."

Believing Athena had altered Myia and Antilochus' memories of the attack, Astrid described the battle slowly, feigning confusion. As she expected, Antilochus grew impatient and told his version of the events as she listened. He remembered neither Swarm's appearance, Phaethon's transformation, nor Athena's intervention. He did not mention the injuries to the two warriors Athena had healed. Myia concurred with his version of events. Astrid noticed they sounded oddly detached, as if they were repeating a story instead of sharing a lived memory.

"We lost a man. The raider slashed his throat," Antilochus said, gesturing at his fallen comrade, "then fled into the sea. I don't know if he drowned."

Nestor walked to the fallen warrior and kneeled to examine him. He looked up and called to Astrid, who kneeled beside him.

"This man was not killed by a sword," he whispered, pointing at the ragged wound where the man's throat was almost completely torn out.

Astrid looked on the face of the young warrior. He was handsome, with an innocence that reminded her of Antilochus.

"This looks like it was done by a wild beast," Nestor said.

"Is there someplace we can talk," Astrid whispered, "alone?"

Spike awoke from a deep sleep. He remembered dreaming he had joined his littermates in their struggle against the man who had taken him, and a wild joy filled his mind. Spike remembered how the woman had shared Swarm's body and remembered the stranger who had stopped the battle and brought them back from death. He had shared their pain, just as he shared the goddess' healing touch. Spike reached forward with his paws and raised his hind legs, stretching his spine in a long, downward arc. Hungry, Spike walked from beneath the outcropping of rocks where he had slept. It was close to the granary with its endless supply of rodents, yet far enough from the spotted tomcat so as not to disturb their uneasy truce.

He slowed as he approached the colony. As usual, the spotted tomcat hissed a warning but did not approach him. Spike lifted his head to test the fragrant morning air. He detected only the lingering smells of mice and rats, of cats returning to their rest after the night's hunting. Spike looked for motion in the shadows and listened for the sound of small feet crossing the rubbish under the building. He sensed nothing and left to search the meadow near the village for birds or other prey.

He saw a bird perched in a low bush, facing away from him. Spike eased into a crouch and silently inched forward, coming almost close enough to strike. He heard a sound behind him, and the bird flew away. Frustrated, Spike turned and saw someone approach, barefooted, wearing a simple kilt, and carrying a clay bowl. As he drew closer, Spike saw it was one of the children who played near the granary.

Spike retreated under the bush and watched the boy come near. He sensed no danger from him but remained cautious. This boy was not like the others who threw rocks at him and the cats in the colony. He moved slowly and spoke in reassuring tones like those Spike remembered from his home. He watched the boy kneel and reach into the bowl. Spike smelled the cooked fish in his outstretched hand.

Emboldened by hunger—and reassured by memories of home and human kindness—Spike approached cautiously. He stopped safely out of reach, staring through sage-green eyes as the boy tossed the fish onto a patch of dry grass and stepped back. Spike approached in a series of shortening arcs, his path shaped by the tension between his instinctive mistrust of strangers and his growing hunger. He took the fish in his mouth and backed away, returning to the bush to eat. He did not take his eyes off the child who sat cross-legged in the nearby grass.

Chapter 29

Phaethon waded ashore at the rendezvous with Proxonos and his raiders. As he lost buoyancy, he stumbled against the stern of their beached ship, exhausted, the welts raised by Athena's insects burning through his concealing enchantments. He lowered himself back into the momentary comfort of the saltwater and cursed softly. "Bitch."

Phaethon fought through his pain onto the beach. Proxonos approached him without speaking, spit into the sand at his feet, and limped away, a dirty cloth binding a gash on his thigh. Less than half of the fifty raiders he had led into the Achaean camp sat scattered across the sand. Many were wounded, their improvised bandages soaked with blood. One man lay delirious on a fleece near a handful of warriors who stared into a campfire, poking the coals with sticks and ignoring their comrade's moans.

"What happened?" Phaethon asked as he collapsed to sit cross-legged among the surviving raiders. Proxonos stared silently.

"Did you kill Odysseus?" Phaethon pressed.

Proxonos stepped forward, his hand on his sword. "You son of a whore."

"I take it Odysseus lives."

"There were too many of them," Proxonos complained bitterly. "You sent us into slaughter."

The raiders around him grunted in agreement. Some stood, hands on their swords.

"Tell me what happened, then you may kill me," Phaethon said.

"An Achaean saw us approach. He cried out before we could reach him. His comrades swarmed over us like ants."

"Like ants . . . it seems to be a common theme," Phaethon mused. He reached down for a handful of moist sand and rubbed it across his welts. "I did not expect there would be sentries."

"He wasn't armed. He'd just left his tent to piss."

Phaethon laughed ironically. "The gods have truly cursed us. And then?"

"We fought well," Proxonos said. "I engaged Odysseus and would have killed him, but the Achaeans kept coming."

"Odysseus' men?"

"And others from across the camp. One called Nestor brought the most."

"Nestor? The old man?"

"That 'old man' fought well. One of my best warriors fell to his spear." Proxonos pointed at the welts covering Phaethon's skin. "It seems you failed as well. Did your girl do this? Or was it her cat?"

"A goddess intervened . . . Athena."

At the mention of the goddess, Proxonos' men took their feet, shouting curses. A short warrior with dark hair and a blood-soaked bandage on his arm forced his way forward. "You said nothing about immortals!"

A tall raider, showing no wounds, drew his sword. "I say we kill him now, leave him for the gulls to feed on."

Proxonos raised his hand and the shouts fell to a low rumble. "It seems you're not popular," he told Phaethon.

"Kill me, and you forfeit your final payment," Phaethon said apathetically.

"I don't care for this fool or his treasure," Proxonos told his raiders as he walked away through the crowd. "You decide if he lives."

Phaethon watched as they argued, a circle of rage closing around him.

"Kill me," he said. "I have nothing left but my shame and nothing to offer you but revenge."

A few of the raiders seemed to listen, disarmed by his indifference to death or his offer of vengeance, but the majority continued to rage at him.

"But, if you come with me," Phaethon said, raising his voice, "I will not only take you to a healer who can treat your wounds, but also I will give you each an additional payment equal to that already promised."

Phaethon watched as the currents of rage running through the raiders seemed to subside. "And I swear, I will give you vengeance on the men who killed your comrades."

Proxonos laughed from the back of the crowd. "You have balls," he shouted. "You are a fool . . . but you have balls."

Although the raiders continued to argue among themselves, Phaethon sensed their sentiment was turning in his favor. "So," he shouted at Proxonos, "it seems your men are considering my offer."

Proxonos stepped to the front of the mob. "No, my friend. They have simply come to realize what I have always known."

"And what's that?"

"That they can always kill you later."

Astrid, Myia, and Antilochus joined Nestor in his tent; Hecamede brought wine and stayed at Astrid's request. They listened incredulously as Astrid finished her account of the battle, including Phaethon's transformation into the lizard creature, the joining of her body and mind with Swarm, their defeat at the lizard-things hands, and Athena's intervention. Antilochus and Myia protested when Astrid's story diverged from their recollections.

"My son, the gods have been known to single out one man in a crowd and help him, while remaining invisible to the rest," Nestor cautioned. "We know the gods favor Astrid. Hear her out."

Astrid described how Athena had healed the fallen warriors and driven Phaethon away in a cloud of stinging insects. When she finished, Antilochus and Myia began to argue.

"Except for the man he killed, my warriors showed no signs of injury," Antilochus insisted. "And we fought a man. I saw no monster, no goddess, no great cat."

"The immortals often cloud men's minds," Nestor reminded him.

"I've seen the great cat take form, as well as other things that make me believe her," Myia added as she turned to Astrid. "But how could you join your body with these animals?"

"I don't know, Myia. It happened once before, and then, like now, the cats made it happen."

"These animals carry powerful magic," Hecamede said, frowning.

"You say we fought a monster?" Antilochus interrupted.

"Yes. Are you sure you don't remember?" Astrid pressed.

"I remember fighting the man you called Phaethon. I remember his speed, his tactical skills. I remember how he killed my warrior with a sword across the throat and fled into the sea."

"My son," Nestor interrupted, "you saw the wound on the dead man's throat. It was no sword wound."

Antilochus frowned.

"And look at your shield." Nestor lifted the bronze disk onto his lap and ran his hand over the gouges that crossed its surface. "Three deep gouges running parallel across the bronze . . . These did not come from swords or spear points, but they could have been come from the claws of some monstrous beast."

"The gouges in the shield could have come from the great cat," Antilochus said, staring down at Audrey, Chessie, and Greystoke, "so could the wound to the dead man's throat."

Nestor lifted Audrey to his lap. She squirmed, then grew calm as he stroked her long fur. He raised her front paw and pressed its center, forcing the claws to extend. Audrey growled a warning.

"Cats have four claws. The two center claws are aligned, with another claw on each side," he said and released Audrey, who jumped to the floor. "It's unlikely they would leave three gouges on your shield—not impossible, but two or four cuts would be more likely. Also, their claws are not hard enough to cut this deeply into bronze; they would only leave scratches. And don't forget, the cat serves and protects Astrid. Why would it attack us?"

Myia leaned forward. "I remember something happening with the cats. I remember them moving together toward the creature—" She stopped herself suddenly.

"No," Astrid said excitedly, "you said 'creature,' not 'man,' not 'warrior.' Do not correct yourself, just let the words out."

Myia stirred uncomfortably. Hecamede placed her arm around her.

Astrid kneeled in front of Nestor's son, her hand on his knee. "Antilochus," she said, "I have an idea. Will you trust me?"

He nodded.

"Don't just tell us what you remember. Try to see the battle in your mind as it happened. Describe what you see, without judgment or explanation."

The young warrior closed his eyes and seemed to struggle with his thoughts. "It's difficult . . ." he murmured after a time. "I remember what happened, but the images . . ."

"I trained you to remember your battles in detail," Nestor said, a look of surprise crossing his face, "to recreate them in your mind and step through each move, to discover what you could have done differently. It's an ability shared by all skilled warriors. Why would it fail you now, if not through some enchantment?"

"I don't know," Antilochus said, closing his eyes in thought. "I can bring images of the battle to my mind, but I feel like I'm making them up to fit some story. They don't seem real; they lack detail—"

"Wait," Myia interrupted excitedly, "I remember now. There was a great cat, the one you call Swarm. I stood beside it as we fought."

"It was to my right," Antilochus said without thinking. He caught his breath and seemed surprised.

"There was a creature," Myia added, "a monster . . . like a snake."

"Or a crocodile," Antilochus said, his voice rising. "It stood on two legs,- like a man."

"It struck me with its tail, and I lost consciousness," Myia added.

"Antilochus," Astrid pressed, "when you fought, where were your men?"

He spoke without hesitation, confusion replaced with the excitement of discovery. "They fought beside me. No, only at first. They were wounded and unable to continue. I fought alone, beside the great cat."

Astrid looked up at Nestor, and he helped her to her feet. "It would seem you have penetrated a goddess' enchantment," he said.

"I did not see you, only the cat," Antilochus continued, speaking excitedly. He looked at Astrid as the realization seized him. "You say you had become one with the animal?"

Astrid nodded.

"But how can that be? Are you an enchantress? Are you an animal yourself, taking the form of a woman?"

Astrid took his hand. "Antilochus, I am neither an enchantress nor an animal, and I do not know how the cats can join their bodies with mine. I do know that they are not evil."

"What was it like?" Myia asked. "Did you become Swarm?"

"It has only happened twice. I didn't exactly become Swarm, but I seemed to share Swarm's body with these cats," Astrid explained, looking at Audrey, Greystoke, and Chessie. "And, I was terrified both times."

"But you controlled the animal," Antilochus said. "When it fought beside me, it seemed to understand what I was doing, to plan."

"I had some influence, but much of the time Swarm—the cats—followed their own instincts." She took his hand. "Antilochus, they helped me save you, Myia, and your men. Please, don't fear them."

Antilochus nodded silently.

"I don't remember seeing Athena," Myia said.

"She came after Phaethon's blow left you unconscious," Astrid explained.

"How is it you remember her?" Myia asked.

"I don't know. Even Athena seemed surprised. Perhaps it has something to do with the cats or the enchantments surrounding them," Astrid said. "What worries me is that Phaethon found us. I didn't think he knew where we were."

"Could he have used the same magic you used to locate your missing animals?" Nestor asked.

"Perhaps . . ." Astrid trailed off, retreating into thought.

"What is it?"

"Nestor," she said slowly, "I'm no longer sure this is your fight."

Nestor ran his fingers over the marks on Antilochus' shield. "It is my fight," he said with conviction, "now more than ever."

Antilochus and Myia shouted their agreement.

"No," Astrid argued. "I asked you to help me fight a man and recover my animals. I assumed that enough warriors could defeat Phaethon—even in his reptilian form—but I was wrong. Your warrior's death is on me."

"The Fates determined his death," Nestor said. "It is my responsibility to avenge it."

Astrid shook her head. "I brought that monster down on him. Phaethon defeated all of us—even Swarm, a creature with the strength of a lion—and he did so easily. Had it not been for Athena, he would have killed us." She took Nestor's hand. "I cannot be the cause of more deaths."

"We won't make the same mistakes," Nestor argued.

"He'll know we're coming," Astrid countered.

"We can plan for that."

"And the raiders you fought in Odysseus' camp?"

"We routed his riff-raff."

"Nestor, please—"

"None of that matters," Nestor interrupted. "I have learned that the gods favor men who act without fear or hesitation. This is my fight now, not just yours—he has attacked my camp and killed one of my men. We leave in the morning. Antilochus, you know what must be done to finish preparations. Hecamede, Myia, go with my son. Help him."

Nestor watched in silence as they left the tent, then sat beside Astrid. "I sense there is more on your mind," he said.

"He uses enchantments to fight. His wounds close on their own. How can we defeat him?"

"He is mortal. You've told me of his injuries, his mistakes. We'll find a way. Besides, you have your own magic." He glanced at the three cats resting at Astrid's feet. Audrey looked up at him and meowed softly.

Astrid shook her head. "When Athena stripped away his enchantments, I saw his injuries in detail. Half his body was burned—charred to the bone in places. But despite that, he raged at her—he raged at a goddess—with no thought for consequences. It was like he hated everything—the world, the gods, even himself. When Athena held her spear point to his throat, he begged her to kill him and cursed her when she refused."

"What does that tell you?"

"He has nothing to lose. He does not fear death or pain, and he will not stop. He fights like a berserker—"

Nestor put his hand on her shoulder. "That kind of rage is not a strength. It clouds the judgment. It causes a man to make mistakes, to take unnecessary risks . . . it can lead him into death."

"Nestor, he terrifies me. He is no ordinary warrior."

The horseman stared at her for a time. Astrid saw something new in his eyes, something hard, merciless—frightening.

"Neither am I," he said.

Spike crouched beneath a low bush away from the granary and his uneasy interactions with the cats of the colony. He knew the boy would come soon. He sensed it from the angle of the shadows around him, from the subtly shifting smells as the wildflowers released their morning pollen, from the hum of flying insects, and a thousand other signs. The emptiness churning in his belly reminded him of the food the child would bring. He scanned the grass through partly closed, sage-green eyes.

As Spike had anticipated, the boy appeared at the edge of the meadow and walked toward him, making soft repeated sounds, much like the woman who had cared for Spike and his littermates. The boy placed the clay bowl on the ground and sat beside it, cross-legged in the grass.

In the days since he had first brought the food, the boy had gradually moved his offerings closer to himself. Although Spike had accepted his proximity, he had remained cautious, always gauging the perimeter of the boy's reach before approaching. Now, Spike noticed that the bowl sat within that circle of risk. He remained a safe distance away as hunger, fear, and growing trust of this human contended within him. The boy sat still, the breeze stirring his dark hair.

Spike stretched his head toward the bowl, took a large piece of fish, and stepped back, still wary. The child smiled as Spike began to eat.

Chapter 30

Athena strode through the hall of Circe's palace, a half-dozen Nereids scurrying behind her, their welcoming intentions swirling like seafoam in the goddess' wake. As she neared the marble atrium, Circe greeted her, throwing her arms around the daughter of Zeus and kissing her cheeks.

"Welcome, cousin," she said, smiling. "You grace Aeaea with your visit."

"As you honor me with your hospitality," Athena said, returning the greeting and the embrace.

"I trust my Nereids have helped you refresh from your long journey?"

"The bath and perfumed oils have washed away the battlefield's dust."

"I see they've found something suitable for you to wear," Circe said, admiring Athena's pale blue gown.

"My armor has always suited me."

"Yes, but the Aegis would have frightened my Nereids." Circe laughed. "And who knows what it would have done to the animals."

Athena smiled as she remembered how bears, wolves, and great cats walked peacefully among the deer, goats, and swine on Circe's island. "I had forgotten Aeaea's beauty," she said. "It is a welcome change from wind-swept Olympus."

"Come," Circe said, taking Athena by the hand and leading her into the atrium. "I've prepared a feast you will find pleasing—even by Olympian standards."

Skillfully fashioned bowls of gold, silver, ceramic, polished wood, and semi-precious stone—filled with fruit, meats, fresh fish, grains, bread, honey, and other delicacies—covered the marble slab that served as Circe's table. A golden bowl of ambrosia—the favored food of the gods—sat at its center. Circe gestured to a mound of tapestries, fleeces, and cushions, all carefully arranged to seem as if they had been scattered artlessly across the stone. Athena took her place as a pair of eager Nereids tried to fluff the pillows for her comfort. They stepped back when the goddess glared at them and arranged the cushions herself.

Circe leaned across the table and set two gold cups between her and the goddess of wisdom. The cups bore images of forests and animals, of warriors and lovers, embossed in the metal with a skill beyond human abilities.

"Is this my brother's work?" Athena asked.

"Yes. Hephaestus' touch is unmistakable and without equal," Circe said. She lifted a green glass bottle from the table and removed the cork with a chrome-plated mechanical extractor.

Athena frowned as she watched the gears and screws of the unknown mechanism at work. "I see you've been traveling," she said.

Circe nodded. "It's a delightful California Cabernet I found during one of my visits. I've saved it for just such an occasion. I find our own wines too simple, like so many of our people."

"My father frowns on such adventures, and he would not care for your returning with souvenirs."

Circe smiled as she filled Athena's cup. "He frowns, but does not forbid."

"He gives you too much latitude."

"Perhaps he sees that pleasure and invention are as essential as law," Circe retorted, filling her cup.

"Perhaps he does not see everything you do."

"One of the benefits of Aeaea's distance from Olympus."

An involuntary smile crossed Athena's lips as she drank from the golden cup. "I enjoy our little games," she said, "but these people you insist on visiting . . . they're lost. They do not honor us, they do not honor each other, they do not even honor their own world." Athena passed the cup under her nose, and inhaled the fragrant vapors, eyes closed.

"It's true," Circe admitted, "they're killing their planet with war and poisons, and their minds with stupidity, hatred, and greed. Still, their world does have its attractions." She raised her cup.

"You don't belong there."

"No, cousin, a goddess of wisdom and honorable struggle does not belong there. I seem to do rather well." Circe gestured to Annape, who walked around the table to refill Athena's cup.

"So would my whore of a sister, I imagine." Athena watched the stream of dark wine shine in the light of Circe's lamps. "Does she join you?"

"Aphrodite? I see her on occasion. We've dined once or twice, but usually, we go our separate ways. She finds my tastes too rough."

"Tastes in men?"

"Among other things . . ." Circe smiled. She lifted the golden bowl of ambrosia, ladled a portion onto a plate of fine silver rimmed with gold, and handed it to her guest. As Athena ate the food of the immortals, Circe offered her a gold platter with a neatly sliced French baguette and an assortment of cheeses arranged across it.

"My ambrosia cannot equal that found on Olympus, but you may enjoy these delicacies I brought back from . . ." Circe smiled as she chose her words, "from my journeys. Try the Camembert. It's ripened to perfection."

"The food of mortals holds little interest for me," Athena said, her eyes not moving from the gold platter.

The enchantress smiled knowingly as she sliced through the cheese's white rind, exposing a soft, ivory center. She placed a wedge of it on a round of bread and passed it to Athena. The goddess of wisdom took a bite of the strange delicacy and washed it down with a deep swallow of California wine.

"My father overlooks these indulgences," she said, "but I think you may have overstepped this time."

Circe did not respond, but prepared additional portions, arranging them on a plate with a selection of fruit. She passed it to Athena as Annape refilled their cups.

"How did Phaethon come to Troy?" Athena lifted another portion of Camembert and held it under her nose, eyes closed. "Why didn't he die when my father struck him?"

"You saw him?"

"He had taken the form of a large reptile—an abomination. He attacked Nestor's camp and killed one of his warriors. More would have died had I not intervened."

Circe nodded thoughtfully.

"You seem surprised," Athena observed.

"I am. Phaethon has learned many things, including how to hide from me. I did not know his location."

"Let's not play games, cousin," Athena said, her voice a mixture of silk and steel. She helped herself to another portion of bread and cheese and ate quietly, her silence leaving Circe room to navigate, her gray eyes leaving her few places to go.

"Cousin," the enchantress said slowly, "have you ever been consumed by love? By a passion that would not release you?"

Athena listened quietly.

"I only knew Phaethon from afar, but I saw his beauty, his innocence, his purity—"

"He was your half-brother," Athena interrupted sharply.

Circe smiled. "Yes, my half-brother, the son of my father, Helios, and a mortal woman, but we may as well have been strangers. Immortals do not smile upon the bastard off-shoots of their adventures, let alone bring them into their homes."

Athena frowned but listened quietly.

"I knew how desperately Phaethon wanted to prove his patrimony to those who mocked him; how he tricked our father into letting him drive the chariot of the sun."

"He was a fool."

"Yes," Circe continued, "but a beautiful fool, and so young. I watched the chariot spin out of control and I saw Zeus strike him with a thunderbolt."

"You were visiting there as well?" Athena said sarcastically.

"I am always there, cousin, as I'm always here, as I am always in that time you scorn—as are you. We are immortal."

"You can choose to remain apart. You can recognize where you do not belong."

"That is a question of perspective," Circe countered, taking a deep drink of wine. "My heart cracked when I heard the thunder of Zeus and saw Phaethon consumed by fire. I waited until his body had fallen from the sky, until the moment before he struck the ground. It was a small intervention—only the slightest unbinding of space and time brought him here."

"You interfered with my father's justice," Athena said sternly.

"No one noticed. Helios recovered his chariot, and the Earth was saved."

"Have you no control over your appetites?"

"He was my blood, he was beautiful, and I loved him." Circe spoke with no trace of apology. "Are you angry because he was my half-brother—or because he was half human?"

"Enough," Athena snapped, glaring at Circe in icy disapproval.

Circe returned Athena's stare without flinching. After a time, the goddess of wisdom relaxed her gaze and nodded imperceptibly.

"My love for him bore no fruit but sorrow," Circe confessed. She drank silently from her cup, staring through the open sides of the atrium into the forest surrounding her palace. "I tried to return him to health, but all my enchantments failed. I could save his life, but I could not undo the terrible effects of Zeus' bolt."

"You did more than that."

"Yes," Circe nodded, "I taught him how to hide his deformity behind a pleasing illusion."

"Or the body of a monster?"

"He was an apt student and threw himself into my library, often without my knowledge—or my approval."

Athena took a deep drink of Circe's wine. "How did he come to Troy?"

"How did he come to defile your precious battlefield?" Circe tore off a piece of bread and chewed it thoughtfully. "There was a girl named Iaria, one of my Nereids. He used what I had given him to seduce her. He left her with child and fled, stealing several books from my library, and covering himself in enchantments I could not penetrate."

"What of the Nereid?" Athena asked warily.

"I was enraged. They betrayed me."

Athena's gray eyes narrowed. "What have you done?"

"What have I done? No more than our male relatives have done countless times. I let love for a mortal blind me, and I let his betrayal drive me to madness."

"You killed her?"

"No," Circe said ironically. "We gods do not kill those we would destroy—nothing so unimaginative."

Athena raised an inquisitive eyebrow.

"I transformed her into a cat, an animal she loved." Circe's eyes shined with unformed tears.

"That is monstrous," Athena gasped.

"It was an impulsive cruelty I will always regret, but it is no more than our male cousins have done countless times. How many young women—beautiful innocents—have been turned into trees, animals, rocks simply to let a lustful god hide his indiscretions? Do you think Zeus would hesitate to transform the most beautiful, the most loving of our sex into some vile, cold creature imprisoned in slime, just to hide his lust from vengeful Hera?"

Athena stared silently.

"Why the Medusa whose image graces your Aegis was once a child serving in your temple—a virgin until Poseidon raped her. Have you forgotten the monstrous transformation you inflicted on her in your rage?"

"Enough," Athena warned. Circe saw a tear fall across her cheek.

"I am not alone in punishing the innocent, nor am I alone in regret," Circe confessed. "I tried to reverse the transformation, but in my anger, I had obliterated Iaria's human form. There was no trace, no pattern from which I could restore her. I took her to a place where she could live, where, in my shame, I would not see her, but where I believed she would be safe—a place far from here."

"Far? In location? In time?"

Circe looked toward the Aegean. "It seems like another life entirely . . ."

"What have you not told me?" Athena pressed.

"Cousin?"

"I saw a great cat at Troy. It took the form of three ordinary animals when I healed its injuries."

"Swarm," Circe acknowledged. "When Iaria became a cat, the child in her womb divided into five kittens," she confessed, "but its essence—its soul—remained intact. You saw three of the five cats. Five individuals joined by one essence, five minds sharing a single sentience, five inconsequential house animals and one great predator—all midwifed by a foolish enchantress."

Athena looked at her in shock. "Tell me no more."

"You know the worst of it." Circe nodded to Annape, who filled both goddess' cups.

"What are you going to do?"

"I am going to restore what I can and protect what I cannot. Do you recall a woman being with the great cat?"

"She was not only with it," Athena scowled, "she had become one with the animal. It is not natural."

"It's not natural, but it's not evil and it may hold promise."

"Promise of what?"

"I do not know, cousin. That's what makes it worth protecting."

"You speak in riddles."

"Riddles? No. Mysteries, perhaps."

"Mystery, riddle," Athena said in frustration, "it makes no difference. How will you set this right?"

"A riddle can be solved, but a mystery must be lived," Circe mused.

"What will you do?" Athena pressed.

"Always the goddess of practical wisdom," Circe said, looking at Athena with deep affection. "As I told you, Phaethon used his stolen enchantments to block me from finding him, but the woman you saw in Troy, she raised these animals and is somehow bound to them. She can sense their minds, their emotions—even their locations."

"And?"

"Phaethon took one of her animals and I took another. The cat who is in my possession will lead the woman to me, who, in turn, will lead me to Phaethon." Circe rested against the cushions as Athena stared at her, judgment and compassion contending in her gray eyes.

The goddesses sat quietly for a time, listening to the songs of the animals and insects that filled Aeaea. Athena emptied the plate Circe had prepared for her and leaned toward the platter of bread and cheeses. She started toward the Camembert, reconsidered, and cut into a wedge of blue cheese with a golden knife.

"You said Phaethon had taken one of the cats. What does he want with it?" Athena asked as she spread the blue cheese on a round of bread and bit into it. Initially shocked at the pungent taste, she closed her eyes, exploring the strange sensation. She smiled and prepared another portion.

"I believe he hopes to use its abilities to heal himself."

"Could that work?" Athena asked in surprise.

"I doubt it. There is something unique about these animals, something that cannot be duplicated. I even asked Proteus to reveal their fate, but he saw nothing beyond conflicting forces and shifting probabilities."

"They have no threads in the Fates' tapestry?" Athena asked, astonished.

Circe shook her head. "Their future remains fluid."

"This instability could alter the unfolding of the universe as Zeus intends," Athena protested, "even tear our world apart. They must be removed."

"They must be removed," Circe agreed, "but they must not be harmed. I promise you, the tapestry of the Fates and Zeus' plans will remain intact, but these animals may be of great importance to their own age—and the woman who followed them here."

Circe leaned across the table and placed her hand on Athena's. "This is mine to bear and mine to set right. The woman is at Troy with three of the animals. She is preparing to sail with Nestor."

"If my father learns of this—"

"I know," Circe interrupted, "but you must give me time."

Athena stared at Circe for a time, her gray eyes revealing nothing. Then, she leaned across the table, filling her plate with carefully chosen delicacies. She lifted the wine bottle, found it empty, and beckoned to Annape. "Do you have more of this wine?" Athena asked.

"Please bring us an open bottle, Annape," Circe said, "and bring my cousin a case of our best as a gift. Include the Cabernet of course; add a few bottles of the Bordeaux, and the Sangiovese . . . Along with anything else you think she will enjoy. She will also need a cork remover, and there is another wheel of Camembert cooling in the caves."

Annape smiled and signaled to a nearby Nereid, They left together.

"You should eat the cheese soon," Circe told Zeus' daughter. "It will not keep for more than a few days."

Athena nodded. "There is one thing more," she said as she set her plate on the marble table and brushed a smattering of crumbs from her lap. "Do not take too long to set this right. I am only a little more patient than my father."

Circe poured the last of the wine into her cup as Annape entered the atrium. "Has our guest departed?"

"Yes," Annape answered.

"With her gifts?"

The Naiad smiled.

"Bring me the orange cat," Circe said.

The enchantress leaned back in the cushions, staring through the arches across the meadow. The atrium's golden sconces shined through Aeaea's forests to grace the ocean with a light invisible to mortal eyes. Circe's mind wandered over the events surrounding her, the probabilities that were rising like walls to narrow the path she walked.

Annape returned with Elizabeth in her arms.

"Thank you," Circe said, smiling up at the Naiad and taking the cat from her. "Leave us now. Take your rest."

She stroked Elizabeth absentmindedly as Annape withdrew, then retrieved a portion of fish from a golden platter. She held it in her hand as the cat ate, her rough tongue crossing Circe's palm.

"Athena has long resented the privileges assumed by our male relatives—it inclined her toward our cause," Circe mused as she tangled her fingers in Elizabeth's soft fur. "She is right to say you do not belong here. Your presence is disruptive and would eventually attract Zeus' attention, but you must return to your time unharmed."

Circe reached across the table for another piece of fish and placed it on a golden dish within Elizabeth's reach. She leaned back on the cushions and watched the cat eat.

"Your journey—yours and your littermates—that is all that matters."

Chapter 31

Phaethon stood in the open space outside Strachys' hut, the wind that followed the mountain ridge rippling his tunic, the welts from Athena's insects still covering his skin. He called out to the seer and started toward his hut, only to fall to his knees in pain. Strachys ran across the open space and guided him to a flat boulder near the trail.

"I failed to capture the animal you needed," Phaethon rasped.

"I know."

"How?"

"My abilities have grown," Strachys answered cryptically. He examined the welts on Phaethon's skin. "These are of immortal origin; they penetrate even the enchantments that cover your injuries. Come, we must go inside."

Strachys helped Phaethon to a chair inside his cabin and handed him a cup of wine. "If I am to treat your injuries, you must remove the enchantments that alter your appearance," the seer explained.

"I understand." Phaethon drained the wine and placed the cup on Strachys' table. "I'm ready."

Phaethon closed his eyes as light surrounded his body, at first a faint glow on his skin, like moonlight reflected from the sheen of sweat, then flaring into a blue gyre that quickly faded, leaving him huddled on the floor. The charred side of his body seemed inert while the rest trembled in pain. The welts from Athena's swarm of insects covered even the most severely burned parts of his flesh. Strachys offered him a cup of foul-smelling tea.

"This will ease the pain."

Phaethon drank and passed into unconsciousness. Strachys raised his eyelid to reveal an unresponsive jelly.

"Some things are not for you to see."

With his eyes closed, the seer moved his hands over Phaethon's unconscious body. His palms passed no more than a centimeter above his flesh, guided not by vision but by a long-forgotten sense—one that required no physical organ. As his hands moved, the scroll's golden writing fell from them, each character landing on a single welt left by Athena's insects. The golden flakes dissolved into Phaethon's flesh, then just as quickly sloughed off onto the floor, removing the welts from both burned and intact skin. They returned to the seer, streaming up his legs to vanish beneath his tunic. Strachys continued his work until the golden symbols found no more bites from Athena's insects. He stumbled to the wooden chair, exhausted.

"By the gods, Athena, your magic is strong." He poured a cup of wine from the clay pitcher, drained it, and closed his eyes as the last of the golden writing returned to his flesh.

Phaethon began to stir. Strachys kneeled and placed his hands upon his shoulders, returning him to the form of a young man. He sat up, still groggy from Strachys' tea, and examined his skin. "How . . ." he stammered, "how did you do this?"

"As I told you, my abilities have grown since we last spoke—and they continue to grow." Strachys poured a cup of wine and gave it to him.

Phaethon drank deeply. "Tell me what you've learned."

"When I observed you at Troy," Strachys said, "I saw the woman join with the animals. That is encouraging. If she can merge with them, so can you. Bring me the animal I need, and you will have your cure."

Phaethon trembled as he heard the seer's words. "Are you certain?"

"As certain as one can be."

"You've changed," Phaethon observed. "You seem . . . stronger."

"It is like a student studying swordsmanship with a master," Strachys explained as he scratched behind his beard. "The student reaches a point where the master can tell him no more, but he remains inferior. As he practices, his skill increases, even as he forgets the letter of his lessons."

"I do not understand."

"Soon, I will remember nothing and know everything." The seer smiled. "Then, I will be the master."

Phaethon stared at him, first in confusion, then with anger, and finally, he began to laugh. "Very well, keep your secrets." He lifted his cup from the table, drained it, and paced the narrow confines of Strachys' hovel. "I cannot return to Troy," he said.

"I know," Strachys responded. "Athena has spread enchantments across the battlefield, but you do not need to return there."

"Why not?"

"Just as I observed you at Troy, so do I know the woman's plans. She and the animals are leaving with Nestor. They have learned how to find the cat that prowls this island. Soon, they will be here."

"My men and I will be waiting."

"Perhaps you do not need to wait."

Phaethon stopped pacing and stared at him.

"My ability to sense the woman and her animals is growing," Strachys explained. "Soon, I will be able to locate them precisely and send you among them. You can take an animal and return here before they can react."

"Why can't you send me now? You said you could locate her."

"I am still unable to guide you accurately across great distances. If I'm even a few yards off, you will lose the element of surprise. You could even appear beneath the ocean or become trapped in rock itself."

"I don't have much time left," Phaethon said, worry shadowing his face.

"My powers increase daily," Strachys reassured. "What of the men on the beach?"

"What do you mean?"

"They are no longer necessary. We can take the animal by surprise."

"No. Nestor will be coming here. Proxonos and his men stay."

"We don't need them," Strachys argued. "I can heal you. We can leave Kyros before Nestor arrives, and if we leave the cats behind, the woman will have no reason to follow."

Phaethon's expression hardened. "Nestor, Odysseus, Circe . . . I will make them pay."

"I said I would heal you. I want no part of revenge."

"You are part of what I choose you to be," Phaethon threatened. "These men will stay, and I've instructed Proxonos to bring more."

"Your lust for vengeance nearly killed the animals who hold the key to your cure."

"I lost control in the heat of battle. It will not happen again."

"Don't be a fool. You can't control these men. They're like a plague."

Phaethon glared at him. "A plague I can turn on my enemies."

"A plague that will end you."

Phaethon lifted Strachys from the chair by his tunic. He drew his dagger and pressed the point to the seer's throat. "You will do what I tell you, seer," he snarled. Phaethon felt the dagger move in his hand. "Do you think you can fool me twice?"

Ignoring the snake hissing in his grasp, he pressed the knife against the seer's flesh, guided by feeling alone. The illusion of the snake vanished as blood trickled down the blade. "You will do as I tell you."

"As you wish."

The voice came from behind him. He turned and saw Strachys standing naked, smiling. Phaethon held only the seer's empty tunic. He threw it aside angrily.

Strachys retrieved the garment from the floor. "You no longer frighten me," he said, pulling it over his head.

"Perhaps that is the reason I keep my little army intact," Phaethon sneered. "Do you think your enchantments could defeat them all?"

Strachys smiled cryptically.

"Proxonos and his men will stay," Phaethon continued. "You will prepare herbs and enchantments and heal his wounded. Do you understand?"

"I will heal your men," the seer said reluctantly.

"Then, I'll take your leave," Phaethon said, starting toward the door.

"Where are you going?"

Phaethon looked scornfully around the room with its simple furnishings. "There is a place where I can rest in comfort."

"Stay here with me," Strachys offered. "I can provide enchantments to ease your pain."

Phaethon shook his head. "There are wounds enchantments cannot soothe," he said as he left through the hut's narrow entrance.

Strachys watched Phaethon start down the trail, then vanish into a ball of light that flew along the mountain face like a sea bird before turning to race across the Aegean.

"Dismiss your raiders or not," Strachys muttered, "it matters little."

He walked back into the hut's dim light and sat in the wooden chair. He closed his eyes and spoke softly as if in prayer. His words did not come from art, faith, or memory but from the ancient writing that filled his body. The words flowed through him like spring water over ice, slowly dissolving all that was impermanent—all that was human.

Claea stood on the wall of Etagama's palace, the wind stirring the fringe of her shawl. The evening twilight hid the faint scars that remained from Akiala's brutality, just as it enhanced the beauty emerging in their place. She watched the people of Etagama's kingdom—little more than a village teetering on the edge of starvation, she reminded herself—go about their lives, their memories of Akiala dissolving in the solvents of time and routine. Claea wondered if they shared the comfort she felt at the coming of darkness, or if their small pleasures and overarching fears kept such thoughts from their minds. She heard footsteps, turned, and saw Etagama approach.

"Do you think he is coming?" The newly-made king asked as he stood beside her, resting his forearms on the parapet.

"I don't know," Claea said. "You shouldn't believe these rumors of some mystic bond between us."

Etagama smiled. "But there is a bond with him—with this stranger?"

Claea looked up at him.

"He does not think of you as anything more than a servant," Etagama said, staring out at the stream that wound through the village below.

"How do you think of me?" she asked softly.

"Sarcasm does not become you."

"No, I owe you more than that," she confessed. "You have been kind."

"I would like to be more."

Claea stared quietly across the plains surrounding the palace. "I know."

"You also know I could take what I want."

"We both know that what you want must be given."

Etagama nodded and stared into the night. "The stranger cannot meet your needs," he said.

"What do you know of my needs?"

"I know there are worse things than being a queen."

"Yes," she said, touching one of the scars that still marked her cheek.

"This one brings darkness with him," Etagama warned.

"I know. I carry my own darkness inside of me."

The king removed his cloak and placed it around her shoulders. "Your shawl is thin; this will keep you warm. I will go to my bed to wait for dawn to drive the darkness away."

Claea smiled at him and took his hand. "You have become a poet," she observed.

"No," he said as he turned to leave, "I have become a fool."

Chapter 32

Astrid stood in front of the low bed, her backpack and its contents spread on a fleece, an inventory of her resources for the coming voyage. She tested the repair where the bandit's sword had cut the pack, pulling against Hecamede's careful stitches. Greystoke slept on the cotton shirts and underwear she had washed the day before. She picked him up and held him close.

Myia held her hands out. "Let me take him. We'll be leaving soon, and you need to finish packing."

"Thank you," Astrid said as she handed Greystoke to her. "Have you gotten your things together?"

Myia nodded toward a roll of bedding that rested nearby. It was larger and heavier than a few blankets and her small wardrobe would explain. Astrid knew it contained the sword, arrows, and bow she had buried in the forest, possibly with other weapons she had hidden in the hills.

"I see you're traveling light," Astrid joked.

Myia carried Greystoke toward the tent's exit. Chessie and Audrey followed behind. "They've grown fond of you," Astrid said as Myia smiled and led the cats through the canvas flap into the sunlight.

Hecamede rose from the bed where she had sat, watching Astrid pack and giving advice about life on Nestor's ship. Astrid saw tears in her eyes.

"Hecamede . . ." Astrid began as sobs overcame her and she threw her arms around her, "I would have died without you."

"No," Hecamede protested, "I did little."

"You risked your life for me."

"We are friends."

"Yes," Astrid said as she relaxed the embrace, "we are friends."

She turned to the clothes she had spread on the bed and picked up the neatly folded sweaters, one black, one dark red. She held them out to Hecamede. "Please take one . . . as a gift. It will keep you warm against the evening chill."

Hecamede took the red sweater and ran her hands over it lovingly.

"It will help you remember me," Astrid said softly.

"I will never forget you." Hecamede held the sweater close to her breast. She leaned forward and kissed Astrid gently on the lips.

Astrid held her close, her tears dampening the skin where their cheeks touched, and whispered, "Nor I, you."

She heard a familiar voice call her name.

"I'm in here," she called back. The tent flap rustled, and Odysseus entered.

"Odysseus," Astrid greeted, still holding Hecamede's hand. "I'm glad to see you. I was worried I might not get a chance to say goodbye."

He smiled broadly. "You needn't have worried. I told Nestor he could not leave before we talked."

"How are preparations going?" Astrid asked.

"He will be sailing shortly."

"Will his sons join us?"

"Antilochus will—I doubt Nestor could have stopped him if he'd tried. Thrasymedes wanted to come as well, but Nestor asked him to stay and remain in charge of his people."

Astrid felt a tightness in her chest as his words reminded her that she was leaving the camp she had come to see as a sanctuary, if not a home.

"Will you walk with me before you go to Nestor's ship?" Odysseus asked.

Astrid turned to Hecamede, their hands still joined.

"I'll finish packing for you," Hecamede said, smiling.

Astrid put her arms around her once more, held her for a time, then turned and followed Odysseus from the tent.

As Astrid and Odysseus walked through the camp, people acknowledged their passing with a nod or a smile. A few women came forward and wished her well; one even embraced her briefly. Gilia, the young girl who had formed an attachment to the cats, ran up to her with tears in her eyes. "Don't go," she sobbed as she threw her arms around Astrid.

Astrid kneeled to look into the child's eyes. "I must find their brother and sister," she said gently, "but I will never forget all you've done for the cats and me."

Gilia smiled, her face damp with tears. She hurried to stay at Astrid's side as she and Odysseus continued their walk. Odysseus saw her struggling to keep up and raised her in his arms. "Astrid has told me you were a great help," he said as he carried her through the camp, "and were very brave."

Gilia pressed her cheek against his, her arms around his neck, a smile on her face. They walked the row of ships that defined the extent of Nestor's camp; when they reached the end, Odysseus put Gilia down on the sand. He kneeled and took her by the shoulders. "You must leave us alone now. Astrid and I need to talk."

Astrid bent down to kiss Gilia's cheek, then watched the child return to camp, limping across the beach.

"I wish you were coming," she said as she walked with Odysseus along the juncture of sand and ocean, the surf flowing around their feet.

"Nestor is a skilled strategist, and his men are experienced warriors."

"Still, I wish you were coming."

"Someone needs to keep an eye on our commander in chief." He saw tears in Astrid's eyes and took her hand. "There has been growing unrest among the Achaeans. You can see it in Achilles, even in Ajax and Diomedes. Nestor and I have worked to keep things from coming apart. We cannot both leave."

"Why do I sense there is more?"

"This is Nestor's journey."

"What do you mean?"

"The gods have chosen him. The horses you gave him were their sign. The honor belongs to him."

Astrid shook her head. "That is such a guy thing."

"I don't understand."

"Odysseus," she said, "I'm afraid."

He stopped and squeezed her hand.

"That thing, Phaethon," Astrid said. "He nearly killed me twice. He broke my wrist the first time, and the last time, when he fought Swarm, he broke my back. If Athena had not appeared, I would have died."

"But she did appear, and you are here."

"I'll have to face him again."

Odysseus stared at her thoughtfully. She had come to recognize his habit of weighing the effects of his words before speaking, even on the smallest matter. It was the habit of a king, and Astrid knew it would serve him well on his journey home.

"You've faced him twice and survived. You will find a way."

Astrid shook her head. "He beat me both times, easily. I'm only alive through luck."

She saw a struggle cross Odysseus' features as if he was grasping for words to express something that lay deep in his essence, buried beneath language, beneath consciousness.

"Astrid, I do not know what will happen when you confront him again—and I believe that you will. It seems to be destined. But, I do know that you are brave and strong. I know that Nestor and his warriors will fight beside you. I know that you are special to the gods."

"I wish I had your confidence."

"What were your thoughts when you fought Phaethon back at the camp?"

"I don't recall . . ." Astrid said, "it's a blur."

Odysseus smiled and nodded. "What you think you will do when you face death means little. When you faced it, you fought without hesitation. That is all that matters. The rest is for the fates to decide."

Astrid looked into his eyes. They rested on her without moving, but now, the mask he often wore—the sense that he was always calculating the risks borne by friends and opponents alike—vanished.

"I've heard that people like you, people who are close to the gods . . . that you know things," he said in carefully measured syllables. "Can you tell me anything about my fate? Will I see my home? My wife? My son?"

"Odysseus—" She stopped and took a deep breath.

Astrid knew from Homer that Odysseus would spend another year at Troy, that his journey home would take ten more years and leave his companions dead, his prizes from the war lost. She knew he would return home to find his palace overrun by unscrupulous men who sought to steal his wealth and kingdom and take his beloved Penelope as their queen. She knew he would defeat them with the help of his young son, Telemachus, reuniting with Penelope to rule Ithaca once more. Although Homer's stories were fiction, so much of what she had seen since coming to Troy—the length of the Trojan siege, the animosity between Achilles and Agamemnon, even the characters of Nestor, Hecamede, Odysseus, Achilles, and the other Achaean warriors—were exactly as Homer had described them.

She also understood the risks of telling Odysseus anything that might cause him to change his actions.

"Odysseus," Astrid said carefully, "word of this war and the men who fight it—Nestor, Diomedes, Ajax, Achilles, you—has reached my homeland. I know stories, that's all."

"Do any tell of my future?"

"Those stories are not yet written."

"I have always believed I shaped my fate, but I also believe that the obstacles I will face already wait for me. Can you tell me anything about them? Anything at all?"

"Odysseus . . ."

"Please," he said softly.

For the first time, Astrid sensed doubt beneath his carefully constructed persona. She gathered her thoughts carefully. "What I know," she said, "is that you will return home. You will rejoin your wife, and you will fight beside your son with honor. You will once again rule your kingdom."

"How soon will I leave Troy? How long will my journey take? Will I return home in glory, rich with treasure?"

Astrid fought back tears. "All I can tell you . . . is that it will be difficult."

He nodded and stared out across the Aegean, perhaps looking toward Ithaca, perhaps contemplating an uncertain future. After a time, he turned back to her.

"It always is," he said softly.

Part IV
Aeaea
Thirteenth Century B.C.E.

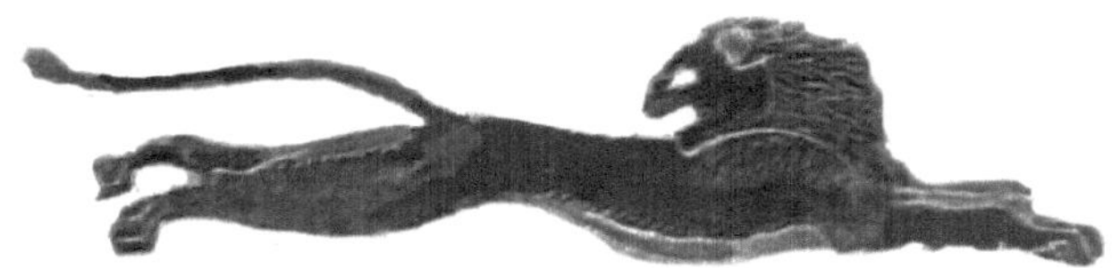

Chapter 33

Astrid rested against one of the scattered trees that forged a liminal existence between the Aegean and the island's arid hills. She closed her eyes and listened to the surf, her heels furrowing the warm sand. After leaving Troy, Nestor had sailed along the coastline for three days, putting ashore each night for rest and fresh water. Finally, the cats' sense of Spike and Elizabeth's locations had pulled them out into the open sea. Astrid stretched her legs as she remembered the nights she had spent on the cramped ship, sleepless as Nestor navigated by the stars and the cats' narrow connection to their siblings. She remembered the smell of salt air mixed with the pitch of the ship's caulking, the restless shifting of bodies seeking comfort on wooden benches, and the sound of waves complaining against the hull. She also remembered the men's elation when they saw the small island rising from the Aegean, their laughter and horseplay as they pulled the ship onto the sand.

She looked across the beach at Nestor's ship. It was larger than she would have imagined from Homer's descriptions—more than sixty feet long and fifteen feet wide amidships, with space for several dozen oarsmen. A warship, it was designed for speed—stripped of unnecessary weight and lacking in creature comforts—and it achieved a stark elegance, riding low in the ocean like a dark seabird, its bow and sternposts rising alertly above the waterline. The ship was devoid of decking, except for the rowers' benches crossing below the gunwales and two small platforms fore and aft. The removable mast rose from a wooden block amidships when favorable breezes filled the sail, or lay along the ship's centerline when the crew stowed it and rowed through calms. Twenty-five men had joined Nestor on the journey. With their weapons, stowed sails and oars, meager personal belongings, and clay jars of water, wine, and food, little open space remained—and almost no privacy.

Astrid turned her attention to the cats prowling the sparse vegetation near the beach. On the ship, inside the small hut Antilochus had built for them on the aft deck, their food bowls and sandbox had marked the poles of a small, dark world. The animals had fallen into an uneasy stupor, and Astrid's sense of their presence had dimmed nearly to silence. Now, as she watched Greystoke chase Chessie around a cluster of rocks and Audrey raise her face to the warm breeze stirring her whiskers, Astrid realized they were reclaiming their feline essences. They were becoming cats once again.

She saw Myia and Antilochus walk up the beach in her direction. Although armed, they walked unhurriedly, almost casually along the shore, the surf teasing their feet. They reminded Astrid of any young man and woman enjoying any beach in her own time. As they came closer, Antilochus saw her and broke into a run, sand flying behind his bare feet. Myia chased him, laughing at first, then straining as she overtook him. She fell to her knees next to Astrid, out of breath, with Antilochus close behind.

"So," Astrid said, "you found me."

"You shouldn't be alone," Antilochus warned. "We don't know this island."

"I thought it was uninhabited," Astrid explained. "We didn't see any signs of people when we approached."

"We can't be certain. We don't know who may be living in the hills."

"I'm sorry, but I've had trouble sensing the cats' connection to Spike and Elizabeth. I almost couldn't sense any direction the last day we were at sea. I needed to get them away from the ship and the men, where they could play and explore—where they could be themselves."

"Are they returning to normal?" Myia asked.

Astrid nodded. "How are the men?"

Antilochus smiled. "They're happy to be away from Troy and grateful for the winds."

She remembered the favorable winds that had filled the square sail, the linen straining at the leather reinforcements that crisscrossed it, and the men's pleasure when they stored their oars under the benches. Astrid smiled as she recalled how they had treated Myia, the cats, and herself with a gentler version of their own boisterous camaraderie—as if the crowded ship left no room for the reticence they had shown her at the camp.

"Sit with me a while," Astrid invited.

Antilochus looked up and down the beach, across the rocky inland, then sat where he could see both the beach and the hills. He carefully placed his sword on the sand within arm's reach. Myia found a comfortable patch of sand and looked out at the ocean, catching her breath from the race up the beach. They spoke about the men's progress in setting up camp, the search

for game and fresh water to replenish their supplies, and Nestor's plans
to give the crew another day and night of rest on the island. Gradually,
the conversation faded to a comfortable silence, and the cats joined them.
Astrid felt Chessie rub against her hip and lifted the cat onto her lap while
Greystoke and Audrey found places to nap in the shade nearby. She leaned
against the trunk of the small tree and closed her eyes, relaxing into the
sibilant rhythms of the surf and Chessie's purrs.

Astrid awoke to voices and the clattering of bronze. She opened her eyes
and saw Antilochus and Myia on their feet, hands on their weapons, attention focused on a figure approaching from the sea. She stared across the
shining water, shielding her eyes from the glare with her hand, and saw
Claire Ortega walking through the waist-high surf.

She jumped to her feet in shock.

"Do you know her?" Antilochus asked. "Is she dangerous?"

"It's all right. She's my friend."

"I remember this woman," Myia said, though recognition did not clear
the apprehension from her voice. "She's the immortal who brought the
horses for Nestor."

Astrid began to shout and wave. Claire saw her and hurried through the
surf. As she drew close, Astrid saw she was wearing an orange tank suit
under a white crochet cover-up, her dark skin shining through the loose
weave. Astrid recognized the outfit from a weekend she and Claire had
spent at Puerto Vallarta.

"Claire, is that you?" Astrid shouted as she approached her friend, first
at a walk, then running into the shallow water. Crying, she threw her arms
around Claire as the Aegean soaked her jeans.

"It's okay, sweetie," Claire reassured her. "What's wrong?"

"Please tell me you're dreaming. Please tell me you're home, safe."

"What are you on about?" Claire laughed. "We didn't drink that much
last night."

"Do you know where you are?"

"Puerto Vallarta . . . same as yesterday."

Astrid felt a wave of relief. "You're safe."

"What are you talking about?"

"Look around," Astrid said.

Claire scanned the narrow strand, the arid hills, and the salt meadow
where she expected to see the shops, bars, and restaurants of the resort.
"Something doesn't seem right . . ."

"Take your time," Astrid reassured.

Claire looked up and down the beach. She stared at Nestor's ship and the activity around the camp, at Antilochus and Myia standing nearby still holding their swords. Astrid took her hand and waited as Claire analyzed her surroundings with a scientist's intensity.

"This has happened before," she said slowly as if thinking aloud. "I remember coffee with you in a forest . . . I gave you two horses. That was a dream. This is the same, isn't it?"

Astrid nodded. "You are dreaming, but you're also here, I believe to give me a message."

"A message?"

"It's hard to explain, and you probably wouldn't believe me if I tried." She took Claire by the hand and led her toward her companions. "These are my friends, Antilochus and Myia."

Myia approached Claire cautiously and asked, "Are you a goddess?"

"No, but I think one sent me." Claire stopped, surprised by her words. "Why did I say that?"

"As I said, it's hard to explain. If any words start to come to you, just let them out."

Claire turned to Nestor's son.

"My name is Antilochus," he said.

Claire seemed to return to her usual self. She took his hand and smiled mischievously. "Where did you find this gorgeous man?" she asked Astrid as Antilochus smiled.

"Come sit in the shade," Astrid said as she led Claire back to the small cluster of trees. She reminded herself that for Claire, this was a dream, immune to the logic of the waking world. She sat quietly as Claire's dream of the familiar resort modulated to accommodate this new reality.

"She wants me to take you to her," Claire said after a time.

"Circe?"

Claire nodded as Antilochus and Myia shifted uneasily.

"I've heard of this enchantress," Antilochus warned. "She can't be trusted."

"It's all right," Astrid reassured him. "I don't think she wants to hurt me."

"That's true," Claire said.

"Does she have Elizabeth?" Astrid asked.

"Yes, she wants to return the animal."

Astrid felt her excitement rise. "Elizabeth's here? On this island?"

"No, but I'll take you to her."

"Do you have a ship?" Antilochus asked.

"No. Circe wants me to take Astrid up the beach." Claire spoke easily as if she had once more settled into her role as the enchantress' proxy.

"I'm coming with you," Antilochus insisted.

"We both are," Myia added, grasping the hilt of her bronze sword.

Claire shook her head. "Only Astrid. You and the cats must stay here."

"What does she want?" Astrid asked.

"She wants you to come to dinner."

"Dinner? Are you shitting me?"

Claire shrugged.

"When will I be back?" Astrid asked.

"In a few days."

Claire turned to Myia and Antilochus. "She will return with Elizabeth. Tell Nestor where we've gone and take care of the cats. Do not let any harm come to them."

They protested loudly, insisting that Astrid should not leave by herself, that she must return to camp and discuss this with Nestor.

"I'll be all right," Astrid said, taking their hands in reassurance—even as she struggled with her own reluctance to trust the mercurial enchantress.

She kneeled among Greystoke, Chessie, and Audrey, calming each of them in turn, both through thought and through touch. She envisioned them staying with Myia and Antilochus and sensed how much their trust in Myia had grown and felt gratitude and relief. She embraced her friends, then took Claire's hand and walked with her along the beach.

As they neared a bend in the coastline, Astrid stopped and looked back. She saw Myia was holding Chessie in her arms. Antilochus stood at her side while Audrey and Greystoke circled their feet.

"Thank god the cats aren't trying to follow me," Astrid said as she waved to them a final time. "Were you really dreaming about Puerto Vallarta?"

Claire nodded.

"I thought I recognized the suit and the cover-up."

"Recognized it? Sweetie, after that weekend, it should be in the Smithsonian."

"As I recall, you practically lived in it for three days."

Claire smiled, took Astrid's hand, and led her into the surf. They walked together quietly as the water flowed around their legs.

"You'll be home soon," Claire said, settling into a dream-like calm.

"Claire, is this you or Circe?"

"It feels like me, but I think it's Circe," Claire said thoughtfully.

"Why can't she send us home?"

"It's not much farther," Claire said. "She will explain everything."

Spike crouched under the bush, watching the boy approach with his clay bowl. After several days, he had come to rely on the boy's morning visits. The bush, the boy, the granary, and the nearby cluster of rocks with the small cave where he slept in the heat of the day defined the circumference of Spike's refuge—the place to which he returned after roaming the coast-line, searching for some way to reach his littermates.

He watched the boy place the bowl on the ground, then sit cross-legged beside it. Spike approached him in what had become a dance of caution and temptation. As he had done for the last few days, the boy sat within reach of the bowl but did not move. Spike eased toward him, stopping warily every few steps to watch the strange child. Finally, the smell of burned meat over-whelmed Spike's lingering doubts. He stepped to the food and began to eat.

Spike heard the boy make the soft sounds of a human reassuring a wary animal and felt the child scratch him beneath his ear, at the hinge of his jaw. For a moment, the urge to run contended with an enduring need for long-absent human contact.

He leaned into the boy's touch.

Chapter 34

Astrid and Claire followed the shoreline until they came to a cliff that descended from the hills to disappear into the sea, a featureless wall of granite blocking their path. They walked along the cliff face, searching for some way past it, and found a cave's narrow entrance.

"This doesn't seem natural," Astrid murmured, running her hands along the smooth rock surrounding the cave's opening. "Is this Circe's doing?"

Claire stopped, listening to the whisper in her thoughts. "Yes."

Astrid kneeled and stared into the narrow tunnel. She saw a light at its end. "I suppose it's safe. If she wanted to kill me, she wouldn't have to drop a mountain on me." She turned to Claire. "Something weird is going to happen, isn't it?"

"Probably. Do you want me to go first?"

"No, I have a hunch this may be where we part company."

Claire paused as if listening, then nodded.

"Is there anything else you can tell me about Circe? About what's going to happen?" Astrid asked. "Even a feeling you might have, anything?"

Claire shook her head. "Her words just appear in my mind. I can't hear her voice or read her emotions."

"She's keeping her distance." Astrid took Claire's hand and saw tears dampen her friend's face. "I hope the next time we meet, I'll be back home, and I hope it's soon."

Claire kissed her on the cheek and released her hand. Astrid entered the narrow tunnel as Claire stood watchfully near the entrance. She shuffled along in a crouch, the rocky ground a painful reminder that she had left her shoes back at Nestor's ship. Several times, she scraped her head on the rough ceiling.

"Why does she have to be so goddamn dramatic?" She continued forward on her hands and knees.

Astrid reached the end of the tunnel, stepped into the sunlight, and waited for her eyes to adjust to the glare. Instead of the island's narrow beach, rocky hills, and struggling vegetation, Astrid found herself in a meadow surrounded by a dense forest. Mature eucalyptus, oak, and cedar rose above small pines, olive, and fig trees, as well as countless species of vines and bushes. Flowers contended for space among the vegetation, their bright blossoms punctuating a wall of green. Astrid looked back toward the rock wall and the cave she had just left, but both had vanished.

She heard flowing water and saw sunlight reflect off a silver band winding through the grasses and wildflowers. A deer raised her head from the stream to examine her with dark, patient eyes, ears pivoting in Astrid's direction. The doe was small, her light chestnut coat marked with white spots, unlike the brown mule deer of Astrid's home. Satisfied that this intruder was no threat, the animal resumed drinking. Astrid continued along the edge of the meadow, keeping a safe distance from the forest and what might lurk within it while staying close enough to take cover in the trees if needed. As she crossed a hill, Astrid saw a fully-grown African lion look up from sleep, a dark mane framing his tawny face, his body sprawled on the grass.

"Not another fucking cat," she mumbled.

Astrid hoped he would return to his nap. Instead, he rolled onto his feet and stretched, claws digging into the turf as his back arched upward to his raised hindquarters. Completing the stretch, he started lazily toward her. Astrid heard a splashing sound from the stream and saw a young woman, wearing only a short tunic, walk unhurriedly through the water. She smiled as the lion turned to greet her, a deep rumble resonating in his chest.

"He looks fierce, but he's quite gentle," the girl shouted across the meadow as she scratched behind the cat's ear, her fingers tangled in his dark mane. She kissed him on the nose. "Loving, actually."

"Is this Aeaea?" Astrid asked.

"You know this place?"

"I've read about it. It's Circe's home."

"I'm Annape." The girl smiled. "My mistress sent me to welcome you."

With a simple gesture, Annape commanded the lion to remain behind. She watched it find a shady spot near the forest and lay down, then she walked to Astrid's side and took her hand. Her grasp was as cool and as compelling as water. "Come," she said.

Annape led Astrid across the meadow, climbing a low hill to look down on a sprawling marble structure. To call it a palace would imply a level of pretense absent from the simple intersecting planes of white stone—and still would understate its beauty. The structure was as elegant and as inevitable as a Euclidean theorem. It rested across the meadow like a lover, conforming to the contingencies of the land without compromising the ratios of its intent. Annape led her down the hillside into Circe's home.

They walked through a long colonnade, its pillars and lintels no more than an implied separation of the interior from the surrounding wilderness. They entered a room, also open to the outside, where two young women—Nereids who served Circe, Astrid assumed—waited near a stone tub. Steam drifted over the flower petals that floated on the water's surface, and soft cloths, sponges, combs, brushes, and clay jars filled with perfumed oils covered a table beside the tub. Astrid noticed the shampoo and conditioner she had used at home and a bar of distinctly modern soap among the ancient vessels. A gown of what looked like silk dyed the silver-green of fresh sage lay on the bed, draped across a mountain of pillows, blankets, and fleeces.

"Where is Circe?" Astrid demanded. "Where's my cat?"

Annape smiled. "Elizabeth is well and waits with my mistress. Let us wash away the dirt of your journey, and they will join you for dinner."

"No, I want to see them now."

"Please. My mistress will answer all your questions, but you must let us honor you with our hospitality."

Sigrid had long ago taught Astrid about the importance of hospitality in the Bronze Age Aegean. It was an essential mercy among the hard realities of the time, a courtesy elevated into law, and an act of honor to the gods. Astrid remembered Homer's descriptions of how Odysseus had formed valuable alliances from such hospitality on his long journey home. She thought of Odysseus—no longer a character in an old story but a friend—and she longed for the counsel of his great heart and labyrinthine mind.

"Please," Annape repeated.

Astrid looked at the steam rising from the water and ran a hand through her hair's oily stiffness. She thought of the dirt, sweat, and ocean salt that covered her skin and loosened the waist of her jeans.

"I don't usually have a chorus when I bathe," she told the two young women who stood watching.

Annape waved the Nereids away. "Can I bring you anything?"

"Could I have some water, please? I'm thirsty."

Annape followed the Nereids from the room as Astrid undressed. She started to lay her clothes on the bed but noticed the dirt they had accumulated and dropped them onto the marble floor. She eased into the warm bath and rested against the tub's stone side. It seemed to conform to the contours of her back, with no points of pressure, only a warm buoyancy enfolding her body. Astrid closed her eyes and tried to envision her upcoming encounter with Circe. The thoughts floated away like the petals swirling on the water's surface as exhaustion overcame her.

Astrid heard footsteps and opened her eyes to see Annape enter with a golden pitcher and a cup. She filled the cup and gave it to her; the water was cold, with a sweet mineral taste. Annape removed her dress and stepped into the far end of the tub.

"What are you doing?" Astrid challenged her.

Annape smiled as she slid into the warm water at Astrid's feet.

"I'd rather bathe alone," Astrid protested. She felt a touch on her foot and pulled it back reflexively.

Annape looked at her in confusion. "I mean you no harm."

Astrid remembered the importance of the bath—often shared—in so many of the world's cultures. She let Annape take her foot into her hands.

"You have many injuries I can heal," Annape said as she skillfully ran her fingers over Astrid's skin and muscles.

"It's nothing. Just a few cuts and scrapes."

"No," Annape said softly, concern marking her brow. "There are deeper injuries . . . Your wrist was broken."

"How do you know that?"

"Every part of the body tells of every other," Annape said as she held Astrid's foot.

"Proteus healed it."

"But the brutality that caused it remains," Annape said. "I also sense the trauma of an attack. Your back was broken . . . your ribs . . . There were other attacks—" she stopped, her eyes widening in horror. "A man tried to rape you."

Astrid pulled her legs back. "That is not your concern. Besides, he failed."

"But I can—"

"No," Astrid interrupted. "I've had enough of you people poking around in my mind."

"I realize it is hard for you to trust me," Annape said, "or my mistress."

Astrid laughed. "You have no idea."

"I will do nothing against your wishes," Annape assured her. "But if you allow me, I will heal your injuries."

"They've already healed."

Annape smiled cryptically and took Astrid's foot in her hands once more, massaging it gently. Astrid tried to ask the questions that swirled in her mind, hoping to learn something that might help her to confront Circe, but the words dissolved like dust in the fragrant bath. She leaned back in the water and closed her eyes as Annape massaged her feet and legs with a strength beyond her slender form. The water lifted her in a weightless embrace as Annape's timeless art and immortal spirit flowed through muscles, tendons, bones, and nerves.

Astrid awoke alone on the bed, wrapped in soft fleece, her skin and hair clean. Although she remembered little of what had happened in the bath—beyond an expansive pleasure that had carried her into sleep—she felt refreshed and renewed. She checked her body for the cuts, aches, and bruises that had accumulated in Nestor's camp and during the ocean journey. They had vanished—even the scars of old injuries had disappeared.

The late afternoon sun had descended into the treetops, casting long shadows across the marble floor. Astrid looked for her jeans and sweater, but they were no longer in the room. She slipped into the gown that lay on the bed, the silver-green silk soft against her skin. She wondered if the cloth had come across the Silk Road from ancient China or if Circe had found it in a boutique in Astrid's own time. She found a brush on the table and brushed her hair vigorously.

Astrid walked barefooted into the empty hall. Gold sconces graced each column, the light of their flames amplified by the polished metal. She saw a flat marble stone piled with fruits, grains, bread, and cheeses. An avalanche of fleeces, brightly colored blankets, and cushions surrounded the table. As she neared the feast, Astrid saw a familiar dark green bottle and picked it up. It was the same Sangiovese she'd found in her mother's pantry the night after Swarm had appeared in the forest.

"What the hell?"

Astrid poured the wine into a gold cup and drank deeply. She heard the roar of a large cat—possibly the lion she had seen in the meadow—and stepped to the edge of the atrium. She stood beneath the marble lintel, staring into the twilight.

"Be not afeard. The isle is full of noises, sounds and sweet airs that give delight and hurt not."

Shakespeare's familiar phrases brought Astrid around to face the woman who had probed her mind at the coffeehouse, the woman who had transformed the unfortunate Scott into a boar, who had stood by while Phaethon broke her wrist and kidnapped Spike, the woman who had taken Elizabeth—Circe, the enchantress.

She wore a gown like Astrid's but colored in the soft pinks of dawn's first appearance. Elizabeth rested in her arms. Circe gently lowered the cat to the stone floor, and she trotted toward Astrid.

"What's going on?" Astrid demanded as she took Elizabeth into her arms and questions that had haunted her for weeks burst forth. "What is happening with my cats? Why did you take Elizabeth? Why did you let Phaethon take her brother? My god, he nearly killed me . . ."

Circe gestured to a place at her table, set with an empty golden plate and a modern silver knife and fork. "Sit, share these gifts, and we'll talk."

Astrid stood trembling as she pressed Elizabeth close.

"Please," the enchantress said.

Reluctantly, Astrid took her place at the table, releasing Elizabeth onto a cushion beside her.

"Why did you use my friend like a puppet rather than come to me yourself?" Astrid challenged, struggling to contain her anger. "Now, you serve me wine my mother liked, you walk in here quoting Shakespeare, you send that woman to bathe me . . ."

Circe took the bottle from the table and filled her cup. She drank slowly, staring through narrowed eyes. Astrid sensed the goddess' silence was a subtle reprimand for her anger—perhaps a warning. She took a deep breath and tried to calm herself.

The enchantress sat in silence, sipping her wine, waiting for Astrid to assert her self-control. "I spoke through your friend in the hope it would set you at ease," she explained finally, "and, I confess, to keep my distance until I could bring you here. I hope you realize how much Claire loves you, how much she has suffered for you since your divorce and Sigrid's death. Sending her to you was as much a kindness to her as a convenience for me. Your presence in her dreams will heal her grief. I had no right to keep her away."

Astrid fought against tears at the mention of Claire.

"I gave you wine your mother enjoyed as a gesture of friendship," Circe continued. "I shared lines from *The Tempest*, a play I know you loved—that I love as well—to set you at ease. As for Annape, she is a gifted healer but something of a free spirit. I only asked her to make you comfortable and prepare you to join me for dinner." Circe smiled. "I'm sure anything else she offered was pleasurable."

"How did you know I was fond of *The Tempest*?"

"When I touched you—"

"You mean at the coffee house, back in Albuquerque?" Astrid interrupted. The enchantress nodded.

"You violated me," Astrid lashed out.

"It was not a violation; it was a question. I hope it was the beginning of a conversation."

"Why did you take Elizabeth?"

"I recognized the bond among the cats," Circe said patiently, lifting an olive from a bowl carved from rose quartz and polished to shine like glass. She rolled it thoughtfully between her fingers before eating it. "I also sensed their bond was beginning to include you. I did not know where Phaethon would take the animal he stole, nor did I know where you would appear when you came to this age." She glanced at Elizabeth affectionately. "The cat gave me the ability to find you and bring you to Aeaea."

"How did you know I would come to your time . . . to Troy?"

"I knew the animals would come after their brother. I followed you into the forest and saw you join with them and pass through the rupture Phaethon had opened between our worlds."

"What do you want?"

Circe refilled her cup and slid a tray of fruit across the polished marble toward Astrid. "Eat, and we will talk."

Nestor stood between Myia and Antilochus and stared out at the Aegean. "You say the woman appeared from the surf? That Astrid knew her?"

"Yes," Myia answered. "She said Circe spoke through her."

"She was strangely dressed," Antilochus added.

"What do you mean?"

He described Claire's tank suit and cover-up. "It was like nothing I've seen on our women. It did not cover her arms or legs—she was almost naked. The color was like saffron but deeper and brighter than any fabric I've seen. The covering was strangely woven."

"You've seen this woman before?" Nestor asked Myia.

"She appeared in the forest with the horses Astrid gave you."

Nestor smiled at the mention of the matched stallion and mare, then looked up the beach. "They went in that direction?"

"Yes," Myia and Antilochus replied, almost in unison.

Nestor's eyes followed the footprints up the shoreline. The tracks meandered through the sand like furrows from an unskilled plowman. He walked carefully to the landward side of the tracks, gesturing for Myia and Antilochus to stay behind him. They followed silently, careful not to disturb Nestor's concentration. They came to a place where scattered sand filled the tracks.

"What happened here?" Nestor asked.

"They turned and waved to us, then moved on," Antilochus answered.

Nestor nodded, then continued up the beach. He saw the tracks disappear where Claire and Astrid had entered the surf, then resume where they had returned to the beach. He followed their trail until the twin furrows stopped, and footprints moved back and forth between the water and the salt meadow that bordered the strand. It seemed as if the women had encountered some invisible barrier.

"What do you see?" he asked his son, like a teacher engaging a student.

"The tracks just end. It seems as if they were searching for something, but the tracks neither enter the water, climb into the hills, nor continue up the beach. It seems as if they just disappeared."

Nestor stood silently for several moments, scanning the hills, the beach, the ocean, staring up the shoreline at the untouched sand where reason said the tracks should continue.

"We should return to camp," he said. "Myia, where did you leave the cats?"

"On the ship. They're safe."

"Can you sense their minds, like Astrid?"

"I don't think so. Sometimes I feel things from them, but they're too faint to understand."

"I want you to open your mind to those feelings. Tell me if you sense anything unusual. Perhaps they can tell us where Astrid has gone."

Nestor turned to his son. "I want two warriors guarding Myia and the cats at all times and additional men around the perimeter of the camp. No one may leave unless necessary, never alone, and then only with my permission."

"Are we going to continue searching?" Antilochus asked.

Nestor shook his head.

"Astrid is no longer on the island. We must wait for her to return."

Chapter 35

Spike felt the boy's touch as he ate, stroking his back, scratching behind his ears. When he finished eating, he moved closer and rubbed his cheek against the child's knee, the longings awakened by his visits resolving into a pattern of trust. The boy took him into his arms as he had before, but this time, he carried him from the field.

Spike did not resist until they approached the edge of the village, and he saw and smelled the people living there. His muscles grew tense, and the boy lowered him to the ground, reassuring him with soft words, his hand on his back. Memories of captivity filled Spike's mind, and he ran under a small structure raised on stilts nearby. Spike smelled drying barley and found he shared his refuge with the granary's protector—an old tomcat sleeping in the shadows, his fur the spotted brown common to Bronze Age cats, his breath an uneven wheeze. The old cat raised his head, hissed indifferently, and lay back down. The boy kneeled outside, trying to lure Spike out, but he retreated beneath the granary, remaining out of reach. Eventually, the boy returned to a small, one-room house nearby.

Despite his instinct to run, to return to his lair near the beach, Spike stayed in his shelter, both drawn to the boy and reluctant to pass among the strange buildings and the people who lived in them. After sunset, as darkness filled the space around him, Spike heard small feet on the dirt. He saw a mouse peek from behind one of the posts that supported the granary and felt his muscles twitch in an instinct of pursuit. Still full of the boy's fish, Spike watched as the mouse saw him and scurried away.

As the night deepened and people disappeared into their homes, Spike heard footsteps and recognized a familiar scent. The boy kneeled and held his hand out, speaking softly. Spike edged toward him cautiously. The child grasped the scruff of his neck and dragged him from his shelter. Spike growled in protest but did not claw or bite. He let the boy carry him into the house, past the curtain behind which the two adults slept, to a small wooden bed in the corner of the room.

The boy held him beneath a fleece that smelled of wood smoke, stroking him gently in the darkness. Eventually, Spike relaxed as the child drifted off, then followed into his own precarious sleep.

After the monotony of the charred meat, boiled barley, and the occasional fig or olive she'd lived on at Troy, Astrid found Circe's table overwhelming. The beautifully wrought bowls overflowed with dishes both familiar and sublime, their origins spanning the ages and the world. Astrid's hunger seemed to increase as she ate. Circe told her the story she had shared with Athena at the same table—the story of an enchantress bound to a doomed demigod by blood, love, and fate.

Phaethon, Circe explained, was the bastard son of her father, Helios, the sun god, and a mortal woman. She told of her grief to see him labeled a mongrel by his immortal relatives and mocked by his human family. She told how he had begged Helios to prove his patrimony to his doubting friends, and Helios had sworn a binding oath—a promise a god cannot refuse—to honor any request he might make. He did not anticipate that Phaethon would ask to drive the chariot of the sun. Realizing this would kill his son, Helios had begged him to ask for anything else, but Phaethon had stubbornly held his father to his oath. Circe wept when she described the horses' panic at his mortal touch—how they had carried the sun so far into the sky the oceans froze, and so low it scorched the ground. She told how the Earth herself had cried out for help and how Zeus had ended Phaethon's ride with a thunderbolt, sending him falling to his death.

Even though Sigrid had told her Phaethon's story when she was a child, Astrid listened in silence, not to hear the tale but to understand the teller.

Circe described how she had spirited away Phaethon's dying body before it struck the ground; how she had saved his life but could not heal the damage of Zeus' bolt—a fire that burned beyond the flesh to char the fabric of reality itself, a fire even an immortal could not survive. The enchantress explained how she had taught Phaethon to hide his deformity behind a pleasing illusion, and she flushed with anger when she revealed his theft of powerful enchantments from her library—enchantments as deadly in mortal hands as Helios' chariot. Circe's voice cracked as she finished her story. She raised her golden cup, took a long drink of wine, and stared between the atrium's marble columns into Aeaea's wilderness.

"What about my cats?" Astrid probed after a time. "What is their part in all this?"

The goddess shifted on the cushions. "There was a young Oread who attended me, named Iaria," she began. "She was born of the winds passing from Egypt across the Aegean, and came to my island to serve and learn. Her beauty was as pure as the desert, and her heart was as vast . . ."

Circe told how Phaethon had used the stolen enchantments to seduce Iaria. She wept when she confessed her rage in learning he had fled Aeaea leaving Iaria pregnant. She stopped, unable to continue.

"What happened to Iaria?" Astrid pressed. "What happened to the child?"

"Confession does not come easily to an immortal," Circe said.

"It does not come easily to anyone."

"No, I suppose not." Circe sat in silence, gathering her strength, then continued impassively as if describing the actions of a stranger. She told Astrid of her rage at Phaethon and Iaria's betrayal and how in a single, irredeemable impulse, she had transformed Iaria into an ordinary house cat.

Astrid immediately realized the implication of Circe's words. "Sigrid's cats . . . they were once Iaria's child," she whispered in shock.

"In my rage, I did not think of the child in her womb. The fetus divided into five kittens, but my enchantment could not divide the essence your cats still share. It enables them to join their bodies and become Swarm, and it binds them psychically when they return to their individual forms."

Astrid stared at her, mute.

"Are you shocked to learn they were once human?" the enchantress challenged, her confession completed, her burden passed to another.

"I—it's disturbing," Astrid stuttered.

"Unnatural?" Circe challenged. "Are they an abomination?"

Astrid lifted Elizabeth in her arms. "No," she whispered, tears forming in her eyes.

"Are their minds so unlike yours?"

"No."

"Do they not feel love? Fear? Hunger? Joy?" Circe challenged.

Astrid remembered experiencing the cat's emotions when she had joined Swarm—and the empathy that had remained even after they had separated. She nodded silently, her fingers tangled in Elizabeth's ginger fur, her thoughts entrained with the cat's soft, rolling purrs.

"What does Phaethon want with them?" she asked. "Why has he taken Spike?"

"He believes their abilities may help him cure his disfigurement."

"Is that possible?"

"It's unlikely. I used all my powers, but nothing could undo the damage of Zeus' bolt. Even Annape tried her considerable skills as a healer—which you have experienced," Circe added with a cryptic smile. "Mere contact with Phaethon's injuries nearly killed her. She only survived by dissolving back into the waters of this island. I did not see her for a month."

"Why don't you stop him?" Astrid pressed. "Certainly, your abilities exceed his."

"The enchantments he stole gave him the ability to conceal himself from me. Elizabeth enabled me to find you at Troy, but Phaethon and Spike remain hidden."

"I can follow the cats' connection to Spike," Astrid finished Circe's thought. "Is that why you brought me here? To lead you to Phaethon?"

"Partly," Circe said as she refilled her cup, "but it's more than that. Since I discovered your animals, I have come to realize that no one recognizes the extent of their potential. I need to learn more about them and their fate, and you are part of that."

"Why? What's my place in all this?"

"The cats have chosen you."

"Because they joined with me?"

"Because they love you."

Astrid felt her breath catch at the enchantress' words. She reached down and stroked Elizabeth, who rested on a cushion beside her.

"Joining with them has changed both you and the animals in ways neither of us understands," Circe said.

She held out her hand and called to the cat. Elizabeth walked across the cushions to rub her cheek against the enchantress' hip. Circe found a piece of fish on the table, and Elizabeth ate it from her hand. "It seems we are both ripples in the wake of their journey," she said.

Elizabeth ate the last of the fish and stood with her front paws on the table's marble edge, surveying the food spread in front of her. Circe smiled and moved her back onto a nearby cushion. The enchantress took a pear from an exquisitely painted bowl and ran it under her nose.

"I've watched humans for millennia—endless repetitions of the same passions, the same self-satisfied pieties, the same greed. Humans no longer surprise me, but sometimes, nature does." She bit into the pear and chewed thoughtfully. "Your animals are unique, five ordinary cats who share the essence, the mind—and sometimes the body—of one great predator. They have opened a new door into the heart of creation; their future must be allowed to unfold."

"What is that future?"

"It has not been written. Neither the fates nor I can see where their promise leads. They may live their lives and be forgotten, or they could change everything. In either case, they are something new in a world that has too long followed the same tragic, predictable path. They must be protected."

"What will happen when Phaethon learns they cannot cure him?" Astrid asked. "What will he do to Spike?"

"The cat is not in danger—not only because Phaethon believes he can help him, but also because he can use the animal to draw me from Aeaea. He will keep him safe until he faces me."

"Why does he hate you so much? Is it because of Iaria?"

"He wants revenge and blames me for his misery."

"But you tried to save him."

"I saved him but could not heal him. He blames me for his suffering—he wishes I had let him die." Circe paused, a barely detectable shiver passing through her slender body. "Also, I am his half-sister, beloved of my immortal parents, but our father was indifferent to Phaethon and his mother. It deepens his resentment." Circe stared at Astrid as if searching for some reaction to her revelations.

"I just want to find my cats and return home," Astrid said.

The enchantress nodded. "He cannot return here," she continued. "I've invoked enchantments that bar him from my island, and I cannot find him. We are in a stalemate until one of us acts."

"Then we should act first. Come with me. I will lead you to Phaethon, and you can end this."

Circe laughed. "No wonder Odysseus is fond of you. You're as impetuous as he is."

"Why won't you help me?"

"Just like a mortal," Circe said sharply. "I sent Proteus to you, and he healed your injury; I showed you how to locate your missing animal; I sent the horses as a sign to Nestor; I watch you constantly and can be at your side in the space of a breath. And now you sit at my table, begging for more. There is no point in my holding your hand on Nestor's ship."

"What aren't you telling me?" Astrid demanded.

"Child, you cannot begin to comprehend the things I am not telling you."

"Things like your feelings for Phaethon? You still love him, don't you?"

"How dare you," Circe challenged angrily. "If it were not for these animals—"

"Is it true?"

Circe took a deep breath, calming herself through a visible effort. She lifted her golden dish from the marble surface, carefully selecting and arranging delicacies from her table on the golden circle like a lost Euclidean diagram.

"Phaethon?" Her tone turned bitter. "Love him? Yes, I love him. Hate him? Yes, I hate him. I saved him, I crippled him, I grieve for him, and I will kill him to set this right." Circe lay back among the cushions and fleeces. "It's enough to put any woman on edge," she complained.

Astrid felt her head spin from frustration, wine, and exhaustion. She closed her eyes and welcomed the breeze that moved through the atrium, cool against her face. She watched it send ripples through Elizabeth's long fur. "How did the cats come to Sigrid's home?"

"I met your mother at the university. I had learned of her course in Homer, and she had a unique understanding of my age. I attended her lectures, and we became friends. After I changed Iaria, I could not bear to be reminded of what I had done. I knew your mother would care for her, and she agreed to take the cat. I did not know of the kittens' abilities; I only knew my shame would be hidden."

"But Phaethon found her."

"Iaria is not the only one of my attendants he had deceived. There is another named Lara, who told him where Iaria had gone."

"That's why he came to my home. To steal one of my animals."

"His clumsy use of my enchantments ruptured the fabric of space and time. I followed the disturbances to Sigrid's home. That was where . . . Well, you know the rest."

"What happened to Lara?" Astrid asked warily.

"Lara? She still serves me," Circe said resentfully. "I'm not a monster; I could not kill another child. Also, now that I know of her tendency to speak indiscreetly, she may prove useful."

Circe rose from the cushions and started across the atrium. "I've answered enough questions for one night. It is not something to which a goddess is accustomed, and I am tired."

Wait," Astrid said, rushing after her. "A few days after the kittens were born, their mother disappeared. I'd assumed she was killed by a coyote."

"I will send Annape to your room in case you need anything," Circe said without stopping.

"It wasn't a coyote, was it?" Astrid pressed, following her into the hallway. "Stealing Spike was not Phaethon's first visit."

The enchantress stopped and turned to Astrid. "I did not recognize the disturbance caused by his earlier visit for what it was."

"What happened?"

"As I had feared, seeing Iaria as an animal enraged him."

"It was him," Astrid whispered. "He killed her."

Chapter 36

Strachys walked beside the quickly flowing stream as he'd often done since the golden text had entered his body. He followed its fractal path up the mountainside to a small stand of trees and thriving vegetation, an island of grace where an artesian spring emerged among Kyros' arid hills. Moss and ivy surrounded the terraced pools through which the water descended to the stream bed, its mossy banks a home for insects, snails, amphibians, and all the creatures that fed upon them. Strachys sat where the stream started its descent, his hand resting on the bag that contained Circe's stolen scroll—the source of the power that filled him and the master whose absence meant death. He watched the water emerge from years underground into the patient sunlight to flow past his home and down the mountain to the village with its groves of stunted olive trees, its goats grazing the wild grasses, its terraced fields of irrigated barley. The sounds of the stream carried him into meditation, his mind as transparent as water.

"Seer," Proxonos' voice interrupted Strachys' tranquility, "the woman weaving at your cabin told me you would be here."

"Yes," Strachys said calmly, watching the mercenary walk the last few yards between them. "I find the sound of the water helps focus my mind."

"Focus on what?"

"On nothing," Strachys said without irony. "What brings you here?"

"One of my men needs your attention."

"I have visited them, treated their wounds."

"His wound is not healing. There's a rot in it," Proxonos demanded.

"I'll bring a poultice this afternoon."

"Come now."

Strachys closed his eyes for a moment, sensing the distant warrior and the state of his injury. "The wound causes him little pain, and the infection is not serious. I will finish my meditation."

Proxonos grabbed him angrily by the arm, lifting him from his seat. "Seer, I'm sick of your excuses. You will come now."

Strachys looked at him, neither in fear nor anger, but with something like curiosity. His eyes moved to Proxonos' hand. The mercenary cried out in pain and lurched back, his right arm hanging at his side, a stilled pendulum.

"Please sit." Strachys said and gestured toward a nearby flat rock.

Proxonos cursed and remained standing. He grasped his bicep desperately with his left hand, then pounded it with his fist. His eyes narrowed, and he glanced at the bag containing the scroll, resting on the stream bank.

"I see our employer has told you about the scroll," Strachys said. "Perhaps he mentioned the bond I share with it?"

"I don't know what you're talking about."

"You lie effortlessly but unconvincingly. If you have any thoughts of removing it from my side, know this . . . I could end you as easily as I froze your arm—and before you took a second step."

"Why don't you?"

"The man who shares this body with me resists the thought," Strachys said abstractly. "I don't understand why."

Proxonos swore and rubbed his right arm vigorously.

"Sensation will return shortly," Strachys said, returning to his seat on the stream bank. He stared at Proxonos abstractly, analytically. "You're unlike the other men I've met—even your mercenaries. All men are violent, selfish, but you . . ." he paused, groping for words, "you seem empty."

"Shut up, old man, or I swear I'll find a way—"

"No," Strachys interrupted. "You'll do nothing, and I will leave soon."

"Why don't you leave now?" Proxonos snarled, slowly moving the fingers of his right hand as sensation returned.

"I have more to learn here," Strachys said, gesturing once more toward the nearby stone.

Proxonos sat warily. "Like what?"

"Little from you, so mind yourself," Strachys warned. "You're a curiosity at best—a man so empty but still able to command others. Our employer interests me more. He knows powerful enchantments but learns little from them. He longs to heal his injuries, but I doubt it will give him peace. He speaks of these gods of yours—even his father—with such rage. I want to learn more about these gods, who are like men but so cruel to them."

"The gods are cruel because they're like men. They're like men because men invented them." Proxonos said, still massaging his arm and hand.

Strachys laughed. "Just when I think you are of no interest, you show genuine insight. Perhaps your emptiness holds lessons after all." He leaned toward the mercenary. "These animals Phaethon seeks interest me a great deal. How can they join their minds and bodies completely and then return to their original forms? How can they merge with that woman . . . that unremarkable female?"

"Be careful what you ask, seer," Proxonos warned. "Phaethon confronted that 'unremarkable female' and her cats at Troy and came back with his tail between his legs."

"There's much I don't understand," Strachys acknowledged. "Perhaps you and I are not so different. Like you, I benefit from letting Phaethon walk his path and following behind him."

The mercenary scowled.

"Come." Strachys stood and placed the bag with its precious contents over his shoulder. "We will go and attend to your man's wounds."

Phaethon crossed the empty megaron of Etagama's palace and entered his sanctuary. He found Claea arranging his bedding. She turned and smiled. "I was preparing your quarters."

Wildflowers fanned from a vase on a small table near the bed, and a candle burned beside them. Phaethon walked to the table and rested his fingers on the rim of the vase, then leaned down to smell the unassuming blossoms. "You picked these for me?"

Claea nodded. "I wanted to brighten your room—to surprise you—but I'm not finished. I thought you would stay longer with King Etagama."

Phaethon sat on the bed wearily. "Etagama honors me, but I come here to rest, not to sit through sacrifices of screaming cattle, endless chants to the gods, and his courtiers' sycophantic, drunken babble. I think I've demonstrated enough gratitude for this visit."

Claea sat on the bed near him. "Why do you come here?"

"Because, gentle Claea, there is no other place I can truly rest, where I can drop my pretense and simply be."

"If that is so, then why do you leave?"

He smiled, struck by the purity of her question.

"Do you look forward to seeing me?" She lowered her gaze.

He lifted her chin and looked into her eyes. "Yes."

"Nothing more?"

"What are you asking?"

"Do you . . . do you love me?" Claea stammered, a flush spreading across her face.

He stared at her for a long time, running his fingertips along the contours of her face, lingering on the fading scars and bruises left by Akiala's brutality—marks that time had nearly erased from sight. She placed her hand on his cheek and kissed him. His lips neither welcomed nor resisted her touch.

"Claea, I cannot."

"Why? Don't I please you?"

"Little else pleases me."

"Then, why?"

"I've told you. I must heal my injuries, and I must punish those who have caused them."

"I see no injuries."

"They are there, deep in my flesh—and in my heart."

"And this revenge?"

"It is my due," he said, metal in his voice, "and it is my duty."

Claea took his hand and held it, her eyes searching his face. "Perhaps learning to live with the injuries of the flesh can itself heal the heart."

She stood to leave, pausing to survey the room and ensure that everything was in its proper order. "I will be nearby, should you need me."

Claea lowered her head in the hint of a bow, then left, closing the door behind her. Phaethon walked to the door and secured the bolt. He saw his shadow appear suddenly on the rough wood as if a fire had ignited behind him. He turned and saw Strachys' image at the foot of his bed, surrounded by a shimmering corona.

"I waited for her to leave," the seer said indifferently.

"Were you eavesdropping?" Phaethon scowled.

"Why is this woman important to you?" Strachys asked, ignoring his question. "You have not taken her as a lover."

"She's none of your concern," Phaethon snapped. He returned to his bed, walking through Strachys' image. His passage disrupted the projection, leaving cubist fragments of the seer's face and body to swirl in his wake. He sat as the image reassembled itself.

"You must be growing stronger," Phaethon said wearily. "You've always appeared smaller than this, like a mouse on my table. What do you want?"

Strachys nodded, either ignoring Phaethon's sarcasm or failing to grasp it. "The woman, Astrid, has gone to the enchantress."

"How do you know?"

"I used my enchantments to follow Nestor's ship. It landed on a small island where a woman appeared to her. They spoke of Circe, then vanished."

"To Aeaea?"

"Only Astrid," Strachys explained. "The other woman was never really there."

"What do you mean?"

"She was an enchantment. She said Circe spoke through her."

"Just like the bitch, hiding behind her illusions," Phaethon swore. "Did the animals leave the island?"

"No."

"Send me there now. I can take one before she returns."

Strachys shook his head. "When the woman and the animals are together, I'm strongly aware of them; her presence seems to gather and focus their minds. When the cats are alone, my sense of them is vague."

"There's always a reason you cannot do as I ask," Phaethon said angrily.

"Animal minds move over their perceptions of the world like water over stones. They are harder to track than humans, whose minds turn inward like flames that fan themselves. If I err when I transport you—"

"Yes. Yes, I know. I could appear under the sea or inside a rock."

Strachys ignored his sarcasm. "You must return at once. I'll know when she returns from Aeaea. The passage will leave her disoriented, and I'll send you to her side without warning. You can easily take an animal."

"Can't you send Proxonos?"

"No. You know enchantments that carry you across space like Hermes himself. I must rely on them to send you to Astrid's side. Proxonos knows nothing but brutality."

"I'm tired. I'll rest the night and return in the morning," Phaethon said. "And seer—no more eavesdropping."

Strachys nodded in acceptance and vanished, leaving the glowing nimbus to fade like a lamp consuming the last of its oil. Phaethon sat on the edge of the bed beside Claea's wildflowers. He stared at them with longing as the blue light flared briefly around him, then faded, leaving his injured body behind. He wrapped himself in the clean fleece Claea had left for him and stared at the flowers in the candlelight.

Chapter 37

Astrid stood barefooted beneath the marble lintel, looking out across Circe's meadow. She raised the cup to her nose, inhaled deeply, and smiled. She had discovered the coffee next to her bed when she'd awakened, steaming in a cup decorated in the Mycenaean style, with a row of maidens carrying gifts to a woman—presumably a goddess—who reclined on a dais. She'd also found a plate of fruit, cheese, and bread, a bowl of cooked fish, and another of milk. She had placed the milk and fish on the floor for Elizabeth. Still full after Circe's feast, Astrid had picked at the fruit, but she surrendered unconditionally to the coffee, this most welcome of the anachronisms that surrounded the enchantress.

She wore the jeans and sweater she had found clean and folded near the bed. Initially, she had thought they were her own but quickly realized they were duplicates. The pants were not denim, but linen, skillfully dyed and woven to match her worn jeans. Instead of wool, her sweater rested against her skin with silk's unmistakable caress.

She felt a pressure against her leg and saw Elizabeth look up at her, purring softly. "Shall we take a walk?" she asked leaning down to stroke Elizabeth's long ginger fur.

Astrid drained the last of the coffee, placed the cup on the floor next to the column, and led Elizabeth into the meadow. She saw two young girls—Nymphs and Circe's servants, she assumed—passing about thirty feet away, dressed in jeans and sweaters like her own, one in the same shades of faded denim and black she wore, the other in wine-colored pants and a bright saffron sweater. Astrid watched them pass, laughing and talking to one another. The girls saw her, smiled shyly, and hurried on their way.

"It seems we've started a fashion trend."

Astrid thought of Elizabeth's littermates. She felt worry for their safety and a deep longing to see them again. A wave of emotions surged into

Astrid's awareness. She sensed they came from Elizabeth, a resonance of her own feelings. Astrid kneeled beside the cat. "What is it, Biffy? Did you feel what I was thinking? Did I remind you of your brothers and sisters?"

The cat looked up at her, copper-colored eyes round with intensity.

"Come, I want to try something."

Astrid led Elizabeth to a fallen tree at the edge of the meadow. She sat on the soft grass behind it, concealed from Circe's palace, her back against the moss-covered trunk. She held Elizabeth on her lap, her eyes closed, her attention focused on the rhythms of the cat's breathing. As Astrid cleared her mind, she felt Elizabeth's sentience—expansive, wordless, flowing like water through her awareness. Cautiously, she opened her mind to the cat's presence. Almost immediately, she felt prick of a thousand pins on her skin, the stripping of her memories, and the terrifying loss of self she had experienced before. She pulled her hands away and opened her eyes. She saw Annape standing a few yards away.

"I did not hear you come."

"You were deep into your sharing with Elizabeth," Annape said as she sat cross-legged in front of Astrid. "I did not want to disturb you." She reached and stroked the cat's soft fur.

"Do I have you to thank for the coffee this morning?" Astrid smiled.

"My mistress said it was a drink from your home. She gave me the beans. I roasted them, ground them between stones, and poured hot water through them the way she told me. Was it to your liking?"

"Delicious. Did you taste it?"

"Yes, but I found it disturbing."

"It's an acquired taste."

"I saw you with Elizabeth," Annape said. "Were you touching her mind?"

"What do you know about that?"

"I know you've joined your body and mind with her siblings."

"I've joined with the cats twice. Both times, it was hard . . . I felt invaded."

"You thought you would try with one cat only?"

"I thought I could explore the change safely—maybe learn to control it better, but it didn't work. Even with Elizabeth, I felt like I was being torn apart, my memories stripped away, like I would lose myself completely."

"I understand," Annape said. "Our memories, our desires, our beliefs are the stories we tell ourselves to understand our life, who we are in the world of men. We depend on them. Looking past them can be frightening."

"Looking past them?"

"These stories are not who we are; they are only reflections of ourselves, like a mirror."

"It didn't feel like I was losing a reflection," Astrid said. "The first time I joined with the cats it felt like I was losing myself, like I was dying."

Annape shook her head. "I have touched Elizabeth. She is a deep and gentle creature. There is nothing to fear."

"Touched her?," Astrid asked. "You mean you—"

"Joined with her?" Annape interrupted. "Not the way you have. I sensed her nature much as I sensed your feelings and past injuries when I joined you in the bath."

The Naiad watched Astrid's face for her reaction. Astrid took her hand and squeezed it gently. "It's all right, Annape."

"May I show you something?"

Astrid nodded.

The Naiad smiled and placed Astrid's right hand on Elizabeth's back. She put her own hand behind the cat's head, where it joined with her spine, and grasped Astrid's left hand with her other, forming a circle of the three of them. Astrid sensed Annape's presence, an impulse without intention, mediating her thoughts and the currents of Elizabeth's sentience. She closed her eyes and felt Elizabeth's presence move through her, a spreading intimacy. Astrid's memories unwound through her awareness as they had before, but without the terrifying sense of their being stripped away. She felt empty but strangely whole.

She opened her eyes. Annape sat before her, holding her hands, smiling. Astrid saw the meadow in sharper definition, in deep shades of blue and green. The motion of trees and flowers in the breeze, the sound of birds' wings against the air, the pungency of moss on the nearby stream banks— all caught her attention immediately, then faded just as quickly. A breeze touched her face, and she could discern subtle variations in its currents. She felt a new strength in her limbs, simultaneously energizing and calming. Astrid looked down and saw her skin covered with a soft orange fur. A rhythmic hum resonated in her throat, and Astrid realized she was purring. She felt Elizabeth's presence sharing her mind—gentle, comforting.

She heard Annape whisper, "Come back now."

Astrid followed the Naiad's voice. Air flooded her lungs, and a spasm ran through her body, simultaneously pleasurable and unsettling. She opened her eyes and saw Elizabeth resting on the grass between her and Annape, looking up with half-closed eyes. "What happened?"

"You joined your body and mind with Elizabeth."

"But I was not overwhelmed," Astrid said. "The other times I joined with Swarm, I felt my memories torn away. When I returned to my own body, I was so disoriented I couldn't speak at first. What did you do?"

"Very little," Annape said. "I helped you see yourself and Elizabeth directly, without fear or illusion. The things you feared losing were only reflections of this deeper reality."

"Did you learn that from Circe?"

"No. My mistress knows great enchantments. I do not."

"How can I do that again?"

"It will come with practice."

"I'm not sure how often I want to do that, even in practice," Astrid said.

The Naiad smiled.

"Annape, when I joined with Swarm before, my vision changed."

"Predators do not need a full range of colors. Their eyes are formed for seeing in darkness and detecting the movements of prey."

"I understand, but this was different. Do you know about Phaethon? How he can become a sort of monster?"

"The shape of a man and the strength and speed of a snake?"

Astrid nodded.

"It's one of the enchantments he stole from my mistress."

"Before I came here, I had merged with Swarm and fought him."

"I found traces of the injury still on you," Annape acknowledged.

"When we were in the bath?"

"Yes," Annape said shyly.

Astrid smiled. "When I merged with Swarm," she said, "I briefly saw the injured man within the monster. I could still see the enchantment that cloaked him, but it was transparent, like a hologram."

Astrid saw the confusion on Annape's face. "I'm sorry. That word, 'hologram,' is from my home. It is an image of a thing, but it is made of light."

"Yes, an enchantment," Annape said enthusiastically. "Animals are less easily distracted by them. Joining your mind with the cats' enabled you to see the reality beneath it."

"But when Swarm attacked the creature, I could no longer see Phaethon's injuries, only the monster. What changed?"

"When you join with the cats—or when the cats join with each other—your minds do not become one so much as they strive for harmony, like the strings of a lyre," Annape explained. "When the cats saw the danger of the monster, their instinct to defend themselves overwhelmed the deeper reality you had seen."

Astrid realized her joints had grown stiff from sitting on the ground. She placed Elizabeth on the grass and stood. "Walk with me," she said.

The sun had climbed in the sky and lifted the dew through the grass into the soft air. The smells awakened Astrid's childhood memories of freshly mown lawns and summers free from school. The lion that had greeted her upon coming to Aeaea raised his head to watch them pass, then returned to his nap, his tail twitching idly.

"Annape, how did an African lion come to this island? Did Circe bring him here?"

"No, he came by himself."

"How?"

"He was the leader of a pride but had grown too old to protect them. When a younger male overcame him, he wandered away to die of his wounds, as nature demands, but his heart remained strong. He walked a path between life and death until it led him here. It happens with some animals, especially those who are strong and wise."

"How did he cross the ocean?"

Annape placed her hand on Astrid's chest, over her heart. "Do not think of oceans and places and distances. The geography that matters is here."

Astrid smiled. "The other animals . . . the wolves I heard howling last night, did they come here the same way?"

"Yes. There is a bear who was injured while she was pregnant. She did not want her cubs to die, so she came here and gave birth."

"Will these animals live forever?"

"No, but they will live full lives and pass gently."

"Could men come here in ships?"

"Only if my mistress or the Fates allow it."

"Will Odysseus come?"

Annape smiled knowingly. "If it pleases Circe."

"I think it will." Astrid laughed. "The swine that roam the island . . . were any of them once men?"

"From time to time, bad men have found their way here."

"And Circe transformed them."

"Their natures were troubled—they're happier this way."

As they continued across the meadow, Astrid found herself strangely reassured by Annape's presence. They climbed the small rise from which Astrid had first seen Circe's palace, stopped, and sat on the grass, looking down at the marble structure that seemed to emerge from the ground like a giant crystal.

"Annape, when you helped me join with Elizabeth, you told me that what I feared losing was only a reflection. What did you mean?"

Annape furrowed her brow once more, struggling for words to describe a concept she found so basic that it rarely entered her thoughts—like a fish trying to explain water or a bird the wind.

"We are born without memories, without stories," she explained. "The world has not marked us, but we are empty and helpless. As we age, we create a story of who we are out of our experiences, skills we learn, people we meet . . . It becomes a self with which we face the world."

"I think I understand," Astrid said. "We look at that story and think we see ourselves, but it's only a reflection of our experiences—it isn't real."

Annape smiled patiently. "It is real but different—and it is necessary. It is what allows us to face the world with its gifts and brutality, but it also confines us. Joining with Elizabeth did not fit your story."

"Because all my experience told me it was impossible?"

"Yes. Like many things, it was impossible until it happened. That is why your stories had to be pushed aside to see a reality they denied. It caused you great distress, but it did you no harm. Now, joining with the cats has become part of your story. It will become easier."

"Annape, what is behind the reflection? A true self?"

Annape shook her head. "One is not truer than the other. They are merely different."

"Different how?"

"I cannot describe it in words."

"Because words are stories?"

"Yes. As soon as we speak of it—it becomes part of another story."

Astrid laughed softly. "But there must be a deeper reality," she said. "Something behind all our stories."

Annape leaned toward her and took her hand. "Of course," she said, "but it cannot be told. It can only be lived."

They sat quietly for a time, watching animals large and small crawling and flying across the meadow as Astrid struggled to absorb Annape's strange, circular reasoning. A flock of robins landed near the stream and searched for worms in the damp earth. Three deer approached the stream to drink. The birds ignored them.

Myia sat in the sand watching Audrey, Greystoke, and Chessie explore each nearby bush, rock, or burrow. Two warriors Nestor had assigned to protect her stood nearby, looking up and down the beach and into the hills. Since Astrid's departure, the cats had grown increasingly uneasy, distracted by the men maintaining the camp and unsettled by Astrid's absence. Eager to test her deepening relationship with the cats, Myia had led them away from camp to the spot where they had last seen Astrid. She watched them explore the area, sniffing the locations where Astrid had rested, where she had rushed to the water to greet her friend, and the path she had taken with the strange woman. Myia felt them grow calm and slowed her own breathing, trying to sense the animals' emotions.

Chessie stopped in her explorations and stared with round eyes toward Nestor's beached ship. Audrey and Greystoke joined her immediately. Myia followed their gaze and saw Antilochus approach along the water's edge.

"Myia," he said as he drew near, "how are the animals?"

"I sensed they wanted to come here. It seems I was right."

"I'll keep an eye on things," Antilochus told the guards. "You can return to the ship."

The warriors hesitated. "Nestor wanted two men to protect her and the animals," one of them protested.

"It will be all right," Antilochus said. "I'll be here, and Myia is armed."

The warriors nodded reluctantly. They walked up the beach toward the ship, stopped a discrete distance away, and sat under a tree to keep protective eyes on Myia and Nestor's son.

Antilochus sat in the sand beside the girl. "Are the cats well?"

"They've been uneasy since Astrid left, but being here seems to help."

He stretched his legs out in the white sand, listening to the rhythms of the surf, watching the cats resume their explorations.

"You've grown close to them," he observed.

"Yes, they trust me more every day."

"I meant something deeper, like with Astrid."

"I'm not sure. I feel things from them, but I don't think it's the same."

Antilochus stared silently across the water.

"Why do I feel there's something you want to say to me?" Myia asked.

Antilochus smiled nervously. "Do you remember when we fought Phaethon back at Troy? How we remembered it one way until Astrid and my father led us to see through Athena's enchantments?"

"Yes."

"Since then, more memories have come to me out of nowhere. I'm not sure which are real and which are not. I find myself asking questions."

She looked at him inquisitively.

"Were you ever at the camp before?"

Myia sprang to her feet, her sword in her hand. "What are you saying?"

Antilochus did not move or touch his weapon. "Myia, I need to know what is true and what is an illusion. I need to trust my mind, and I need to trust you. Are you the woman who disappeared from camp a few years ago?"

"Am I the woman who saw her family slaughtered? Who was brought there as a slave," she replied angrily, "and given to a man to use as he pleased?"

Antilochus closed his eyes and nodded.

"Did I kill the man who tried to rape me?"

"Myia . . ."

"What are you going to do?"

"Nothing. I just needed to know." Antilochus stared at her for a time. "I would have done the same thing. The man you killed was—"

"He was a pig. He deserved to die," Myia interrupted. "Are you going to tell the others?"

"No," he said softly. "Back in the camp, when Phaethon attacked, you fought beside me. You could have died, but you fought anyway."

Myia stared at him, her breathing slowing. She sat near him on the sand. "Can an Achaean warrior call a woman a comrade?" she asked.

"That is the easy part. What comes next is harder."

Antilochus and Myia sat together in silence, staring quietly across the water. After a time, he took his feet and held his hand out to her. "We should return to the ship."

Myia let him help her up, and they started up the beach, the cats following close behind. He did not release her hand, nor did she pull away.

Chapter 38

Circe watched a Nereid struggle to uncork a bottle of wine. It was from Astrid's time, a Bordeaux, and it looked expensive. The enchantress frowned as the extractor pulled out, scattering fragments of cork onto the marble table.

"It's all right," she told the Nereid, her frown giving way to a patient smile. "Nothing has fallen into the wine. Just finish like I showed you."

The young woman gathered the bottom of her tunic in her hand and used it to wipe the fragments of cork from the mouth of the bottle. She reapplied the extractor with intense concentration, and the remaining cork emerged in one piece. She filled Circe's crystal glass—another souvenir from Astrid's age. The enchantress smiled and nodded.

"I understand you spent time with Annape this morning," Circe said.

"She showed me how to merge with Elizabeth without . . . well, with less fear of losing myself."

"She is unique, a gift."

"I'm not sure I'll be able to do it again without her," Astrid said as the Nereid filled her glass. At Circe's request, she'd left Elizabeth in her room with one of her attendants.

"Annape's gifts often exceed my own abilities," the enchantress admitted. "What I achieve through art, she does effortlessly, through her nature, but she leaves a mark. You won't forget. It will return to you when you need it."

Astrid sipped the wine, masking her doubts. The glass was as thin as an eggshell and shivered like a living thing as it brushed her lips. She held it by the stem in front of one of the gold sconces that lined the atrium and watched the wine refract the light like a ruby floating in space.

Circe smiled. "I wanted to celebrate. You'll be leaving soon."

Astrid sat up on the cushions. "Leaving? Back to Nestor? But I have so many questions."

"I'll answer as many as I can."

"I still don't know how I'll get home."

"I'll return you once you reunite the animals."

"Will it be like before?" Astrid asked.

"What do you mean?"

"When I came here, it was difficult, disorienting. I didn't even know I had left my own time. I was still in my house, then it disappeared. At first, I couldn't speak at all, then I couldn't speak your language . . ."

"When I send you home, I will ease your passage," Circe reassured, "sliding you through gaps in space and time. Phaethon does not understand the enchantments he stole. His clumsy efforts created a rupture between our worlds, and you fell through it without protection. It could have destroyed your mind, possibly killed you."

"I think it almost did."

"Your will is strong, and it brought elements of your world through the rupture with you—your house, your belongings. They insulated you from the change. As your mind aligned with this reality, your home and possessions vanished."

"Is that why it took me a while to understand your language?"

"You were adapting to the transition," Circe said. She gestured at the food covering her table. "Eat, and we'll talk."

Astrid thought of the sparse fare waiting for her on Nestor's ship and eagerly filled her plate.

"What's on your mind, child?" Circe asked as Astrid began to eat.

"I'm not ready to leave here . . . to face Phaethon."

The enchantress leaned forward and arranged a selection of fruits on her golden plate. "You must trust me," she said. "It is time."

"Time," Astrid said ironically.

"What is it?"

"You travel in time. You've visited Phaethon in the distant past, and you've also been to my home. You must know something about the future, about what will happen to my animals and me, but you've told me nothing. What is it you're not saying? Am I going to die? Are Nestor and his men in danger? What about Myia and my cats?"

Circe glanced at her attendants. "Could you leave us alone, please?"

The Nereids hurried from the atrium, except for Annape, who looked at her mistress inquisitively.

"You too, Annape. We'll be fine."

Annape nodded, glanced at Astrid, and left. "I wonder if my fondness for Annape hasn't gone to her head," Circe mused.

"I doubt it," Astrid said, "she seems beyond such things."

"I suppose she is," Circe acknowledged. She sipped her wine thoughtfully. "You talk as if I could visit the future, then come home and draw a map."

"Can't you?"

"'Travel' is a poor metaphor for an immortal's experience of time. You think of time as something orderly, with each action creating a new branch that moves on its way—tidy causes and effects we can analyze and manipulate. I think you read too much science fiction."

"All right then, what is time?"

"Child, time is a tangle, a hopeless tangle, a tangle of tangles." The enchantress cut a slice of cheese, placed it on a fresh fig, and nibbled thoughtfully. "I can move through time, alter this or that outcome, but every action I make sends ripples through time and space—even into the past, such as when you came to Troy—endless tangles of shifting, interconnected probabilities. Even the present shifts constantly under my feet, like a raft in a whirlpool."

"I don't understand."

"Try to think of time as a maze that continuously reshapes itself as we pass through it—whether through the normal flow of time or other channels, like those that brought you here. The complexity is more than even Zeus can untangle. As an immortal, I see it all—and I see it all at once."

"Still, you move through time," Astrid challenged.

"Immortality would be unbearable if one were forever trapped in the present." Circe raised her glass and drank deeply. "But that does not mean the future is spread out before me, waiting to be shaped to my ends."

"But you do act. You followed Phaethon to my time."

"I also went to the past and intervened in his death. My indiscretion has brought this danger, just as it produced your remarkable animals. But I foresaw neither. I acted impulsively, and I was arrogant. Experience has made me cautious. Unlike an immortal, your ignorance gives you greater freedom to act."

"I'm flattered," Astrid said sarcastically. She leaned toward the enchantress. "These philosophical questions are interesting, perhaps important, but I have to leave here and fight for my life—for the cats' lives. What can you tell me that will help us survive?"

Circe leaned back among her cushions, staring out into the night. She seemed to be weighing her words as if misspeaking could lead to disaster. "I've searched the probabilities that surround both of us, the potential outcome of every action I could take—they all tell me the same thing. Letting you and your animals pursue your future alone is our best hope."

"That's our best hope?"

"Perhaps our only hope. I am the object of Phaethon's hatred. Any further intervention on my part will only draw his attention to you. Even bringing you here created risks, but it was necessary. You must believe me; I will come to you at the proper time."

Astrid nodded, then rose from the table and walked to the edge of the atrium, staring out into the darkness.

"I've faced Phaethon twice," she said without turning, "and he almost killed me both times. The second time Antilochus, three of his warriors, Myia, and Swarm fought beside me. He would have killed us all if Athena had not intervened. What chance do I have?"

"You're not the person who fought him. Each time you fight and survive, you grow stronger, and so does Swarm."

"So, are we wearing him down?" Astrid asked ironically.

Circe smiled. "For all their abilities, your cats are still animals. They are incomplete in so many ways. Merging with you has started to complete them. It has brought a human mind into the equation—"

"Equation?" Astrid interrupted angrily. She returned to stand beside Circe's table. "Is that all this is to you? An equation to be solved? All this talk about fate and probabilities, the unfolding of the universe . . . What about my animals?"

"Watch your tongue," Circe snapped.

"What about Spike?" Astrid challenged, ignoring the goddess' warning as anger grew within her. "What about Elizabeth? What about Audrey, Chessie, and Greystoke? They're just cats. They don't understand any of this. They just want to live—they deserve to live."

"If you were not Sigrid's daughter . . ." Circe said, her voice quivering with anger. "You are just like your mother—stubborn, determined, infuriating, always drawn to homeless cats or injured birds, lonely people, mad people, lost causes—"

"My God," Astrid interrupted, her breath catching in her chest as the realization seized her. "I've been a fool. How could I not have seen it?"

Circe stared silently.

"You and Sigrid were lovers," Astrid said in a rush of understanding. "It's obvious. In everything you've said, in the way you speak of her, trusting her with Iaria. Why didn't I see it before?"

Astrid's words flew through Circe's atrium, running desperately behind her thoughts. "I found a picture among her possessions, a picture only a lover could take," she said. "There was a note with it—something about 'a spirit shining across time and worlds.' That was you, wasn't it?"

"It means nothing."

"No. That's not true. My mother and I shared everything. She wouldn't be ashamed to tell me of a lover—she had before. It could only have been something she believed I wouldn't understand, like a love affair with a Bronze Age goddess."

The enchantress seemed to relax as if in surrender. She took a deep sip of wine and held it in her mouth for a moment before swallowing. "Well, the age difference would have been hard to explain," Circe confessed, her voice softly ironic. "Sit down. Please."

Astrid did not move but stood trembling with emotion.

"Please," the enchantress repeated.

Astrid took a deep breath and returned to her place at the table. Circe refilled both their glasses. Astrid drank deeply as the enchantress stared between the columns, out into Aeaea's darkness.

"Your age fascinates me," she began. "An explosion of science, art, and invention among people whose capacity for brutality exceeds even Agamemnon's. I visit often, and on one of my visits, I learned of your mother's course at the university—her course on Homer. I could not resist the chance to hear her speak of my age . . . and of me."

"So, gods have egos."

"Child, you cannot imagine—but your mother saw through that. She saw through me. We fell in love immediately."

"Did you love her?" Astrid asked. "Truly?"

Circe stared out into the night as a tear inscribed her cheek with the signature of grief.

"I can only hope you will find a love like ours, and I tremble in fear for you should it come."

"Did you bring her here?"

"Oh yes, she visited often. She ate at this table and shared my bed. I asked her to stay, but she refused."

"Why?"

"She loved the life she'd made—like I said, she was stubborn. Most of all, she loved you."

Astrid felt the muscles in her chest tighten, her breath catching, tears moistening her cheeks. "What happened?" Astrid pressed.

"Like all things human, it ended."

"I was with her in her last months. Why didn't you come to her?"

"I was there constantly," Circe said softly. "I visited during the day when you left on errands. I was one of the rabbits she watched playing in the grass when she sat on her porch, wrapped in her blanket. I was among the birds on her windowsill, and I came to her in the scent of the flowers you placed near her bed. I came as rain, as cooling breezes, as sunlight on her skin, and she knew I was there. I was with her the night she died."

"How could you have been? I was in the room."

"I remained unseen to all but her, but I held her close, and her spirit passed through me as it released."

They sat together in silence for a time, touching neither the food that covered the polished marble nor the wine glasses that stood like two dark moons above an abandoned field of plenty.

The enchantress took Astrid's hand. "Child," she said, "even an immortal can love, and I can grieve. I can also make mistakes, but you must trust me when I say I've done all I can to help you and your animals—and I will continue to do so."

"But I don't know what I'm supposed to do."

"You will know when the time comes. I promise." Circe squeezed Astrid's hand. "Astrid, it's time for you to leave, and you must make a decision."

"A decision?"

"I can return you to the beach where Nestor and your friends wait, or you can take a more difficult route."

Astrid looked at her inquisitively.

"There is one named Tiresias, whose ability to see into the tangle of time exceeds my own—he exceeds even Proteus. I can see possible futures, even see into the tapestry woven by the Fates, but Tiresias sees the patterns that bind all realities, all worlds—that bind spacetime itself. He may see something of use to you."

"He's in the underworld, in Hades," Astrid whispered.

"Death is the source of his power," Circe acknowledged.

"I've read that you will send Odysseus to him after he visits you."

"Yes, for reasons much like yours."

"There are dangers . . ."

"To your life? Few and easily avoided. Do not eat food from Hades or you will be unable to leave. Do not linger; keep moving, or the shades of the dead will overwhelm you. The dangers are to your mind; no one passes through there untouched."

"Could Tiresias help me face Phaethon and end this?"

"Possibly."

"What about Elizabeth?"

"She'll be safe. Animals do not see death until it comes to them. To her, it will seem strange, and she'll stay close to you."

"What's it like? The underworld?"

"You cannot experience it directly—you would go mad. It will come cloaked in metaphor, emerging from the depths inside you. Each person's experience of it is their's alone."

"Are you sure Tiresias will tell me what he sees?"

"Yes, he is bound by Zeus' law and his own nature. He cannot do otherwise—although he can be difficult."

"How will I find my way?"

"I'll send a guide."

"I'll go," Astrid said without hesitation.

Circe rose and walked to where Astrid rested on the cushions. She leaned down and placed her hand on her cheek, turning Astrid's face toward hers. She kissed her gently on the lips—a kiss filled with sorrow and longing.

"I will come to you when it is time," the goddess said. "Do not fear."

Circe turned and crossed the marble floor. She did not follow the hall that led to her bedroom but walked down the steps into the night, crossing the meadow in her bare feet, the hem of her gown dragging through the damp grass, alone—all too human.

Astrid remained at the table for a time measured by the wine remaining and the food she ate without thinking. When she emptied the bottle, she waited for one of Circe's attendants to appear with a replacement. She hoped she might see Annape. No one came.

"Dinner must be over," Astrid said as she rose from the cushions. She walked down the hallway, past the golden sconces, and entered her room.

She stopped in shock.

Claire Ortega sat on the edge of the bed, stroking Elizabeth who rested at her side. She was dressed like a model in an overpriced outdoor outfitters catalog, wearing neat khaki shorts and a bright orange nylon shirt. Both garments had too many pockets and zippers. Instead of her high heels or the athletic shoes she chose from her seemingly endless collection, she wore hiking boots with red-topped gray socks. Her black ponytail passed through the back of an Albuquerque Isotopes baseball cap, shining like a comet on a moonless night.

"What do you think? Not my style, but I make it work."

"What's going on?" Astrid asked, her voice a faint rasp.

"Anthony wanted a camping vacation—Pecos Wilderness. We outvoted him three to one, but he dragged us there anyway."

"So, you're dreaming?"

"When I can sleep. Can you believe the man has me on the ground in a fucking sleeping bag? When I'm not getting poked by rocks, I'm being eaten by insects, and I haven't bathed in days. There isn't a restaurant, spa, or store within fifty miles. He doesn't know it, but the next vacation is going to be San Francisco—and he's paying."

"Wait, I remember this trip, but it was years ago," Astrid said.

"Do I survive?" Claire asked.

"Yes, and so does your marriage. I also remember Anthony does take you to San Francisco."

"Oh?"

"I don't want to spoil it. Why are you here?"

"I have to take you on a hike; hence, the girl scout outfit."

"You're my guide through Hades?"

"I guess so."

"You're guiding me through hell?" Astrid repeated in disbelief.

"Sweetie, it can't be worse than camping."

Claire looked longingly at Astrid's silk gown as she gestured toward the jeans and sweater folded neatly on the bed. Astrid saw a pair of hiking boots and socks on the floor nearby.

"You're overdressed for where we're going," Claire said. "You'd better change."

Chapter 39

The raid began just after dawn. Spike had seen such attacks before, watching from his hiding place outside the village. He remembered the terror of armed men coming from the mercenary camp to steal food and supplies—or worse. He huddled in the house next to the boy and his parents, staring out the door at the villagers running in terror. The boy's father held a short sword.

Spike saw a dozen mercenaries cross the open ground. A young villager rushed at them with an ax. One of the warriors struck his head with the flat of his sword, and he fell unconscious. The old tomcat dragged himself from under the grain store, his crippled leg trailing behind, and hissed at a raider who kicked him brutally, sending him skidding across the dirt to land motionless near the boy's home. Another warrior forced his sword between the slats of the small grain store, prying until the wood gave way and precious barley spilled onto the ground. Laughing, they scooped it up and filled a woven basket. Others stole vessels of oil or wine from the villagers' meager stores. A fat mercenary saw a girl hiding near a hut and ran after her. She escaped, leaving him cursing and panting for breath.

When the mercenaries had what they came for, they left; the entire raid had taken only minutes. Spike saw the boy's father step out in front of the home, holding the sword at his side, shoulders slumped forward in the contours of shame. Spike saw the boy kneel beside the dead tomcat. His cries joined the chorus of grief that filled the village.

Charon, the boatman who ferried the souls of the dead across the river Styx into Hades, pressed his oar against the riverbed to steady his boat as Astrid jumped ashore. Claire handed Elizabeth to her, and Astrid climbed the gravel bank, the cat in her arms. She turned and saw Claire take Charon's hand and step gracefully from the boat. Claire took a wallet from the pocket of her shorts, removed a bill, and handed it to him.

"Did you just tip the boatman of hell?" Astrid whispered to her as Charon rowed into the fog that hugged the river.

"Well, it seemed like the right thing to do. He did row us across in the dark. Besides, he seemed lonely."

"I imagine he is," Astrid said. "Actually, once they invented money, both Greeks and Romans would place coins in the mouths of their dead as payment for the crossing."

"I guess I started something," Claire laughed.

A dim light from no discernible source formed a circle on the dust and gravel where they stood. Outside it, the darkness was complete, as if reality itself had ended. Astrid could not see the cavern's roof or the broader contours of the riverbank, only a path that disappeared into nothingness. She followed behind Claire, holding Elizabeth in her arms, her steps unsure as the gravel shifted under her weight.

"Be careful," Claire said. "The people who usually walk this way are dead—or dreaming like me—they don't weigh anything."

"Claire," Astrid asked, "did Circe just speak through you?"

"I'm not sure . . . I just seem to know."

Astrid followed Claire up the path, the circle of light moving with them to illuminate their steps. Ten yards above the river, the trail broadened into a stone stairway. As Claire started up the stairs, Astrid heard voices behind her. She turned but could not see through the darkness.

"You should hurry," Claire warned. "We don't know who's behind us."

An opening appeared as they climbed the steps, framed in columns and a stone lintel. Drawing closer, Astrid realized the columns and lintel were carved into the rock itself, rising above the debris at their base. Astrid followed Claire into a wide, dimly lit passage that seemed to carry forward endlessly. Shadowy figures passed silently around them, burdened with colorless sacks and boxes. Astrid squinted up the tunnel and saw faint, almost unreadable writing on the walls, high above the cave's floor.

"Come on," Claire said. "This gives me the creeps."

"Wait . . ." Astrid said, "something's familiar."

She gently set Elizabeth on the ground. Unlike the path from the river, it was smooth, like polished concrete. She walked to the side of the tunnel, and Elizabeth followed closely, just as Circe had promised. As she neared the wall, Astrid saw large windows filled with objects of no recognizable function—gray, unmarked boxes and sacks. A shade walked by her without acknowledging her presence, turned into the wall's glass face, and disappeared. A few seconds later, he reappeared, arms laden with objects devoid of either purpose or value, possessions that served only as burdens. Astrid squinted at the faint writing above the windows, unable to quiet a nagging sense of its familiarity. Suddenly, like realizing a face in a crowd belonged to a dimly remembered acquaintance, Astrid recognized a series of corporate logos.

"Claire," she said, "I think we're in a shopping mall."

"I see it," Claire said slowly. She pointed to a bold script covering the wall some twelve feet above the floor. The writing was at least twenty feet across and three feet high. "Isn't that the department store we used to have in Albuquerque . . . before it went bankrupt and got bought out?"

"Apparently, it died and went to hell," Astrid said. "Circe told me that this place would take on the form of something I hated."

Claire laughed softly, as if not wanting to disturb the passing shades. She stood with Astrid near the wall, watching the dead pass around them. The shadows moved quickly, compulsively finding and carrying their meaningless acquisitions. Claire took Astrid's hand and led her forward. Elizabeth walked between them, protected from the passing shadows. As they continued through the tunnel, the shades flowed around them like a muddy river, driven by desires beyond understanding.

After they had walked for almost a hundred yards, the tunnel widened into a large area filled with tables and chairs—all the same, gray color as the walls and floor. A heavy dampness and vague smells of dough cooking in rancid oil filled the air. Astrid recognized the universal layout of a shopping mall food court, and the smells stripped of any recognizable aromas except starch, salt, sugar, and fat—the essence of corporate cuisine. Scattered individuals sat at tables alone, eating mechanically.

A woman approached from among the shades. She pointed at Elizabeth and spoke too softly to be understood. As she drew close, she fell to her knees, weeping, and Elizabeth trotted toward her. Astrid stared in shock as the woman took Elizabeth into her arms. The gray wash that covered her skin, hair, and clothing took on the colors of a young woman—little more than a girl—with dark hair and pale skin, wearing a soft yellow gown and a necklace of lapis beads. She held the cat in a desperate embrace, tears covering her face as Elizabeth rubbed her head against the girl's cheek. The girl responded with a series of purrs and soft meows.

"It's Iaria," Claire whispered in Astrid's ear.

Astrid felt her heart skip. She kneeled in front of the girl, and Iaria opened her mouth in a feline hiss. Astrid held her hand out, palm up. Iaria turned her body sideways, sheltering Elizabeth behind her arm and shoulder.

"It's all right," Astrid reassured. "It's your baby."

Iaria responded dimly to her words.

"I won't hurt you. She's your baby," Astrid repeated.

"Baby," the girl said as an expression of recognition crossed Iaria's face. She rubbed her face against Elizabeth's fur, the cat's soft purrs mixing with her own.

"It's all right, Iaria," Astrid spoke as if comforting a frightened animal. She felt a hand on her shoulder as Claire bent toward her.

"I can keep an eye on Elizabeth," Claire whispered.

"It's okay. Iaria seems comfortable with me."

"No," Claire said, tilting her head toward another approaching shade. "I think you should pay attention to this."

Astrid looked over Claire's shoulder. Her breath caught in her chest as she saw the unmistakable shape of her mother approach from the shadows.

As she ran to the shade, it resolved into the form of Sigrid Lund—not the gaunt, pain-wracked figure Astrid remembered from the months before her death, but a vital woman in her forties. She wore a loose-fitting white blouse over a pleated, dark blue skirt of a style traditionally worn by Navajo women, with a simple necklace of turquoise beads around her neck. It was an outfit she often changed into after a day spent in jeans, a work shirt, and a toolbelt. Astrid reached out anxiously, afraid that her hand might pass through a phantom. Instead, she felt warm flesh against her fingers. She sobbed as she threw her arms around her mother and held her close.

After a long embrace, Sigrid placed her hands on Astrid's shoulders and looked into her eyes. "My darling Astrid," she said softly.

Astrid stared in silence, unable to speak, unable even to breathe.

"My God. Is this where you . . ." Astrid's words trailed off as she began to sob.

"No, darling," Sigrid said, smiling, "this is not where I spend eternity. I'm only visiting . . . to see you."

"I don't understand," Astrid said, the words like dust in her mouth.

"It's hard to describe." Sigrid looked down at her body, at the hands she held palms up before her. "I remember this person, Sigrid Lund, but I am no longer her."

Sigrid paused, struggling to express something that defied explanation. "I was in a place that had no dimensions in the sense I remember them, but where I moved freely. I don't recall time, but I do remember contentment, even joy. I experienced physical pleasure but don't remember this body. I seemed to be formless—no, it's more like my form had no boundaries or edges."

She spoke haltingly, struggling with her words. "Fuck it," she said finally. "I'm fine, honey. Did you finally get rid of that bum of a husband?"

"You sound like Claire," Astrid said, laughing through her sobs as she held her mother close. "But yes, I'm single again."

She felt her mother's body grow tense as Sigrid released the embrace and held her by the shoulders in a desperate grasp. "How did you get here? Please, you didn't ..."

"No, I'm alive."

"But how?"

Astrid breathed deeply, calming herself. She started to describe the events that had brought her to Troy but stopped herself. "It's not important," she said. "I met Circe, and she sent me here to see Tiresias."

"Circe," Sigrid said thoughtfully, searching her memory. "I remember her, too." A look of longing crossed her face.

"She told me she loved you."

"We loved each other ..." Sigrid's words trailed off, and she stared into the darkness. After a time, she looked at her daughter with concern. "Honey, I'm sorry I didn't tell you."

"I understand."

"It isn't that I didn't want to," she said. "I didn't know how."

"I hope it wasn't because she was a woman," Astrid said.

"No," Sigrid laughed. "I remember the people you used to hang out with." Her voice echoed through the tunnel, but the shades did not react. "It was something else, something beyond words, something I couldn't share—not even with you."

"Did she make you happy?"

Sigrid smiled. "Oh, yes. So much has faded from my memory. Only you and Circe seem real to me. You were my greatest love, and she was my last."

Astrid smiled.

"Is that Biffy?" Sigrid said, looking toward the cat resting in Iaria's arms.

"Yes," Astrid said.

"Circe brought me a cat," Sigrid said slowly, struggling to reconstruct the memory. "She didn't tell me much, only that she needed a home. It's strange, but I recognize her in that girl."

Sigrid smiled at Iaria, who stared back, her round eyes narrowing slowly in a cat's expression of familiarity.

"Mother, I need to know something," Astrid began. "The cat that Circe brought to you, she had kittens ..."

"Yes, I remember them. Their mother disappeared, and we raised them," Sigrid said, smiling. "Elizabeth was one of them."

"Do you remember when they grew up? Do you remember anything unusual about them?"

"No," she said. "They were loving, intelligent, and very close to each other. Why do you ask?"

"It's nothing," Astrid said.

Sigrid looked at her knowingly. "You never could fool me. What is it?"

Astrid embraced her mother. "I wouldn't know where to start," she said. "I just want to hold you."

"Honey, you cannot stay here. Circe sent you for a purpose, and it wasn't a family reunion. You must move on."

"No," Astrid insisted as she began to cry once more.

"My darling," Sigrid whispered, holding her close, "neither of us belongs in this dark tunnel. Don't grieve. I loved my life, and I love you. Return to the living. I will always be with you, and we will see each other again."

Astrid threw her arms around her mother in a desperate embrace. She buried her face in Sigrid's hair and wept. She wept for her regrets, for words she wished she had said, and for words she wished she had not said. She felt her mother's body grow thin in her arms and slip away in a mist. Astrid fell to her knees, sobbing.

"It's okay, sweetie. I'm here." Claire kneeled beside her, holding Elizabeth in her arms. "They've gone, Sigrid and Iaria."

Astrid stood unsteadily. "I didn't expect that," she said, breathing deeply, searching for the calm center Annape had shown her and failing to find it.

"I know," Claire said, "but we can't stay here."

Astrid saw shadowy figures gather around them and remembered Circe's warning not to let the dead overwhelm her. Still numb from meeting Sigrid, she followed Claire like an automaton across the food court into another tunnel of shadowy stores.

Astrid heard wheels on the hard floor and saw a figure emerge from the crowd of shades. It was a boy of about thirteen, riding a skateboard. He wore baggy denim shorts and a long black T-shirt. Greasy blonde hair fell from beneath the green ball cap he wore turned backward. When he drew close, Astrid noticed his canvas high-top sneakers were tearing at the seams. He stopped in front of her, landing on one foot as he flipped the board into his hand with the other.

"The old man wants to see you," he told Astrid.

She looked at Claire, who placed Elizabeth gently on the floor beside her.

"This is where I get off, honey," Claire said. "He'll take you to the man you came to see."

"Claire . . ."

Claire kissed her cheek. "Good luck," she said as she stepped back. "I'll see you soon."

"Follow me," the boy said.

Astrid turned toward his voice without thinking, then back to Claire. Her friend was gone.

"Follow me," the boy repeated as he walked toward a small kiosk. Its bright colors stood out against its gray surroundings.

As they drew near to the kiosk, Astrid noticed the sign above it. The word 'SUNGLASSES' was drawn in a sweeping script beneath a bright yellow, stylized sun. Sunglasses of every design filled two cylindrical displays and a flat glass case between them. An elderly man sat on a stool beside the kiosk. He held a white cane with a red tip and faced the length of the tunnel, sightless behind black-framed glasses with opaque lenses, wide temples completely hiding his eyes. He wore an immaculate gray suit, a pale blue plaid shirt, and a navy-blue bow tie. His brightly polished shoes reflected the dim light down the endless tunnel. His gray hair and neatly trimmed beard framed a face as weathered as eternity.

"This is the woman you asked me to find," the boy said.

The old man smiled and placed his hand on the boy's shoulder, turning toward him as if their eyes could meet. He took a worn leather wallet from the inside pocket of his suit jacket, removed a bill, and held it out. The boy took it from his hand.

"Now go on," he said, smiling, his teeth like ancient ivory but clean and even. "Buy yourself something to eat and stay out of trouble."

He listened to the wheels on the stone floor as the boy vanished into the crowd, then turned in Astrid's direction. "He's a good boy, but he spends too much time on that damn skateboard."

She touched the wrinkled parchment on the back of his hand. "Are you Tiresias?"

"I most certainly am," he said, smiling broadly.

"Do you know why I'm here?"

"You need a pair of sunglasses."

"No," she said gently. "They tell me you can see the future."

Tiresias laughed and tapped a rhythm on the concrete floor with his cane. "Honey, I can't see shit, but I do recognize a pretty woman."

"Do you know why I'm here?"

"I suspect Circe sent you," he said. "She takes in strays—doesn't matter what kind—and usually winds up sending them on to me, at least the people. Were the two of you lovers?"

"No," Astrid said impatiently. "I need your help."

Tiresias nodded. "That's a nasty business with Phaethon." He turned toward Elizabeth as if he could hear her breathe. "Is that one of the cats?"

"Yes, it's Elizabeth."

"Let me hold her," he said.

He rested his cane against the display and held out his hands. Astrid placed Elizabeth in his arms, and he stroked her fur, smiling like a child.

"Now, this is a nice cat," he said. "Nothing's better than a nice cat, but some of them are nasty."

"Spike, her brother, was stolen. Can you tell me anything that will help me find him?"

He shook his head, still stroking Elizabeth. "You have everything you need," he said, "except a nice pair of sunglasses."

"No, thank you. Can't you tell me anything?"

"All day on a ship, the sun glaring off the water . . . Did you know that even your retinas can get sunburned? Not to mention cataracts. Come close."

Astrid stood silently.

"Don't be afraid, honey. I love the ladies, but I am a gentleman."

Astrid stepped toward him. He placed Elizabeth on the floor and reached out to touch her face. His fingers were softer than she would have expected from their desiccated appearance, and he ran them over her face gently, lingering on each feature of interest. She closed her eyes as his fingers traced her brows, brushing her eyelids softly. He ran his fingers down the side of her nose and across her lips. His hands stopped their explorations as he felt the breath of life. A smile lit his face.

"You're an artist," he said. "Young, but not too young; pretty, even beautiful to people who know how to look; a bit of a rebel, but you're serious, too. Maybe too serious. I have just the thing."

He took a key from his shirt pocket and unlocked the display that stood between the rotating carousels.

"I keep them in here with my special stock," he said as he removed a pair of black-rimmed sunglasses. "Just the thing for an artist like you. Classic, simple, but a little edgy. These will loosen you up, I promise. A lot of jazz guys wear these . . . rockers, too."

"I'm sorry, but I don't think . . ."

"Would you rather have tortoiseshell? A lot of ladies prefer tortoiseshell—"

"No, thank you," Astrid protested as he spread the temples and slid the glasses on her face. She felt his fingers gently move against her skin, over the temples, adjusting their position.

"Now those do your pretty face justice," he said.

As the glasses passed over her eyes, Astrid saw the dim light of Hades grow brighter. She looked down the tunnel of stores and saw each logo, each storefront, each desperately wandering shade clearly, in bright colors. All at once, the images faded, collapsing into a bright aperture surrounded by darkness.

The light flared, and she found herself standing at the edge of a forest, looking across the open space toward her home. Swarm ran ahead through the sparse grasses and mesquite and pawed at the door, tail twitching as Astrid felt the joy of knowing she had returned home safely. She saw Swarm leap off the porch and run toward her, stopping in the nearest mound of dry grass to roll onto her back, paws opening and closing against the sky.

The sun struck her face, and she closed her eyes from the glare. When she opened them, Astrid found herself in almost total darkness. She shuffled forward, the ground dry beneath her feet. Her foot struck something soft. She reached down and touched a small, fur-covered body, its joints frozen in the rigor of death. She could not recognize it in the darkness but knew it was one of her animals. Grief overcame her as she realized that one of the cats had not returned home—an animal she had sworn to protect had died.

Astrid pulled back in reflex and fell hard on the ground, dust swirling around her. A painful light exploded in her eyes, then collapsed into a single line thrumming in a black void, a wire that shined like burning magnesium and hummed with a thousand dissonant voices. The line exploded in a blinding light, followed by darkness unlike any she had known, a weight of emptiness that pressed against her, forcing her limbs into the ground, constricting her breath, splitting her joints. Absolute silence screamed through her ears, driving all thought and sensation from her mind.

Astrid knew it was the darkness of death—her own death, a bitter certainty. Struggling against the weight of the void, she tore the sunglasses from her face.

Chapter 40

Phaethon sat beside the loom Strachys' woman had abandoned, running his fingers over the unfinished fabric as if he might find his future in the weaver's interrupted plan. Proxonos stared at him from the doorway. "He's a strange one," Proxonos muttered as he walked back into the seer's hovel. "He's been sitting like that for hours."

He looked over Strachys' shoulder into the dome of light that covered the table. He saw nothing. "Is anything happening?"

Strachys did not answer but sat at the table as if in a trance, staring silently into the shining hemisphere, hands cupped on each side of it.

"You're worse than him. You haven't moved all night," Proxonos complained as he sat on the edge of the bed. "Don't you ever have to piss?"

Strachys did not respond. Mumbling to himself, Proxonos began to sharpen his sword, drawing the stone rhythmically along the blade, the rasp of the stone and the ring of bronze partitioning the silence.

"Bring him," Strachys shouted, "quickly."

"What is it?" Proxonos leaped to his feet, his sword in his hand, the stone clattering on the floor.

"She's returning."

Proxonos ran to the doorway and called out.

"Is it time?" Phaethon shouted as he crossed the dirt between the abandoned loom and Strachys' hut.

"Hurry," Strachys shouted, knocking his chair on its side as he rose from the table. He walked to the center of the room, passing through the sunlight that came through the small window. Phaethon took his place before him, his short sword drawn, his hand flexing nervously around the hilt.

"You don't need that." Strachys gestured at the weapon. "I can place you among the animals and bring you back as soon as you take one—before anyone can try to stop you, even before the great cat can take shape."

"Quiet," Phaethon said grimly.

Strachys frowned and grasped Phaethon by his shoulders. He looked into his eyes. "Remember what I said. Prepare yourself to move across space as you have in the past, but do not envision your destination. I will guide you."

"Yes. Yes. Get on with it."

Strachys closed his eyes and pressed his fingers into Phaethon's arms. Phaethon stared intently at the seer, his eyes narrowed, jaw set, right hand clenching his sword as a blue vortex rose from the floor to enclose them. Proxonos stepped back in reflex, shielding his eyes with his hand. The column of light collapsed, and Strachys stood alone.

Phaethon's bronze sword dropped to the floor, its point digging a hole into the dirt before it fell impotently to the ground.

"Elizabeth?" Astrid called out as she fell to her knees, disoriented, head throbbing, her fingers digging into the dry gravel as the mountain seemed to move beneath her. Elizabeth stood beside her, crying in distress.

"Thank god you're safe," Astrid said, pulling the cat close and closing her eyes as she reassembled the fragments of her consciousness. The sense of her body returned by degrees, first in the awareness of gravel digging into her knees, then in the press of Elizabeth against her, in the sun glaring in her eyes, and most insistently, in her breath, an uncontrollable series of gasps. Astrid fought to control her breathing, pulling the air deeper into her lungs, struggling against the shock of returning to the bright reality of the living world. Slowly, her breath became slower and more regular.

She found herself on a ridge overlooking the beach and Nestor's ship. Astrid saw Audrey, Chessie, and Greystoke race toward her up the rocky hillside, with Myia and Antilochus close behind. She heard shouts and saw Nestor and a dozen warriors farther down the slope, following them up the hill. She shouted in joy and waved at them.

As the cats drew near, Astrid saw a distortion in the air, a dark oval forming between her and the approaching men and animals. She felt a disturbance, like an echo of her ejection from Hades, and Phaethon stepped from the oval onto the hillside below her. He stood unsteadily, disoriented from his transport, fighting to regain control of his body, cursing as he stared down at his empty right hand. He turned in place, searching the ground for his weapon, stopping for an instant to glare at her with rage. He froze when he saw Chessie, Greystoke, and Audrey on the hillside below him.

Overcome by panic, Astrid watched Phaethon stumble toward the animals. She ran down the hill and struck him in the back with her shoulder. Pain shot down her side as she fell in the rocky dirt. Astrid saw Phaethon roll several yards down the hillside as Chessie, Greystoke, and Audrey ran past him. The cats slowed briefly as they passed her, then ran to greet Elizabeth.

Astrid struggled to her feet and saw Antilochus and the Achaeans run up the hill. She knew she must keep Phaethon from the cats until they arrived. She searched for a stone, a tree branch, for any weapon she could use against the man lurching up the hill toward her. Astrid felt the ground shift beneath her, and a flash of light inscribed her shadow on the hillside. She looked over her shoulder and saw the four cats press together in the now familiar blue gyre. Astrid heard a shouted curse and turned back to see Phaethon lift a jagged stone from the hillside and throw it into the center of the transformation.

The light collapsed as Astrid felt four minds cry out in pain, splitting her consciousness and driving her to her knees. Phaethon pushed her to the ground as he ran past her, closing on the cats who circled in confusion. Without stopping, he grabbed Chessie and continued forward with the frightened animal howling in his arms. Phaethon leaped through the portal in the air, and Astrid saw him fall into the interior of a crude hovel, still holding Chessie. The opening collapsed, and the bright fire of Chessie's mind vanished from Astrid's awareness.

Astrid scrambled up the hillside to the cats, her feet slipping in the loose dirt. Elizabeth lay motionless beside the stone Phaethon had thrown, blood pooling from her nose and mouth. Audrey and Greystoke circled in confusion around her. Calling her name repeatedly, Astrid touched Elizabeth's side, feeling for a heartbeat. She found nothing but broken ribs and unresponsive flesh. The vision of the dead cat from Tiresias' prophecy flooded her mind.

"Gods," Myia cried as she reached Astrid's side, "what happened?" She saw Elizabeth's inert form. "No, no, no."

"She's not dead yet," Astrid shouted. "I can sense her presence, but it's faint . . ."

Antilochus kneeled and put his hand on the cat's side. "Astrid," he said haltingly, "her rib cage is crushed. Her heart has stopped."

Astrid stared at him and then at Myia sobbing beside Elizabeth's body. Her mind cleared of all thoughts but one. "No. Her heart has stopped, but her cells still live. I can still sense her faintly. We must move quickly."

Antilochus and Myia stared frozen, uncomprehending.

"Bring the other cats to me," Astrid shouted at them.

They continued to stare.

"Now!"

Shocked into action, they grabbed Audrey and Greystoke and brought them to Astrid's side. They drew back as she gathered the cats together around Elizabeth's broken body, her back arching over the three animals as the blue vortex once more swirled around them. Astrid felt her memories fall away and forced them from her consciousness, clearing her mind and once more releasing the sense of her physicality into the tangle of nerves at her brainstem. Astrid could feel Elizabeth's fading sentience, as well as Audrey and Greystoke's panic at the tide of death moving through the minds and bodies they shared. She took control of Swarm's emergence.

As Astrid confronted the wave of cellular death spreading through Elizabeth's tissues, the slowing of the cat's infinitely complex biochemistry, a terrible clarity filled her mind. She could sense Elizabeth's individual cells, each of them struggling for nourishment within a collapsing physiology. She untied the knot sequestered in her brainstem, letting her life force flow through the metamorphosis. Astrid felt her awareness divide, then divide again and again, spreading exponentially as she embraced each dying cell, nourishing it from her own biochemical fires, then releasing it as its metabolism reignited. As Swarm began to take form, she guided the transformation to repair the anatomical damage left by the stone's impact—the broken ribs, damaged organs, torn nerves, and ruptured blood vessels. Astrid felt a surge of strength and realized that Swarm had instinctively engaged with her, their shared vitality flooding Elizabeth's dying tissues like water renewing parched soil.

An intense closeness enfolded the three cats; Astrid sensed it was the memory of Iaria's womb. She felt Elizabeth's flame grow steady as Audrey and Greystoke joined her with an intimacy born of that memory—an intimacy Astrid could not share. Drained by her struggle with death's currents, knowing that Elizabeth would survive, she released the animals and returned to her remembered self.

For an instant, Astrid sensed Annape's presence. She recalled her words, the sound of her voice, and her liquid touch as she fell into an impenetrable sleep.

Nestor and the warriors who had followed him up the hillside stood in silence beside Myia and Antilochus, watching the vortex of blue light envelop Astrid and the cats as Swarm took shape, her fur a deep black. They stood helpless as the great cat screamed in agony, legs spread for stability, gasping for breath, tongue extended, eyes narrowed to slits, struggling against an unseen enemy. Suddenly, Swarm's fur turned pure white, her eyes as black as death. The colors of the individual cats begin to appear like brush marks on a blank canvas—Audrey's orange and brindle, Greystoke's smooth gray, and finally, Elizabeth's bright ginger. Swarm vomited a black liquid across the rocks, then fell onto her side, exhausted.

The blue light appeared once more, surrounding the motionless animal. When the transformation ended, Astrid and Elizabeth lay unconscious on the rocky mountainside. Audrey stood unsteadily nearby as Greystoke crouched beside her, crying softly. Nestor rushed to Astrid's side and felt her throat for a pulse. "Thank the gods. Her heart is beating," he said.

Myia lifted Elizabeth in her arms. "The cat is alive, too," she said between sobs and laughter. "She is unconscious, but she breathes."

"Quickly," Antilochus said to the soldiers who had followed him up the hill as he gestured toward Astrid's unconscious body. "Carry her back to the camp . . . carefully."

Myia emerged from the tree limbs and sailcloth of the hastily erected shelter. She walked to where Nestor, Antilochus, and the Achaeans waited near the ship.

"How is she?" Nestor asked.

"She's in a deep sleep. She does not respond, but she breathes, and her heartbeat is steady."

Nestor exhaled a release of tension. "I've seen this before in injured men. It is a healing sleep."

"The orange cat rests beside her," Myia continued. "She does not awaken, but she stirs from time to time, usually to draw herself closer to Astrid."

"And the other animals?" Nestor asked.

"They are fine but will not leave her side, not even to eat or drink."

"Antilochus," Nestor said, "I want four men guarding the shelter at all times. Myia, take whatever supplies or people you need to care for her. When you leave the tent for any reason, make sure Antilochus or I replace you at her side."

"We will remain on this island until she recovers," Nestor declared to his gathered warriors. The men shouted their agreement, then gathered in groups of two or three, speaking in hushed tones as word of the events on the hillside spread among them.

Part V
Kyros
Thirteenth Century B.C.E.

Chapter 41

Phaethon fell to his knees on the dirt floor, trembling from the effects of his sudden transfer through space. Only his right arm remained free of spasms, pinning Chessie against his chest with a desperate rigor. As Phaethon regained control of his body, Proxonos took the disoriented animal, cursing as she clawed and bit him. He threw her roughly into one of the two reed cages Strachys had placed on the floor.

"If they did not need you . . ." Proxonos swore at the hissing cat, rubbing his forearm and smearing blood across the skin.

Phaethon turned toward Strachys angrily. "Why did you strip me of my weapon?"

"If I hadn't, you would still be fighting Achaeans instead of standing here with your cure at hand."

Phaethon searched for his sword. He saw it leaning against the wall and crossed the room to retrieve it.

Strachys kneeled to examine Chessie, who tore at the sides of her cage. It was one of two identical enclosures he had constructed, woven of straight reeds he had gathered from the stream bank and secured with leather bands. The cats' prisons were thoughtful in design, immaculate in construction, and left no opportunity for escape. They stood a few feet apart in the center of the room, away from the light that shined through the doorway and the small window, carefully aligned, framing a portal into darkness.

"If you ever do anything like that again, I swear I will end you," Phaethon threatened, waving his sword menacingly at the seer.

Strachys ignored the threat and motioned Phaethon toward the small table. The surface was littered with plates, cups, and scraps left from recent meals; wine stains marked its surface. The order that once graced Strachys' home had vanished with the woman who had shared his bed. "When you took the animal," Strachys said, "you threw a stone to disrupt the great cat's formation. It struck one of the animals, killing it. Watch what happened after you returned here."

Strachys cleared a space on the stained wood and raised a dome of light against his palms. He moved his hands along its circumference until they rested on the table. Phaethon stared into the glowing ball and saw the hillside where Elizabeth's crushed body lay. He watched Astrid gather her and the two remaining cats into her arms. He saw Swarm take shape, struggle, then separate, leaving Astrid and three living animals.

"I was correct; merging with these animals can heal injuries," Phaethon said as he stepped from the table.

Phaethon turned to Proxonos. "Take your men to the village," he told the mercenary. "Bring back the other animal—Strachys can show you where it hides—"

"It is in the village, an a small house near the granary," the seer said, reluctantly.

"I know the one," Proxonos said. "My men told me they saw the cat during their last raid."

"Bring back five or six hosts for my cure," Phaethon continued. "Make sure they are young and healthy. Include a woman or two as well."

"The villagers will resist," Proxonos warned.

"Make sure they cause no further trouble," Phaethon said icily.

Proxonos grinned and walked outside. He spoke to the small group of mercenaries who had camped there, and two of them followed him down the hill to their main encampment on the beach. Phaethon watched him disappear down the path, then turned to Strachys. "Seer, do not cross me again."

"You will have the cure I promised, and then I will leave this island."

"And the scroll?" Phaethon asked. "My scroll?"

"A reward for my services."

Phaethon took the carved spindle with its blank parchment from the shelf and turned it in his hands thoughtfully. He returned it to its resting place. "Very well," he said, "it will no longer be of use to me. But remember—its destruction will be your reward if you fail."

Spike heard the shouts and the clash of metal before the smell of the fires reached him. He saw the boy's father take a sword from its place near the table and run outside. He watched the boy's mother run through the hut, throwing food into a sack. Spike realized that this was no ordinary raid and hissed loudly. The boy lifted him with one arm and followed his mother toward the doorway.

A mercenary blocked their exit, sword in hand. The boy released Spike to the floor as two more mercenaries appeared in the opening. Spike bolted toward a narrow gap between the legs of one man, only to become entangled in a crude net. He howled as the twine cut into his skin, and a warrior lifted him to dangle helplessly in the air. The mercenary carried Spike from the cabin, holding him like a trophy for his comrades to see. Chaos swirled around him—the burning homes, the screams of dying villagers and slaughtered farm animals. He saw a mercenary cut down the boy's father with a single blow of his sword.

Spike saw another mercenary back out of the doorway. The boy stepped from the hut, holding his dagger in front of him. The man lunged, and the boy slashed at him. Cursing, the warrior stepped back, blood dripping from his forearm. A second raider knocked the knife aside with the edge of his shield, grabbed the boy by the arm, and threw him onto the dirt next to his father's body.

The boy screamed, and another mercenary grabbed him. He clawed at the man's face until the warrior struck him on the cheek with the pommel of his sword, blood spraying from his mouth. He dragged the stunned child toward four men and a woman—all young and healthy, their hands bound together and secured with rope. They tied the boy to the line as two mercenaries dragged his mother screaming back into the darkness of her home.

Chapter 42

Strachys moved the two cages—one holding Spike, the other Chessie—closer together, the woven reeds cutting furrows in the dirt floor. He stood between them, closed his eyes, and extended his arms toward each animal. Cold fire surrounded the seer's hands as golden filaments extended from his fingertips, snaking through the air as if seeking nourishment, only to wither and return to his flesh. He moved the cages a fraction of an inch closer, careful to maintain their alignment—and to avoid the cats' attempts to strike him through the reeds. He returned to his position between the cages, and the filaments extended once more from his hands. Strachys closed his eyes, evaluating the forces contending between Spike, Chessie, and himself in a calculus of enchantment only he understood.

Phaethon and Proxonos sat at the table, watching the seer who remained oblivious to them and the half dozen mercenaries camped outside in the night. The prisoners—including the boy who had befriended Spike—stood terrified, tied to the tree where Strachys' woman had spent her days weaving. The loom lay in pieces, scattered under the branches, the unfinished cloth rippling over the dirt with each breeze.

"Is he going to take all night?" Proxonos complained.

Phaethon shrugged and leaned toward him. "We have time. Nestor and his men remain on the island where I took the cat. Once they leave, their journey here should take a day or two, depending on the winds. You have time to prepare to face them."

"I'll have my men move up the mountain to protect the house."

Phaethon shook his head. "I want you to confront Nestor and his men on the beach and stop them from coming here."

"I would prefer to keep the high ground, face them when they are tired from the climb and confined on the narrow trail."

"No. I have plans . . ."

"Do they involve Circe?"

Phaethon nodded. "She will follow the cats here. I must face her alone, without being distracted by your fight with Nestor."

"You cannot kill an immortal," Proxonos challenged. "You should find your cure and leave."

"Anyone can be killed. I have learned much from the enchantments I stole from Aeaea—and I will be even stronger once I am cured." Phaethon paused as he watched Strachys' methodical labor. "Whatever happens, I must face her alone. Can you keep Nestor away?"

"The Achaeans will probably land on the beach near the village," Proxonos thought aloud. "The rest of the shoreline is too rocky to land a ship safely; even if they did, they would have to come overland, through rough and unfamiliar terrain."

"Then you can face them on the beach—as they land."

Proxonos nodded reluctantly.

Phaethon turned his attention back to the seer, watching Strachys continue his experiments, moving the cages closer by a barely perceptible distance each time. Proxonos sat sullenly at the table, drinking wine from the clay pitcher. Suddenly, a blue glow ignited around each animal, the joining of their bodies driven by instinct, and frustrated by confinement. The golden filaments extended from Strachys' fingers into the blue gyre surrounding each cat, multiplying as if they were alive, swaying like seaweed in a tidal shallow. The light moved up the golden web to engulf the seer in a blinding corona. Spasms shook his body as if they would tear him apart. Suddenly, the light collapsed upon itself like a dying star, disappearing into his flesh for an instant, then flaring through the room as if it would ignite the air itself. The light faded to darkness, and Strachys fell to the floor.

Proxonos kneeled and probed him for signs of life. The seer stirred, and the mercenary jerked his hand back in fear.

Strachys sat up like a man waking from a nightmare, eyes darting around the hut. He touched his face, fingertips dancing across his eyes, ears, nose, and mouth as if he had discovered his body for the first time. He stood and ran his fingers over his arms, his chest, his hips. The lamp flickering on the tabletop caught his eye, and he reached into the flame. Jerking his hand away, he laughed at the burned flesh.

"What is going on?" Phaethon shouted at him.

Strachys turned to him, the fires of discovery burning in his eyes. "This body . . ." he said, struggling to speak between spasms of laughter, "I've worn it like an ill-fitting cloak since the seer awakened me. It's been so long, I had forgotten that flesh could bring such pleasure."

Phaethon grabbed him by the shoulders and shook him roughly. "Can you cure me?"

"Cure," the seer repeated like a man awakening from a deep sleep. "Yes. That is what you want, isn't it? I remember now. You're burned, disfigured, dying." Strachys stumbled to the chair and sat, eyes closed, forcing himself to breathe regularly. "Since the night I awoke from the parchment, I shared this body with the seer. Over time, I learned to command his limbs, speak with his voice, and see through his eyes, but the body was not truly mine. I moved it like a puppeteer moves a wooden doll. I tasted his food and shared his rest and his pleasure with the woman, but everything seemed as if it were cloaked in a drunken insensibility. But now, I feel my strength, my life—"

"The blue light did this to you?" Phaethon interrupted.

"Yes. I am finally one with this body."

"Then Strachys is gone?"

"No, but I am no longer a stranger sharing his body, his will hanging like a shroud around my every move. He remains a part of me but nothing more. "

"Then who are you?" Phaethon asked.

"You can still call me Strachys. It will be simpler."

"Can you use this magic to heal me? Do you know how to join my body with another?"

"An enchantment surrounds the beasts when they merge." Strachys spoke as if thinking aloud. "Within it, the laws of nature become fluid. Things— even people—lose their solidity, their substance; only their forms remain, sustained by thought. The animals desire to join together, and their bodies follow that desire."

Strachys saw a cup on the table. He held it beneath his nose for a moment, then sipped the dark wine. He closed his eyes, and his body trembled with pleasure. He smiled and took another swallow.

"As I had hoped, my experiment enabled me to enter the enchantment," he said. "The animals opposed me—their wills were stronger than I had anticipated. But I could control it long enough to free myself from the seer."

"Then you can join me with another?" Phaethon repeated. "Like you took the seer's body?"

Strachys closed his eyes in thought. After a time, he looked up and nodded. "Yes. I see how I can use the cats' abilities to meet your needs."

Phaethon turned to Proxonos. "Bring me one of the men . . . a strong one."

Proxonos and two mercenaries threw a young man through the door of the cabin onto the floor. The youth rose quickly to face them, lifted by the reflexes of an untrained warrior, his empty hands held ready to engage his kidnappers. Phaethon approached him, holding out a cup of wine. "Take it," he said, "drink."

The youth ignored the offering. "What do you want with me? Why did you attack my village?"

Phaethon smiled. "I have chosen you."

"You destroyed our homes. You killed my people. You left nothing. Why?"

Phaethon shrugged, drained the cup himself, and placed it on the table. "Do you believe in the gods?"

The villager stared at him silently.

"We can become gods, you and I."

The youth spat on him. Phaethon wiped the spittle from his face.

"I had hoped you would accept my gift with gratitude," he said dispassionately, nodding at Proxonos. "Nevertheless, it is a gift you will accept."

The villager turned to face the approaching mercenary. Proxonos hit him before he could react. He recovered and struck back. Proxonos dodged the blow easily and hit him again, knocking him to the floor. As the youth struggled to take his feet, Proxonos kicked him viciously in the head.

"You've brought me a fighter," Phaethon said. "He'll be worthy."

Strachys stared grimly at the unconscious youth.

"Don't look so unhappy," Phaethon told him. "He won't feel the transformation and will awaken to a greater existence than he could have imagined."

Frowning, the seer took his place between the cats' cages. He gestured to the floor in front of him, and Proxonos dragged the body into place.

"Lay beside him," Strachys told Phaethon.

Phaethon did as the seer asked, letting Strachys guide him into position, his chest conforming to the curve of the youth's back, their hips and thighs touching like sleeping lovers. Strachys moved Phaethon's hand around to clasp the villager's, his face brushed by the villager's hair. Satisfied that the two bodies were positioned correctly, the seer extended his hands toward the cages where Chessie howled in fear and Spike growled imperceptibly. Once more, the golden filaments grew from his fingers to drain the enchantment rising around the animals. As blue fire swirled around him, Strachys turned his palms toward the men at his feet, one trembling with hope, the other lost to mercy.

Golden filaments grew from his palms to pierce their flesh. The fire burned through them, passing into Phaethon and the villager. The enchantment that cloaked Phaethon's deformity dissolved, revealing his charred flesh and twisted limbs as the blue vortex enveloped him and the unconscious youth. The light collapsed into their bodies, then exploded through the room, leaving a single form, naked, alone on the floor. For a moment, features danced across the contours of his skull like sunlight through a tree's wind-shaken leaves before settling into a face of unmarred beauty. It was Phaethon's face, but it bore traces of the village youth, like grace notes on a musical passage.

"Well, seer," Phaethon said, laughing as he took his feet. "It seems you have succeeded."

"What do you feel?" Strachys asked with a dispassionate curiosity, like a clinician examining a patient.

"I feel whole, strong. The pain is gone." Phaethon walked briskly around the small hut. "I am whole," he repeated. "I am healed."

The seer checked the two cats. They appeared to be unharmed but lay panting, eyes narrowed to slits. He stepped in front of Phaethon. "What about the villager? Is he part of you?"

"I sense his presence, but only faintly."

"He remains unconscious," Strachys said, concern thickening his voice.

Phaethon walked through the doorway, naked into the night. He held his arms wide and raised his face to the sky, laughing. The mercenaries gathered around him as if he had lost his wits to drink or madness. Some of them laughed while others stepped back in fear. A few looked to Proxonos, who stood near the doorway, his hand resting on the pommel of his sword.

His grasp tightened as Phaethon began to scream.

"By the gods, what is happening?" Phaethon cried out. He clawed at his face, gouging tracks of blood across his cheeks, his features twisted by panic. He fell to his knees as his body shook like a soul in hell. The light of the transformation surrounded him for an instant, and he screamed again—a single cry parting into the anguish of two dying voices.

As the mercenaries drew back in a ragged perimeter, two bodies collapsed near the campfire. Phaethon's burned husk trembled, and the young villager lay beside him as if asleep. Strachys rushed to them and placed his fingers on the youth's throat, seeking a pulse. "He's dead. What happened?"

Phaethon raised onto his unburned arm. "I don't know," he repeated, his voice cracking with pain.

"Think," Strachys demanded.

"The body was mine. I was strong, free of my injuries—"

"He awoke?"

"I felt pain . . . unbearable pain . . . panic, terror," Phaethon stammered. He fell back in the dirt, breathing heavily, as the mercenaries stared at his burned form. When his breath slowed, the blue light surrounded him, covering him once more in stolen enchantments.

"Bring another captive," he told Proxonos.

"Wait, we do not know—" Strachys began.

"Silence your righteousness," Phaethon interrupted.

The man who had been Strachys stared at the remaining captives from the village. He felt a sickness through his body as Proxonos gestured to his men. Two of them grabbed the dead youth by his arms, and dragged him out of the firelight. Four others walked to the remaining captives, who pulled against their restraints, crying out in terror.

"Come, seer," Phaethon said as he started back into the hut. "We have work to do."

Myia left the improvised shelter, walking through darkness into the campfire's light. Nestor and Antilochus rose as she approached.

"Has anything changed?" Nestor asked.

She breathed deeply, lack of sleep showing on her face. "She remains in a deep sleep but stirs from time to time."

"Does she wake?" Nestor asked, hopefully.

"No, she seems to be dreaming. I think they're nightmares; her movements are troubled."

Nestor nodded. "Myia, you are tired. You should rest. I will sit with her."

"That would be unwise," she said. "When she began to stir, the cats joined to become Swarm. The animal seems agitated and will not leave her side. Swarm knows me, but I cannot assure your safety."

Nestor looked thoughtfully toward Astrid's shelter. After a few seconds, he nodded to Myia, then turned and walked up the beach alone.

Chapter 43

Phaethon vomited clear liquid streaked with blood onto the hardened earth of the cabin's floor. The body of a young woman, strong from the labors that fell to youth in the struggling village, lay motionless nearby. Strachys kneeled beside her body and searched for a pulse. He frowned and rose wearily to his feet. Phaethon trembled in the darkness, his enchantments stripped away. The seer reached into Spike's cage and rested his hand on the unconscious cat. He did the same with Chessie, then walked to the doorway and stared out at the four bodies lined up at the edge of the firelight.

"We're finished," Strachys said as he collapsed into his chair and filled his cup from the clay pitcher.

"No," Phaethon screamed, his voice an anguished rasp, only vaguely human. He made no effort to reassert the enchantments that hid his injuries.

Strachys took a swallow of wine and looked at him in pity. "It's no use," the seer said softly.

"Why do you defy me? The woman joins with these animals," Phaethon said hoarsely, "and she takes on their power—she even brought the orange cat back to life after it had died."

"Yours are not ordinary injuries," Strachys said in an exhausted whisper. "They carry the effects of Zeus' bolt, a fire that can kill even an immortal. Your injuries attack your hosts, driving them to madness and death. You you cannot remain joined to a dead man." He swirled the last of the wine in the clay cup, staring into the blood-red vortex. "We're done."

"No," Phaethon repeated angrily and turned to Proxonos. "Remove the woman's body and bring the boy."

Proxonos started toward the hut's rough opening. Strachys stepped in front of him. "He's only a boy."

"I've killed younger," Proxonos said coldly.

"Not like this. You've killed in battle, in revenge—there was a purpose."

"There is gold, and there is seeing you die if you interfere with me," Proxonos snarled as he pushed him aside. "That's purpose enough."

Exhausted, Strachys steadied himself against the wooden table. Two mercenaries removed the woman's body, and Proxonos walked to the tree where the boy remained—the last of Phaethon's hosts.

"I will not help you," Strachys said, his voice hardening. He collapsed into the chair.

Phaethon restored the enchantments that covered his injuries, though they did not hide his exhaustion. He limped to the table and looked down at the seer. "Old man, do you think I still need your help? Do you think I've learned nothing this night?"

"What are you talking about?" Strachys rasped.

"I can do nothing as elegant as your golden threads," Phaethon said, "but I have learned from these animals."

"You can join your body with that of another?"

Phaethon nodded. "That and more—much more. I no longer need you. I may not even need them," he said, staring at Spike and Chessie, lying exhausted in their cages.

"You do not understand . . ." Strachys protested. "Your injuries—"

"I will continue until I'm healed."

"You'll only bring death. You must stop."

"Let us test your newfound conviction," Phaethon said as he limped to the shelf and took down the scroll. He carried it to the mud-brick fireplace where the fire had burned through the night and held the scroll just outside the flames. "Do you want to take this and leave? Or will you stay here and fight to save this boy?"

Strachys closed his eyes for a moment, then held out his hand. "Give me the scroll," he whispered. "I will go."

"I expected as much." Phaethon smiled and threw the scroll into the fire.

Strachys screamed as the flames danced across the carved olive wood and ancient parchment. He felt the presence inhabiting his body convulse in agony and lurched forward onto his knees. He crawled toward the fireplace as if he would reach into the flames themselves and collapsed, his fingers inches from the fire, his face in the dirt.

Proxonos appeared in the doorway, holding the boy. The child struggled against the mercenary's grip, his hands still bound. The brightening fire caught Proxonos' eyes, and he saw the blackened scroll fall into ash. He saw Strachys' trembling body and smiled broadly. The boy kicked the distracted mercenary in the knee and bolted toward the doorway, only to be blocked by one of the warriors waiting outside. The warrior beat the boy into unconsciousness, then threw him onto the floor where the woman had died.

"Perhaps a younger mind, one still adapting to a changing body, will be easier to shape to my needs," Phaethon said, his voice a hoarse whisper.

"But the seer?" Proxonos asked.

"I no longer need him. I've learned to use the enchantments myself."

Proxonos smiled as he lifted the dying seer by his tunic and dragged him to the doorway and threw him out into the night.

Strachys writhed in the dirt as the mercenaries gathered around him, some laughing, others remaining in the shadows to hide their revulsion. He struggled to stand, feet parted, hands on his knees to brace his trembling legs. The ancient, indecipherable writing—once golden, now the color of dried meat—appeared on his skin but did not fall away. Having no parchment to accept it, the writing melted back into the seer's body, like a demon casting off its flesh only to feed on it without shame.

Strachys lurched into the night, and the mercenaries returned to their fire to continue drinking, boasting, and waiting for Proxonos' next command. A long-dormant instinct drove the seer to the stream that flowed past the hovel, and he stumbled along its bank. Blinded by the flakes that covered his eyes, deafened by the once-golden writing filling his ears, insensible to the branches and thorns that tore at his skin, the seer followed a genius older than the Earth itself—a sense beyond instinct, beyond physical organs. It led him to the spring at the stream's source, and he fell onto the moss surrounding it.

The dark, indecipherable symbols continued to form on Strachys' skin like scabs from an unknown pox, but his body no longer reabsorbed them. Instead, they fell to the soft moss as his flesh decomposed, crumbling into a mound beside the stream. Centipedes, spiders, beetles, worms, and other things that crawled in darkness dropped their eggs among the brown flakes. Moss covered the seer's remains, roots growing into them as if they were fertile dung, achieving months of growth in minutes, enclosing it all in a living blanket as insects swarmed across the shifting surface.

"How is she?" Nestor asked Myia as she sat down. He ladled a bowl of the thin stew that boiled on the fire and passed it to her.

"She rests peacefully." Myia took the bowl and blew on it to cool the broth. "The dreams that had troubled her have passed. She rests calmly." She raised the bowl to her lips and drank deeply.

"And the animals?"

"The great cat sleeps at her side."

Nestor leaned toward the fire; worry and exhaustion shadowed his face.

"You should rest," Myia told him.

"I cannot," he said, smiling wearily. "It's an old habit."

"Habit?"

"I can't sleep the night before a battle. Rest belongs to soldiers, not kings."

"But there is no battle."

"She fights one now," Nestor said, nodding toward Astrid's shelter. "Ours will come soon enough."

Myia remained beside him, drinking the warm broth, watching the surf's encroachment on the beach. They heard a rustling from the improvised shelter, and the guards cried out as Astrid emerged from the makeshift tent. She crossed the beach toward them, Swarm walking at her side. The cat was as dark as Audrey's brindle and Greystoke's gunmetal gray, but Elizabeth's copper streaked her fur like burnished bronze.

"Nestor," Astrid said. "We must leave as soon as possible."

Nestor hurried toward her. "Are you all right?"

Astrid nodded, her hand resting on the cat's shoulders. "We are well, but we must leave as soon as possible."

"Why?"

"Something is happening . . . something terrible."

Chapter 44

Spike felt the pull to join with Chessie. It was not the intimacy of a littermate's embrace, nor was it the painful incision of the golden filaments. This came like a hand closing on the scruff of his neck and pressing his face into the dirt. Tears blurred his eyes as he stared at the man's shadow in the glare of transformation, the man who had taken him from his home long ago.

Spike felt the man draw life from Chessie, from the boy, from himself, and rage overcame him. It burned through his awareness of the dimly lit room, through the will of the man trying to twist Swarm's appearance into something evil. It consumed Spike's mind and muscles in a final, desperate explosion. He screamed and felt the man withdraw into darkness, the joining incomplete. Spike pushed through his exhaustion to touch Chessie's mind with his own. He found her unharmed. He sensed the boy, unconscious but alive, and he released himself into unconsciousness.

Phaethon collapsed, his enchantments stripped away. Proxonos felt for his pulse. Awakened by the touch, Phaethon crawled to Spike's cage. He stared at the unconscious animal, watching the rise and fall of his flanks. "You have beaten me," he whispered.

"You should have kept the seer," Proxonos said coldly.

"It would not have mattered," Phaethon said, rolling onto his back. "The child—or perhaps it was the cat—rejected the merging as soon as it began. There was no point in continuing."

"Now what?" Proxonos asked.

Phaethon restored his concealing enchantments and limped to the remaining chair. He rocked the pitcher back and forth and found it empty. He stared through the small opening above the table into the twilight.

"'Now what?'" Phaethon repeated. "It seems, my taciturn friend, that you have stated the problem eloquently. 'Now'—this moment of defeat. 'What'—what must I do?"

Proxonos stared blankly.

"Now what? What now?" Phaethon mused. "'Now what, now what . . . what now, and on in an endless stream of moments and questions."

Proxonos scowled at him. "Shall I dispose of the boy? And the animals?"

"Let the boy go."

"He'll tell the villagers what has happened."

"It doesn't matter."

"We should kill the boy and the animals and leave."

Phaethon shook his head. "You see, my friend, it is not the boy or the animals I must end; it is the endless stream of moments and questions." He leaned forward and held his head between his hands. "It splits my mind like Zeus' bolt."

"You've gone mad," Proxonos sneered.

Phaethon looked up at him. "It is only logic. I suppose logic is a form of madness. Do you understand?"

"I understand you've failed."

"It's not a failure, only another step in proving a final theorem. Your logic is too direct, a geometry of force and desire," he said slowly as if contemplating a mathematical problem. "Mine is a logic born of clarity."

Phaethon watched the boy regain consciousness and crawl to Spike's cage. "I must end the bitch who brought me to this," he continued. "That is an inevitable conclusion. I cannot be released from my pain while she lives. But, what of the woman who joins with these animals at will, a consequence of her effortless ignorance? What of Nestor and the Achaeans who accompany her?"

Proxonos stared at him impatiently.

"The witch must die. Therefore, by extension, the woman and the Achaeans must die as well," Phaethon said abstractly, like a geometer concluding a proof. He turned to Proxonos. "Leave the animals in their cages. They will bring Nestor and the woman to us, then I will dissolve the enchantments that have hidden me from Circe. She will come."

"How do you know?"

"The bitch would not miss this for all the wealth of Egypt."

"And the boy?"

The child kneeled next to Spike's cage, pulling on the leather straps, struggling to unbind Strachys' indecipherable knots.

"Go, boy," Phaethon shouted. "Go before I change my mind."

The boy rose and faced him. "I want my cat," he demanded, "both cats."

"You are a brave one," Phaethon said as he limped to the child's side. "What's your name, boy?"

"They call me, Hector."

Phaeton laughed. "Like the protector of Troy. How fitting." He placed his hand on the boy's shoulder and stared into Spike's cage. "People are searching for these animals, people I must bring here. So long as the cats serve my needs, I will not harm them. You can return for them when I am finished, or you can stay here, and your cats can watch my friend skewer you on his sword like a roasting pig."

Proxonos grinned and moved forward, his hand on his sword.

The boy rose and backed toward the door. "I will come back for you. I promise," he shouted to the cats as he ran into the dawn.

Phaethon took two cups from the table and filled them from the water jug that sat near the door. He held one out to Proxonos. "We started our partnership over two cups of wine. Can we renew it over water? Will you help me bring this to an honorable end?"

"Do you expect me to join you in a death pact?" Proxonos scowled, "to send my men to fight an immortal and a swarm of Achaeans?"

"No," Phaethon said calmly. "Nestor only brings two dozen men. You have twice as many. There will be no Odysseus, no 'swarm of Achaeans' to help him. You can face them on the beach while they are still struggling through the wet sand. You can avenge what happened at Troy and leave. As for the witch, my business with Circe is here, and it is mine alone."

"What about my payment?"

"Always the mercenary." Phaethon smiled. "I must leave to settle a personal matter. When I return, I will bring more . . ." he paused, struggling to find a word to express a value he no longer found meaningful, "more trinkets to please your men."

"A personal matter?"

"Yes. There is someone I must release from her obligation to me."

"A woman." Proxonos grinned, teeth white against his dirty face.

"It's not what you think."

"If it's not, then why do you go to her?"

"There is your logic once more, desire and force," Phaethon frowned. "She was kind. I owe her the freedom that has been denied me."

"How do I know you'll return?" Proxonos pressed.

"Because it is all I have left. The Achaeans will be here in two days," Phaethon said. "I'll return before they arrive, and I'll bring your payment— swords and armor, skillfully wrought cooking tripods, bolts of fine cloth, gold and lapis jewelry—as promised. While I'm gone, care for the animals, give them food and water—I will need them to lure Circe to me."

"And what will you do when she comes? You cannot kill an immortal."

"I've learned much in the course of this night, much more than the futility of my search for a cure," Phaethon said as he drained his cup. "I have become a weapon. I have become death."

"What are you talking about?"

"I've learned to join with another, even without Strachys or the cats, but I do not bring life to the union."

Proxonos stared inquisitively.

"I carry the wounds Zeus has inflicted on me, the untreatable burns of his immortal fire. I carry them into all I touch—human or immortal—and no one can survive them," Phaethon said as he placed his cup on the rough wooden table.

"It seems, my friend, that these beasts have given me the means to kill a goddess."

Chapter 45

Nestor spoke to Myia, his voice thick with concern. "How is she?" Myia looked up the length of the ship, past the warriors talking in groups of two or three or performing the endless chores needed to maintain the vessel against the insistent ocean. She looked to the aft deck and the shelter where Astrid had secluded herself with the animals.

"She has recovered, but she seems distant," Myia said.

"Is it because of Elizabeth's injuries? The way Astrid saved her?" Antilochus suggested.

"That seems likely."

"Could you ask her to join us?"

Myia stood and started aft. She had only taken a few steps when the cloth flap of the shelter entrance parted, and Astrid stepped onto the deck, raising her hand to shield her eyes as they adjusted to the sunlight. The constant rumble of voices dropped as she picked her way through the crowded ship. Astrid did not hurry but paused and asked after the well-being of each man she passed, smiling and addressing them by name. She helped a warrior move a large jar of water to reach his personal belongings. She took his hand as he thanked her.

"It seems she knew we wanted her," Nestor observed.

"Since she awoke," Myia whispered, "she seems to know what is happening on the ship without looking or being told. It's hard to explain, but she has changed."

Nestor watched Astrid as she slowly made her way toward him. She took his hand, and he helped her onto the foredeck. "We seem to be making good progress," she said as she sat cross-legged across from him. Myia and Antilochus sat to each side.

Nestor nodded. "Are you well?"

Astrid rested her hand on his. "Dear Nestor, I'm fine."

"You were unconscious for days."

She looked out across the ship, past the straining sail to the improvised shelter where she had left the cats. "It was necessary for my recovery. Thank you for caring for me."

"And the cats?"

"Elizabeth, Audrey, and Greystoke are well."

"What about the stolen animals?"

Astrid closed her eyes and frowned. "They are alive, but they've been through something terrible. They are confined and are in pain."

"Do you know how far we must go to reach them?" Nestor asked.

She closed her eyes as if listening for a distant voice. "Not exactly, but I know we are growing closer."

"Can you tell us more?" Antilochus asked.

Astrid shook her head. "I can't sense distance accurately, but my connection to Spike and Chessie grows stronger. I think we'll arrive tonight."

"Will you know when we're close but before we can be seen from the shore?" Nestor asked.

"I think so."

"I want to stay out of sight until after midnight and approach in darkness," Nestor explained.

"What are your plans?" Myia asked.

"I'll take a small party ashore and send the ship away. With luck, no one will see us land. We can scout the island and learn what we face. We'll rejoin the crew the next night and make our plans."

"I want to go with you," Astrid said.

"I don't know if that's wise," Nestor cautioned. "You're still weak, and it would put you and the animals at risk."

"I've recovered fully. This is my fight, and Swarm could be a great asset. Once we get close, I'll be able to sense Spike and Chessie's location. They can join with Swarm when we find them. It will protect them if they are weak or injured, and they would strengthen Swarm. Also, a cat's vision, smell, and hearing would be useful."

"Can you control her?"

"We've grown much closer, especially after . . ." Astrid's relaxed manner dimmed into shadow.

"After you restored Elizabeth to life?" Myia finished her thought.

"I'm sorry," Astrid said, gathering her composure. "Yes, I'm more closely bound to the cats—and to Swarm—than before."

"Very well," Nestor said. "Antilochus, select two experienced warriors who know how to remain unseen."

He turned to Myia. "I understand you're skilled at concealment?"

"Yes."

"Good. You may join us." Nestor smiled ironically. "I'm certain you would sneak ashore anyway. You can help Astrid with the animals."

Claea walked with Phaethon beside the stream that flowed through the valley of Etagama's small kingdom, staying in the shade of the cypress and fir trees that lined its banks. From time to time, they passed the wooden gates that diverted water to irrigate the olive groves that had grown there for generations. Phaethon stopped near a large oak where the stream widened and the currents slowed. He sat with Claea in the shade, resting on the soft grass among the wildflowers. They looked back at Etagama's palace, where the stream flowed under the city walls to fill the public basins and replenish the cisterns against drought or siege.

"You've been quiet, my lord," she said.

"Why do you call me 'my lord,' Claea? I'm your friend."

She smiled. "Because you've never told me your name."

Phaethon laughed in surprise. "Is that true?"

"I fear it is, my lord," she said mischievously.

"Forgive me. I did not want Etagama and the others to spread word of my presence."

"What about me?" she teased.

"Claea, my name has been a curse. It's not something I share easily."

"Perhaps sharing will ease the burden."

He picked up a handful of pebbles and threw them thoughtfully, one at a time, into the stream. "My mother named me Phaethon."

"After the old stories?"

"Yes," he answered bitterly. "The bastard son of a god."

Claea took his hand. "There is no shame in being named after a demigod."

"No shame? A bastard who squandered his gifts to impress his friends? Who tricked his father into letting him drive the chariot of the sun and scorched the Earth's garden before Zeus struck him with a thunderbolt? A presumptuous, greedy child who threw his gifts away; who spread death and sorrow wherever he went?"

"It's only a name."

"Claea, I can no more escape that name than I can overcome my fate."

"Why not?"

"Because of all I have done since my mother gave me that name."

"That's in the past," she said. "It doesn't matter. I only see the good you've done. You found me broken and healed me. You found me ugly and made me beautiful. You found me scorned and gave me a home." She paused, looking into his eyes. "You found me alone and gave me love."

She leaned across and kissed him, her lips lingering on his.

"Claea, I cannot . . ."

"Why?" A shadow crossed her features.

"Do you remember when I last left? How I told you I had to set certain things right?"

She nodded.

"I have failed."

"I don't understand. You are here with me, you are well, and I love you. What else matters?"

"Claea, I've seen how Etagama looks at you. He treats you well and can give you a life I cannot."

She stared at him in silence.

"If you follow this stream to where it falls from a cliff into this valley, then track the cliff north until you reach a thick stand of scrub oak, you'll find a cave hidden behind the brush. I've hidden treasures in it—gold, bolts of dyed cloth, weapons, and armor—enough to make Etagama the ruler of a prosperous kingdom." He reached out and touched her cheek. "And you can be his queen."

"I do not care for treasures, and I do not wish to be a queen."

"I must leave soon."

"Let us leave together," she insisted.

"No. Where I must go, what I must do . . . you have no place there."

"I have no place here without you."

He stood and looked down at her. "I'm sorry. I must go. I will not return."

He held his hand out to help her to her feet. She did not take it but struggled to her feet alone, grass and mud staining her knees. "How can you leave me?"

"I had hoped it might be different, but fate opposes me."

"Don't blame fate," she cried. "Fate has given me pain, but it has not closed my heart."

Claea ran along the stream bank. Her foot slipped on a patch of damp grass, and she slid into the stream, soaking much of her gown. She cursed, climbed up the bank, and ran toward the palace.

Phaethon watched as she disappeared through the palace gates. He followed, back bent as if from an unseen weight. As he neared the palace, he frowned suddenly and reached across to grasp his left elbow. A blue glow engulfed his hand and arm. "It comes sooner each day," he said abstractly, like a physician examining a wound.

He closed his eyes, and the blue glow faded, quelled by an act of will as he hurried into the palace to collapse upon his darkened bed.

"Claea, what is it?" Etagama asked, blocking the narrow hallway. "Why are you crying?"

She carried a bronze tray with a clay pitcher of wine and two matching clay cups. "Let me pass," she begged. "Please."

"Has the stranger hurt you? Done something to upset you?"

"No. Let me pass. I must speak to him before—"

"Before what?"

"Please," she repeated as she pushed past him. He grasped her arm, but she shook free and hurried through the great hall to the throne room and Phaethon's sanctuary. Etagama followed, his guards hurrying behind. He saw her pull the door open and rush inside. She neither knocked nor called out.

Etagama heard her scream through the shattering of cups and the clash of the bronze tray striking the floor. He ran through the open door and saw her standing in horror before a burned, broken creature who struggled to rise from the bed. Claea stumbled back as the deformed body fell to the floor, his feet tangled in the bedding like an animal caught in a snare. Phaethon cursed her, cursed himself, his cries clashing with Claea's screams as a blue fire surrounded him, restoring the enchantment that hid his injuries.

"I told you never to come in here without asking," Phaethon shouted.

He swung his arm through the fog of his horrors as if it might erase this moment from time itself. He struck Claea on the side of the head, shattering the fragile bones of her face, breaking her neck, and driving her against the stone wall to fall like stone.

"Monster," Etagama cried out, taking a sword from one of his guards.

Phaethon rushed toward him with the speed of thunder, ducking under the king's raised arm before he could strike. He grabbed the wrist of his sword arm with one hand and broke the bone. Phaethon's other hand closed around Etagama's throat and jerked his head sidewards with a terrible snap. He threw his body against the wall to crumble before Claea's sightless eyes.

Phaethon ran from his sanctuary, past the guards who stood frozen, unmanned by the horrors they had witnessed.

Chapter 46

In the darkest moments of the night, the rocks, soil, and vegetation surrounding the spring swarmed with creatures that build a world from the stirrings of blind senses. The darkness that nourished them nourished another. The body that had belonged to Strachys, that had hosted the scroll's ancient text stirred beneath the moss. He struggled through the green blanket that had been his refuge, his medicine—his womb. He tore away sections of the moss until his head pushed through, gasping in the dark air. His body followed, breaking the enfolding tendrils to fall naked, exhausted on the bank of the stream like an unlicked newborn animal. As he crawled across the ground to drink, creatures formless, strangely formed, and familiar welcomed him as a brother. He remembered how he'd come to this place—golden words carried by a dying seer like seeds in a bird's belly.

He swayed on his feet as sense contended with memory to shape his newly awakened mind. Memories of a half-life trapped between the twin prisons of the seer and the scroll passed through a mind too fluid to crystallize around them, a mind free of Strachys' conflicted will, free of the parchment that had bound him for millennia. He remembered his distant origins, how he had first been called from darkness by a worshiper of darkness thousands of years before men raised the monuments of Sumer, of Egypt, of Minos and Mycenae, of Troy. He remembered moving freely through the hearts of men who walked the land like dark gods until they were subdued by the priests of a forgotten Pharaoh—until those priests had imprisoned him in lifeless marks on a dried animal skin. Confined to parchment, he sensed the agonies of the men who had once worshiped him. He grieved to know they had been stripped of his animus, conscripted to serve in farms, quarries, and temples, made to construct vast mausoleums and be buried alive within them, their wild imaginations surviving only in dreams.

He shared the agony of the sorcerer who had written words that would awaken him in the parchment's margins—before dying at the hands of the inquisitors who served the new gods. He remembered the millennia of his confinement to symbols on the dry animal skin—stolen from tombs, bartered for trinkets, hung as a decoration in the cells of kings, peasants, priests, and prostitutes until it was left to rot in the ruins of some forgotten empire. He recalled the illiterate shaman who had discovered the parchment—a book he revered but could not read—and attached it to an olive wood spindle.

He remembered the enchantress who had found the scroll, and Circe's presence touched him as in a dream. He remembered how she had hidden it among books, both exalted and forbidden, taking it down from time to time to contemplate its promise. He remembered how her touch quickened his dim existence as her passion for the power it contained contended with her fear of the chaos it could unleash. Each time, she had returned it to its resting place, the liberating words unspoken.

He remembered the final theft that brought the scroll to Strachys, who spoke those words without comprehension, giving him a half-life in the seer's body, even as the half-death of confinement continued to bind him. He remembered the scroll's destruction and how he struggled through death to this rebirth. He remembered these things as a newborn remembers his origins—shadows flashing across an unformed consciousness to rest in hidden parts of the soul. Only one memory continued to shadow his awareness—one shackle bound him to the past. He remembered the men who had tried to kill him, who had burned the scroll, who had thrown him in the dirt to die, and a new sensation stirred in his immaculate mind.

Rage.

Nestor and his companions approached the island after midnight, the mountain range occluding the low stars. They rowed along the coastline until it curved inward to form a small bay lined by a white sand beach. Fires burned at one end of the beach, and dark shadows intruded from the water onto the sand—the ships of Phaethon's mercenaries. Nestor directed his men to row quietly past them and around the point that marked the far end of the beach. Out of sight of the mercenary camp, they approached the rocky shore as close as safety permitted. Several warriors lowered themselves into the water to hold the ship steady while Nestor and his party waded ashore. In addition to Astrid, Myia, Antilochus, and the animals, Nestor had chosen two warriors, Amphides and Ekhinos, to accompany them. After they watched the ship depart, Astrid spoke to them.

"What do you know about my cats?"

"I've been told they can join together and form a great cat and that it follows your will," Ekhinos said.

"I was at Agamemnon's council when she summoned the animal," Amphides added, "and I saw it again when she healed the orange cat."

"Then, you should not fear what you are about to see," Astrid reassured.

She kneeled and called in her thoughts to Audrey, Greystoke, and Elizabeth. The cats swarmed around her, rubbing against her legs, leaning into the touch of her hands like ordinary housecats begging for food or affection until a blue light smoldered around them. Astrid guided them to a spot just in front of her, then stepped away, watching the flowing colors of Elizabeth's ginger, Audrey's tortoiseshell, and Greystoke's gunmetal blend into Swarm's reasserted existence. Despite Astrid's warnings, Amphides and Ekhinos stepped back in fear.

"Are they . . . Are you gods?" Ekhinos asked.

Astrid shook her head. "I'm only a woman. As for the cats—and the great cat—the gods have touched them, just as they touch the warriors they hold dear, but they are still creatures of flesh and blood. The great cat will walk with us as our companion, and she will protect us. Do not fear her."

Nestor put his hands on their shoulders. "Believe what she says," he told them, "and remember who you are. Warriors of Pylos . . . *my* warriors."

Astrid saw the calming effect of Nestor's touch on the men, a transformation as remarkable as Swarm's. The landing party prepared the weapons and armor they had brought from the ship. Astrid watched Myia adjust the greaves and cuirass that protected her shins and torso, pull a leather helmet with bronze plates over her short black hair, then take spear in her hand, her sword at her side. Astrid felt a mixture of pride and sorrow as she realized Myia would never accept the role the world required of her.

As the sky lightened to the deep blue of early twilight, Nestor led them over the ridge to a point overlooking the beach. Astrid stood beside Swarm, her hand on the great cat's shoulders. Her experience in restoring Elizabeth to life and her time with Annape had deepened her bond with the cats. Her sense of Audrey, Elizabeth, and Greystoke, the distant presence of Spike and Chessie, and even the deep resonance of Swarm's awareness no longer lingered at the edge of her mind. They had joined her own stream of consciousness as nearly equal voices.

Astrid had come to think of this new, plural sentience as a six-part harmony, not unlike the Bach fugues Sigrid loved—multiple melodic voices moving through a shifting tonal landscape. Although her own stream of consciousness continued to control her thoughts and actions, Astrid had started to explore the cats' constant, psychic presence. On the ship, in the quiet of the night, she had let her thoughts entwine with their liquid minds, experiencing an alien emotional palette and novel forms of perception and understanding. Her consciousness had danced with theirs in counterpoints of two, three, four, or more voices, and beneath it all, Swarm's constant presence hummed with a deeper resonance, the fundamental of their shared awareness.

She longed to explore this new sentience, this new form of life. But, as she looked up the mountain where Spike and Chessie remained imprisoned, and down to the beach where they would face Phaethon's deadly mercenaries, Astrid knew it would have to wait. She asserted her human reason, even though the animals' voices continued to call her with seductive songs and unexpected harmonies.

"Are you all right?" Nestor's voice interrupted her reverie.

"Yes," she answered. "I'm ready."

"What about Swarm? Can you control her?"

"Our minds entwine constantly."

"But can you control her?"

"Do you remember the mare and stallion I gave you at Troy?" Astrid whispered so only he could hear.

"Yes," he said, smiling at the memory.

"My bond with Swarm is like yours with those horses."

Nestor looked thoughtfully across the beach, then took her hand and squeezed it.

"I will not fail you," Astrid promised.

The mountains formed a rough arc around the beach, with the rocky outcrop where Nestor and his party hid at one end and the mercenary camp at the other, approximately a mile away. Grass grew along the foothills, a buffer against the encroaching sand. A stream descended from the mountain to bisect the beach and enter the Aegean, slowing and widening to spread its alluvium across a fertile patch where the village once stood. In place of the once-living community, Astrid and her companions saw burned huts, abandoned possessions, carcasses of dead animals, and bloodstains left by the bodies mourners had removed in the darkness of night.

"Phaethon's mercenaries did this," Nestor told Astrid, answering her unspoken question. He pointed to the columns of smoke rising near the ships. "Judging by the fires, the bulk of the raiders are camped on the beach. I would guess a smaller force guards your animals."

"Do they know we're here?" Astrid asked.

"Perhaps, but I think not. Can you sense Spike and Chessie?"

Astrid pointed to the top of the mountain that circled the bay. "They're on the ridge. I think near where the stream starts down the mountainside."

Nestor surveyed the mountain face. "We should find any surviving villagers," he said. "They know the terrain. They can help us. But be careful; they may not welcome strangers."

They continued along the path as it crossed the face of the mountain above the beach and the remains of the village. They walked quietly where boulders or vegetation could hide them and hurried low across exposed sections of the trail. Canyons cut through the mountain face, bringing water to the brush that struggled on the dry slope. Groves of trees marked places where water accumulated—likely hiding places for refugees.

Astrid drew close to Nestor. "Swarm senses something," she whispered. "I think we're being watched."

"We have been since we started along the trail," he said.

Astrid followed his gaze up the mountainside. She saw the villagers appear from among the rocks, trees, and other hiding places on the mountain face—men and women, children and the elderly, healthy and infirm, the remains of a shattered community. Most held clubs, spears of sharpened wood, or other improvised weapons, although a few of the men carried short swords. One woman, younger and stronger than the rest, held a bronze sword and a crude wooden shield.

"Stay here," Nestor commanded. "Do not draw your weapons or move unless Antilochus so orders."

He stepped forward on the narrow path as five men—village leaders, he assumed—descended from the hillside, loose rocks and gravel sliding around them. They gathered just ahead of him, where the trail dipped into a small hollow and a scattering of small trees provided added concealment. Nestor removed his sword and lay it carefully on the ground beside his bronze-tipped spear where the villagers could see them. He stepped away from the weapons and approached them, his hands open at his side.

"What do you want, Achaean?" one of the villagers challenged.

"Do you know who we are?" Nestor asked calmly, stepping toward them.

"We saw you land during the night. What do you want?"

"We come for the men who attacked our camp at Troy. We want to recover what they have stolen and avenge our dead. I believe the men we seek are the same men who destroyed your homes."

"Why should we believe you?"

"You were correct to call us Achaeans. If you saw us land in the night, then you saw our ship depart with the bulk of our forces. If we were raiders,

wouldn't we have brought a larger force?" He gestured toward the mercenary encampment at the far end of the beach. "Or landed on the beach to
join the others?"

"Perhaps you wish to deceive us." The leader pointed at Astrid. "The
woman who walks with the great cat . . . Is she a witch?"

"She is human as you and me, and the cat is only an animal that serves
her, just as your beasts serve you," Nestor said.

"The men who destroyed our village followed a dark magician. This cat
could be his doing."

"What is your name?" Nestor asked him.

"Klymenos."

"I am Nestor of Pylos. Perhaps you've heard of me?"

"You're one of the Achaeans who have besieged Troy."

"Then, you know I'm an honorable man."

"I know your name and a few stories," Klymenos said, "that's all."

Nestor pointed back along the path to where his party remained. "That is
my son, Antilochus, and my men, Amphides and Ekhinos. Astrid and Myia
are our companions. They have trained the great cat to walk at their side,
like your hunting dogs."

"Why do these women travel with you?"

"The same men who destroyed your village attacked our camp and robbed
this woman," he said, pointing to Astrid. "The younger woman is her friend
and was also attacked."

"And thinks herself a warrior," one of the village leaders mocked. Myia
bristled but remained silent.

"She does what she must to avenge her injuries. She is no different from
your women," Nestor said, pointing up the mountainside at the woman
holding the sword and shield.

"What do you have to say, woman?" Klymenos challenged Astrid. "Are
you an enchantress hiding behind men you have possessed?"

Astrid silently directed Swarm to remain with Myia and stepped forward.
"Nestor of Pylos does not travel with dark enchantments. The men who
destroyed your homes also stole two of my animals and tried to kill me."

"What kind of animals?" Klymenos pressed.

"Cats. Not like this great cat, but small, like the cats that guard your gra-
naries."

"Why do you care about them?" He smirked. "The cats that beg near any
village would easily replace them . . . whether you want them to or not."

"These animals are unique. They are beloved of a goddess who has sent
me to recover them and who will reward all who help me."

Astrid's mention of an immortal seemed to silence the men as talk of it stirred among the villagers. She heard a shout up the hill and saw a boy around twelve years old run from behind the rocks, escaping several adults who tried to stop him. He slid down the hillside's loose dirt and rock, alternately on his feet and backside, until he reached the path and stood between Nestor and Klymenos.

"I've seen your cats," he shouted to Astrid.

Klymenos ran forward and grasped him by the arm. "Silence, boy," he commanded, then turned to Astrid. "What do your animals look like?"

She described Spike and Chessie. The boy looked up at Klymenos and nodded. Klymenos led him back to the rest of the village leaders. They spoke for a while, their voices and gestures growing increasingly animated. Eventually, Klymenos returned, still holding the boy by the arm.

"The boy had been captured by the men on the mountain, but he escaped. He said your cats have magical powers, that they were held in cages and used in dark rituals that killed my people."

"The cats have certain abilities," Astrid conceded. "The sorcerer who lives on the mountain used them for his dark magic, but the cats did not cause your people's deaths. They are in danger themselves."

"That's what the boy has told me," Klymenos said.

As he spoke, the boy broke from his grasp and ran to Astrid. Klymenos shouted at him to return but did not pursue him.

"What's your name?" she asked, kneeling to face him.

"My name is Eumenes, but my friends call me Hector."

Astrid smiled. "After the defender of Troy?"

He nodded.

"You must be brave to earn a name like that," she mused.

He looked nervously at the Achaeans. "It's all right," Astrid reassured. "They respect courageous men—even the Trojan Hector. Tell me what you saw."

Hector told how he had befriended Spike and how Proxonos and the mercenaries had kidnapped him when they raided his village. He described Strachys and Phaethon's dark magic, the deaths of the abducted villagers, and his escape. The surviving villagers wept openly as he spoke.

"Are the animals well?" Astrid asked.

"They are not hurt," Hector said. "The man who killed my friends said the cats would lure his enemies to him—into a trap."

"Then you know where they are?"

He pointed to the mountain's crest. "They're caged inside a house."

"How many mercenaries are there?" Nestor asked the boy.

"Less than ten at the house, but many more are camped on the beach."

"More than fifty," Klymenos added.

Nestor frowned. "I have half that many men on my ship," he said thoughtfully. He turned to Klymenos, his posture and expression indicating it was time to end their negotiations.

"Will you help us? Can we fight together to avenge our losses? We can give you weapons and help plan a strategy."

Klymenos retreated to speak with his people. After several minutes, he called out to Nestor. "Very well, we will hear what you have to say."

Astrid, Swarm, and the Achaeans remained behind, watching Nestor speak with Klymenos and the other villagers. A few adults came down from the mountainside and stood around them in a restless circle, but most stayed back, watching cautiously. Nestor sat on a rock among the trees, his manner relaxed and confident. Even though Astrid could not hear all they were saying, she followed the conversation from scattered phrases and the men's body language. At first, Nestor simply listened to their accounts of the tragedy that had befallen the village. Gradually, he began to talk, turning mistrust into a discussion of common interest and strategy. After a time, Nestor returned, accompanied by the boy and the village elders.

"When our ship returns tonight, we will arm the villagers with our extra weapons." He saw the concern on Amphides' face.

"We must trust each other," Nestor told him.

"What is our strategy?" Antilochus asked.

"We have little time to plan, and the villagers are not experienced warriors, so it must be simple. We are outnumbered, but we may be able to draw Phaethon's raiders into a trap. When our ship returns tonight, part of our forces will stay here in the mountains to prepare the villagers and to fight beside them. The rest of my warriors will take the ship out to sea and wait for dawn. Klymenos' people will conceal themselves in the foothills above the beach, with our warriors spread among them. My ship will land and draw Phaethon's men to attack. When they come, our people in the hills will go down on their flank, trapping Phaethon's men between them and my warriors from the ship."

"What if they learn of our alliance with the villagers? If they suspect the trap?" Ekhinos asked.

"If they do not enter our trap," Nestor said, "we will gather our forces and move up the beach to face them."

"What if they try to move behind us?" Amphides asked.

"They will have to cross the foothills, and the terrain is difficult," Klymenos said." My people will stop them. We know the land; they do not."

"It's not perfect," Antilochus observed, "but it could work—and it's all we have time to prepare."

"Astrid," Nestor said, "When the fighting starts, Antilochus will take you and a small party to recover the animals. Do not leave until I tell you."

"If you follow us across the beach as we drive the raiders back, you can take the trail that follows the stream," Klymenos explained. "It is an easier climb than the trail that crosses the mountain and it will take you to the sorcerer's home."

Hector stepped forward from the crowd. "I want to come."

"You're too young," Klymenos said.

"No," the boy insisted, tears filling his eyes. "They killed my father, and they hurt my mother. I want to fight."

Nestor looked inquisitively at Astrid.

"He knows the layout of the sorcerer's home," she said, "how Spike and Chessie are being held. He could help us." She turned to Klymenos. "I will protect him."

Klymenos nodded reluctantly, and Astrid kneeled in front of the boy.

"Hector, I know you are brave and want to avenge your family, but you must do as I tell you. If I tell you to wait, you must wait. If I tell you to run, you must run away. Do you understand?"

"I promised the cats I would come for them," he argued.

"And we will, but you must obey me, just as these warriors and I obey Nestor."

Hector nodded reluctantly.

Chapter 47

Proxonos walked into Strachys' hovel, a dark shadow framed by the sunlight glaring through the doorway. "The Achaeans are here," he said.

Phaethon sat up in the seer's bed. He checked the cages where Spike and Chessie remained confined. "Are you sure?"

"One of my men in the hills saw a single ship land in the night and drop off a small party. They are on the hillside above the village. The woman and the great cat are with them."

"Are they coming here?" Phaethon asked.

Proxonos shook his head. "They're a small force, probably scouting the island. Most likely, they'll rejoin the men on the ship and attack tomorrow. My man saw Nestor meet with the villagers. They'll tell him how many of my men are here and how many are camped on the beach."

"How many warriors does he have?"

Proxonos took a chair near the wooden table. "About twenty on the ship," he said, "and a half dozen in the scouting party."

"We have twice that," Phaethon said. "What about the villagers? Will they join him?"

"I assume they'll help, but the villagers are weak and untrained—many are sick. They don't worry me." Proxonos paused, considering his plans. "Nestor will try to find some advantage in the terrain—perhaps create some sort of trap. We should strengthen our positions and wait, force him to act first and show his intentions."

"Shouldn't we attack his men when they're leaving their ship, while they are slowed by the surf and wet sand?" Phaethon asked impatiently.

Proxonos shook his head. "Do not underestimate Nestor. He'll expect us to attack the beachhead, and it could draw us into a trap. We should make him come to us so we can meet him on our terms and take advantage of our superior numbers," Proxonos explained. "I will spread some of my men in the trees above the beach. If he attacks our camp, they will come down on his flank."

Phaethon nodded reluctantly.

"How many men should remain here with you?" Proxonos asked.

Phaethon shook his head. "My business is with the woman and her cats—and with Circe. I must face them alone."

"As you wish, I'll place warriors on the path that follows the stream, and on the one that crosses the mountain, in case any of Nestor's men try to sneak past us. I'll also leave a few warriors nearby should you need them."

"I don't want any interference when I face the enchantress."

"Don't worry." Proxonos stared at Phaethon grimly. "I'll tell them to leave the witch to you."

Nestor had taken his men, Myia, and a few dozen villagers to where the mountain met the ocean, to wait for his ship to return. Astrid had taken Swarm and found a place where she could be alone with her thoughts, away from Nestor and the others but still within hearing distance of them. Since arriving on the island, Greystoke, Audrey, and Elizabeth had remained joined as Swarm, partly from Astrid's wordless suggestion and partly from their own unease. She found courage in the sleeping cat's regular breathing, and she rested her hand on Swarm's shoulders, gently stroking her dark fur. She heard a rustling of branches and saw Nestor approach. He wore a woolen cloak over his linen tunic and carried his sword in his hand.

"Nestor," she said, "Is everything all right?"

"My men are keeping watch," he reassured. He looked at Swarm and smiled. "The cat is resting. I think that's a good sign."

"Yes," Astrid said, running her hand down Swarm's back. "How long do we have until the ship returns?"

"Long enough for you to get some sleep. I'll come for you when it is time." He removed his cloak and draped it over her shoulders. "Keep this against the chill."

She smiled at him and gathered the cloth around herself.

"Please sit," she invited him. "I have a feeling there is something you want to talk to me about."

He sat in the small patch of grass, laying his sword nearby. "You are as aware of my thoughts as you are of Swarm's."

"What is it?"

"Myia told me you had given her instructions on what to do with the animals should you be killed."

Astrid took a breath and exhaled slowly. "It seemed prudent. I told her that Circe would find her and take the cats if I died."

Nestor stared out at the ocean. "You've seemed different since you awoke from the deep sleep."

"I feel fine."

"Astrid, we must be honest—"

"Nestor, I'm fine," she insisted.

He sat beside her for a time, then spoke slowly, in measured phrases. "I have led many men into battle. It's been my experience that when a warrior shows no signs of fear but tells his friends his wishes should he be killed, he usually dies. It is as if he has made peace with the idea."

He looked Astrid in the eyes, but she did not respond.

"Fear is not your enemy," Nestor continued. "It strengthens courage, but you must believe you will survive—and triumph."

Astrid pulled her knees to her chest and stared out across the water. "When I disappeared on the island where we had stopped to rest," she began, rocking almost imperceptibly on the sandy ground, struggling with her emotions, "when the woman came out of the surf for me . . ."

"I remember," Nestor said.

"She led me to Circe's palace."

"As you have told me."

"What I didn't tell you was that Circe sent me back through the underworld to find Tiresias. She said he could see my future."

"That is dangerous knowledge—and a dangerous journey."

"I should have told you."

He shook his head. "There are things one keeps to oneself."

"Tiresias told me two things. The first was that one of my animals would die. That has happened."

"When Phaethon almost killed Elizabeth?"

"He had killed her. He'd crushed her rib cage, and her heart had stopped. By all appearances, she was dead. It was only by joining with Swarm that I was able to revive her." Astrid continued, speaking softly. "His second prediction was that I would die before I returned home."

Nestor's breath caught in his chest, and tears formed in his eyes. "Elizabeth lives in spite of his prophecy," he argued. "These things are often nothing more than stories intended to influence your actions. Sometimes, they are deceptions that send you to destruction. Other times—if the gods favor you, which I believe to be true—they guide you along a wiser path. Mostly, they are simply puzzles to be solved, as you saw with your cat. I remember a story that was told to me a long time ago—"

Astrid leaned over and pressed two fingers to his lips.

"Dear Nestor, I know what you are trying to say. I know the stories, and I know that Tiresias' words are not a death sentence, but I don't want to think about it. I just want to rest. I want to forget about all this for a few hours—and just be."

Nestor took her hand and squeezed it. "Astrid—"

She silenced him once more and leaned across to kiss him. "Did anyone ever tell you that you talk too much?"

"Often," he said ironically.

Astrid placed her hand on his cheek and kissed him again. He returned the kiss as a lover would, lingering on the touch of her lips. He grasped her arm and pulled her close. She rose and straddled his outstretched legs, removing the cloak he had draped over her shoulders and laying it to the side. She stared into his eyes, then took his face in her hands and kissed him deeply.

"Astrid," he whispered.

"It's all right," she smiled.

Nestor pulled her close, and they kissed again. She released his embrace, straightened her back, and pulled her sweater over her head, laying it on the grass beside them. Still straddling his legs, she leaned forward and kissed him once more as he grasped her sides, caressing her body with hands that had grown strong from breaking horses and fighting men. He kissed her lips, her throat, her breasts, running his palms along the soft sides of her belly to grasp her hips, her pelvic bones hard beneath her denim jeans.

Astrid tugged on his linen tunic—pinned beneath him, it did not move. Laughing, she raised her weight from his thighs, and he lifted his buttocks to let her slide the cloth from beneath him. He leaned forward, his arms raised as she pulled his tunic over his head. She threw it aside to drape randomly across a tree branch.

Nestor kissed her once more, and she pushed him playfully onto the rough grass. He grasped her sides, her stomach, pressing his thumbs into muscles grown taut from her time at Troy. Astrid's breath caught in her chest, and she moved her pelvis against him. She bent forward and kissed him again as he stroked the side of her face, as he caressed her breasts.

Astrid ran her hands over his body, touching each of the scars that marked his skin. She found the crease of a once deep wound on his stomach and kissed it gently as he rested his hand on the back of her head. She kissed a faint scar, the width of a dagger's blade, over his lowest rib. She kissed each mark that life had left upon him and playfully ran her tongue around his nipples before stretching forward to kiss his lips once more, her body against him, his fingers pressing into the muscles along her spine. She felt him hard against her and smiled.

Astrid pushed herself away and took her feet. She released her belt and the metal button of her jeans, lowered the zipper, and removed them as if she were preparing to sleep in the safety of her home. She laid her jeans on her sweater, placed her panties on top of them, and returned naked to Nestor's arms, finding the joy of life in the arms of a king out of distant Pylos, a warrior out of legend, a man she had grown to trust—and to love.

Astrid slept in Nestor's arms, her head on his chest, his cloak covering them from the night's chill. He felt a disturbance and saw a blue glow as Swarm returned to the forms of Astrid's three small cats. Audrey lay down near Astrid's head, her soft fur touching Nestor's shoulder. Greystoke and Elizabeth found places to rest along Astrid's back. Nestor closed his eyes but remained alert, marking the time until he would rise to meet his ship and gather his warriors, as he had done so often before.

Chapter 48

Astrid and Swarm hid in the twilight with Nestor, Myia, Antilochus, Amphides, and Ekhinos at one end of the beach, some fifty yards up the mountainside. Klymenos and six villagers had joined them. They stood at the junction of two trails. One descended from where they stood to the beach, passing along the foothills through the village's remains, then turning to follow the stream up to its source. Behind them, a harder trail ascended through the rocks, crossing the mountain face in a long climb.

Eight Achaean warriors who had landed in the night joined the villagers hiding in the rocks and scattered vegetation, waiting to flank the mercenaries when they attacked Nestor's ship on the beach. Nestor had provided enough weapons to arm almost half of the villagers, most of them with bronze-tipped spears. He had cautioned them against throwing the spears since their clumsy attempts would almost certainly miss, leaving them unarmed. Instead, he instructed them to remain together and form a phalanx from which they could thrust their weapons. They quickly grasped his intent, with many improvising wooden shields to strengthen their line.

Nestor had distributed the swords from the ship among those who had fighting experience, with any extra going to those who seemed most capable, many of them young women. The ship also carried a dozen bows and a supply of arrows. He had given bows to Myia, Amphides, and Ekhinos, and the rest to village fighters. He instructed them to fire down on the mercenaries from the rocks above the beach—and to avoid hitting their own people. The rest of the villagers carried clubs, knives, farm tools, and other improvised weapons. Finally, Nestor had taught them simple hand signals.

"Are they ready?" Astrid asked him as they waited for daylight.

"No," he frowned, "but there is nothing more I can do."

"How bad is it?"

"The villagers are neither trained nor experienced. Many are sick and weakened from living in the hills. But they will increase our numbers, and will fight with a passion to avenge their losses."

"Will it be enough?"

"My men are strong, skilled, and disciplined," he said. "With the villagers' help, we will prevail, but . . ."

Astrid saw the concern in his face. "But?"

"Many will die, mostly villagers," Nestor said as Astrid took his hand.

As the twilight grew brighter, Astrid found her dread of the coming battle reflected in Swarm's growing agitation. She massaged the muscles in the cat's neck and shoulders and sensed the rise of her predatory instincts. Even as she tried to calm the great cat, Astrid felt a now-familiar longing to release herself into Swarm's emotions. She had felt it after the attempted rape, and when she had joined with Swarm to fight Phaethon at Nestor's camp. She fought this desire once more, her efforts to calm the restless animal becoming one with her own struggle for self-control.

The beach remained in the shadow of the mountains as Nestor's ship approached through the morning sunlight, his warriors rowing slowly to conserve their strength. Astrid heard a noise from the trail that crossed the mountain face and saw a young man run toward them. He was from the party Klymenos had sent to scout the mercenary encampment. A blood-soaked cloth bound his upper arm.

"What have you seen?" Klymenos asked urgently.

Exhausted from his long run, the youth answered in a breathless staccato, "We followed the trail then crossed the stream and hid in the rocks and trees above their camp. As soon as it became light, we saw them. They had spread out in the foothills. Only half their force remains near their ships. It is a trap."

Nestor frowned as he listened to the boy. "We have men in the foothills as well. Why didn't we see them?"

"The raiders remain near their camp but are ready to attack."

"Where are your companions?" Klymenos asked.

"A group of mercenaries saw us when we started back," he said, his voice cracking. "My friends told me to run here to warn you while they fought to cover my escape." He stopped as tears cut tracks through the dirt and blood on his face. "They . . . they did not survive."

Nestor glanced at Klymenos and saw the grief on his face. It was a feeling he understood too well.

Astrid pointed to the boy's bandaged arm. "You're hurt."

"An arrow nicked me, but it's nothing."

Nestor turned to Klymenos. "They know we're here," he said, frustration in his voice, "and they've guessed our plan. They will not enter our trap, and it seems they've set one of their own."

"What are we going to do?" Klymenos pressed.

Nestor placed a hand on Klymenos' shoulder. "Your people know the terrain—that gives us some advantage. Take my men who left the ship last night and your strongest fighters into foothills. Try to remain unseen. Stop short of the mercenaries' position—do not engage them. The rest of your people will remain with me, my sons, Amphides, Ekhinos, Myia, and Astrid. When the ship lands, we will join my warriors from the ship and move up the beach to attack the mercenary camp. As soon as we move, attack the mercenaries in the foothills to protect our flank."

Klymenos nodded and smiled grimly. "We will face these dogs like men."

"Spread word of the new plan among your people," Nestor said, "but be sure to tell them not to attack until I command it."

Nestor turned to Ekhinos. "Take two of my men and three villagers for protection. Go to where the ridge meets the ocean but stay hidden. When our ship draws close, signal them to land at the end of the beach farthest from the mercenary camp, and tell them of the change of plans."

Ekhinos nodded and gestured to two of Nestor's men and three villagers. Nestor watched them run across the mountain face, then he spoke to the wounded scout. "How many raiders guard the hut at the top of the trail?"

"We saw only a few when we passed in the night, less than ten."

"Can you give me five of your men?" Nestor asked Klymenos.

"Yes."

He turned to Astrid. "You and Swarm will go with Antilochus, Amphides, Myia, and Klymenos' men to recover your cats, just as we had discussed. Wait until we drive the mercenaries back from the streamside path. Then follow it up the mountain. Antilochus will decide what to do next."

"What do you mean 'decide what to do next?'" Astrid asked with concern in her voice.

"That depends on what happens on the beach," Nestor said grimly. "Either you will join us in victory or hide until this scum leaves the island."

"I can't leave you here."

Nestor glanced at Antilochus, who understood his father's silent request and took the others aside to plan their ascent of the mountain. Astrid followed his father a short distance from the others, where they could talk alone. Swarm followed restlessly.

"I must take command of my men when they land," Nestor told her.

"I know," she said reluctantly. "Nestor, do you really think you can defeat the mercenaries?"

He smiled at her and nodded. "Yes we will prevail."

"Protect yourself," Astrid said, taking his hand.

"I'll be all right," he reassured. "But promise me you will not take any foolish risks."

Astrid nodded.

"Remember, you are a warrior," he told her, "I saw it in you the day we met." He glanced down at Swarm and rested his hand on the great cat. Swarm leaned into his touch, and Nestor smiled. "The heart of the great cat beats inside you."

Astrid stretched up and pulled Nestor's head toward her. She kissed him, holding the embrace until he gently pulled away.

"Do not worry," he said. "These raiders have grown overconfident slaughtering farmers. Soon they will face warriors of Pylos."

"I worry about one warrior of Pylos," she said. "Be careful."

"I have not led three generations of men into battle just to fall to a mercenary blade." Nestor smiled, taking her hand. He glanced toward the young man who had scouted the raider's position, then back to Astrid. "Perhaps you could tend his wound?"

Astrid realized Nestor needed to gather his thoughts free of distraction; she also sensed that he wanted to give her some task that would keep her from worrying about the upcoming battle. She kissed him and walked to the wounded scout

"What's your name?" Astrid asked the boy.

"Nikostratos."

"May I look at your arm, Nikostratos?"

He nodded. She removed the bandage to reveal a deep puncture wound in his bicep. The injury was torn as if he had removed the arrow by force. It had stopped bleeding, but dirt covered the open wound. She washed it and bound it with a clean cloth from the supplies they had brought ashore.

"How old are you?"

"Fourteen."

Astrid felt her anger rise at all this child had suffered and would continue to suffer. "You must rest."

"No. I must fight. I will join my people."

Astrid suppressed her feelings and bandaged his arm. As she worked, she felt a growing tension fill her mind, tightening the muscles in her neck and shoulders. At first, she thought it came from her anxiety over the battle or compassion for the injured child she treated, but she quickly realized it came from Swarm. Astrid finished bandaging the boy's wound and watched him join the other villagers. She kneeled in front of the cat and took her head in her hands.

"What is it, honey?" She rubbed her fingers across the cat's jawline, feeling Swarm's anxiety swell in her mind.

The great cat growled and stared up the mountainside. Astrid followed her gaze and saw a mist form along the ridge, moving down the path that paralleled the stream's descent. It moved through the trees toward the far side of the beach and the mercenary camp.

"Nestor," she called out, "do you see that?"

Nestor looked up the mountain. "It looks like fog, but it's too warm for fog, the air's too dry."

Myia and the others gathered at his side. They watched the mist spread across the foothills, curving toward the mercenary camp as if nudged by a breeze, although the air remained unnaturally still. The fog rolled over the mercenaries hiding in the trees, down to their camp, seemingly guided by will rather than by nature. As the cloud passed over Phaethon's mercenaries, Astrid heard them cry out—at first in surprise and warning, then intensifying into cries of rage and panic.

The clash of bronze striking bronze echoed across the beach, and Astrid saw men run from their hiding places onto the sand. Some of them stumbled, and others looked back over their shoulders as the mist overtook them. The fog thickened into a dark cloud above the raiders, a cloud from which only the sounds of metal and madness escaped.

"They are fighting among themselves," Nestor said in astonishment.

Astrid felt Swarm's tension increase, the low rumble in the cat's chest threatening to turn into a scream. She looked up the mountain, unconsciously guided by Swarm's gaze. She saw a man standing on a rise, looking down at the source of the mist. A dagger of sunlight passed through a gap in the mountains to illuminate him. He stood naked, his arms extended toward the mercenary camp.

The boy, Hector, ran toward her. "That's one of them," he shouted, pointing at the man, "one of the men who hurt the cats . . . He's the sorcerer, the one named Strachys."

"Antilochus," Nestor shouted, "run to our people on the beach. Signal the ship to land as far as possible from the fog and tell the men to stay with the ship. If the mist spreads toward them, they must take as many of our men and villagers as they can and row out to sea. They must avoid that mist, no matter what. Then return here with Ekhinos."

He watched Antilochus run across the hillside.

"Send word among your people in the foothills," he told Klymenos. "Tell them to pull back. They must not go near that cloud."

Klymenos shouted to his people, and word spread among the people on the mountainside.

The mist darkened over the mercenaries as the clash of metal and screams of the dying filled the beach. Astrid remembered reading of something like this long ago, but she could not recall where. Was it the Old Testament? Some ancient epic? For an instant, she wondered if she might be witnessing the origins of the legend.

Astrid looked at the man standing naked on the ridge above them, the man the boy had called Strachys. He stood with his hands at his side, his eyes locked on the slaughter. She reached into the turbulence of Swarm's emotions with her thoughts, comforting the cat. She sensed a hatred of the man on the mountain. It did not come from the cat beside her, but from Spike and Chessie.

After a time, the man on the mountain turned and crossed the ridge to disappear into the island's interior. As he left, the mist dissipated like an ordinary fog in the morning heat.

"By the gods," Nestor whispered as he stared at the carnage left by the receding enchantment. Bodies littered the beach, blood staining the sand beneath them. The few mercenaries who remained staggered among their dead comrades, their weapons lowered, pulled down by the weight of madness and death.

Nestor heard shouts and saw Klymenos give his people the sign to attack.

"Klymenos, no," he shouted. "It is too soon. We don't know—"

"It's our time," Klymenos shouted back as a terrifying smile crossed his face. "Good luck, Achaean. I hope you find your animals and return home."

Nestor watched Klymenos join his people as they swarmed onto the beach. The villagers who had offered to help Astrid recover the cats broke away and joined them. Only Nestor's warriors and the child, Hector, remained. Men, women, children, and the elderly ran into the ruins of the mercenary force, thrusting spears into the bodies that littered the sand. Those who had no weapons retrieved the swords of the dead and turned them against the dying. A handful of surviving raiders formed a defensive circle, only to be overwhelmed by the mob. Astrid watched an old woman who had limped behind the others pick up the sword of a wounded warrior and hack into his body. She saw villagers loot the dead, searching corpses for any valuables they might have carried into battle, cutting off hands for the rings on their fingers, slicing hair and scalp away for the beads woven into men's braids.

Astrid heard a sound on the path and saw Antilochus had returned with Ekhinos at his side. Nestor looked across the hillside and saw the rest of the Achaeans move to join him—the disciplined warriors had not followed the villagers onto the beach. As his men worked their way across the mountain face, he asked Ekhinos about the ship.

"The ship landed safely near the ridge," Ekhinos explained, "but as soon as Klymenos attacked the raiders, the village men left to join the others."

"Do my men remain with the ship? Are they safe?"

"Yes, all of them. They wait just offshore."

The last of Nestor's warriors crossed the hillside and gathered around him. Nestor counted the men to ensure all were present. He motioned to a man who wore a boar's tusk helmet and carried a sword and bronze shield, gray streaks running through his hair and beard.

"Lead my men back to the ship," Nestor instructed. "Row out and wait offshore. Some raiders may have survived, and I'm not sure if we can still trust the villagers."

The gray-bearded warrior nodded. "Aren't you coming with us?"

Nestor shook his head. "Antilochus, Amphides, and Ekhinos will join me to take Astrid, Myia, the boy, and Swarm up the mountain to find the animals. If we do not return by sunset tomorrow, leave and don't return."

The warriors protested, demanding to stay with Nestor. Astrid felt Swarm grow uneasy at the sound of so many voices and kneeled beside the cat, her arms around her neck. She looked up at Nestor and shook her head.

"You must do as I tell you," Nestor commanded. "You must protect the ship. Antilochus, Amphides, Ekhinos, Myia and I are enough to handle any raiders who survived the mist."

A few of the Achaeans continued to protest.

"You heard Nestor," graybeard said in a steady voice. "Do as he tells you." The men grew quiet, and graybeard clasped Nestor's shoulder. "Good luck. May Athena watch over you."

Nestor watched his warriors start back to the ship. When they passed out of sight, he turned to Astrid and Swarm, Antilochus, Amphides, Ekhinos, Myia, and Hector. "I think it best we take the trail across the mountain face. The trail by the stream may not be safe."

The rest of his party looked down at the carnage below and made their agreement clear.

"Come," Nestor said as he started up the trail, "let us find Astrid's animals and leave this cursed place."

Chapter 49

Astrid and her companions followed the narrow path across the mountain face. Occasionally, picking their way through the rubble where landslides had covered the trail. Nestor and Antilochus led them, discussing tactics as they climbed. Astrid and Myia followed with Swarm, trying to reassure the increasingly restless cat, while Hector, Ekhinos, and Amphides walked at the rear. Everyone except Astrid and Hector wore the armor they had brought from the ship. Astrid had refused it and the weapons with which she had no skill. She believed the ability to move unhindered gave her a better chance of recovering her animals—and surviving the day. At Nestor's insistence, she carried a bronze-tipped spear but hoped she would not need it for anything more than a walking stick.

As they followed the trail across the mountain face, they could see the beach and the devastation below. The villagers had completed their rampage through the dead and dying mercenaries. Most sat dazed or wandered aimlessly through the carnage. Others walked along the ocean's edge, alone or in small groups consoling one another. A few waded into the Aegean to cleanse themselves in the waters of creation.

Swarm had grown increasingly agitated as they neared Spike and Chessie. Astrid sensed that the two cats were uninjured, but she also felt the lingering effects of their ordeal. Her anger grew, stoking Swarm's rage. She slowed her breath, and kneeled beside the great cat, her arms around her neck, speaking soft syllables in Swarm's ear as she struggled to calm the animal—and herself. Nestor, Myia, and the Achaeans waited silently until Astrid indicated she was ready to continue. Nestor dropped back to walk at her side letting Antilochus take the lead.

"Can you still control the cat?" he whispered.

"Our minds are connected," she said, leaning close to him. "It's as if her emotions have become my own."

"Does that make it easier?"

"I'm not sure," Astrid said, forcing a smile.

Swarm grew calmer as they continued up the mountain and moved away from the carnage on the beach. They climbed steadily and reached the top of the ridge. When they approached an outcropping of rock, Astrid felt Swarm become agitated and cautioned Nestor and the others. They rounded the outcropping with their weapons ready. The trail widened into a flat area of dirt and dry grass where seven armed men blocked their way. Proxonos stepped forward, carrying a shield and spear, a short sword at his side.

"If it isn't the great Nestor of Pylos," Proxonos shouted, his lips drawn into a grim smile. "Are you disappointed I survived the seer's fog?"

Nestor approached him as Astrid pulled the cat close to her.

"You know me?" Nestor asked.

Proxonos' smile gave way to a scowl of resentment. "Do you forget, Achaean? How you led your men against me at Troy?"

"Were you part of the attack on Odysseus' camp?" Nestor asked calmly.

"I led the attack," Proxonos sneered. "Now, you must face me without your friends."

"What is your name?"

"Proxonos."

Nestor gestured toward the beach with his spear. "Haven't you had enough slaughter, Proxonos? I only wish to recover this woman's animals and be on my way."

"Does the great Nestor fear a fight?"

"You know my reputation." Nestor smiled. "I would gladly pass in peace, but if you choose a battle, I will not turn away."

As he spoke, Nestor's companions moved forward. Ekhinos took a position to Nestor's right; Antilochus took the center, standing beside his father, with Myia and Amphides to his left. Astrid stayed back with Swarm and Hector.

"Listen to me," she whispered to the boy. "If the fight goes badly, or if I tell you to run, go down the trail as fast as you can and don't look back."

As she spoke, Astrid heard the shouts of men and the clash of bronze. She saw Nestor's warriors engage the mercenaries as Swarm's bloodlust rose, straining against her control.

Amphides hurled his spear at a mercenary who challenged him. It entered the man's throat just above his shield, and he fell back, drowning in blood. Amphides drew his bronze sword and moved beside Myia to engage one of the two warriors she faced, allowing her to fight a single opponent. Antilochus fought two raiders, keeping them at a distance with disciplined thrusts of his spear and parries with his shield. Ekhinos fought the remaining mercenary, skillfully driving him back. At the center of it all, Nestor and Proxonos stalked each other patiently, experienced warriors evaluating tactics in their minds, envisioning possibilities that others could only measure in bronze and blood.

Astrid watched Myia confront a mercenary who stood at least six inches taller than she. Myia threw her spear, only to have him knock it aside with his shield. He laughed as she drew her short sword. His laughter died when she attacked him with no regard for her own safety, striking two blows to his one. Caught off guard by her untutored ferocity, he stepped back and tripped on a rock protruding from the brown sod. Myia hacked his body savagely as it convulsed in death. She screamed as if all the brutality she had faced in her young life—her family's slaughter by Agamemnon's men, the years of hiding in the forest, the constant fears of rape and death—all exploded from her at once.

Swarm's rage intensified with Myia's fury—a reflection of the bond that had grown between them. Astrid opened her mind, trying to bring the great cat's rage into her own self control, to stop her from running into the battle to fall to a mercenary's spear or blindly attack one of her companions.

"Stay beside me," Astrid repeated, both silently in her mind and speaking softly in the cat's ear. She rubbed Swarm's chest, hoping to calm her through physical contact as well as their psychic connection. She drew on all she had learned since first joining minds with the cat, but realized she could only delay Swarm's surging bloodlust for a few moments more.

She saw Proxonos drive Nestor back, the strength of his youth prevailing against the older warrior's skill and resisted her desire to run to Nestor's side. She knew she would only distract him—and lose control over Swarm.

One of the men who fought Antilochus broke free and stalked toward Astrid as his companion continued to attack Nestor's son. As he approached, she stepped away from Swarm and thrust at him with her spear. He stepped back in surprise. She lunged forward, pressing her advantage, but he pushed her spear aside and struck her with his shield, knocking her to the ground. As he raised his sword to strike, a deadly shadow engulfed him.

Swarm's unleashed fury filled Astrid's mind, and she felt the cat's jaws close around the man's throat, crushing muscle and bone. She experienced an involuntary thrill at the taste of blood and, without thinking, placed her hand on the cat's shoulders—Swarm turned and screamed, teeth bared. Astrid threw herself back on the dry grass, stunned, as the animal she had known for so long threatened her with uncontrolled rage. She froze, and Swarm turned back to the dying warrior, tearing at his throat.

Astrid looked toward Nestor. The horseman stood opposite the mercenary, breathing heavily as Proxonos taunted him.

"Where is the great Nestor now?" Proxonos shouted, beating his shield with his spear's wooden shaft. "Where is your strength now that Odysseus does not fight at your side?" He pointed toward Astrid with his spear. "Are you waiting for your girl to rescue you, old man?"

Nestor did not react to Proxonos' taunts but seemed to turn inward, gathering his strength, his chest rising and falling as if drawing power from the air itself. He lowered his shoulders and stepped back, shifting his weight onto his right leg, compressing his muscles as he moved his spear from a thrusting grip to one meant for throwing. Proxonos recognized his intention and raised his shield as Nestor pushed forward, his right arm arcing overhead. As his hand crossed the top of its curve, Nestor released the spear, his arm following through in a perfect arc, his right hand skimming the ground, his shoulder, back, and hips forming the fulcrum of power. For an instant, the wooden shaft seemed to vibrate in the air like the plucked string of a harp, then it accelerated toward Proxonos' shield. It penetrated the cowhide covering, splintering the wood beneath it, and continued through to strike the mercenary in the center of his armored chest, bronze against bronze.

Proxonos stared at the spear protruding from his chest. No emotion seized his face, nor did blood spread from the point of penetration. There was no gap between the bronze spear tip and the armor's surface; it appeared as if they had been welded together. Astrid feared that Nestor's spear had stopped short of Proxonos' flesh until she saw blood flow from beneath his bronze cuirass like wine spilling from an overturned cup, soaking his tunic and covering his thighs. The mercenary fell to the ground, motionless.

Nestor stood over him, breathing heavily, his empty spear hand at his side. "Who are you calling an old man?"

Once more, Astrid felt a surge of animal emotion crash through her awareness. She turned and saw Swarm run up the trail toward her littermates. Hector ran behind.

"Go after them," Nestor shouted. "We'll follow."

Astrid scanned the clearing and saw all her companions had survived. The remaining mercenaries ran, scrambling down the hillside, feet slipping on the loose gravel, courage drained by the Achaean's disciplined attack, Swarm's ferocity, and Proxonos' death. Myia stood over the man she had killed, rage distorting her face. Astrid saw Antilochus approach her slowly, repeating her name. His voice seemed to cleanse the madness from the girl's face, and she responded with a nod to his touch on her shoulder.

"Go," Nestor shouted to Astrid.

She ran after Hector and the now uncontrollable Swarm.

The man who had been Strachys continued his passage across the island, the mercenaries' destruction already fading from his newly-formed mind. He had only dim memories of his life in the seer's body—constrained by the weaknesses and desires of the aging human, forced to obey Phaethon's dark plans. Each step carried him into a new world, a world of wonders large and small, wonders of water and stone, of earth and sun, of life burning in the plants and animals he passed. He constructed a self from these discoveries and the traces of memory that flowed beneath his awareness.

He stopped suddenly, his breath catching in his chest. He realized through an ancient, non-physical sense that the man who had mocked his agony as the scroll burned, who had thrown him like garbage into the dirt had died. Strachys felt Nestor's spear point as it entered Proxonos' heart and clutched his chest in reflex. Immediately, the pain gave way to joy. He stood naked on the mountain, laughing.

A bird flew noisily from a tree, nearly striking his face as it passed. Strachys saw a tangle of sticks in the crotch of a limb and found three ivory ellipsoids at its center. He ignored the bird's desperate efforts to lure him from her nest and removed a single egg. He broke the shell with his thumb and examined the small creature that lay in the fluids pooling in his palm. He compared it to the bird scolding him from a high branch and recognized the homomorphic structures of their bodies—and their similarity with his own.

He added this new pattern to the patterns that had started to connect his experiences. He felt no grief at the death of the small creature, no empathy for the mother's loss, only the joy of discovery filled a mind as innocent as the dead chick he held. The mother flew down, desperately trying to lure him from her remaining eggs, and she reminded him of the seabirds he had seen from the mountain's ridge. He climbed to the top of a boulder overlooking the water and contemplated the gulls flocking above it. He watched them gather over the ocean, then surge into the sky as if of a single mind.

He remembered a time before the priests had imprisoned him in the golden writing, a time when he'd moved freely through the world—sometimes formless, sometimes occupying the forms of creatures he loved. He remembered flocks of seabirds as uncountable as the stars in the sky, how he flew among them with white wings and a hunger for things that lived in the ocean. He remembered the exhilaration of the flock's intention emerging from the resonance of many minds—a single will contained by many vessels.

He looked down at his body—at Strachys' body. It had been his liberation from the scroll and his shelter when the scroll burned, but it was not the resting place of his being. It was only a rung on a ladder he would climb forever, like the currents in the air that pushed him to join the birds circling over the bay.

He felt the substance of his flesh disperse as the idea possessed him. He looked down at his arms—the arms Strachys had once cherished for their strength and the muscles' pure curve of intention. He saw through them to the ground as flesh dissolved in his expanding will. He felt a thrill of release as he spread unencumbered, invisible into the air, riding the warm currents rising from the beach, joining the chaos of seabirds. He touched each animal's bright consciousness as the churning of white wings carried him from the island.

Chapter 50

Astrid ran along the ridge, trying to catch Swarm and Hector. She stopped in shock when she rounded the boulder where the trail ended at Strachys' hovel. Instead of finding Swarm tearing at Phaethon or struggling against his dark enchantments, Astrid saw Hector sitting among her five cats as they circled each other in a feline ritual of greeting. Spike and Chessie moved nervously among their littermates, touching noses as if they had just returned from a visit to the veterinarian. Astrid watched Chessie stop and crouch sphinx-like, eyes closed as Elizabeth groomed her face with impenetrable feline concentration. Spike stood beside Hector as Audrey rubbed against the boy. Greystoke sat nearby, alert, eyes wide, fixed on the man sitting alone in front of Strachys' abandoned home.

Phaethon sat motionless, his back against the hut's wall, his hands resting in his lap, contemplating the five animals. Astrid heard Nestor and the others come up the trail behind her and held up her hand for them to stay back.

"They're remarkable creatures, aren't they?" Phaethon mused, seemingly unaffected by the violence that had swept the island.

Astrid cautiously approached Hector and the cats. She let the animals' individual streams of consciousness rise in her mind and confirmed they were uninjured. She sensed their joy at Spike and Chessie's return and their fear of the man sitting in front of Strachys' house.

"It's odd," Phaethon said, "but I knew the great cat was coming. I sensed it from the two that were here, so I opened their cages. Can you sense their emotions like that?"

"Sometimes. What did you do to Spike and Chessie?"

"That awareness, that intimacy must feel wonderful," he said, ignoring her question. "Did you know that as soon as the great cat saw its siblings, it separated into the individuals? Why is that?"

"I don't know," Astrid said as she walked toward him. She motioned for Hector to remain behind her and silently instructed the cats to stay with the boy.

"Perhaps they can only greet each other by returning to their individual forms? Could it be that physical separation is necessary for emotional intimacy? It's a paradox, don't you agree?"

Astrid did not respond.

Phaethon stood from the bench and stepped into the clearing. He stared into the distance as if at a gathering storm. "She's coming, you know. She will be here soon."

"Circe?"

He nodded.

"What did you do to my animals?" Astrid asked, speaking softly, hoping not to provoke him.

Phaethon shook his head. "I did not harm them. I only wanted to heal my injuries."

She glanced at the five bodies lined up beside the broken loom. "By using their abilities to merge yourself with another human being?"

"It failed . . . miserably. They died as soon as I joined with them. It's as if I was poison—as if I have become death." He paused thoughtfully. "Do you think I would bring death to an immortal?"

Astrid realized that Phaethon's injuries from Zeus' bolt had killed the villagers—and given him the ability to kill Circe. "You don't have to do this."

"No, I do."

Phaethon saw Astrid glance at the cats. "I may end them, too," he said, "and you." His voice seemed abstract, detached, his words more a conjecture than a threat.

"They were once your child," Astrid told him.

"That child was lost. Circe killed it. They're just animals."

"They're more than that, Phaethon. When Circe transformed Iaria into a cat, her child—your child—became five kittens."

"Lies," Phaethon shouted. "More of the bitch's lies."

"No, I saw Iaria. She recognized Elizabeth. She embraced her."

"You're lying. Iaria's dead."

"Circe brought me to her island and told me everything. She sent me back through Hades so I could visit Tiresias. I saw Iaria."

"That sounds like something the bitch would do," he snarled. "What did Tiresias tell you?"

"What matters is that Iaria and Elizabeth recognized each other. Iaria knew Elizabeth was her child."

"Stop," he shouted. "I will not listen to this." He paced angrily in front of Strachys' hut, tears dampening his face. "The bitch must die. It's the only way."

"The only way to do what?"

"To end all this!" Phaethon pressed his hands against his head, palms pressing his temples, pulling the skin back, narrowing his eyes to slits.

"I know Circe hurt you, but she meant you no harm. You can stop this. It's not too late."

"You have no idea how late it is," he snapped. His features relaxed as his thoughts turned inward. "You have no idea of the things I've done . . ."

Astrid stepped toward him. "I don't care what you've done. These animals deserve to live."

"Then, take them and go, but I will end the bitch."

"You can't," Astrid pleaded. "Circe is the only one who can send us home."

Phaethon began to speak, then stopped and stared past her across the clearing. Astrid turned, following his gaze, and saw the enchantress standing a few yards away.

"She's telling the truth," Circe told him as she drew closer. "I mean you no harm."

The goddess stopped beside Astrid. Instead of the simple attire she had worn on Aeaea, Circe was dressed in traditional Mycenaean style with a flounced skirt the color of the Aegean, each layer lighter than the one below it, and a wine-red, fringed kilt around her waist. She wore a white blouse embroidered with forest scenes. Astrid recognized lions, deer, bears, and other animals she had seen on Aeaea. A plain gold headband held her braids; gold rings and bracelets decorated her hands and bare feet. "I thought the occasion called for something formal," Circe told her ironically.

The enchantress kneeled as Elizabeth rushed to greet her. She took the cat in her arms as the other littermates gathered around her, and she stroked each animal in turn, gently calling them by their names.

Phaethon stood frozen, jaw clenched, the muscles of his face trembling with rage. Circe released Elizabeth to the ground and approached him. "I am sorry for what I've done to you."

"Sorry, sister?" Phaethon said coldly. "Do you think that matters?"

"Return with me to Aeaea. I can ease your pain."

"You expect me to follow you to my death?"

Circe stopped in front of him. She reached out and caressed his cheek. "I will end your pain gently. It's the only way."

Glaring at her with rage, Phaethon grabbed her wrist and pulled it from his face. "Bitch," he cursed, "I'm no longer the child you took as a plaything."

Circe tried to pull away, twisting her arm in his grasp, but he did not release her. Revulsion distorted her features—the disgust of a goddess constrained by a mortal—as the gyre of metamorphosis swirled around Phaethon. Astrid knew he had learned to duplicate the cats' transformation, and she watched in horror as it spread over him to engulf Circe's wrist and move up her arm. The enchantress closed her eyes; when she opened them, her gaze had hardened, her eyes the color of steel. The blue gyre stopped its spread. For a moment, it seemed as if she had ended his attack until Phaethon's enchantments exploded with blinding incandescence to engulf them both.

Nestor and the others stepped back in reflex. Astrid squinted into the glare. Although she could not see the figures contending inside it, she heard their screams, male and female in bitter dissonance. Without thinking, she ran into the cold fire. Astrid realized that Phaethon was attempting to join mind and body forcibly with Circe, just as he had done with the unfortunate villagers. She knew she must stop him from projecting his injuries— the deadly consequences of Zeus' bolt—onto the enchantress. Eyes closed against the glare, Astrid found Circe by touch and joined her struggle to escape Phaethon's grip. Circe responded with renewed strength. Together, they stopped Phaethon's intrusion, but even their combined wills could not free them. Locked in a stalemate, Astrid felt her muscles weaken, her concentration waver, worn down by Phaethon's unyielding attack.

As Phaethon began to overcome them, and the deadly chill of his injuries grazed Astrid's flesh, she felt a new presence enter the transformation. A crushing impact knocked her and Circe to the ground, and the blue gyre dispersed. Astrid saw Nestor standing between her and Phaethon, rubbing his shoulder where he had struck them. Circe rested on her hands and knees, gasping for breath, convulsions shaking her slender form. Phaethon lay in the dirt, his enchantments dissolved, his injuries laid bare, screaming in a voice stripped of language, of humanity.

The blue vortex swirled around him again, and Astrid prepared to face the reptilian monster she had fought in her home, the same one who had nearly killed her and Swarm at Troy. Instead, Phaethon returned to the shape of his youth.

"You expected me to become the reptile?" he cursed. "You expected me to use the vulgar enchantment I stole from this woman? You have no idea what I've become."

Myia and Nestor's warriors rushed forward, joining Nestor to attack with swords and bronze-tipped spears. Phaethon's wounds closed as soon as the weapons passed through him. The blue vortex rose around him once more, then exploded outward, scattering Nestor, Myia, and the Achaeans like leaves in a whirlwind. Only Astrid, Circe, and the cats remained, trapped with Phaethon inside a luminous blue dome.

"This is not their concern," Phaethon scowled.

"How did you . . ." Astrid stammered.

"Your animals have shown me powers you cannot imagine. You tried to control them. I would have set them free."

"No, you would have killed them."

"Then take them and walk away."

Phaethon gestured toward the shimmering wall. An opening appeared, the clearing's dust and scattered clumps of brown grass framed in blue fire. "Consider it a gift."

Astrid glanced at Circe. The goddess remained on her hands and knees, struggling to recover from Phaethon's attack and the transitive effect of his injuries—of Zeus' lightning—on her immortal flesh.

"She cannot help you," Phaethon said coldly. "Go while you can. Leave her with me."

"I won't let you do this"

"As you wish." Phaeton nodded, and the opening vanished. Astrid sensed the cats' anxiety as Audrey pressed against her leg, and she felt the spreading tingle that preceded Swarm's appearance. Astrid resisted the transformation, pushing Audrey and the others behind her.

"You refuse to take them away to safety, and now you pretend you can protect them," Phaethon mocked. "They're only animals. Use them. Use them against me."

"Help me," Astrid shouted as she ran to Circe. She helped the enchantress to her feet and pointed toward where Nestor and the others had regrouped, striking at the dome without effect. "Open the barrier."

Astrid's voice seemed to revive the weakened enchantress. Circe limped to the shimmering wall and placed her palms on its surface, eyes closed, head lowered in concentration. Astrid watched the blue shimmer darken where she touched it, solidifying against the pressure. Suddenly, Astrid felt a hand grasp her shoulder from behind, threatening to crush her bones. Phaethon threw her across the dirt to strike the dome's opposite wall. She collapsed at its base. Fighting back from oblivion, Astrid saw him walk unhurriedly toward the enchantress. Circe retreated along the dome's perimeter, a cornered beast testing the boundaries of her confinement.

As Astrid found her feet, she saw the cats gather, and a blue corona flared around them. She sensed the urgency of their transformation and saw Swarm take shape almost instantly. Instead of the lithe predator that had followed

Astrid up the mountain, Swarm appeared as she had in the forest near Sigrid's house—a golden giant with a heavily muscled chest and shoulders, the full embodiment of all five animals. Even though she had not joined with Swarm herself, Astrid felt the great cat's strength surge within her.

She watched Swarm leap onto Phaethon's back, jaws closing on his neck, claws raking his shoulders, arms and chest. Each laceration closed immediately, but Phaethon could not throw the cat from his back. Suddenly, he vanished, and Swarm fell to the ground, turning in confusion, finding nothing. Phaethon reappeared behind the cat, grabbed the scruff of her neck, and threw the giant predator against the dome's wall as if she were no larger than a kitten. Swarm cried out in pain and struggled to take her feet. Her hindquarters did not respond.

Phaethon turned his attention back to the weakened enchantress, following her slowly along the dome's perimeter rather than cutting across to attack her directly. He laughed, mocking her as she retreated.

"What would our father think if he could see us now?"

"Phaethon, it doesn't have to end like this."

"No, sister," he cursed, "it can only end like this. This was destined the moment Helios bedded my mother."

Her strength returning, Circe stopped retreating and stepped away from the shimmering barrier. "Stealing the chariot of the sun was your choice, just as intervening in your fate was mine." Her voice carried neither argument nor anger, only grim resignation. "We created this destiny together."

As she spoke, a barely perceptible flush shined from her skin, growing in intensity to blaze through the barren air. It filled the dome, reflecting from the blue shimmer of its walls like sunlight on the Aegean. Phaethon raised his arm to cover his eyes, blinded by the goddess' terrible beauty.

"I will show you how a goddess faces death," she said calmly.

Astrid ran to Swarm and touched her gently on the shoulder, wary that the injured animal might strike out in pain. Instead, Swarm leaned into her touch, and Astrid welcomed the tingle of metamorphosis, releasing herself into the transformation. The years of her memories unwound, and the structures of her physicality collapsed into her brainstem's impossibly tangled networks. Astrid had never joined with all five animals. For the first time, she experienced Swarm's full strength as her own, both terrifying and exhilarating.

As she adjusted to the dimensionless space she shared with Swarm's five minds, Astrid felt the paralysis that gripped the injured cat's hindquarters, the pain that cut through Swarm's pelvis. She extended her will into the injury just as she had reached into Elizabeth's dying flesh. The pain faded as muscle, tendon, and bone re-aligned. Astrid felt Swarm's strength surge through her consciousness, and a feral scream exploded from the body she shared with the cat. Phaethon turned to face her.

As Astrid adjusted to sharing the great cat's body, she felt Swarm drive with her back legs, claws extended to close on her prey. Phaethon swept her aside with a single blow and fell upon her back, one arm around her chest, the other closing on her throat. He pulled her close, and Astrid felt pinpricks across her skin where it contacted him. She realized Phaethon was not trying to defeat Swarm but to join his body with hers, carrying his deadly injuries into her flesh.

Astrid felt her body twist as Swarm turned in a cat's loose skin and clawed savagely at Phaethon's belly with her hind legs, snapping at his face with jaws that could sever the keel of Nestor's ship. Phaethon fell back in surprise, pain contorting his features. Just as quickly, his wounds closed, and he took his feet to face the great cat. Swarm's faceted awareness narrowed into a predator's single-minded focus, a low growl rumbling in her chest, head lowered, muscles bunched under her shoulders.

Astrid struggled to control her shared physicality as the chorus of Swarm's rage surged around her. She searched for some weakness in the man who faced her, studying him through feline eyes that intensified every perception in a spectrum of green and blue, that traded color for sharpness, breadth of field for an unshakable focus. Astrid found what she had hoped for—a barely noticeable ripple in the skin of Phaethon's belly. She narrowed her gaze, staring through his enchantments as if through a tunnel. Phaethon's perfect body faded to a milky corona as her focus intensified, and she saw the shadow of the broken demigod convulse at its center.

Astrid held her focus and silently called to the five animal minds with whom she shared Swarm's body. Chessie was the first to answer, her attention shifting to Phaethon's human form. Audrey embraced Astrid's vision next, and the others followed, eyes locked on this new target, sensing its vulnerability. Astrid felt her muscles tense as Swarm drove forward, penetrating Phaethon's illusions to strike the broken man within them. She shared the thrill of jaws closing around flesh, the taste of blood filling her mouth.

Astrid felt a tingle against her skin once more, and the blue light covered her vision. Her breath caught as she realized that Phaethon was ignoring the cat's attack, sacrificing his physical body as he projected his mind, his body, and his injuries, into Swarm. Astrid felt the freezing void of Zeus' bolt and knew she could not let Phaethon merge with the great cat.

A sudden clarity filled her mind. It was the same clarity she had felt on Aeaea when Annape guided her through the metamorphosis, the same clarity that had pushed back the spread of cellular death and restored Elizabeth's life. Astrid found herself moving freely through the transformation's blue corona, unconstrained by time, space, or form itself. She seemed simultaneously within the metamorphosis and outside it; simultaneously existing as pure thought and inhabiting Swarm's muscle, bone, and nerve; simultaneously part of the cat and wholly herself. Astrid continued to guide Swarm's attack, even as she separated from the cat, drawing Phaethon to follow her.

She faced his intrusion without resistance.

As Astrid had hoped, Phaethon's attack flowed away from Swarm to herself, like water moving through a break in a levee. She felt his darkness surge across the network of habits, memories, skills, emotions, and histories that defined her, from the neural shadows left by infancy to the incandescent topography of her adult mind.

Astrid confirmed that Swarm remained unharmed and knew that Phaethon's physical body would not survive the cat's rage much longer. As the tide of death engulfed her, Astrid sought some protection, some shelter until Swarm could end Phaethon's attack.

She sought sanctuary in the memories she loved most—the voices of Sigrid, Claire, and all the people she'd cared for, the pleasures of physical love, the joys of work, the comfort of her home. She embraced the tangled songs of Swarm's consciousness, the softness of the cats' fur against her cheek, the strength she found within herself at Troy, the joy she'd found in Nestor's arms. All of them endured briefly, then dissolved in the acid of Phaethon's rage and the terrible chill of Zeus' bolt.

All forms of refuge fell away, leaving only a nameless soul among the ruins of Astrid's mind and body—ruins quickly colonized by the dying demigod.

Astrid found herself young, male, and alone, accepted by neither human nor immortal. She experienced the ridicule Phaethon had endured as if it was her own, a child's longing hardening into a man's bitterness. She shared Phaethon's excitement as he tricked his father into letting him drive the chariot of the sun.

She watched Helios' fiery horses strain against their harness and felt Phaethon's exhilaration as they bolted into the sky. The exhilaration turned to terror as the horses flew out of control, panicked by a mortal touch. She dropped the reins as the flames burned her face, and she held onto the sides of the chariot in desperation. She gasped for breath as it plunged toward the Earth, threatening to crash into the boiling ocean. The horses turned at the nadir to explode back into the sky, and a crushing force pressed her against the floor, forcing the air from her lungs. She saw stars flicker through the glare of the chariot and felt the bitter cold of space on her face.

A shadow surrounded her. She sensed the wrath of Zeus and frantically turned in the darkness, searching for the father of the gods. She found no persona to beg for mercy, no comforting face, only the amoral power of raw creation as Zeus' bolt struck, penetrating her soul with a terrible emptiness.

As she fell from the heavens, Astrid felt the sense of herself return for a final moment, and she touched Swarm's five-part mind. She found it whole, safe, and clear of intrusion. She realized that Swarm had ended Phaethon's attack. Her sacrifice had succeeded. Astrid released the cat and fell, trembling into the void, a dying animal.

Part VI

Home
Present Day

Chapter 51

Astrid awoke to Nestor's touch on her cheek. He raised her head and shoulders, his hand supporting her back, and held a waterskin to her lips. She drank deeply.

"What happened? Is everyone all right? Where are my animals?" she asked as her strength returned.

"Everyone is well," Nestor said, smiling, "and your animals are with you—all of them. You must rest."

"Nestor . . ." she began, but words eluded her. She squeezed his hand.

Astrid felt a pressure against her thigh and saw Audrey standing with her front paws on her leg. It was not the pressure of Swarm impinging on her awareness; it was only the touch of a cat demanding affection. She took Audrey in her arms, pressing the soft fur against her cheek. Spike, Elizabeth, Chessie, and Greystoke approached and circled around her.

"What happened?" she asked.

"Do you remember joining with Swarm?"

Astrid nodded. She tried to stand, but her limbs did not respond. She felt as if she were recovering from anesthesia.

"The cat attacked Phaethon, but with no effect," Nestor recounted. "Each wound healed immediately. Then Swarm stopped, like a warrior rethinking a tactic. She attacked once more but passed through Phaethon's body to strike at a shadow inside it."

"Yes, I remember. I saw through Phaethon's enchantments. I saw him as he was. I saw his vulnerabilities, and the cat followed."

"When Swarm attacked him, the blue light returned. Its intensity was greater than I had seen before, almost blinding. Circe ran into it, and then the light vanished, along with the dome. She held you in her arms, unconscious, and the cats were clustered around you. Phaethon was on the ground nearby, mauled by Swarm's attack."

"That's it?"

"It happened in an instant."

"No, that's not right," Astrid said, shaking her head. "We fought for a long time . . . for minutes. Phaethon tried to merge with Swarm and force himself and his injuries into us. He would have killed us, but I was able to separate myself from Swarm and draw him away while she attacked."

"I saw none of that. It was over so quickly."

"I don't remember Circe," Astrid continued, talking frantically as if words were her only refuge from madness. "I only remember Phaethon engulfing me in his rage. It seemed to go on forever. I could feel his injuries . . . Zeus' bolt, falling, the pain—"

The memories rushed through her, overtaking her words. She began to cry, sobs convulsing her body. Nestor held her close.

"Where is Circe?" she asked after a time.

Nestor nodded toward where the enchantress sat in the dirt, Phaethon's head in her lap. As sensation returned to her limbs, Astrid limped to their side and saw the consequences of Swarm's attack. The cat had torn the burned side of Phaethon's body from throat to waist and all but separated the blackened stump of his arm from his shoulder. Only a few remaining tendons, the pale gray of a shark's belly, held the bones together. His unburned flesh had not escaped; a brutal bite had torn away much of the trapezius muscle, and blood flowed from claw marks that crossed his chest.

"I am sorry, my beautiful boy, my brother, my love." Circe whispered in a voice like a lover's apology. "I should never have brought you to Aeaea."

The enchantress stroked his brow gently. "I thought I could make you whole, but I could not heal the burns of Zeus' thunderbolts." She spoke haltingly, as if grief would overwhelm her. "In my arrogance, I condemned you to a bitter half-life, imprisoned in an illusion of all you had lost. It is a cruelty only a god could devise."

Circe comforted him, stroking his forehead, murmuring soft reassurances. Eventually, she began to speak again, struggling with her words as if each syllable cut into her immortal flesh. "I must end this . . . You must complete your fate."

Phaethon tried to reach toward the goddess; his muscles only trembled.

"It's all right, my love," Circe said softly.

"Not like this," he rasped.

The goddess nodded. She kissed his burned lips and laid his head gently on the ground. Kneeling beside him, Circe moved her hands over his body, cloaking him once more in the naked perfection of her enchantments. She held her hands above him for a moment, then closed them into fists. Phaethon vanished, returned to the moment when Circe had taken him from Zeus' terrible justice, sending him to complete his fall from the heavens.

Circe stood and walked away, her back arched in spasms of sorrow, ignoring the mortals and their stares. As she entered the grove that surrounded the cabin, the people in the clearing, the birds, the animals—even the rustling of tree branches in the wind and the rippling voices of the stream—all grew silent, shamed by the goddess' grief.

Gradually, Astrid's companions began to talk. It was not the celebration of men who had won a battle but the whispered gratitude of those who had survived a disaster. Astrid thanked each of them, sharing embraces, smiles, and the comforts of friendship.

"Will you leave soon?" Nestor asked her. "You've recovered your animals."

Astrid seemed shocked by his question. "Nestor, I've wanted to go home for so long, but now it feels . . ."

He took her in his arms as her voice trailed off. Astrid heard a voice behind her and turned to see the enchantress.

"Walk with me," Circe said.

Astrid looked anxiously at Nestor.

"It's all right," the goddess reassured. "You will have time to say goodbye."

Circe led her into the trees that surrounded Strachys' hut. They stopped at a large, flat stone and sat in the shade.

"What do you remember from when you fought Phaethon?" the enchantress asked.

Astrid described the struggle, from merging with Swarm to Phaethon's effort to penetrate the mind she shared with the great cat. She told how she had guided Swarm to strike past Phaethon's enchantments at the vulnerable flesh within them, and how she had separated from the cat and drawn Phaethon's attack to herself, freeing Swarm to strike without interference.

Circe listened quietly.

"How could that have happened? How was I even able to do that?" Astrid pressed as she finished her account.

"The transformation suspends the laws of physical reality," Circe explained. "That's what permits the cats to join and become Swarm. Everything that is normally unyielding—physical laws, the processes of life, the essence of your existence—becomes fluid within it. It allowed you to separate from Swarm and draw Phaethon away while remaining bound to the cat and guiding her attack. Your essence had become two. I would not have believed it possible . . . even for an immortal."

"Nestor told me it all happened in an instant," Astrid said, "but it wasn't that way. We fought for a long time. He said you entered the vortex as soon as it appeared, but I don't remember you."

"The transformation suspends natural laws—that includes time," Circe said patiently. "Your experience of a struggle spanning many minutes and Nestor's memory of it happening in an instant are both correct—they simply reflect different frames of reference. Tell me what you do remember after Swarm penetrated Phaethon's enchantments."

Astrid's words came slowly as she recovered her memories of the struggle's final moments. "Phaethon seemed to enter my mind. I felt him tear at my thoughts, at my memories, obliterating everything I was." She began to tremble as she relived the encounter.

Circe took her hand as Astrid composed herself. "Do you trust me?"

Astrid nodded, and the enchantress placed a hand on her brow. The tension seemed to leave her body, and she recounted the events without reliving their horror. Astrid described her sense of moving freely within the transformation, the feeling of power and unlimited possibility. She told the enchantress how she had simultaneously guided Swarm's attack and drawn Phaethon's intrusion into herself, protecting the animal. Astrid described how Phaethon's rage had flowed around her, stripping away her memories, her sense of her mind and body. Despite Circe's soothing enchantments, Astrid shuddered as she described the pain of Phaethon's injuries.

She suddenly opened her eyes. "I remember now . . . the last thing before I awoke. It was as if I'd become Phaethon. I remember—no, I experienced the chariot of the sun, the flaming horses, the loss of control, the sun's heat, the chill of space—" She stopped, struggling to control the spasms that seized her body. "I felt Zeus strike. I felt his fire."

"Astrid," Circe explained gently, gauging Astrid's reactions as she spoke, "these were Phaethon's memories of his theft of Helios chariot and his injuries at Zeus' hand. You experienced them because he had merged his mind with yours as his life was ending—he relived them and so did you."

"I experienced his death?" Astrid whispered.

The enchantress nodded. She did not speak but let Astrid sit undisturbed, absorbing all she had said. Astrid saw Circe stare past Strachys' hut, past the clearing, into the sky's blue mysteries.

"There's something you aren't telling me."

"Yes. You have the right to know," Circe began slowly, gauging the effect of words yet unspoken. "But you must not let it overwhelm you."

"What do you mean?"

"I was able to bring you back."

Circe held her hand silently as Astrid realized what she had found so difficult to tell her. "Are you saying he killed me? That I died as well?" Astrid absorbed the enchantress' meaning slowly, like the stirrings of a forest in spring. "No. This can't be."

"What is it, child?"

"When you sent me through Hades . . ."

"You met Tiresias," the goddess finished her thought.

"He told me I would die."

Circe nodded as if the words completed a puzzle only she understood.

"Did you know this would happen?" Astrid pressed.

"No, only Tiresias and you knew his prophecy. I understood the risks, the probabilities of different outcomes. It enabled me to prepare—"

"Prepare?" Astrid interrupted. "Prepare for what? What did you know?"

Circe spoke slowly, carefully as if one wrong word could destroy her intended meaning. "I saw possibilities—different choices you could have made. I could have placed you on a path that would have insured your survival, but one or more of your cats would have died. I knew you could not accept that. I saw the path you were taking—your judgment, your commitment to saving these animals you loved—and realized it was our best hope. I did not intervene until the end—when everyone was safe."

"Why didn't you tell me what you saw?" Astrid spoke with a forced calm in her voice, an excess of self-control. "I had a right to know."

Circe nodded slowly. "Yes, you did, but knowing what you would face could have made you fearful, caused you to hesitate or doubt yourself. The path you had to walk was narrow and dangerous, and any deviation would have meant disaster. My knowledge of the risks let me prepare. I was always watching, ready to intervene—" Circe stopped, a tear tracking the curve of her cheek. "I could never have let you die, Sigrid's daughter."

Astrid took the enchantress' hand and they sat together in silence. After several minutes, she began to speak. "Tell me what happened when I died. Tell me what you did. I need to know everything."

Circe nodded. "When I entered the transformation, you were passing into oblivion. Your mind was shattered, fragments swirling in the vortex. Your body was a fading impression in what remained of your brain and nervous system. I gathered them together, your memories, the sense of your body, habits, abilities, the patterns of your emotions . . ."

"How is that possible?"

"I've gained certain skills over the millennia," the enchantress said cryptically, "but it was the suspension of reality within the transformation that made it possible. Some things may have been lost—"

"Lost? What do you mean—lost?"

"Parts of your mind had already been obliterated by the effects of Zeus' bolt and the experience of Phaethon's last moments."

"My mind?" Astrid gasped.

"I drew upon my understanding of you to complete what was missing—memories of touching your mind at the coffee house, our time on Aeaea, things Annape shared with me, even things Sigrid had said about you—"

"But how could you have recovered everything I was from so little?"

"I also drew on Swarm's memories. Much of what you'd lost was beyond language—habits of perception and emotion, muscle memory, patterns of behavior. Since Swarm was not constrained by language and had shared body and mind with you, her impressions were superior to mine."

"Oh . . . the cats. Well, that's different," Astrid said sarcastically.

"You must trust me. It was enough. When Swarm returned to her individual forms, your body took shape along with theirs. You are intact, perhaps improved. Your reflexes may seem faster, your hand-eye coordination more accurate than you remember." Circe smiled. "You may even be more impulsive—if that's possible."

"This can't be real."

"Astrid, the cats love you. Their minds and yours have been bound since you first joined with them. This is their gift to you."

Astrid started to speak, but words did not come. She looked back toward Strachys' hut, where the five animals waited with Myia. "You said parts of me were missing? What the hell am I, some sort of half-baked Frankenstein? Will I forget Sigrid? Claire? The people I've loved?"

"The fact that you ask those questions means you will not."

"That doesn't make me feel better."

"People think their essence—their character, their soul—is permanent, eternal, hard like a diamond, but our essences change constantly. Life is a constant process of death and renewal. Cells die and are replaced; memories fade, giving way to new experiences; the passions of youth yield to the wisdom of old age—even death is no more than another transition. You're not the woman who came to Troy. Just as you are not the woman you will be a year from now. Even if you had not—"

"If I had not died?"

"Yes. Even if you had not died, the woman you were would have been lost through time. Please trust me. You are alive, you are yourself, and you will return to your time and the life you had there."

"But I didn't just change," Astrid repeated, "I died. And I still don't know what it did to Swarm—to my animals."

"You protected them, and they were not harmed," Circe reassured. "In a sense, you completed them."

"What are you talking about?"

"Your cats do not understand what their abilities mean—what they could mean for the future, but you do. By sharing Swarm's metamorphosis, you have changed that, as they have changed you."

Astrid forced herself to breathe deeply, slowly. "What the hell am I? What do I do now?"

"Those questions are yours to answer—and yours alone." Circe squeezed her hand. "Sometimes, if we are to become something new, what we were before must die."

Astrid heard a rustle in the trees, turned toward it, and saw Athena approach. Instead of her armor and the Aegis, she wore a plain tunic of undyed linen and sandals. A rope woven of gold held her braids.

"That was lovely," Athena said to Circe. "I didn't know you were capable of such eloquence."

Circe nodded graciously and Astrid took her feet as Athena drew near.

"So, cousin, does this return the universe to order?" the enchantress asked.

"You have restored Zeus' justice, but these animals remain."

"And so, they must," Circe asserted. "The possibilities they bring to the world cannot be denied."

"Perhaps," Athena said sternly, although Astrid thought she saw a smile flash across her lips.

"I will return Astrid and the animals to their own time," Circe said. "Our world will not be affected, and they may be of value to their future."

"And I will help Nestor and his men return to Troy," Athena told her. "They have business there on my behalf. I must be certain they will not become entangled in another of your schemes."

"Schemes?" Circe smiled ironically. She accompanied Astrid and Athena back into the clearing where Nestor and the others stared, shocked to see the two immortals. When Athena neared the cats, they looked up at her in round-eyed curiosity. Audrey rubbed against her ankle as the others drew close. The goddess of wisdom looked down at the animals circling her feet, kneeled on one knee, and touched each of them. The cats followed her as she approached Nestor and the Achaeans.

"Return to your ship and prepare to sail," Athena told the Achaeans. "I'll ensure that the sea will be calm, and the winds will carry you to Troy. I will also replenish your supplies of food and wine."

She gestured toward the bodies of the villagers Phaethon had killed, bodies still unburied, covered only by rough blankets. "Return these unfortunates to their families and ensure that their remains are treated properly. Also, attend to the mercenaries you killed on the ridge and those who died on the beach. Although they lived outside Zeus' law, they died as warriors."

"I will do so," Nestor said lowering his head in respect for the goddess.

Astrid felt a nudge as Circe leaned toward her. "Just like an Olympian," the enchantress whispered in her ear, "turning up after the work's finished and grabbing the credit."

Athena approached Myia.

"I remember your courage when you fought Phaethon back at Troy," she said. "Seeing you now, in bronze greaves, sword at your side, brings joy to my heart. What will you do now?"

"She can return with me," Antilochus interrupted.

Athena stared at Nestor's son as if looking into his soul, then turned to the enchantress. "There seems to be no end to the mischief you've fostered."

"This was not my doing," Circe protested.

"You know I cannot return to Troy," Myia told Antilochus.

"I can protect you," he insisted.

"I do not need your protection," Myia said, her voice hardening, "and I won't go back there."

"You can come to Aeaea," Circe offered, "and join my attendants."

Athena laughed. "This woman was not made to serve." The goddess of wisdom placed her hands on Myia's shoulders. "There is an island of women warriors," she said. "They are called Amazons and are beloved of me. If you wish, I will take you there. They will teach you to fight at their side."

Athena waited as longing and fear, hope and bitterness contended within the girl. Myia turned to Antilochus. "I won't go back to Troy."

"Myia . . ." He protested briefly, then surrendered.

The girl kissed him softly on the lips, then turned to Athena. "I would like to join these Amazons," she told her, "and become a warrior."

Athena nodded and turned to Antilochus. "Do you want me to erase the pain, the memory?"

"No. I want to remember her. I want to remember everything."

"I expected no less of Nestor's son," Athena acknowledged. "Very well, I will give you time to say goodbye. Myia will remain with you until Nestor departs—it will take him a few days to prepare his ship and complete the tasks I've given him. Then, I will come for her."

Athena turned to Circe. "I hope you find that satisfactory."

"Of course, cousin," the enchantress said. "And, as I promised, I will return Astrid and her animals to their own time." Circe put her hand on Astrid's shoulder and nodded toward the trees. Claire Ortega entered the clearing, wearing the white spring dress with daffodils and orange tulips she had worn to the coffeehouse the day Astrid had come to Troy.

"Do you know how much I've missed you?" Claire asked, smiling and holding her arms open. "It's time to go home."

Astrid ran to her, and they embraced. "I know," she said, "but first I need to say my goodbyes."

Claire smiled as Astrid walked to where the Achaeans had gathered. She took Amphides and Ekhinos' hands.

"You barely knew me, but you risked your lives for me. I will never forget you," she told them, kissing each man on the cheek. They accepted her kisses with brotherly affection. "Give my thanks and my love to all your crewmates."

Astrid kneeled in front of the boy, Hector. "Thank you for helping save my animals."

He took Spike in his arms and rubbed his cheek against the cat's golden fur. "He is my friend," the boy said sadly.

"He will always be your friend, but he must return home."

Hector held the cat closer as Astrid waited. Reluctantly, he set Spike on the ground.

"I must go as well," he said in a determined voice. "I must help rebuild my village and care for my mother."

"One day, you'll be a great leader of your people," Astrid told him as she rose to her feet. "Do not forget what you have done here."

Astrid looked around for Antilochus and Myia. She saw them walking beside the stream, talking earnestly as they disappeared into the trees.

"I will share your thanks with them," Nestor said.

Tears filled Astrid's eyes as she took his hand and led him around the side of Strachys' hut, out of sight of the others. The cats remained with Athena, Circe, and Claire as if they sensed Astrid's need to be alone with him.

"I don't know what to say."

Nestor drew her close and kissed her deeply. "You must return home, and I must return to Troy."

"And then to your home," Astrid added.

"If the gods allow it."

Astrid remembered Homer's account of how Nestor returned home with honor to rule for many years with his queen.

"I know they will," she said. "Your story will be sung by poets, and people will remember King Nestor of Pylos forever." She paused and looked into his eyes. "And I will never forget you."

She began to cry; Nestor held her close and kissed her once more.

"Please, tell Hecamede how much she means to me," Astrid asked him.

"She knows," he said, "but I will remind her. I will also tell her everything that happened here."

"Give my love to Odysseus, to Thrasymedes and the warriors who fought at my side, to the women in the tent . . ." Astrid began, the words coming in an uncontrollable torrent.

Nestor laughed. "I won't forget. I will thank everyone you have touched."

"And you must help Gilia."

"Gilia?"

"A young girl in the women's tent. She was kind to the cats and me, and she is more vulnerable than the others. I fear for her."

"The girl who'd been injured, who walked with a limp," Nestor acknowledged. "I will see that she is cared for. When the war ends, I'll take her to Pylos to live in my home."

"Nestor . . ." Astrid felt her words die in her throat as she began to cry. He held her close.

"When you came to me, I thought you were an immortal," Nestor whispered, his cheek touching hers, his lips brushing her ear. He released their embrace and looked into her eyes. "I still think so."

Astrid kissed him softly. "Goodbye, my king, my friend."

She heard footsteps behind her. Claire drew near, the five cats following. "It's time to go home," she said.

Circe and Athena watched Claire and Astrid walk into the forest. The goddesses had made themselves invisible to human eyes and watched the mortal rituals of parting with a curiosity unique to the gods.

"How soon will you return for the girl?" Circe asked.

"It will take a few days for Nestor to prepare his ship," Athena said. "She and Antilochus will have some time."

"It's not like you to care about such things," Circe goaded. "Has the goddess of wisdom become sentimental? Are you becoming a romantic?"

Athena bristled. "You know Antilochus' fate as well as I," she said. "He will die at Troy. He deserves these days."

"You know Myia won't stay with the Amazons," Circe taunted.

"I know nothing of the kind."

"She'll soon tire of the discipline."

"Are you proposing a wager? Perhaps another case of your wine from California?"

"If she stays with the Amazons, it will be yours," Circe said. "And if she does not? What will I receive?"

"Well, cousin," Athena said, "I'm sure it won't be long until you need my help again in hiding your mischief from my father."

Circe laughed. "You are as wily as Odysseus."

"What of these cats?" Athena asked, growing serious.

"Cousin?"

"Why do they matter to you? You've spun your webs around them and the woman since before they came here."

"Webs?" Circe said, feigning injury.

"I know your schemes—in spite of your efforts to conceal them," Athena scolded. "What are you planning now?"

"Plans, cousin? Perhaps we should say I have hopes—for Astrid, for her cats, for her world that has turned away from so much of what we have given them. Return with me to Aeaea," Circe offered. "It's much closer than wind-swept Olympus, and we can wait there until you return for Myia. My ladies will prepare a feast for us, and I will answer all your questions." The enchantress smiled conspiratorially. "Perhaps we'll spin some webs together."

"I should return home," Athena demurred.

Circe took her hand.

"Zeus and the universe will survive your absence. Besides, I've found a wonderful Bordeaux that I'm sure you'll enjoy."

Chapter 52

Astrid stared across the mesquite and dry grass that surrounded her home. She turned to thank Claire, but her friend had vanished. It was early morning, barely past dawn, and she imagined Claire's family was calling her into waking reality. Astrid carried the shotgun that had been left behind when Swarm had taken her through Phaethon's rupture in time. She'd found it laying on the ground where it had fallen when she'd first joined with Swarm and traveled to the Bronze Age.

The Bronze Age, she thought. After the weeks she'd spent with Nestor, Hecamede, Odysseus, Circe, Annape, and all the people and struggles she had experienced there, her once familiar forest seemed strange, unaccustomed. *Will this ever be the same to me?*

As Circe had promised, Astrid had experienced no discomfort from the transition, only a subtle change in the forest vegetation, in the dryness of the air, and the contours of the light. She and the cats crossed the open space, passing Scott's BMW still in her driveway, and entered the house. The devastation from her encounter with Phaethon remained, and memories of it engulfed her. The dry grassland, her wooden porch, and the shambles of her home seemed like a dream as Troy, Aeaea, Kyros, and everything that had happened there held her like a deeper reality.

Astrid leaned the shotgun against the wall and looked at the digital clock with its time, date, and temperature display. It showed that she had only been gone for a day. Her strength left her—she did not know if it was an after-effect of her passage through time or her feelings at finally returning home. She stumbled to the old blue recliner and sat, eyes closed, her mind focused on the rhythms of her breathing. After a time, she walked into the kitchen and fed the cats. Their experience with burned beef and raw fish in the Bronze Age had not dulled their fondness for their favorite food, and they ate ravenously. The cats finished their meal and dispersed through the house to become reacquainted with their surroundings, groom themselves, use their familiar litter boxes, and ultimately, sleep.

Astrid lifted the receiver of her mother's old phone—she had lost her cell phone and wondered if it remained in some ruin, waiting to be uncovered by an astonished archaeologist. She dialed Claire's number and felt a rising joy to hear her friend's voice. Astrid did not mention Claire's appearances in the Bronze Age. She understood that those experiences were buried in Claire's unconscious and were best left undisturbed. They made a date for lunch, and Astrid replaced the receiver.

As she began to straighten the rubble of her living room, Astrid heard a weak knock at her door and a voice calling for help. She opened it cautiously and saw Scott—the man whom Circe had transformed into a boar—standing naked, trembling in the doorway, covered with dirt, garbage, and manure. He held his hands across his genitals and looked up at her in desperation. Astrid helped him to the blue recliner, then retrieved a blanket from the bedroom and arranged it around him.

"What . . . happened?" he stammered. "Where am I?"

"You're safe now, but I think you're in shock. What do you remember?"

"There was a woman," he said slowly. "She brought me here . . . then something happened."

Astrid took his hand. "I think she drugged you," she said, grasping at the seed of an explanation.

"What?"

"I'd come home and found a strange man here," she improvised. "He'd torn my house apart—I don't know why—and he held me here by force. Later, you came with the woman. She and the man were accomplices."

She hoped he would believe her hastily constructed deception.

"Yes," he said, accepting her story, "I remember the house was ransacked."

"I think they were thieves, or drug dealers, or something," Astrid said. "I don't know what they wanted. The man held me until the woman came, and that's the last I remember. They must have drugged me, too. I woke up a few minutes ago, and they were gone. Then, I heard you at the door."

Scott nodded silently.

"I'll call the police and an ambulance," she said. "Also, you look like you could use a cup of coffee."

He nodded, and Astrid walked to the kitchen to prepare a pot of coffee—and the rest of her story.

In his weakened, suggestible state of mind, Scott had accepted her account of a home invasion by a gang of criminals. Astrid had convinced him that they'd both been drugged and that she had awakened only a few minutes before he'd come to her door. He even helped her fill in the blanks, 'remembering' things about Circe that he now took to be evidence of a darker purpose. By the time the police arrived, Astrid's fiction had solidified.

Faced with the house's devastation, Scott's concurrence with her story, and their memory of Sigrid as a long-time pillar of the community, the police had accepted her fabrications. She'd felt a deep sense of relief as they helped Scott into an ambulance and promised a thorough investigation. Astrid hoped their promise would pass into the oblivion of insufficient evidence and overworked detectives where most of the county's burglaries languished.

After they left, Astrid surrendered to exhaustion. She postponed clearing the devastation of her home, took a long hot bath with an excess of bubbles, and crawled into bed for a deep afternoon sleep. She awakened as the sun was setting. Ravenous, she consumed two microwaveable dinners from Sigrid's freezer, along with the last bottle of her mother's wine.

After an hour on the porch and a second bath, she returned to bed, pulling the strangely luxurious bedding around her. Gradually, Astrid drifted off, eased into sleep by the comfort of her home, by the five cats taking their familiar places on the bed around her, and by the memory of Nestor's embrace.

As she relaxed into sleep, Astrid felt the strange music of Swarm's plural sentience rise from her unconscious to sing in her dreams.

Epilogue

Sarah sat on the stool she had moved behind the bar, staring across the deserted rooftop lounge, through the rain-glazed windows at the reflection of city lights on the bay and the cars crossing the Golden Gate Bridge into Sausalito. It was late, past midnight, and the only other person in the bar was a woman who sat alone by the window, sipping her drink, and contemplating the view. The woman had come in by herself a few hours earlier when the crowd had started to thin. She was dressed beautifully, even by the standards of the elite San Francisco hotel. Her peach-colored silk gown draped from a single shoulder in a cut that seemed simultaneously fashionable and timeless. She wore little jewelry, only a green teardrop pendant with matching earrings. Sarah had recognized them to be genuine emeralds—probably worth more than her house. The woman wore neither rings nor a watch.

What had struck Sarah most was her beauty, a grace in voice and gesture, in movement and repose that raised unsettling desires—even in the straight, happily married mother of a small child. The woman spoke with an accent Sarah did not recognize, despite conversations with thousands of customers from dozens of countries over the years. Still, Sarah had recognized the emotions that brought her into the deserted bar—a familiar pattern of loss, a longing that could not be born in solitude but that barred human contact like a wall. It had kept most of Sarah's male customers from approaching her and turned away the few who found the courage to try.

Sarah heard the bell of the elevator doors and saw a man step into the bar. She recognized him from earlier in the evening. He scanned the empty room before his eyes rested on the woman near the window. He stared as if in a trance. He was young and athletic; his suit hugged his body in ways that suggested a tailor's hand and a young man's vanity. The sleeves of his jacket revealed the correct length of shirt cuff, the semi-circle of his gold wristwatch showing perfectly beneath the white cloth. He wore no tie, leaving the top buttons of his neatly pressed shirt open. His face was handsome under his dark hair, with dark eyes, sensual lips, and high cheekbones. The muscles in his cheeks alternately flexed and relaxed as he stared at the solitary woman. After a time, he walked to the bar and took a seat.

"Card game over already?" Sarah asked.

"What?" he asked as if she'd pierced a spell that had possessed him.

"The poker game," Sarah reminded. "You were here earlier and told me you were going to a game on the seventeenth floor—high stakes."

"Oh yeah," he said, glancing at the woman by the window. "I didn't like the action, so I thought I'd see what was happening here."

"Fair enough," Sarah said. "What will you have . . . Ray, is it?"

Ray smiled at her. "Good memory."

"Goes with the job. What are you having?"

"What's she having?"

Sarah shook her head. "Bartender-client confidentiality," she joked.

"Come on, Sarah," he pressed, glancing at her name tag.

The bartender smiled ironically as she took a bottle from the rows behind the bar and placed it in front of him.

He whistled softly. "The lady has taste. Give me two glasses."

Sarah placed two tulip-shaped whiskey glasses in front of him and poured two generous shots of the expensive single malt. "Shall I run a tab?"

"Nah, it's getting late," Ray said as he took a money clip from his jacket pocket and left a hundred-dollar bill on the bar.

Sarah smiled as she picked it up. "I see they didn't clean you out on the seventeenth floor."

"I know when to quit. Keep the change." He glanced at the woman by the window. "For luck," he added with a smile.

He pivoted on the barstool and walked across the empty room, a glass in each hand. "Is this seat taken?" he asked as the woman looked up at him.

"I'm sorry," she said. "I just want to enjoy the view."

"Then what am I going to do with two of these?"

The woman looked at the crystal glasses but did not react. He placed one of them in front of her and sat down before she could protest. "Ray," he said, holding his hand out. She did not take it.

"I'm up from Los Altos Hills on business," he said. "I thought I'd stay the night in the city."

The woman did not respond but stared at him with narrowed eyes. She glanced at the clock behind the bar. "What brought you up to the city, Ray from Los Altos Hills?"

"Business," he said.

The woman lifted the glass from the table and held it under her nose, resting the edge on her upper lip, eyes closed as she inhaled deeply. She surrendered and took a sip.

"I didn't catch your name," he said.

"I didn't throw it. Are you a venture capitalist, Ray from Los Altos Hills? Maybe you have a startup. The next Google? Maybe marketing? You don't look like a coder."

He laughed. "Nope, real estate. What brings you to San Francisco?"

"How do you know I don't live here?"

"I would have already met you if that were so."

The woman laughed.

"I bet you sell a lot of houses with that line of bullshit."

"Office space," he said unfazed. "I do all right."

"That's refreshing," she said. He either missed or ignored the sarcasm in her voice.

"It's gotten too hard to make it in tech," he said. "The low-hanging fruit's gone, the boom's over, but companies are growing, and they'll always need a roof over their heads."

She took another sip and seemed to relax. They sat silently, staring out the window, the lines of light inscribed on the bay refracted by the raindrops on the glass. The woman drained the single malt and pushed the glass back on the table.

"Thanks," she said. She stirred in her chair as if preparing to leave.

"Where are you from," he asked, trying to prolong the encounter. "Wait, let me guess . . . Singapore?"

She shook her head and smiled. "I haven't heard that one before."

"Okay, how about . . ." He leaned back and stared at her contemplatively.

"Try Greece," she said.

"Greece. That was my next guess. What brings you to San Francisco?"

"The weather," she said ironically, looking at the rain on the window.

Ray laughed. "What do you say we get out of here and let Sarah go home. Come to my room; we can finish this conversation over the mini-bar."

"Sorry, Ray, but I don't think you're going to close this sale."

"What do you mean?"

"You've been fun, even made me laugh—and I needed that," she said as she stood to leave. "I appreciate it. Another time, maybe, but not tonight."

He leaned back in his chair, looking up at her. "What's wrong?"

"It's nothing personal," she said. "Just bad timing."

"Maybe I can help," he said earnestly.

She walked around the table, bent down, and kissed him on the cheek. "Take it home to your wife."

Ray glanced down at his left hand.

The woman laughed. "Don't worry. You're not wearing your ring."

"What made you think—"

"Call it a sixth sense. Besides, you looked at your hand when I mentioned your wife. Isn't that what the guys on the seventeenth floor call a 'tell?'"

"No, you got it wrong. I just got divorced. I'm lonely. I just want to talk."

"Sorry, Ray, I'm not looking for office space."

Ray frowned. His eyes followed her as she walked down the short hall to the ladies' room.

The enchantress stepped from the ladies room into the narrow corridor and found Ray leaning against the wall, flipping his car keys. He smiled at her inquisitively. "I thought you might have changed your mind—now that you've had time to think."

"You are persistent," she said.

"I didn't get where I am by giving up," he said. "Look, I don't usually do this, but I think there could be something between us—something special."

"Are you kidding me?"

"Give me a chance," he said.

"Okay, Ray," she said in mock surrender, "I got you all wrong, and I'm sorry. But I'm just not interested—nothing personal. Let's leave it there."

She turned to leave. Ray put his hand on the wall and leaned toward her, blocking her way.

"What are you doing?" she said coldly.

"I deserve better than this."

"You don't want what you deserve. Move your hand," she demanded.

Suddenly, Ray coughed and raised his left hand to cover his mouth. His right hand continued to block the enchantress's way. Circe's eyes turned the color of polished steel, and he doubled over, struggling to breathe. He began to shiver as if from the chills of some sickness, dropped his car keys on the carpet, and fell to his knees, spasms running through his spine.

Circe watched his body contort, his limbs shorten, his features blurring into an elongated snout and ears, his head bald but for a few coarse bristles. The seams of his expensive suit strained as his back arched convulsively. After a final spasm, a full-grown boar appeared where he'd stood, its short, fat legs tangled in Ray's clothing. Circe reached down, grabbed the collar of his jacket, and gave it a tug. Loosened by her enchantments, the clothes fell away from the animal.

"Sorry, Ray," she said, "I just wasn't in the mood."

She reached into the jacket pocket and removed the money clip as the boar snorted and ran into the bar. She heard hooves cross the tile floor, followed by Sarah's scream. She retrieved Ray's keys from the floor, saw the logo on the car key, and smiled. His car was Italian, expensive, and fast.

"What the hell just happened?" Sarah shouted incredulously as Circe walked from the narrow hall. "Where did that thing come from?"

"It was in the ladies' room," Circe explained. "I didn't notice it until I came out of the stall."

"How the fuck did it get there?"

"I don't know. You didn't see it go in?"

"Are you fucking kidding me?"

"It was probably some frat-boy stunt, maybe an initiation ... kids up from Stanford or Berkeley."

"They couldn't have gotten that thing past me," Sarah protested.

Circe smiled. "Never underestimate the ingenuity of young men, particularly when they're up to trouble."

She counted five one-hundred-dollar bills from Ray's money clip, laying them side by side on the bar. "Do me a favor. Make sure they take proper care of the animal. Don't let them send it to the pound. He's just a randy young boar who wound up in the wrong place. He'll be back to normal in a day or two, and someone will come looking for him. Call the Humane Society or something."

Sarah took the bills and stared in shock as Circe walked to the elevator and pressed the call button. The enchantress looked down the hall and saw Ray standing beside a large Ficus growing from a wine-colored pot, panting and snorting softly.

"For what it's worth, Ray, you did cheer me up."

Circe watched the animal walk back toward the bar. It saw Sarah, then walked back to stand in front of her, staring up through small dark eyes.

"This will wear off in a few days," she whispered. "Try to behave yourself."

The elevator doors opened, and she stepped in. Circe contemplated the rows of glowing numbers, then pressed the button for the parking garage. She twirled Ray's keys in her hand.

The elevator descended, carrying her down to Ray's car, to the city's temptations, and to the possibilities awaiting her in this age of spreading chaos and desperate pleasures.

The End

Greek Character and Place Names

The myths of ancient Greece have given humanity a powerful set of archetypal characters and narrative frameworks that have inspired writers from Homer through the Romans to the work of Shakespeare and modern storytellers ranging from James Joyce to Star Wars. One of my goals in writing *Swarm Metamorphosis* was to use these archetypes as a vehicle for my explorations of the differences and similarities between human and animal intelligence, the love that humans and animals so often share, and our capacity for transformative change. My other goal was simply to tell a story that would engage and entertain the reader.

Like the writers who have preceded me, I have done my best to stay true to the legacies of the ancients while bending them to my narrative purposes. I hope that I have achieved these goals without doing too much damage to my sources. I also hope that my work will encourage the reader to discover—or revisit—this rich legacy herself. There is no better place to start than Homer's twin masterpieces: *The Iliad* and *The Odyssey*.

I have added this list of character names to provide an additional bridge from my story to the treasures that have inspired me. I have written the names of characters I borrowed from Greek Mythology in **Bold Roman** font; those I invented for this story are *italicized*.

Achaeans – The name Homer used to describe the Mycenaean Greeks.
Achilles – The greatest of the Achaean warriors at Troy. His dispute with Agamemnon led to his refusal to fight and turned the war in Troy's favor. When he returned to the conflict, his killing of Hector, the leader of Troy's defenses, ultimately led to the Achaean victory.
Aeaea - Home of Circe, the enchantress.
Agamemnon – A powerful, although foolish and selfish, Mycenaean king who led the Greek coalition against Troy.
Ajax – Huge in stature, strength, and courage, Ajax was one of the Achaean's greatest heroes.
Akiala – The cruel, foolish ruler of an impoverished kingdom near Troy.
Amphides – One of Nestor's warriors, he assisted Nestor and Astrid in fighting Phaethon on Kyros.
Annape – A Naiad, or freshwater Nymph. A servant of Circe, she possessed powerful healing abilities and an intuitive, almost erotic connection to all living beings. She was also something of a mystery—even to Circe.

Antilochus – Nestor's son who fought and died at Troy.

Aphrodite – The goddess of love, she was responsible for Paris and Helen's affair and took the side of Troy during the war.

Apollo – One of the most important Olympian gods, his abilities included archery, healing, prophecy, music, and poetry.

Arsinous – Hecamede's father who died defending his home from Achaean raiders.

Artemis – The goddess of the hunt, nature, wild animals, and chastity.

Athena – The daughter of Zeus, Athena is one of the most important Olympian deities. She is a goddess of wisdom, the practical arts and handicrafts, and warfare.

Briseis – Although taken as a spoil of war, Achilles soon came to love her. When Agamemnon took her for himself, the great warrior refused to fight.

Charon – The boatman who ferried the souls of the dead into Hades.

Circe – An enchantress who famously turned Odysseus' men into swine. Odysseus persuaded her to restore them to human form and later became her lover. He remained with her for a year.

Claea – A slave of king Akiala, she later becomes a servant of Phaethon.

Diomedes – An Achaean warrior, second in prowess only to Achilles.

Dymenos – AKA Plumed-helmet. Swarm killed him when he attempted to rape Astrid.

Ekhinos – One of Nestor's warriors, he assisted Nestor and Astrid in fighting Phaethon on Kyros.

Etagama – Originally the captain of Akiala's guards, he became king when Phaethon killed Akiala.

Eumenes – A boy who befriended Spike on Kyros. He was nicknamed Hector for his bravery.

The Fates – Three powerful sisters who spin the threads of life into each person's destiny, from birth until death.

Gilia – A young girl and slave of the Achaeans, she showed a fondness for Astrid's cats.

Hecamede – Taken as a spoil of war by Achilles, she was given to Nestor to be his servant. Her grace and intelligence earned Nestor's respect and affection.

Hector – The defender of Troy, Hector turned the tide of war against the Achaeans until his death at the hands of Achilles.

Hector – The nickname given Eumenes, the boy who befriended Spike, in honor of his courage.

Helen – The wife of Menelaus, Agamemnon's brother. Her seduction by the Trojan prince Paris resulted in the Trojan war.

Helios – An immortal who drove the chariot of the sun across the sky. He was the father of both Phaethon and Circe.

Hephaestus – The god of blacksmiths, metal workers, and artisans, he was unmatched in his skills in these fields.

Hera – The wife of Zeus and goddess of marriage and the family.

Hermes – The herald of the gods, Hermes was known for his ability to travel quickly to any location.

Iaria – A Nereid who served Circe. Her seduction and abandonment by Phaethon led to Circe's tragic reaction and Swarm's creation.

Idomeneus – The Cretan king who fought at Troy.

Klymenos – A village leader on Kyros

Kyros – The island where Strachys lived and where Astrid, Nestor, and Swarm confronted Phaethon.

Lara – A Naiad who was famous for her loquacious nature and inability to keep a secret. Although not associated with Circe in Greek Mythology, I found her interesting enough to include her among Circe's attendants.

Medusa – A monstrous creature with venomous snakes for hair, the sight of whom would turn onlookers to stone. In Ovid's version of her myth, Medusa was a beautiful maiden serving Athena until Poseidon raped her. Enraged by what she regarded as a betrayal, Athena transformed her into a monster.

Menelaus – The brother of Agamemnon and husband of Helen. The seduction of his wife by the Trojan prince Paris led to the Trojan war.

Minoans – A people named after King Minos of Crete. The Minoans formed one of the earliest of the Aegean's great civilizations.

Myia – A young girl who fled enslavement by the Achaeans and lived in the hills above Troy.

Naiad – A freshwater nymph.

Nereid – A ocean nymph.

Nestor – One of the kings who accompanied Agamemnon to Troy, Nestor was known for his skill with horses, his wisdom, and his strategic judgment—as well as his long-windedness in council. Although he is older than his companions at Troy and was no longer a match in combat for younger men, I disagree with the common image of him as frail and elderly. A weak man could not have spent ten years living in a rough encampment and driving chariots across a battlefield. Instead, I chose to portray him as a man nearing sixty who remained strong, vital, and hard as nails, even as he came to long for something more than constant war and brutality.

Nikostratos – A young villager on Kyros, he heroically discovered the trap set by Proxonos and his raiders and reported it to Nestor.

Nymph – A female nature deity, usually associated with a specific place or natural feature. Nereids, Naiads, and Oreads are different types of Nymphs.

Odysseus – King of Ithaca. Odysseus is a prominent character in *The Iliad*, and his ten-year struggle to return home after the war is the focus of *The Odyssey*. He is known for his intelligence and his skill as a warrior and tactician.

Oread – A mountain Nymph.

Paris – A Trojan prince, whose seduction and abduction of Helen, wife of Menelaus, led to the Trojan war.

Phaethon – The half-human son of Helios and a mortal woman.

Proteus – A sea god, Proteus was known for his shape-shifting abilities and his prophetic gifts.

Proxonos – A mercenary, nicknamed 'the ambassador,' Proxonos worked for Phaethon in his efforts to steal one of Astrid's cats.

Strachys – Originally a petty thief and fraud of a seer, Strachys becomes something more when he unleashes the power of a scroll Phaethon stole from Circe.

Thrasymedes – Nestor's son and Antilochus' older brother, he accompanied his father and brother to Troy.

Tiresias – A blind oracle who is unequaled in his powers of prophecy. Odysseus visited him in Hades after he left Circe.

Zeus – The king of the Olympian gods and the most powerful of Greek deities.

Thank you for reading
(And for sharing) Swarm Metamorphosis

If you enjoyed reading *Swarm Metamorphosis* as much as I have enjoyed writing it, I hope you will tell your friends about it. You can also ask your local library or bookstore to place *Swarm* on their shelves (they can contact us at https://practicaltales.com for information).

I would especially appreciate a review on Amazon, Goodreads, or your favorite book site, and don't forget to mention *Swarm Metamorphosis* on Facebook, Instagram, Twitter, or other social medium you enjoy.

For more of my writing, including short fiction, poems, and essays, please visit my website: https://wmstubblefield.com. Also, to stay informed on coming publications, please sign up for my mailing list at https://wmstubblefield.com/mailing-list-signup/.

Acknowledgments

I would like to thank Professor Brooks Otis, who taught Homeric and Roman epic poetry when I was an undergraduate at Stanford. His class started my lifelong love of Homer. I also owe a debt to Diane Middlebrook, Kenneth Fields, and Ronald Rebholz, who taught me how to write and to understand the ways literature can shape and inspire the human soul.

During the ten years it took me to develop my story of Astrid, Nestor, Circe, and these improbable cats, I became indebted to Merry Stubblefield, Jess and Morgan Langer, Juan Kleban, Lawrence Marrich, Edmund Urbanski, Maddie Fuertsch, and others who encouraged me through conversations about my nascent ideas, and later by reading and commenting on part or all of this work. I hope that anyone whom I have forgotten to name here will accept my apology.

As my story took shape, I was fortunate to meet Professor Lorenzo Garcia of the University of New Mexico, who graciously listened to my ideas for the novel, and who pointed me toward the scholarly literature on Homer and the Bronze Age.

I'm grateful to Tony Kline for letting me use his translation of lines from Ovid's *Metamorphosis* as one of the epigrams at the start of this book.

Jeff Myers of Wilcox and Myers, P.C. was extraordinarily generous in helping me with legal issues surrounding business and intellectual property.

I owe a special thanks to Silvia Curry for her skills as an editor and for her patience and generosity in helping me to give birth to *Swarm*. I also want to thank Kristen Weber, who advised me in my early efforts to find a publisher for my book.

I would like to thank the novelists, poets, and researchers I have not been blessed with meeting but who have shown me, through example and commentary, how to carry these ancient inspirations into the modern world. These include Ovid, Tennyson, Louise Glück, Wallace Stevens, Ezra Pound, Ted Hughes, Madeline Miller, Adam Nicolson, J. V. Luce, Bettany Hughes, Alan Wace, Frank Stubbings, Lionel Casson, Richmond Lattimore, Robert Fagles, Peter Green, Caroline Alexander, and Emily Wilson.

I would like to thank my wife, Merry, for her patience and understanding as I pursued this lifelong dream of writing a novel. Finally, I owe special gratitude to our cats, Elizabeth, Chessie, Audrey, Spike, and Greystoke, for being the real-life inspiration for Astrid's impossible, magical felines and for showing me the rewards that friendship with animals can give us.

Author Biography

William Stubblefield has spent his professional and intellectual life exploring the intersection of humanistic and scientific modes of thinking, and the often-surprising ways each perspective can enrich the other. He received a B.A. in English Literature from Stanford University, which gave him a lifelong love of the written word, and a Ph.D. in Computer Science from the University of New Mexico, which led to a career in Software Design and Engineering, and Artificial Intelligence. He has worked as a jewelry designer, musician, consultant, textbook author, a visiting professor at Dartmouth College, and a researcher at Sandia National Laboratories.

In addition to *Swarm Metamorphosis* he is the author (with Merry Stubblefield) of *How Mother Rat Invented the World*, and (with George Luger) of the first three editions of the textbook *Artificial Intelligence: Strategies and Structures for Complex Problem Solving*, and *AI Algorithms, Data Structures, and Idioms in Prolog, Lisp, and Java*.

When not writing, he enjoys playing guitar and relaxing with his wife, Merry, and their various critters. For more of his work, including poetry, essays, and short fiction, visit https://wmstubblefield.com.